where
the sun
rises

~From Kona with Love ~

Other Books by
Anna Gomez and Kristoffer Polaha

From Kona with Love Series
Moments Like This, Book 1

Forthcoming from Anna Gomez

Eight Goodbyes

From Kona With Love

BOOK TWO:
KAUAI

Here I am, the beauty of Kauai converging around me. It's called the Garden Isle, but its true meaning is seen in the jagged mountains and the strange beauty of the greenery on its dramatic shoreline. There are mountains to the right and tide pools to the left. Tropical forests, covered with giant ironwood trees lie behind the stretch of sandy beach, their branches thick and grand. The scene is a contradiction on its own. In a few steps, the clear blue sky and powdery white beach would transform into a lush, green jungle made impenetrable and mysterious by rich and exotic trees.

ANNA GOMEZ

KRISTOFFER POLAHA

where the sun rises

~From Kona with Love ~

Where the Sun Rises

Cover design Hang Le
www.ByHangLe.com

Kristoffer Polaha Photo Credit: Kailey Schwerman
www.KaileySchwerman.com

ISBN: 978-1-64548-080-8

Published by Rosewind Books
An imprint of Vesuvian Books
www.RosewindBooks.com

Printed in the United States

10 9 8 7 6 5 4 3 2 1

To those who watch the sun rise.

Table of Contents

Prologue

I t was supposed to be the perfect wave.

Though most of her peers would never be good enough to be there, she was. Surfing the Pipe, wrapped in a thick coil of water and counting the seconds in her head, was a dream come true. Although the waves she'd trained for weren't as high as the twelve-foot swell she now faced, she knew about the shallow base and the razorblade reef. She was prepared.

She raised her hands and lifted her head to the heavens in gratitude. Her balance was perfect, the roar of the tube music to her ears. The clouds looked like angels, and the sun's light embraced her with grace. The cadence of her movements was marked with precision. Time was on her side.

But it wasn't.

The board's fins scraped loudly against coral just before she was catapulted into the air. With the leash still wrapped around her ankle, she did what she always did—dove headfirst to get under the wave—except there wasn't enough distance between her and the ocean floor.

Her vision was blurred by a thick smog of sand when her head hit the sandbank. The weight of her shoulders kept her close to the ground. Boxfish fluttered about like birds with transparent little wings, and she watched as an eel burrowed itself under a rock. Sea anemones and corals glowed in indescribable colors, swaying gently in an imaginary breeze, keeping her calm and then making her sleepy.

Her legs were suspended above her, but faced the other way. Panic rose in her throat. When she tried to lift her head, she heard a snap. A dull, tingling feeling traveled through her body, starting at her chin, then moving down her neck and to her shoulders. She froze except for her eyes, which followed the movement of the sand as it slowly drifted down like snow.

Snow. She'd always hoped to see it one day.

She fought hard to keep her eyes open, knowing the green hue of the ocean and the dizzying sand might be the last thing she'd ever see. All her life, she had lived in the ocean's majesty. She was an island girl born and raised in paradise. Her fear quelled by that thought, Maele closed her eyes and allowed the darkness to take over.

It was supposed to be the perfect wave.

Until it wasn't.

PART ONE:

Wedding Bells

Maele & Adam

Same, Same but Different

In Oahu, the sunrise was a sacred time. Sure, sunset was when traditional Hawaiians sang the Oli and blew the conch to gather their mana, but beginnings—those were what really mattered. The glorious sun, the world's preface, created a wave of light, black before and gold behind, breaking over the entire planet with the warmth and guarantee of another day.

Dawn was also twenty-two-year-old Maele's favorite time of day. She stood tall and lean at five feet eight with eyes as brown as the earth, rich and organic, like a source of life. Her skin golden and her hair dark, Mae was a Hawaiian native.

The North Shore of Oahu wasn't just a magical place, it was the perfect place to watch the sun take its shift over the world. Although she was born in Kauai, Oahu was her adopted home, the island where she had parked her hopes and dreams six years earlier.

The sunrise had always been a symbol of birth and reawakening. It was also a symbol of Maele's old life.

So, each morning, she sat on the beach at Waimea, watching the early risers who worshipped the ocean just as much as she did. She looked just like them—the locals or kamaaina, clad in hooded sweatshirts to combat the early morning chill. The young generation whose faces were filled with excitement as the waves rolled to form random, unpredictable swells. She knew all about dropping in, aerials, barrels, lineups, and carves. Yet, there she was, sitting on the hill, hungry for some connection, some semblance of the past.

Despite the exciting day ahead of her, she'd woken early to welcome the sunrise, say her prayers, and meditate. Maele may have been a Christian, but she'd always enjoyed the story of Kane—the highest of the three major Hawaiian gods—the father of life, the dawn, the sun, and the sky. The idea that she was on the same shore where her ancestors once stood reminded her that past and present are woven together.

She rubbed her neck as the surfers played among the waves. She believed that one day she'd be in the water again, surfing with the rest of them.

Her plan was to go back to the place where it all began, to the waters of Kauai, where her love for surfing had been born. She wanted to visit the beach where her hopes had been broken, along with her neck. Maele had been a hairline fracture away from being paralyzed and two breaths away from drowning. It was the last time she'd been in the water. But, lately, something in Maele drove her to go back to the Kauai beach to face her fear.

"Good morning, Mae," Lolana, her mother, greeted when Maele walked in through the front door. "How was the sunrise today?"

She wanted to say how eager she was for the big day to unfold, how it felt like a holiday for her. But Maele had taught herself, out of fear, not to get too excited or expect too much of anything, really. Today was no different. Andie Mathew's wedding was the social event of the year and Maele wasn't going to do or say anything that might ruin it. But inside, she was bursting at the seams with giddiness.

"Same as always. But different. Today, the streaks were more purple than red."

Maele followed her mother into the kitchen. She grabbed three brown woven placemats and set them on the table. Without a word, the two women went about their morning routine. Breakfast was ready in ten minutes. Maele sat on the wooden bench, her feet tucked under her. Her mother poured two cups of coffee before taking her place across from her daughter.

"It's still early. Already getting ready?"

Maele reached for the utensils in the center of the table. "I'd like to be there early to help out."

"That's fine."

Both mother and daughter heard the footsteps descending from the staircase and the soft slamming of the front door.

"Papa?"

Her mother nodded. "They're still harvesting today. Which reminds me, would you check and make sure the animals are fed before you leave? Also—"

"I'll stop over and leave some sandwiches for Papa, Duke, and Kukane. I made them last night."

"Thank you, dear daughter. You're always so organized. And helpful."

The family had five chickens, three pigs, five cows, and four horses on the farm. Maele only had weekends to help her parents out. Throughout the week, she was either at the coffee shop or taking night classes at the community college. That hadn't always been the plan. She'd intended to go to the University of Hawaii; with a 32 on the ACT and a full scholarship to boot. Then life had happened and there she was, at home with her parents, doing what she could to appease her mother, who would not let her out of her sight. Her mother hadn't always been that way, either.

Maele nodded, taking a sip of her coffee before using a fork to cut her egg. She moved the food around her plate, distracted with thoughts and plans she wanted to discuss with her mother, but cared too deeply to dare mention. She'd never been a bridesmaid before, and her friend, Andie, was going to be the most beautiful bride in the world.

Maele was employed at Beans and Books, a coffee shop owned by Andie's friend, Apikelia Flores. She had watched Andie turn the ailing coffee shop around into a thriving business, seeing firsthand how Andie had put her heart and soul into the plantation and its people. Andie became the reason Maele had changed her major to business. She wanted to be as strong and confident as Andie. From Andie, Maele learned that every risk in life was worth the moment, the experience. If you believed in something enough, there would never be any regrets.

One day, she would be just as brave as Andie.

Not while her fear of the water still overtook her love of the ocean and manifested itself into her nightmares, but one day.

What had happened to Andie confirmed Maele's faith that there was a master plan for her own life. She was excited enough about having had a few spa days in Maui with the other bridesmaids, but who would have guessed Andie and Warren would choose Kauai for their reception?

Kauai. Maele hadn't been back to the island she was born on in six long years. She had family over there that she longed to see, and yes, she had her fear to face too.

She noticed her mother's furtive glances. She watched her as she ate and then avoided her eyes whenever Maele tried to hold her gaze.

"Mama, what's wrong?" Maele began. Her mother looked up from her coffee cup with the same big brown eyes that matched Maele's. "You look sad."

"Maele." Lolana's face grew stern, lips fixed in a straight line and tone flat. "I'm not sure it's a good idea to spend Christmas in Kauai. I feel like your cousin put you up to this."

Maele shook her head. "No, no."

Her mother rolled her eyes.

"I mean, we text regularly, but Koa doesn't even know I've decided to come. It just works out perfectly, since I'll already be in Kauai for Andie's wedding reception. It's only for the holidays and a couple of weeks after the New Year. I'll be back January fourteenth. There's something I need to do on the thirteenth. I won't even be missing school."

Lolana stared at her. Maele knew her mother was wading in the memory of the time and place where she'd almost lost her daughter.

The clinking of silverware, the loud sips of coffee, the smacking of lips, and the crunch of a napkin against her mother's chin were the sounds that drowned her hopes of spending Christmas in Kauai. Of seeing her cousin, Koa, and of reclaiming the courage she'd lost. What if her parents changed their minds? She would have to relegate herself to working on the plantation, which wasn't so bad, really. Her father was an honest, hardworking man. And she was proud to see the fruits of his labor.

Finally, her mother spoke. "Mae, I am worried. You're doing so well, you know? Being there, I'm afraid you'll regress and feel the trauma of your accident all over again."

"I won't."

"And how do you know that?"

Instinctively, Maele brought her hand to her neck. Lolana reached over and gently held her fingers.

"Because," Maele began, "there's no escaping what happened, and

I don't want to run away from it forever." She stood and walked over to her mother, who held her arm up so that Maele could mold herself into the space between. "I just want to see my cousin. I've missed home so much."

"This is our home. It's been our home for many years."

"It's our second home, Mama. You miss your sister too."

Lolana smiled, gently tapping her daughter's nose. "Sometimes life is just what it is."

"I'm okay. Look at me. I made it to twenty-two-years old, fit and healthy. Nothing will happen, I promise. Please. Be happy I'm doing this for myself."

Lolana studied her daughter for a moment in thoughtful silence. "Fine, then. You go and do what you need to do, but I will be happy once you're back home safe and sound."

She pulled Maele's head down so it settled in the crook of her neck. Maele responded by wrapping her arm around her mother's waist. "Don't worry about cleaning up around here," her mother said. "Go. Go and get ready. *I kēia lā e nani.* Today will be beautiful. And you are a fitting bridesmaid."

2

Daddy's in the House!

A dam was on a plane to Oahu, first class all the way.
He had decided quickly. Shame and anger made him wish he
could skip Warren's wedding, but that would be a slap to his brother's
face. And Andie, Warren's bride-to-be, had always been so good to him.
He knew what he had to do, swallow his pride and apologize. Hence, his
double whiskey and Coke.

He settled into his comfy seat and mentally prepared for the
important days ahead.

Adam's meeting at Universal had gone well. The movie was on track
for production, and the script notes were good. They touched mostly on
tone and dialogue, which was a huge win. The studio brass seemed
convinced that this script, his idea, was going to be their next big
franchise. It was a dream come true, and he knew what he had to do to
make his new colleagues happy. They had cut him a check for more
money than he'd ever made in his life. Adam may have come from
money, but he'd earned that check on his own. From an idea he'd
thought up, from the sweat off his own brow. It felt good. He just wished
Warren had stayed in town to celebrate with him. The wedding was no
place to celebrate Adam's victory, it was Warren's time. Again.

The plane touched down at one o'clock Hawaiian time and the
December heat washed over him. California was warm, but home sweet
home was warmer. The balmy smell of the ocean filled his nose, the
moisture in the air dampened his skin and clothes. Stepping out of the
cold, dry air of the airplane, he felt at ease immediately.

Adam rented a car and drove to the address his brother had texted him—the Flores manor. While there was lots of new money on the island—and his father was a part of the nouveau riche class with its grotesquely large homes, fast cars, and loud toys—the Flores family was from a very select and small group of generational wealth. Or, at least, wealth that had been in the family long enough to help Hawaii become what it was, for better and worse. The Floreses had been pioneers in the early days of the island, and their roots were firmly established in the land they'd built and cultivated.

Society was a funny thing. You might have the most money, but when someone comes along with less money, but more seniority, deeper roots, and a richer family name, you weren't the top dog anymore. That's why Adam had made up his mind early on, not to play the game. He wanted to make his own way—his own name, build his own legacy. The irony was, if Warren had a child on Oahu, that kid would be a third generation Yates of the highest order. Society would bend his way. The only way Adam could beat that was to marry into a local family that had equal or better standing.

"You can't marry below your station, Adam, remember that," his dad used to say. "She needs proper breeding, an education, class, and she should come from money. Otherwise, you won't be equally yoked—you will be the one pulling all the weight. You'll be paying for her and her brothers, sisters, parents, and cousins. And be careful not to knock someone up along the way. That's the last thing we need in this family, a little bastard Yates on the loose."

Pearls like these flowed off his father's tongue freely. Adam never understood why his father said those things. His mother didn't come from money, but he liked to think she'd helped his father accumulate what they had.

Adam had decided he wasn't going to get married until he was at least thirty-eight. That was a decision he'd made the summer he turned eighteen and had his heart stolen by a brown-haired girl he'd never even met. A beautiful surfer he'd watched every early morning for two years. A girl who moved like a goddess on the water.

In the autumn of his senior year at boarding school, the goddess disappeared, just like a dream.

He often thought of this childhood crush and wondered where she was, or if she was even alive. It was the closest thing to love he'd ever known, and Adam had remained on the lookout for her ever since—six years of scouring social media for clues—but she never reappeared. Mostly, he wondered what would have happened if he would have just talked to her, if he had just said, "Hi."

Not speaking to the girl on the beach had been his first act of self-betrayal, his first act of cowardice, but it hadn't been his last. After that last year in high school, he'd sworn off love and set a plan to become the biggest writer, director, and producer of his generation in Hollywood. Adam had a superpower—when he made up his mind to do something, come hell or high water, he would do it. His downfall was that he never made up his mind to do much of anything at all. His time at boarding school had also been the time in his life when he'd picked up smoking cigarettes and weed, and when he'd started drinking to forget, and trying all sorts of drugs for "recreational" purposes. His acceptance into NYU had him swearing he'd leave the islands and never return until he was famous.

Of course, he had come back, long before fame, to teach surfing and live on Warren's couch and to write screenplays without having to pay rent. These islands had given him the idea for *Oceana* in the first place, sitting at his special spot near the base of the lighthouse on the edge of a bluff, overlooking the sea, or perched on his board, facing the open ocean. He'd always feared being pulled away from the shore by a riptide, but also excitedly wondered what would happen if he was—how far he would go. Could he make it to Japan or China on his surfboard, riding a current like an underwater river? Growing up in the middle of the Pacific Ocean made the world seem like a very small place and a faraway place at the same time. Out of sight, out of mind, so it was easy to let the islands be the only thing in his world.

Adam was happy to be back. He was also running late. The wedding was going to start in two hours, and he had to get to the Flores's house and into his tuxedo. He was the best man, after all.

When he arrived at the residence, the guard at the gate asked a few too many questions. Adam took a deep breath. "I'm Adam Yates, the best man in the wedding."

"Let me see … Yates. Adam Yates." The guard scanned the names on his clipboard. "Oh, here you are. If you're the best man, aren't you cutting it a bit close?"

"Well, that's a long story."

The guard tapped his pencil against the clipboard. "I have time."

He gave Adam a suspicious stare. "Besides, my list says the best man is already inside."

Adam's jaw set as he tried to keep his temper under control. "Look, I'm clearly not already inside, and I'm late, and I still need to put this on." He held up a suit bag before pulling out his driver's license.

The guard squinted at the license and then at Adam's face. "It looks like you, right enough." He ran his finger down the list on the clipboard. "And the name matches the one on my list. Someone must have gotten checked in under the wrong name. So … you're good to go. Have a good time. Aloha."

Adam sped toward the house in his rental car, parked, and grabbed his backpack and suit bag. He made his way inside, checked in with someone near the front door, and was directed to a place where he could change his clothes. He mumbled to himself, rehearsing what to say to Warren and how he would apologize for what had happened in L.A. He turned the corner in a hallway lined with rooms and glanced up toward the courtyard full of guests, hoping to find his brother.

Instead, what he saw stopped him in his tracks. His world was about to implode.

Standing no more than six feet away was the mystery girl from the beach all those years ago. She was more stunning than he even remembered. When she looked his way, he clumsily dove out of sight, almost knocking a flower arrangement over in the process.

"Adam," he muttered to himself, crouched behind the flowerpot, "I don't know what freak of nature event this is, in which that girl is standing outside this room, but you better say hi and get her name. It's time to put childish things away." He slapped himself in the face for good measure. "Do not mess this up."

As he was changing his clothes, his phone went off. The caller ID showed the name Shelly. Ah yes, Shelly. The young blonde woman to whom Adam had promised a lead in a romcom he had written, which took place in Hawaii. The girl he liked to hook up with when he came home. The girl he'd invited to his brother's wedding a month ago. She texted him, next.

WHERE ARE U? I'M HERE. R U HERE?

He quickly called her back.

"Aloha, Shelly. I'm here. You're here?"

"Aloha, baby. Yes, silly. Of course I'm here. This wedding is the social event of the season—I wouldn't miss it for the world—and you are here, which means that you and I are gonna have some fun. Mama missed Daddy."

Oh no. She was already talking in *mama* and *daddy* terms. That's how she flirted. Adam knew if he wanted to right the wrongs of his past, if he wanted to kill the coward inside of him and break this spell he was under, he needed to be free to talk to the mystery girl. Shelly would blow the whole thing up even before it began.

"Daddy is in the house, but … I'm not feeling so well, and I don't want to get you sick. So, I might have to play it cool tonight, okay?"

"Well, what about the reception on Kauai? I can only stay three of the five days. Are we gonna have a chance to hang out? I mean, I'm kinda planning on crashing with you."

"Well, I'm really bad off and I don't want you to get sick, so let's just see. I'll find you after the wedding. I gotta go now," he said, and took her off speakerphone.

"Okay. Love you, baby."

Ugh, there was that word. Why did they always throw that word out there like a hand grenade?

"Okay, yeah, okay. Bye."

Adam hated that he'd have to juggle. Why was he so afraid of being alone? He hadn't needed to invite her. "Yeah, but I didn't know my mystery girl was gonna be here," he argued out loud. He looked at himself in the mirror. "Look, Adam, you don't owe Shelly anything, and you don't even know who the mystery girl is. Maybe she's not who you remember. Or not even her. Relax and enjoy yourself."

He dug into his only piece of luggage, where he found what he was looking for—a little bottle of pills. He popped the cap, shook one into the palm of his hand, and tossed it into his mouth. He closed his eyes and swallowed.

"It's showtime!"

The garden was decorated like a matrimonial paradise, like a wedding fit for royalty. Flowers seemingly hung from thin air and white wooden chairs were perfectly lined up facing an altar which blossomed with gardenias, lilacs, and orchids. There was a painting at the back of the altar.

Adam recognized it as the one that usually hung on the wall in Warren's office. Then he saw Warren. He steeled himself as he made his way over.

"You're here," Warren said, sighing with relief.

"I'm here."

"Good. Lucas was here last night for dinner, so I asked him to stand in as best man for just this portion. He'll walk first, followed by Graham, then Mike, then Andie's brother, Steven, and then you, okay? But don't worry—you're still gonna give the best man's speech if you want to. I mean, look, they are already lined up. They were at the rehearsal—they know what they're doing. You'll walk down with a bridesmaid. Her name is Maele. All you have to do is follow. You good with that?"

"Yeah, of course. I've gotta be, but I'm still your best man?"

"Adam, you'll always be my best man." Warren started toward the altar.

"Warren."

Warren turned and the two brothers exchanged a look of understanding. The look that renders words useless because, in the end, they were family, and family wasn't perfect.

Still, Adam wanted to clear the air. "I'm sorry for being such a clown the other day," he began.

Warren wrapped his arms around his brother, shaking his head at the same time.

It signaled forgiveness, and Adam let it go. "Have fun today, you deserve the best wedding ever, and you look ... you look awesome." Adam stepped back and adjusted Warren's tie as the photographer took a candid shot.

Then Adam made his way to the lineup of groomsmen and bridesmaids.

"Ah, geez, you're here, Adam. Nothing like making an entrance. You take my place, then, no?" Lucas asked.

There was a time when Adam was jealous of his friendship with Warren. Another ex-bachelor who became a family man.

"No. You get to walk out there first. He asked me to walk last. Being late and all, and I just wouldn't know where to go, stop, or line up. I'm still making my best man speech, so don't get any ideas."

"Sounds good to me. Happy you made it. I know it means the world to Warren."

As if fate itself had reached down and planned the whole thing,

Adam saw who he was lined up to walk down the aisle with. It had taken six years, 9,916 miles, and a lot of stupid choices to put Adam smack dab in front of his mystery girl.

But fate gets what fate wants.

Adam looked her straight in the eye and said, "Hi."

This Kind of Love

The girls had an early start to the day. As a bridesmaid, Maele had to be at the venue by 9:30 in the morning. The late afternoon wedding would ensure guests could hop the thirty-minute charter to Kauai, where a week-long reception would take place. After that, Maele would remain on the island for the rest of her Christmas break.

Technically, this was the first full wedding at Mrs. Flores's home. Two years ago, her daughter Api had gotten married, though she almost hadn't. Beset with inconsolable grief about her father's death, she'd doubted her reasons for marrying her fiancé. It was Andie who had convinced her the love she had for James hadn't been brought on by loss, but because they fit so perfectly together. And although all's well that ends well, instead of a gathering of a hundred and fifty, five people had witnessed the ceremony. Evening had fallen, and the rest of the guests had gone home. Every gift was returned, and an apology letter was mailed to those in attendance. Ultimately, there had been no regrets. James had taken his fellowship at the Queens Hospital in Oahu and Api was now three months pregnant. Andie was now fulfilling Mrs. Flores's dream of having a wedding at the sprawling grounds of their Kailua home.

When everything seemed settled, Maele took her stance at the end of the expansive garden aisle, observing the crowd of people who bustled around while waiting for the ceremony to start. Her feet throbbed, caused by the inordinate amount of tissue paper she'd stuffed in her shoes to make them fit. She was a size seven and a half, but the shoes were size nines. Or maybe even a half size larger—the numbers on the bottom of the soles too faded to discern. The resale store had a limited number of styles, and these—white satin pumps with a pointy toe and two-inch heels, which she had dyed to match—had been perfect for the dress. She had practiced pushing her heel against the back of the shoe to keep her feet from slipping out.

The happy moments of the day were enough to make her forget about the pain she endured in those shoes. When Andie had come running to show off her blue necklace, Maele had thought she would cry with joy. Seeing Warren and his father, standing on the balcony overlooking the ocean in quiet conversation, was too beautiful to be overshadowed by ill-fitting shoes. Or Lani's excitement as she'd pointed out the Waterford place settings on the tables. Shoes two sizes too large were the least of her concerns.

This event wasn't a replay of the past. The décor was definitely understated—white hibiscus and colorful hydrangeas covered every post and column around the garden. There were lilies floating in the pool. To the right of the makeshift podium was a life-sized painting Warren's mother had created before she'd passed away. It was the perfect backdrop, placed right as the focal point where the bride and groom planned to recite their vows, with his mother looking on as their main witness.

Maele shifted her weight uncomfortably from one foot to the other. Families from the plantation were not workers that day, but valued guests. Maele beamed with pride as Duke, Kukane, and Kaku walked past her, looking so dashing in their slightly wrinkled suits. Around her were pleasantries, well-wishes, and shrieks of joy for those reuniting. Hugs and kisses and gentle pats on the back. From the far-left corner, someone shouted Warren's name as he walked in her direction. Another man wearing the same style tux with tails and gray piping said something before Warren stepped in to embrace him. Then the stranger fixed Warren's tie while the photographer caught the moment on camera.

As the sound of violins began to fill the air, she painstakingly pinched her toes and walked to her place at the end of the line. Mrs. Flores and Mrs. Matthews took their seats, while Mr. Matthews made his way to Andie's dressing room.

Warren stood proudly beside the preacher.

Out of nowhere, a guy—the one who had fixed Warren's tie—appeared at her side, frantically combing his fingers through his hair before looking her straight in the eye.

The guy looked frazzled, with thick brown hair askew and a five o'clock shadow. When he stared back at her, she turned away. But not before noticing his piercing green eyes. He must be Warren's younger brother—long ago he'd been in the coffee shop once before, with Warren. But, those eyes, she'd never noticed them before.

"I'm Adam."

She nodded slightly, acknowledging him. He offered her his arm and she hesitated. When she looked in front of her, Api and Lani were doing the same thing with their partners. Reluctantly, she placed her fingers on his forearm as they began the procession.

"My brother said your name is Maele. Is that right?"

She nodded again, lost for words. Wasn't she supposed to walk down with Mike, Warren's buddy? What was happening? There had been no rehearsal with the groomsmen—just a basic rundown, yesterday. What would it have mattered, anyway?

He's Warren's brother and best man, so why is he walking in the back of the line with me?

More importantly, why was she so nervous?

Api turned around from the front of the line to smile at her. It was a sly one. A mischievous, one-sided upturn of her mouth, paired with one wiggling eyebrow. When it was their turn to move, Maele made sure she led the pacing, and Adam followed. One foot in front of the other, a second to pause.

It was excruciating, walking in oversized shoes stuffed with tissue paper next to someone like Adam Yates. She took a deep breath and allowed the soft voices of the choir to carry her away. She quickly forgot about the agony in her toes and glided down the white velvet carpet, as if lifted by invisible wings. When they reached the front of the congregation, she removed her arm from her partner.

Warren's smile shone like a lighthouse as he saw his bride for the first time in fourteen days. Andie's father slowly walked her down the aisle, beaming with pride as he brought her to the man she loved. Gently, he lifted her veil to whisper something in her ear. Andie giggled and kissed her father before moving toward Warren. And when she reached him, he closed his eyes and let out a deep breath. When Warren took Andie's hand, Maele decided she wanted that kind of love.

In her experience, men had always gotten in the way of what she wanted. As far as she was concerned, the ones her age were too self-centered. She saw that every day in her interactions at the coffee shop, or on the beach, where she'd sit in the early mornings and watch her peers attempt what she could do in her sleep. Their air of invincibility used to bother her. But, after a while, she'd made peace with the fact that life wasn't fair. She was done questioning why fate randomly bestowed its wrath on her. She just wanted peace in her mind, body, and soul.

Several times during the ceremony, she locked eyes with Adam, though she convinced herself he was looking at someone behind her. The thought made her less self-conscious. Besides, why would a Yates man even want to socialize with her? He was being nice and courteous. Their family had always been kind to the staff. Or, worse—he had mistaken her for one of Andie's rich socialite friends.

After the final blessing, Warren kissed his bride. When the clapping died, Warren handed Andie a bouquet of lilies tied in a large velvet ribbon emblazoned with the name Catherine Lillian. The violinist began to play the wedding march. Slowly, Andie and Warren walked to the end of the beach, and after a moment of silent prayer, tossed the bouquet into the air, far out into the ocean.

Drinks and hors d'oeuvres were served while groups organized into shuttles that would take them to the airport. The island of Kauai was waiting to welcome them—to a lavish, weeklong reception full of celebration.

The Speech

I t had been six years since Adam had last seen the surfer girl from the beach. His boarding school had been a ten-minute walk down the banks of the Puukumu Stream to the ocean. He would walk to the beach at sunrise or after school to look for the girl who danced on waves.

She was stunning. A work of art. Her small body in a bright-colored bikini that barely covered her up. He had been a teenager then, filled with teenage desires, and would watch her extra closely in hopes that a wave would knock her off her board. He'd eventually carried a sweatshirt for just the occasion, fantasizing about running up and covering her golden flesh with his bright yellow hoodie, thus saving the day. The fantasy often led to the surfer girl being so grateful that she reached up, shivering and wet and kissed him on the mouth. Adam would work himself up sitting on the beach, fiddling with seashells, and playing with the sand, daydreaming. Now, here she was—on his arm as they marched down the aisle together, sitting across from each other on the plane ride to Kauai, and now sitting inches away from her where he couldn't stop staring.

Shelly sat on the other side of him and nibbled his ear as they waited for the speeches to begin. He shot a look at Shelly and back to Maele, who seemed to be looking right at him. To escape from his situation, Adam grabbed a knife and rapped it on the wine glass in front of him.

"Time to give a speech," he said as he stood.

The entire party grew quiet. Over one-hundred and fifty faces looked his way. Warren and Andie smiled at him in encouragement. He saw his dad shake his head in what Adam could only interpret as stern disapproval. Was he too early with the speeches? No matter, Adam pushed on and looked toward the back of the dining area, meeting the eyes of a man in khakis and a white shirt. The man gave Adam a thumbs-up. Adam nodded in acknowledgment.

"I, um, I know I didn't get to stand next to my big brother today during the ceremony, so it may come as a surprise to all of you, but I am, in fact, his best man. And, as the best man, I have some serious duties and obligations, most of which I have either missed or messed up. But the best man speech, I think, is the best job the best man gets. All the other stuff is just a lot of planning and work. So, thank you, Lucas, for stepping in and sharing the responsibility of sending Warren into marital bliss with me." Adam raised his glass to Lucas and the wedding party laughed and clapped. Adam got the crowd to sing "For He's a Jolly Good Fellow!" The song rang out and then it went silent again. All eyes were on Adam.

"So, the speech. I am not really someone who likes to get up in front of large groups …" At this, he made eye contact with Maele. Her face was pure and full of wonder. He really had felt love for her all those years ago, and dammit, if he didn't feel love for her all over again right then and there. She hung on every word, as if willing him to be brilliant. Her apparent faith in him made him want to be brilliant, so he dug deep. "However, this is a once in a lifetime moment. I know some people make it a habit of getting married but lack the follow through, and a messy divorce isn't really Warren's style. So, I can pretty much guarantee he's a one-and-done kinda guy, but I'm getting off track here. What I'm trying to say, in my way, is this; Warren, there is not a man on this planet I look up to more than you."

Adam's father looked down at the tablecloth and swept breadcrumbs to the floor.

"You are integrity, strength, class, cool embodied, and defined. Your loyalty is unmatched, except maybe by Andie's, and your kindness is inspirational. I see a table of kids sitting over there who can testify to how much you give and how deeply you are capable of loving. I love you and I'm so proud of you." The table of Warren's YMCA buddies yelled loudly at the mention of them.

Adam choked on his emotion as he looked over to his brother, whose eyes were starting to flow with warm, happy tears.

"I know that you and Andie will have a happy journey on this crazy ride called life. She is the perfect partner for you. I am also proud to be the first Yates to welcome the Matthews family to our tribe. Mom, Dad, brother Steven, to his wife and kids ... and finally, to my new sister, Andie, welcome to the family."

The crowd went wild with a huge cheer. After a moment, the noise subsided.

"Andie, I remember when you came back last December for Api's wedding, you stormed onto the beach looking for Warren. What you didn't know was that I saw you coming, which means, yes ... I saw you trip, fall, and roll down that little hill, but I turned away because I didn't want to embarrass you. Not then, anyway. But now that you're family, I'm cool with it."

The party laughed.

"You asked me about Warren, and I told you he was in the water. Before you left, you told me a story about a woman you met on the plane, the first time you came to Hawaii. Do you remember?"

Andie, who was also crying with joy nodded yes, smiled and blew a kiss to Adam.

"You told me the woman you met on the plane ride said the spirit of Hawaii can help you find love, can guide you to your soul mate, that love itself was born on these islands. I grew up here, but you made these islands seem enchanted and beautiful, you and your story changed the way I see my home. Your love did the same thing for my brother. He is a better man because of you, maybe too good sometimes. I tried to get him to have some fun in L.A. and he just said no, like always, but that's fine because his self-control is this beautiful quality he now has because of you. I have been running away from anybody who could have that kind of sway in my life for a while, but in truth—I guess, deep down, if I'm honest—I want somebody to do that for me someday. I really do. Here's to all of us finding our Andie."

Involuntarily, he shifted his gaze to Maele. She met his eyes without wavering.

"Like I said, I'm no public speaker, but I do know how to make a movie, so, with no further ado, here's a little movie I put together for the newlyweds. Hit it, Omari."

The man in the khakis gave another thumbs-up and a screen slowly rose out of the dance floor, a nice feature of the resort. The hanging lights dimmed, and music filled the area, a split image appearing on the screen. On one side was baby Andie with baby Warren on the other. What followed was a twelve-minute short film, behind-the-scenes footage Adam had taken of Andie and Warren's courtship. Lost little moments found again through his lens. Gestures and looks that told a love story.

The room fell silent as everyone watched Adam's work. When it was over, the warm yellow lights strung across the patio came back to life and the wedding party stayed quiet. Warren stood and walked over to Adam, embracing him in a huge hug, followed by Andie. Even his dad stood, wiping tears and clapping proudly. Adam had a gift and when it was used purposefully, it had a profound impact.

"That's twice now you've used your gift to bless me and memorialize a special moment in my life on film. You know we will watch this every year for the rest of our lives, right?" Warren whispered as he held Adam close.

"I hope so. I love you and I'm so happy for you guys." Adam shed enough tears that night. Now it was time to let loose.

"Who's ready to party? Let's celebrate these two knuckleheads!" Adam shouted as he raised his glass. Everybody lifted their glass in response and the band started to play a boogie.

"Well, hold on, wait," Lucas yelled, waving a piece of folded printer paper. "Hold on, everybody! We have a few more speeches to hear. I've got a speech! We still have more speeches!" The band quieted, everybody laughed as they took their seats again. Maele watched Adam and smiled.

Chucks in a Jar

The plane landed and the guests were immediately shuttled to the resort. Maele was so excited to be on Kauai, she could hardly focus. This wedding reception was the last of the series of gatherings before she could take the time to see her family. Come to think of it, she'd never asked Andie why they had decided to have her reception here. Maybe because the reception was the most picture-perfect Maele had ever seen. But the beach itself, with its golden crescents of sand lit up by a thousand tiki torches, was a major must-see for people who visited the island.

The wedding party was housed in various villas owned by the resort. Maele opted to stay in the same one as her parents, since they would only be there for three of the five days. Afterward, Maele would move out of town to her aunt's home.

That same pair of too-big shoes made its way to the reception in Kauai. Guests were given some time to settle in, but Maele wanted to make herself useful by assisting the resort staff in their venue preparations. She helped the wedding coordinator by making sure the place cards and lists were ticked, tied, and updated. She then snuck off to hide a little post dinner treat for herself in a nearby antique jar. By the time she was done, guests were taking their places at the tables. And her toes had swollen enough that she probably no longer needed the tissue paper, but why tinker with something that had worked so far? So, she limped along, thankful to finally get a chance to sit after being on her feet all day.

The bridal party was seated at a long table set on top of a low wooden platform. Since Maele had never been to a wedding reception like this, she was fascinated by the sights, the sounds, the humanity of what surrounded her. She tried to count them all but couldn't, this sea of people who seemed to have a genuine love for the bride and groom.

When it came time for the best man's speech, she glanced toward Adam, who clanked on a wine glass. He stood and moved to the front to speak. Maele shifted in her seat, turning her back on the young lady who was seated on the other side of Adam. She was pretty, perky, blonde, and too perfect. But Maele forgot about that young lady the moment he offered a toast to his older brother. He'd caught her eye for a brief second before raising a glass to the bride and groom.

He wants a love that can change his life. What needs changing?

Then she'd thought about the way Adam had looked at her. Aside from the initial feeling of self-consciousness, it had felt familiar. She felt like she had seen him before, and she was comfortable with him looking at her.

The night wore on, until finally, servers in white tuxes paraded down the middle of the dance floor carrying the biggest wedding cake she had ever seen on a silver tray. Layers and layers of white frosting sat underneath what looked like a forest with palm trees and volcanoes and shimmering lights hanging on thin branches.

As the band began to play the song for the couple's first dance, Maele quietly pushed her chair back and slipped away, weaving around the servers who approached their table. Not far from the central area of the party were dimly lit pergolas with trellises full of colorful vines in bloom. Maele removed her shoes and crouched. Immediately, she felt her toes expand, the blood rushing back to them as she wiggled and stretched them on the ground. She dipped a hand into one of the large antique jars and pulled out what she'd hidden there when she'd helped the staff set up. She smiled to herself, filled with relief, as she began untying the Converse sneakers she'd intended to put on after the festivities.

She heard someone cough.

Maele realized she wasn't alone and drew in a surprised breath. That's when she smelled it. Someone was having a smoke.

"Smart," the voice said. How she knew who it was before even turning around was a mystery to her. He leaned on the edge of the post, so cool and collected, no longer the nervous, shaking guy from the ceremony. She could feel the heat of his gaze on the back of her neck as she tried to focus on tying her shoelaces.

"Hi, again."

"Hi," she answered. "Adam."

"Yes. Hi, Maele. What am I missing out there?"

"They served a wedding cake as tall as a building," she said. "And now they're dancing."

"Huh. So other than skyscraper cake, nothing, then?" He stubbed out his cigarette. Then those green eyes zoned in on her once more. "Maele. Maele. Maele."

"Adam, Adam, Adam. Why do you smoke? It's a bad habit."

"It's a filthy habit."

They looked at each other for a long moment. Maele felt awkward, like she knew him, or he knew her, somehow.

"You know we've met before, you and I," Maele said.

"Where?" He froze, waiting anxiously for her next words.

"At the coffee shop. You came in once with your brother. I thought you were stoned, the way you acted. You just stared at the scones the whole time."

"I might have been, one can never tell."

They stared at each other for a while longer.

She saw him look at her as if he was putting a puzzle together, and she stared back at him as if she were studying a map. She admired how his nose folded so neatly into his cheeks. He had a beautiful nose. How his eyebrows were strong and thick and a little menacing, like Jack Nicholson's or Gregory Peck's, and his lips were full and pink. His top lip was shaped like a bow, with a little dip right in the middle. His bottom lip was plump. He was beautiful. And those green eyes were somehow so familiar.

He smiled as wide as he could.

"Hi," he said again.

"Hi," she replied.

It was his eyes that got her. *Watch the eyes*, her mother always said. *If he laughs with his eyes, it means he is real, genuine.*

Adam was real and very attractive. His hair was still a mess, but the way he carried his clothes, you would have thought he was a model. Just as quickly, she remembered—*he's like his brother*. Way, way out of her league.

"I'm going to go back now," she said, too nervous to say anything else. "I just came to get my shoes."

She hiked her skirt above the ground, careful not to trip over herself.

"Maybe I'll catch you later," he said, lighting a fresh cigarette as it dangled from the side of his mouth, à la James Dean. He caught her eye one more time before she turned around and walked back toward the music.

"Where've you been?" Lani stood on the side of the dance floor, watching as the bride and groom swayed in the midst of the other guests.

"I went to get my shoes." Maele gestured at her feet.

"Well, I've been waiting for you to dance with me. Let's go."

Maele and Lani joined Andie and Warren on the dance floor. By then, Mrs. Flores and Mr. Matthews were doing some sort of boogie. As Maele twirled around the dance floor, she noticed Adam taking a seat at the guest table. The young lady she'd seen earlier was hanging all over him again.

Not that Maele had been staring, but she had seen that woman stick her tongue in his ear right before he'd made his speech. It had been hard to miss.

Not five minutes later, Adam cut in between her and Lani, turning and spinning until Lani found another partner and moved away. He was a good dancer. People like him—pampered, social, and confident—were naturals. Maele was enthralled with the way he bobbed up and down, the way his eyes never left her face, even if she found every excuse to look away.

Maele leaned in and yelled in his ear, "Shouldn't you be with your girlfriend?"

"Ouch." He playfully rubbed his ear.

"Sorry," she shouted.

"She's not my girlfriend." He changed places with her, causing her to look in the opposite direction.

"I saw her licking your ear earlier tonight." Maele smiled. "Not to mention, she called you 'daddy.'" Something about him made her feel at ease. She figured it was because he was Warren's brother, and Warren and Andie were like family to her. That kind of made him family too, she guessed.

"Yeah, and that was just the half of it. You should have seen what she did to me under the table." He wiggled his thick eyebrows. "Besides, don't friends lick each other's ears all the time?"

She looked at him, eyes wide, incredulous. Was he joking?

He laughed. A loud guffaw that rang above the noise of the music. Maele joined in his mirth. She realized she was taking things too seriously. Girlfriend or no girlfriend, he was family and they danced well together.

The ice had been broken. He grabbed her hand and spun her around, her eyes wide with surprise when she didn't lose her balance. She giggled when he turned into a robot. He gave her a thumbs-up when she flapped her arms like a chicken. Two full songs later, Warren appeared in front of them.

"May I cut in?"

"I'll find you again," Adam whispered in her ear before he released her when Warren offered her his hand.

"Smart move with the sneakers, Maele," Warren said as they began to dance. She felt slightly ashamed at being called out, but his look reassured her that it had, in fact, been a smart move.

Maele watched Adam disappear into the darkness. *What a funny man*, she thought, smiling as her dance with Warren ended. The music began to swell, and laughter brimmed over the quiet night, making it feel festive.

Later on, from her private corner of the party, she saw some of the staff walking back toward the kitchen, laughing and eating some of the food. She remembered working at a restaurant on the beach in Honolulu one summer, and being so hungry, she had been tempted to eat the leftovers. She'd never done it, although her peers had. Somehow, she felt it wasn't classy—not beneath her—just not okay. A job was a job, and she never felt right about giving in to her personal needs, no matter how tempting or acceptable. She never passed judgment though, because she'd been there, and she knew that story.

The thought of work—waiting tables, picking coffee, serving coffee—in the wake of this weekend was a heavy burden. She became keenly aware of her place. Maele had been born into a poor family, and they did the best they could to help her raise her station. They always said that if she married well ... But Maele didn't believe in raising her status by marriage. She wanted a shot at a good life based upon her own merit. She would be the first person in her family to have a college education. And when she had been surfing full time and surf companies had wanted to sponsor her, she'd become the first person in her family to travel outside of the islands. First person to fly on a plane. She'd only traveled to Fiji to surf Cloud Break for the Women's Championship Tour, but that was farther than anybody else had ever gone.

As she listened to the revelry, she felt a stirring in her soul. She yearned for more and felt worthy of having it. She had helped set up the party tonight—she'd done the work she always felt obligated to do, but now she would act like a guest and do what guests did—dance! She ran toward the dance floor in her Converse sneakers without a care in the world.

That night, she danced as if her life depended on it, not as part of the staff, but as a full-fledged guest.

Finding Her

Adam had walked off the dance floor and away from the girl who had set his teenage heart ablaze all those years ago—the girl he'd dreamt about, fantasized about—and here she was, within reach. He wondered if she had ever seen him sitting on the beach at sunrise way back then. On some days, he'd show up and she was nowhere to be found. But on other days, she'd been there, solo in the water, just like a dream. Then, during his senior year, she'd vanished. He'd heard rumors she had drowned while surfing one morning, but the details had been unclear. There was a huge buzz at school about a local surfer breaking their neck at the beach and dying, but the stories changed as they churned through the rumor mill for weeks.

What Adam had found curious, at the time, was when the stories about the dead surfer started circulating, his mystery girl stopped showing up at Secret Beach. After a while, a small part of him had accepted the fact that she was gone for good. There had been moments in his senior year when he'd started to think she'd never really existed anywhere outside of his mind in the first place. That he had invented her to escape his loneliness. Before he knew it, he'd been accepted through early admission to NYU, graduated from Puukumu Prep that spring, and then he was off on the grand adventure of his life. The surfer girl, his mystery girl, became the dream of a dream.

Except, now she wasn't. She was a living, breathing manifestation of his childhood love, and Adam was determined to learn everything there was to know about her.

First, he had some business to attend to. Adam had found his way back to his blonde friend in no mood to flirt or argue—he just wanted to set her free.

"Hey, Mr. Disappearing Act. Where've you been all night?"

"I was just helping Warren, taking care of best man stuff. You look good. It's good to see you again."

"It's so good to see you, Adam."

Adam looked at her for a minute and smiled. "You know, in the past, I would have tried to seduce you, and we would have talked about the movie I wanted to make here on the islands and how you were gonna be my star. We'd latch on to this dream, this enchantment, as a shared purpose. Something to look forward to. It would ward off our loneliness and kill time for both of us. But, I gotta be honest with you, it's not fair of me to do that to you. I'm sorry. I'm so glad you're here, and you do look beautiful. You *are* beautiful. I promise that you are my actor for the film, if and when I can get it made. In the meantime, you don't owe me a thing. Have fun tonight. That bloke over there has been eyeballing you for the past eight hours, so go talk to him. I went to school with him, and I happen to know he is a very cool dude."

Adam pointed to Danny Wong who, caught in the act of looking, glanced down and tucked his long black hair behind his ear.

"Seriously?"

"Yeah, no, I'm being serious. You and I have had this vague relationship ever since my time at NYU, and I feel like you are missing out because of me. You're wasting your youth on me. Don't do it. I'm not worth it. You should be available, in your heart and your mind, to find a love worthy of you."

"But what about our movie?"

"I told you, the movie still stands. You are the only one for the role, one hundred percent. I promise."

"Adam, you … Ugh. You infuriate me and yet you never stop surprising me. Yes, I have waited for you. Do I date and have fun? Of course I do. That guy you pointed out is kinda like my boyfriend. I mean, he is my boyfriend. I snuck him in by telling the guard he was you."

Adam shook his head, now understanding the mix-up with the guard.

"He just knows that whenever you're in town, you and I have a long-standing thing. He understands."

"Well, we should end that. It's not fair to Danny."

She took a step back and looked over her shoulder toward Danny. "Are you cool with that?" he asked.

"I'm cool. You're one of a kind, Adam. Guess I'll see you on set someday." She kissed his cheek and skipped away.

"Someday. That's a promise."

And the Shelly problem was eliminated.

The dance floor was raging with young people. The older members of the wedding party either stood on the side or gathered their belongings and headed out. Andie and Warren had yet to retire. Earlier in the evening, after dinner and cake, the couple walked under a canopy of sparks and light. It was a magical moment, the bride and groom looking perfect in their second outfits of the night, holding hands while running through a tunnel of their friends and family with long-stemmed sparklers held high.

Maele, arms outstretched, hopped and whirled next to the newlyweds. Her body and the freedom with which she moved made Adam's heart beat faster. He was used to watching her dance on the waves, but here she was, tangible for the first time. Adam watched her for a bit longer, until he could no longer stand it, then made his way over to her.

"Adam is here. Now the party begins." Warren moved Andie across the dance floor, leaving Adam in front of Maele.

Adam smiled. "I told you I'd find you again."

"What about your friend?"

"Do you see that handsome guy she's dancing with?"

Maele peered through the crowd. "Yes."

"Well, he's an old schoolmate named Danny Wong, and he is her boyfriend. She and I are old friends, and she'll star in my island romcom someday. Nothing more."

"Your movie, huh?"

"Yeah." Adam hoped the mention had impressed her.

They locked eyes. She smelled like orange blossoms and coconut—his senses were in overdrive.

"So, if she's just your friend, would you like to dance?" Maele smiled shyly.

"Love to."

The music ranged from classic rock to house music and flowed well into the night. Maele was barefoot by then, and looked happy. Adam had taken his jacket, vest, and shoes off long ago, wearing just slacks with his white shirt tucked in and half-unbuttoned, sleeves rolled up. Maele twirled and spun while Adam marveled at her.

A slower song called "Mississippi Moon" began to play, and the whole party ground to a slow shuffle. People paired up, heat rising off their bodies in the refreshingly cool night air. Couples held each other tightly, gently swaying to the music. Adam kept a respectable distance between him and Maele, at first, but as the song progressed, he took one step closer and then another. Adam gently placed his hand on Maele's lower back, making contact with a small sliver of exposed flesh. A spark ran through his fingers. At the same time, her eyes went wide and her cheeks flushed. Fueled by her reaction, he pulled her closer.

She allowed him, sliding her left palm into his right hand like a scene out of an old movie, and, gently, they swayed to the music.

Can we dance,
The dance
The night
Away

The two were locked in a moment. Adam watched her pulse vibrating like a drum in a small part of her long neck. He followed the line down to her collarbone, angular and ornamental, before ushering his eyes to her shoulder and down her toned, lean, long arms to a place on her wrist, damp with sweat and reflecting the warm light from the hanging bulbs above. Adam felt her chest rise up and down as she pressed closer to him, and for a second, he thought he could actually hear her heart beating. There was something so serene about her, her eyes closed and a smile gracing her scarlet lips. Adam, who had been with dozens of women at this point, felt new again. Not just the excitement that came with newness, but the fear and uncertainty that accompanied it, as well.

She opened her eyes and looked up at him. He met her gaze. Brown eyes stared at him, the color of earth, and Adam saw home.

"Adam Yates, you smell like frankincense and sandalwood." She paused to take one more whiff. "And cigarettes."

"Your hand is rough," he responded, living in his own dream, hearing nothing but the sweetness of her voice.

"Sorry?" She pulled her hand away.

"No, no, I don't mean it that way. Take my hand."

She placed her palm back on his and closed her fingers. Adam relaxed.

"I'm a writer, and my hands are soft. I'm really aware of it. In fact, I hate it. I take dirt and rub it between my hands to try and rough them up."

"Huh." She tilted her head as if waiting for him to continue.

"So, when I say your hands are rough, please know that in my world, that's a compliment. My mom's hands are rough. It means you use your hands—you are useful, not lazy. I know too many lazy people, and they make me sick. Like earlier tonight, when all the other guests were getting ready for dinner, you helped the staff set up. I saw you."

"You spied on me?"

"Maybe, just for like a minute or two. Or ten. I was curious. And you were kind. It's funny, people serve me all the time, and I never stop to think they are anything more than a means to an end. Necessary, but disposable. Until this afternoon, when I was made aware that the people who serve us are just that—people. Kids I went to school with, daughters, fathers, brothers, and aunties. I know I must sound like a total asshole, but that's …"

"That's how you see it," she said as a matter of fact. "Yes, Adam, I work, and I have worked my whole life. My parents pick coffee, and I serve it at Api's coffee shop. My hands tell that story. So …"

"That's your truth."

She looked up at him like she wanted to say something, but then she must have changed her mind, because she only exhaled.

They held on to each other as the song played. The heat from their bodies made the air around them humid. Adam felt beads of sweat misting on her skin.

They danced quietly for a while longer.

Can we dance,
The dance,
The night

~ 37 ~

Away
Can I find
A way
A way
To make you stay
Stay with me

"Did you used to live on the island?" he asked.

"Yes."

"When you were in high school?"

"Yes."

"So did I. I went to Puukumu Prep. I was a boarding school student."

"Oh yeah? I used to surf on a beach next to that school. All you Haoles on the surf team used to clog up the break, so I tended to head out at sunrise to beat the rush."

"I know." Adam looked at Maele. Their bodies gently swayed as if they were seaweed tethered to rock, gently moved by the tides in the sea.

Within seconds, Adam felt her stiffen. Maele took a step back, arms outstretched, holding a distance while she looked at him square in the face. They both froze for a long beat as the world danced slowly around them.

"Adam, did you used to wear a bright yellow sweatshirt?"

Without denying or confirming, he smiled.

"Hmm," she sighed, arching an eyebrow and puckering her lips in disbelief.

She had to know.

What funny games fate played. Fourteen days ago he was confirmed bachelor selling his first script in Hollywood, and then this wedding tore into his life like a whirlwind. And now, suddenly Maele. Andie was right— the islands were magic after all.

PART TWO:
Looking Back
(Exactly Fourteen Days Ago)
Maele & Adam

All That's Changed

"Anybody here?"

Maele jolted up in surprise, smashing her head on the open drawer. She hadn't expected anyone at Beans and Books this early. It wasn't even her day to work. She'd snuck in hoping to retrieve the only good pair of shoes she owned from under the counter. After spending hours riffling through the racks at the Salvation Army for outfits, she had finally found two dresses to wear to Andie's wedding festivities. In many ways, finding them had been a huge accomplishment. Most of the items had already been picked over, leaving her with few choices. Her next quest was to find the perfect pair of black heels, except resale shops only seemed to stock shoes donated by women with big feet. If worse came to worst, her backup pair sat in a grocery bag tucked deep under the cash drawer. She had big plans with Andie today—plans to shop for a bridesmaid dress—which left her both excited and dubious.

Maele crept up from under the counter, massaging her head as she stood. The bump caused tingles to reverberate down her neck. It always made her nervous when she hit her head now. Instinctively, her hand would fly to her neck, wrapping around it as if keeping her head from falling off.

The woman in the store had her back turned to her, long brown hair in that familiar French knot. Except she was no longer dressed in overalls and a T-shirt. She looked right at home in wide-legged pants that swept the floor, her bare midriff showing in a tasteful crop top. Maele's breath hitched, and tears formed in her eyes.

Two years ago, it had been here, at the only coffee shop and book nook on the island of Oahu, where Maele and Andie had started working together. Where, at the behest of her best friend, Api, Andie had moved to get away from her problems in Chicago. What had quickly turned into a business challenge ended up reviving the coffee shop, restoring a coffee plantation, and saving an entire community—a way of life.

"Maele," Andie whispered, stretching out her arms as Maele flew into them. "It's so nice to see you."

"Oh, Andie, I didn't know you'd be here so early. I thought I was going to have to wait until this afternoon to see you." She smiled through her tears.

"Don't cry, Mae. I couldn't wait until our fitting. My morning was open, and I wanted to see my friends. And this place. Ah, it looks so good."

"I'm sorry I'm crying. I just missed you, that's all." Maele's words were muffled against Andie's shoulder.

They held each other for a while.

Andie brought the sunrise to their lives when she was there, and her absence was a nightfall that left Maele with a chill.

When Andie had left, Maele had been left to face the fact she had yet to figure out her life. And she'd been right. Two years later, she was stuck in the same rut. Spending time with her cousin in Kauai was a last-ditch effort to regain some semblance of who she'd been before the accident.

Maele stepped back, arms still around Andie's shoulders. "It's so early," she said. "Did you want to open the store?"

"How did you know?" Andie joked in response. "Best job ever."

A rustling by the kitchen door sobered their moment. "I'm not on shift today, but the others are here. Come. Meet them. They've heard so much about you."

"In a minute," Andie said, walking toward the bookshelves, which had not only been expanded but built into every panel. Books spanned from wall to wall, sorted by color and size. "Beautiful," she whispered, running her fingers along their spines, taking a deep breath. "Smells amazing in here."

Maele smiled. From the time Andie had installed the first bookshelves, she used to close her eyes and breathe in the smell of books. She followed Andie as she walked from corner to corner, pausing at times to read the signs on the shelves.

"Wow. This place has turned into something truly impressive," Andie gushed, clasping her hands while scanning her surroundings.

Aside from the built-in bookshelves, a narrow, winding stairway led to a newly lofted second level with more tables, couches, and private reading pods. Though the color scheme remained all blue and white, it now had touches of red, yellow, and orange.

"Look here," Maele said, taking her hand and leading her to the center of the room.

"Andie's Picks?"

"Your favorite books," Maele answered.

"Wow, there must be about thirty books in here." Andie gently removed one of the books and held it close to her face. "Ah, The Thorn Birds. Good choice." She turned to Maele, smiling. "One too long for Api to read."

They laughed. Andie took another book. "Yes. Great Gatsby. Oh, and some indies."

"And this." Maele waved a book in the air. "A haiku book. Small Rooms."

"Hmm, yes," Andie responded, holding the book. "Actually, this may be a collector's item by now. The author wrote a haiku every day for one year and then printed them in this one and only first edition. It's signed, too. I remember where I was when I bought this."

Maele teased Andie with an impromptu haiku.

> "Hot guy waits for you
> His smile just like the sun
> Turning dark to light."

The girls giggled.

"Who doesn't love a good tiny poem?"

Maele's ribbing referred to a time that seemed so long ago. When a mysterious man named Warren Yates had stood outside the coffee shop, waiting for Andie to get off her shift.

"I'm marrying him."

"Yes, you are."

Andie and Maele turned toward a familiar voice. With Lani's arrival, their trio was complete.

Maele and Lani had been Andie's first friends on the island. They'd treated her like family, welcomed her into their homes. Now Andie was sharing her most important moment with them. Maele, Lani, and Andie's best friend, Api, were all bridesmaids at what the social posts had officially dubbed Oahu's Wedding of the Year.

Maele moved aside as Lani and Andie greeted each other. Lani was older—not quite as old as her mother—though a mother of two preteens herself. Her face and hands were lined with decades of hard work from years on the plantation. But her spirit was young. She was the force behind her husband, Duke, keeping him on his toes and on his game by welcoming change and innovation when others declined it. Lani had the courage and drive to protect her family, her culture, and two years ago their livelihood.

"So, what's up for the day?" Lani asked. "I'm on shift, but I'll meet you in the late afternoon here at the shop?"

"Well, yes, we have our fitting this afternoon, but the morning is wide open," Andie answered. "I just wanted to see you both as soon as I arrived. I'm staying at Api's place, but I'd thought I'd spend the day here before heading to Kailua. It's been too long. We have so much to do to get ready and I'm excited to get started."

"I'm game," Maele squealed. "Where should we go?"

"First order of business—to the beach. My body misses the water. I can't wait to get wet and catch some waves."

Maele froze, blinking, heart racing. Today, of all days, was not the day for her to catch some waves. She wondered whether Andie had noticed her reaction.

Just as quickly, she composed herself. She wouldn't let the chance to spend time with her friend pass her by because of some stupid fear of the water.

"Okay," she agreed, pasting on a smile, acutely aware of Lani's eyes on her. "But let's sit down and have a cup of coffee first." If she couldn't avoid it, she might as well delay it.

"Coffee and ..." Andie rubbed her hands together.

Maele knew exactly what she meant.

"Today's delivery of fresh malasadas doesn't come until ten," Lani said. "Sorry, Andie."

"Oh." Andie feigned disappointment. "I guess I shouldn't be eating too much anyway. I've got a wedding dress I need to fit into."

"I did happen to bring the freshest batch of coffee beans with me. Duke sent them just for you."

"And that," Andie said, making her way to the kitchen, "is better than anything else."

Room 64

Bang. Bang. Bang.

The muffled pounding on the door roused Adam Yates, but he couldn't pry his eyes open.

"Adam. Wake up, Adam!"

The voice came to him as if from a great distance through his deep, blackout-induced sleep. After someone slapped his face hard, Adam cracked one eye open. A stunning, raven-haired woman straddled him, but he had difficulty placing her. Was she a model or a waitress?

His night on the town replayed itself in his mind. A steak dinner where a contract had been signed, lots of drinks, several bars, a limo service, conversations with women, and a house party where he'd met up with a group of friends who had a lot of drugs. Wait. The last stop before the house party was the Viper Room—the woman hovering over him worked there.

"Adam!" The thumping on the door continued and the person on the other side knew his name.

"Are you still alive?" The raven-haired woman leaned across his chest and lifted his shoulders and shook him, but his head hung loosely like a ragdoll. She shrieked.

"Stop shaking me. I'm awake." He had mumbled the words, or thought he had. But she continued shaking him.

The knocking on the door grew louder. "What's going on in there? Open the door, Adam."

His heart raced and the blood pounded in his ears. Warren. A vague memory surfaced of his brother calling him after his flight from Chicago had landed. A sinking sensation settled in his stomach. He and Warren were supposed to do something today, but he couldn't remember what.

Adam scanned the room through his half-shut eye. A pile of drugs and a bottle of vodka were on the glass coffee table. Had he passed out in the living room? He ran a finger over the sofa cushion. Definitely not his bed.

The raven-haired woman's skin glistened in the sun burning through the open balcony door. He still couldn't remember her name, but it had something to do with wine. Brandy? A giant billboard with a tall, thin, wet woman dressed in a black swimsuit peeked through the gossamer curtains blowing in the wind.

The pounding on the door grew louder and harder and the girl slapped his face again.

"I. Am. Awake." Adam rubbed a hand over his face.

She let him go and leaned back. "Oh my God, Adam. You scared me. I thought—" Her lower lip trembled.

He shielded his eyes from the sun. "What?"

"I thought you'd had too much and was, like …" She glanced at the pile of drugs on the coffee table, then clutched her hand to her chest.

Adam rolled his eyes. Did she have to be so dramatic? His gaze was drawn to the famous Room 64 balcony of the infamous Chateau Marmont, which overlooked the notorious city of dreams, the idealized city of stars—his Los Angeles.

"I'll go get my things," she said flatly. "And someone's been knocking at the door."

"It's my brother, Warren." Adam sat up, swung his legs over the side of the couch, and groaned. Last night had been one for the books and now he was paying the price.

At a fresh bout of pounding on the door, Adam stood and padded down the long marble checkerboard hallway to the door and opened it. Warren stood on the other side, frowning.

The girl, the one whose handprints still inflamed Adam's cheeks, came out of the spare bedroom, and sidled past Adam.

"Good morning. Or afternoon, as the case may be. I'm Warren. Adam's older brother." He politely offered her his hand. "Sorry to intrude. I wasn't aware he had a guest."

"Lisa," she answered, ignoring Warren's outstretched arm, and scurried past him, carrying her shoes.

Adam rubbed his face with both hands as she walked away. Her name has nothing to do with wine. He opened the door wider, inviting Warren in.

Warren paused halfway down the hallway. "I'm lucky your neighbors didn't lodge a complaint of disturbing the peace. What took you so long?"

Adam closed the door and followed him into the living room. "Rough night." It had been a combination victory lap and a last hurrah before his time with Warren, after which, they'd be chartering a flight from L.A. to Honolulu for Warren's wedding.

As angry as Warren was at being kept waiting, Adam was happy his big brother was in town. He had a long list of sights he wanted to show him before they headed off to Hawaii. He was also excited for a change of pace for the next two weeks. Plus, he had incredibly good news to share.

When they reached the living room, Adam hugged Warren, who turned his head to the side, avoiding the smell of alcohol, weed, and God knows what else. "Welcome to L.A. Man, have I got a story for you."

Warren took a seat in one of the chairs and cast an eye over the stash on the coffee table.

Though Warren didn't say anything, Adam's confidence ebbed as old feelings of inadequacy surged. As far as the family was concerned, Adam was a disappointment—a rebel and a misfit—who would never belong in the Kingdom of Yates. There had always been a war raging inside Adam, a struggle of identity and purpose. He had waged battle alone ever since he'd been shipped off to boarding school at the age of fourteen. Lately, he felt like he was losing the war.

At least the sibling rivalry everyone talked about was no longer true. In the past four years, they had grown close and had become true friends. And ever since Warren had met Andie, things had been even better. She was this perfect mix, not just of culture and heritage, but of beauty and brains.

Warren cocked his head toward the bedroom. "Get dressed, we have suits to try on."

Adam snapped his fingers. "I knew we had something planned for today, but couldn't remember what."

Warren and his bride-to-be, Andie, had devised "a new deal" for their wedding. They would go their separate ways for two weeks prior to the wedding and not see each other until Warren watched Andie walk down the aisle. Warren chose to spend the time with Adam, and they'd have a grand L.A. adventure together.

"I'm gonna take a quick shower," Adam announced, heading to the bathroom.

"Please do." Warren grinned. "I'll make coffee."

As he soaped up, Adam thought about the changes in his brother since meeting Andie. Warren had changed almost overnight—stopped drinking excessively, stopped serial dating, stopped being a fixture on Page Six of the local paper. He'd also stopped stressing out and worrying about his future. Ever since Andie had come into Warren's life, he'd begun going with the flow, taking it slow, and savoring every moment.

Adam would never let a girl change him. He was going to remain single and become a successful screenwriter in Hollywood. Plus, he'd had a taste of love while in high school, but Adam had to convince himself it couldn't have been true love because "how could you love a person you've never even spoken to?" That he had never spoken to that girl on the beach still haunted him. He'd spent the last six years building a giant wall around his heart. A woman would just slow him down and then what? Marriage, kids, and the obligation to provide for his family. No thank you.

He laughed at the idea of providing for a family. Warren and Adam hailed from the wealthiest family on Oahu, one of the richest in the state, and had landed on Forbes's Top 50 Richest Families in the World every year for the past two decades. He was half Yates, but also half his mother, who was working class and practical and who had taught him that the most valuable quality in a man, besides trustworthiness, was to be a hard worker.

Adam emerged from the shower like a new man, then dressed, ready for the day.

Warren put his phone in his pocket when Adam entered the room. "We missed our appointment with Wanda, but she let us reschedule. It's now at four."

"Let's rock and roll. I got lots for you to see."

Every Breaking Wave

Maele sat on a little mound of sand facing the beach, far enough from the water, but close enough to feel the light spritz that came with every breaking wave.

It's too late to drive all the way home to get my swimsuit, she had said, hoping this excuse would get her out of going into the water. I'll sit on the beach while you go for a swim.

For almost an hour, she'd watched Andie frolic in the water, diving in and out like a fish and lying on her back with outstretched arms, her lightness buoyed by the waves.

Now Andie sat next to her, leaning back on her elbows, her skin glistening from the water and her chin tilted up.

"What a workout. I've missed this place so much. And this weather. December in Oahu is the best. Eighty-four and sunny."

"Was it really cold when you left Chicago?"

"We had our first snow in November, and it was a balmy thirty degrees when I left."

Maele smiled. "I'd love to go to Chicago one day."

"You can do anything, go anywhere, Maele. There's a big, bright world waiting for you."

"I wish. Sometimes I …" Maele wanted to say she felt strangled by her obligations to her family. Her mother and father have given her the best they could, but the best they could offer had come crashing down six years ago. Before she could finish, Andie sat up abruptly, fishing inside her beach bag to find her phone. She suppressed the continuous dinging of notifications.

"I wonder who this is," she said, breaking into a wide grin seconds before dropping her phone back into the bag.

"Everything okay?" Maele asked.

"Oh yeah," Andie said, clutching her bag to her chest as if holding close a lovely secret. "Warren's just checking in."

"Lani told me you guys have this two-week rule or something. That you're not seeing each other again until your wedding day?"

"Well, it's not really a rule. I have a ton of things to check off my to-do list before the big day, like our hunt for your perfect dress. Warren had to go to LA and get fitted for his suit and hang out with his little brother. Who is very handsome, Maele, but not for you, he's a bit of a bad boy."

She made a goofy face and a silly noise. Maele laughed, feeling like a younger sibling being teased.

"Anyway, if he had his way, we'd be flying together here, there, and everywhere. So, I kind of made it like a challenge. Why don't we take these two weeks apart? It will make our wedding day that much sweeter. Warren thrives on challenges."

Maele laughed. "Hence, no rehearsal dinner?"

"Hence no actual rehearsal dinner. It just gets so stressful when everyone has to socialize the night before. Instead, we are getting together with our loved ones separately. Warren arranged for his guests to stay at the Four Seasons. Our group will all be staying at The Kahala Mandarin, and we chose several options for a few days of relaxation. All my dad wants to do is play golf. My mom is going to an orchid show in Honolulu with Auntie Mel." Andie looked directly at Maele. "But I regret our deal now. I miss him."

No one in Maele's family, maybe in her generation, had ever been to the Four Seasons, let alone the Kahala Mandarin. When she was in high school, there was talk of a classmate holding her debut there, but Maele hadn't been invited.

"Someone once told me that good things come to those who wait."

"Oh." Andie laughed. "Most of the time, that's true!"

Maele's insecurities resurfaced. What was she doing here, sitting on the beach with her boss? Why on earth is this woman, ten years her senior, wasting precious time on her? She was a farm worker, a coffee server. This woman beside her, showing her so much warmth and love, was marrying the richest man in Oahu! Maele pulled at the edge of her shorts, immediately conscious of a loose thread hanging from its seams. If she pulled it, would it all unravel? She wanted to try.

Just like her life, with its neat little routine, she felt it was time to untangle it.

After a few minutes of comfortable silence, Andie asked, "Mae, are you okay? What's new? How are you enjoying school?"

"Oh." Maele snapped out of her thoughts. "Sorry. Yes, one more year to go and I get my associate's degree."

"That is wonderful. You were always meant to be a businesswoman. Lani tells me you'll probably graduate at the top of your class. I'm so proud of you."

"Thank you. I wish I could transfer my credits over to a real university."

"You can do anything you want, and I'll always be here to cheer you on," Andie said. "I know Warren keeps pestering me about that mentorship program at Apex. We think you'd be a great candidate when you're ready. We've tapped some local industry leaders to act as advocates."

I would never make that program. They probably look at young, promising talent. All my promise has been crippled.

To interrupt her self-pity, Maele looked up and happily waved at a bearded man in a baseball cap and board shorts who slowly approached them from the shore.

"Oh, it's Emerson," Andie said.

Emerson trudged through the sand, his loose, worn flip-flops making it difficult to maintain his balance. Sprays of sand went every which way as he walked. He balanced a huge vase of flowers in one hand and a paper bag in the other.

Andie waved. "Hi, Emerson. What are you doing here?"

"Hi, Ms. Andie. Hi, Maele," Emerson greeted. Beads of sweat rolled down his forehead. "Ms. Andie, Mr. Warren said I'd find you here. He wanted me to give you this." Emerson held out the flowers. "And this." He dangled the paper bag from his other hand.

Andie jumped up, shook the sand off her swimsuit, and covered herself with a sarong. "Thank you so much, Emerson. These are beautiful," she said, admiring the hydrangeas. "What's in the bag?"

"Malasadas. He asked me to make you some fresh coconut ones."

"Ooh." She squealed in delight. "I'm so grateful you took the time to come all the way here."

"It was no problem. My truck is parked down the street from your shop." He removed his cap and smoothed his hair before replacing it. "I'm going to run. Don't want any island rats stealing the stuff in my truck."

Andie laughed. "Thank you again, Emerson."

Maele started packing up the towels. She took the flower vase from Andie. "Here, let me help you. We'd best get going. We have a big day ahead."

"Wait, wait. Let's take a couple of bites." Andie handed Maele a donut slathered in powdered sugar. "What a wonderful way to start the day."

"It is. I'm so glad you're here."

Time Peace

Adam and Warren pulled out of the private chateau driveway, turned right onto Sunset Boulevard, and headed west toward Beverly Hills. Adam liked nice things and he could afford them. He stayed at the Chateau Marmont because of its history and location, but also because the price point meant nothing to him. It was the same reason he drove a cherry red convertible 1963 Porsche Carrera 2—something only a handful of people could afford. He'd bought the car when he was twenty-three because he could, with his dad's money.

Adam wanted these next two weeks to be special. He was going to host his brother, who had become more like his best friend, around the city he loved. First stop would be Rodeo Drive to buy wedding suits, but after that, the sky was the limit.

The car purred as it climbed Sunset Boulevard, passing the Viper Room on their left, the infamous, black and purple place once partly owned by Johnny Depp—where River Phoenix had taken his last breath.

On the right was another famous club. "That's Whisky a Go Go, the birthplace of Janis Joplin, Mötley Crüe, and Guns N' Roses," Adam said over the hum of the Carrera's engine.

They made their way into Beverly Hills where Sunset Boulevard widened and was lined with towering jacaranda, palm, elm, and oak trees. High walls surrounded the mansions maintaining the residents' privacy.

They stopped at a light to turn left. The green arrow allowed Adam to gently pull the car onto North Beverly Drive with its rows of towering palm trees.

"Did you remember watching L.A. Story, that movie by Steve

Martin, with me?"

"Yes, we watched it together before you left for NYU. You told me it was Martin's answer to Woody Allen's Annie Hall."

"Exactly!"

"You said it was the kind of movie you wanted to make."

"Well, I said I wanted to be able to pivot like Martin did. Tell all kinds of stories in all kinds of ways, but do you remember the scene where all the cars were waiting at a six-way stop and all the drivers were waving to each other to go first, but then they all pulled out at the same time and crashed in the middle? Well, this is that intersection," Adam explained as they pulled up to a vast six-way stop where Lomita Avenue runs parallel to Sunset which is bisected by a giant X made by Canon and Beverly.

Then the little car blasted down the road, passing houses and parks and crossing Santa Monica Boulevard as it tore down Beverly Drive, where Adam abruptly pulled into a covered parking lot.

"I figured we'll just walk for a bit."

"Sounds good," Warren said.

It was a nice winter day. The sun was out and it was close to seventy-eight degrees, a typical winter day for L.A. The brothers turned heads as they made their way down the street, bystanders mistaking them for movie stars. Both tall and lanky, hair floppy and full, they looked like the best of the beach, city, and the silver screen. As they passed a jewelry store, Warren wanted to drop in and buy Andie a wedding gift.

"What are you thinking about getting her?"

"A little post-wedding, pre-honeymoon gift. A watch to match mine."

Once the purchase was made, the brothers were off to Armani, but decided to stop for chocolate and coffee at a little sweets shop on the corner before heading in to buy some suits.

Secret Society

After a quick change and cleanup back at the coffee shop, the girls made it to the next stop on their whirlwind adventure—a bridal boutique in Honolulu, for their fittings. Exclusive and private, the windows were shrouded in secrecy by fine silken drapery to protect the creations from the outside world. The décor was minimal; white marble floors, pristine ivory carpeting, and luxurious velvety couches placed strategically around mirrors and pedestals. But what caught Maele's eye were the giant, luminous crystal chandeliers that dangled from the ceiling. They reminded her of Christmas lights, silvery fish, and moonlight shining on the water. And, of course, everyone was dressed to the hilt. The saleswomen wore shoes like Andie's—the ones with the colored soles—which Andie said hurt her feet more than anything.

Maele sat in the fitting room by herself, waiting for them to bring her dress. Her mother had taken her measurements and sent them to Andie's team. Had she mentioned that Andie had a team? It was composed of Diana, her wedding planner, and a cast of hundreds. Okay, maybe a cast of seven, which seemed like a lot to her. Then again, one only gets married once, fingers crossed. Andie had handpicked a friend and Filipina designer named Amarie, who incorporated artisanal materials in her wedding collections. Andie was proud of her country's handicrafts and wanted to showcase their art.

But, to Maele, the intricacies of high couture posed a problem. She was paralyzed by the whole dress situation. She'd never really thought about the economics of participating in such a huge event, let alone being front and center. She'd need two dresses at the most, since Andie had assured her there would be no bachelorette party—just a beach day and a simple dinner. Then a thought made her heart sink. If that "simple" dinner was as fancy schmancy as this place, then she'd really need to step up her game ... Maele had been diligently saving for her Kauai trip, so after paying for her tuition and helping her parents with groceries, a hundred dollars was literally all she had left to spend.

A wedding during the holidays was a beautiful thing, but only if you were the bride.

Her mom had beamed at her the morning she'd tried on the simple dresses she found at the Salvation Army. With her ebony hair cascading down her shoulders in loose curls, her eyes made up, her lips lined and full—even the strangers in the common fitting room stopped to watch her in the mirror. She'd worn one of her dresses—a floral printed jersey dress that fit her figure so perfectly. It was a little long, which made her look short, but she loved the way it made her feel. She wore the dress and the little blue diamond around her neck. The one her grandfather had won from the plantation's patriarch, Mr. Flores, in a game of fan-tan close to seventy years ago. It was the only thing of real value owned by her family and the only heirloom they had to pass down from generation to generation. Worn by her grandmother, who had passed it on to her son, who gave it to his wife, her mother. It was Lolana who gave it to Maele right after her accident. The women in her family believed it was a lucky omen that brought healing and strength to the person who wore it.

The reality of it all—this wedding and her planned stay in Kauai—began to hit Maele as she sat on the spotless velvet couch waiting for a dress to be brought to her. She had developed a nervous tick in recent years, picking at things whenever she was anxious—mostly loose pillow threads, rough pieces of fiber on her bed. Today she took her nerves out on her necklace, pinching and pulling at the little blue diamond while sliding it up and down its golden chain. Furiously fidgeting and wishing it would magically banish her fears.

Three knocks.

"Maele Moana?" A woman in a white suit peered through a crack in the door.

Maele sat up, hands in her lap. "Yes?"

The woman let herself in, hoisting a long, white chiffon gown, belted at the waist, its lace edges dragging along the floor.

Maele stood.

"I am told this is yours," the woman said. "What a gorgeous dress. Good choice! Try this on, honey, and we'll be waiting outside for you."

Maele nodded, walking toward the mirror as the woman softly closed the door behind her. The satin bodice fit her like a glove, feeling like butter as she slipped into it.

What she saw in the mirror stunned her. The girl in front of her was a stranger. The soft lighting and the beautiful dress combined to make her look like someone who was made for this sort of attire—someone whose skin was smooth and soft, not tanned and weathered like lava rock from working under the sun. Rich people skin. It was a rich girl's dress, and she was an imposter.

Maele grabbed the tag sewn to the dress's side and brought it to her face, adjusting its angle and counting the number of zeroes.

"Mae, are you ready?" Lani knocked on the door before letting herself in. Maele couldn't define the look on her face. Lani gasped loudly, her hand flying to her mouth at the same time. Maele thought she was going to cry.

"Oh my. You look like a princess. That dress fits you so well," she gushed. "I wish your mom and dad could see you. You are no longer a girl, but a beautiful young woman."

"Let's go," Maele said tersely, stepping off the platform. "I don't like this dress." She proceeded to bunch up the edges and shuffle out the room.

Lani followed her. "Wait. Why? What's wrong, Mae?"

"Nothing," she said as she marched across the spacious dressing room. "I just want to go home after this."

Andie and Api were waiting in the sitting room. Both women had the same reaction upon seeing Maele, except that Api was more vocal, as always. Sometimes Maele thought the reason Andie and Api were best friends was because they were polar opposites.

"OMG, Maele! You look like … well, you look like a beauty queen."

Maele exhaled loudly. "I'm sorry, I don't like it."

A seamstress and two assistants fenced her in, waiting anxiously.

Maele tugged at the strap across her chest. "It's tight."

A seamstress checked the fit. "No, ma'am. It fits fine."

"Well, it's itchy."

"We use the finest fabric. There shouldn't be any itchiness."

Maele stood on her toes and her socks bunched around her ankles. "It's too long."

"We can hem it."

Maele looked directly at Andie. "I just don't like how it looks on me."

"But you look perfect," Api said.

"No, I don't like it."

Andie stood and motioned to the seamstress. "Okay, let's find something else. I'd like some alternative dresses for her, please."

"No, no," Maele objected. Then she whispered so only Andie could hear. "I can just go to another store and get one that looks like it. Or have Mama sew me one. We still have a few days."

Andie waved her hands, turning to the seamstress. "Can we have a minute here, please?"

The two women nodded, glancing at each other before leaving the room.

"Api, Lani, can we meet you in front?" Once everyone left, she turned to Maele. "What's wrong? Talk to me."

"It's just …" Maele began to cry. "That dress is two thousand dollars. I don't have that much." Her eyes welled up as embarrassment gnawed at her.

Andie placed her hands on Maele's shoulders, before gently touching her face. "Listen, Mae. You're right." She paused to look her in the eye. "The dress costs a little more. But I was looking at how the style would fit my theme. I also considered that the girl who will be wearing it is someone very special to me."

"Thank you," Maele sputtered between sniffs.

"So, what price would you be comfortable with?"

Maele laughed. "One hundred dollars?"

Andie laughed before she pulled Maele close. "I'll tell you what. This store won't have anything at that price, but what if I pay for it? You can owe me if you want, but you don't have to. It'll be my wedding gift to you." Maele looked at Andie with a look that said it all. "Or pay me back once you're successful." She paused and held Maele's face in her hands. "And you will be. Once you become a well-seasoned young woman in business, you will pay me back. You're like a sister to me, Mae. I intend to be in your life forever."

That last line meant the world to Maele. She didn't want Andie to ever forget her. And if she owed Andie money, it would tie them together for as long as … well, forever.

"Okay, deal." Maele said, bobbing her head, comforted by the belief Andie had placed in her. "Okay."

The Tux

The world is a funny place—levels, clubs, secret societies. Some are pure fiction, but the more money one acquires, the more they become a reality. Take Armani. The average suit costs more than an ordinary person's monthly rent.

In Beverly Hills, on the second floor of the North Rodeo Drive store with its 90210 ZIP code, was Wanda, Head of Armani Talent, well into her sixties, with a head of fiery red hair and an expertise at separating the rich from their money. One of her assistants served water, coffee, wine, or bourbon, while another took measurements. All this happened while the privileged were treated to a glimpse of the season's latest fashions as well as a preview of what was to come. If you lived in that universe, someone like Wanda was the gatekeeper who kept everyone else away.

Warren surrendered to the world she created, and Adam was under her spell, too. But getting married, wedding suits, and all the rest of the romantic hogwash didn't fit in with Adam's plans to be the greatest filmmaker in Hollywood. First step, sell a screenplay and win an Oscar for it. Next step, direct one of his screenplays and win an Oscar. Third step, repeat until the legacy was undeniable.

Adam sat on a deep brown leather couch, drink in hand, as Warren interrupted his thoughts of Hollywood domination by discussing what he'd like to wear at his wedding with Wanda.

"I have two ideas in mind for a winter wedding in Hawaii," Warren said. "I want either a tuxedo with tails, like the one John F. Kennedy wore for his wedding, or a khaki suit, to fit the beach vibe."

Wanda acted like she and Giorgio Armani were lifelong friends and he was in the back room sewing suits on request, ready to make adjustments. She made shopping an experience—personal and specific. Used to dealing with high profile clients, she made them feel special.

"Hmmm." She tapped a pencil against her notepad. "Different rules apply in places like Hawaii, so I think you can get away with a light suit."

Warren pressed his lips together for a moment. "Are you sure? The photos will be published in society rags, and I hate giving the press an easy target. I want this day to be bulletproof, not something I 'get away with.' Plus, I want to surprise Andie with something special."

"I have an idea." Wanda grabbed an album and flipped through the pages. "Giorgio has a vintage suit with tails from one of his early lines." She flashed a photo of a black suit with gray piping. "We could have some made for you and your groomsmen."

He nodded. "This will suit me just fine."

They all politely laughed at his pun. Adam was sure that was the first time anyone in a suit store heard that joke.

"I have the measurements for my groomsmen, and this guy will be standing up for me, as well." Warren hooked a thumb toward Adam. "He's my best man."

Warren had chosen family over his longtime friend for the role of best man because blood counted for something. And Adam accepted because Warren had become his best friend. So, being his best man only felt right.

"So, I'll need six suits in total for me and my groomsmen. I'll need them in Oahu on the eighteenth of December. Can you do it?"

"Of course, we can, Mr. Yates. We can do anything."

That was the kind of confidence that money afforded, and for a special occasion, it was worth it.

When the Wanda show was over, Adam raised his eyebrows like a villain, giving Warren a furtive look and a crooked smile. "Sushi?"

"You look like you're asking me to rob a bank with you. Sure. Sushi sounds good right now," Warren said.

"Awesome. I know a place. It'll be the perfect place for me to tell you my news."

13

Us Who?

"**M**ae, come see what Papa has brought home." Lolana's voice skittered through the walls like a megaphone. Maele was busy pinning the receipt of the bridesmaid's dress on her corkboard, running her fingers across it like it was gold. As days went by, she felt less and less guilty about allowing Andie to buy her the dress. Maele considered it an advance. That dress was a work of art. She would keep it and treasure it, pass it on for future generations.

Maybe a bit overdramatic, yes, but a dress that cost so much should last until the end of time. Or, at least, until she had her own bridesmaid. Which, at the rate she was going, would probably never happen.

"Coming." Maele crossed the hall and tore down the stairs, two steps at a time. She landed on the bottom step with a thud. Her mother stood by the open door, hands on her waist, apron blowing in the wind. Their home was set up like a narrow townhouse. To the left of the stairs was the living room, and to the right, the kitchen. But the view of the land surrounding it, with its lush, thick coffee trees and breathtaking combination of hills and valleys and ocean from behind, was out of this world.

"Papa," Mae greeted, and kissed her father on the cheek right before he climbed out of his truck.

Slowly, he shuffled to the truck bed and pulled on its door.

"Look what I found today," Kaku said, smiling. His hair had grayed in recent years—still thick and unruly—but lately salt and peppered in more places.

She leaned in and found a wooden bookshelf, painted white and anchored on four sides by frayed rope.

"Picked it up when doing my rounds of Kailua. The rich people leave their used furniture on the curb, and we pick them up." He slid the cutting blade across the crisscrossed jute fibers, tugging them loose. "Matches your room, no?"

She wanted to say he didn't have to worry about her room; that she didn't intend to stay much longer. But she loved him so much, she would save those words until the time was right.

Saving words. She was a master at keeping things to herself. Maybe because she didn't think anyone would listen—mostly because she'd learned keeping words in her mind somehow kept them alive longer. Once uttered, words became real.

"Thank you, Papa. I love it. Let me get the guys to help you bring it into the house." Maele pulled out her phone and typed a text.

In a few seconds, two burly younger men rushed out from the neighboring townhomes to assist. She followed them as they brought the new bookcase into the house. She knew its material was of good quality—one, because it was from Kailua; and two, because the weight of the solid wood caused her friends to grunt as they carried it up the stairs. She watched them position the shelf in the corner before helping her lay the books from the old shelves on the floor. The frame was thicker and clunkier than she would have chosen, but her father was right. She needed more shelf space.

The guys carried out her old bookcase with ease. It was a far cry from her new one, made of particleboard and stuck together with tape. When she was left alone in her room again, she sat on the floor and began sorting through her books and cards.

An old leather notebook caught her attention. It was brown and weathered, etched with thin white lines, and creased in places that shouldn't have been. Maele drew a breath before leafing through the pages, which were bookmarked with pictures and postcards. They made her smile. Gently, she laid the notebook on the table by her bedside. She felt ready to relive the memories and read the words she had saved for a very long time. She was ready to continue her story.

"Lana, this is probably the best adobo you've made in a while," her father noted as he scooped another spoonful of rice on his plate. "Don't you think so, Mae?"

Maele nodded, her mind somewhere else.

"I marinated it longer this time, with the vinegar and soy," her mother said, proudly taking the serving spoon and twirling it around the bowl to pour more sauce on the chicken. "But when did you not like my cooking, Kaku?"

Dinners at their house were full of life on weekends, when friends from the plantation—especially Duke and Kukane—spent the night playing cards and drinking coconut rum or vodka. That night was a quiet one, a work night. Not only was it the tail end of harvesting season, but orders for their coffee products were also through the roof. Merely two years ago, their future had been uncertain. Not anymore. At least her father's generation had gained the right to retire in their own time.

"Do you like your bookshelf?" Lolana pulled Maele out of her thoughts.

"Yes. It's great."

"Ha." Lolana snickered. "It was probably in their maids' quarters."

"Mama, they don't have those anymore. That's so 1940s."

"You'd be surprised. A lot of the colonialism from Spanish times has stayed with rich people. I remember my mom, your lola—she lived in one of those houses with a separate wing for the help. My dad grew up right here on this land. Same as me."

"But you said they were nice to her." Mae spooned another helping of pork onto her plate. She'd never seen such treatment from the Floreses. Come to think of it, she didn't think they had a separate home for their help. None of their help lived in—everyone was bused to and from the residence during the day.

"Yes, but they were still separate. The rich will always be separate from us." Lolana stood, filled a pitcher with water, and poured a glass for her husband.

Maele's blood rose to her face, her cheeks growing hot. "Us who?"

"Poor people."

"Mama, we're not poor. We have everything we need. Rich people can't buy what we have. Look at what happened to Mr. Flores. No matter how much money they had, his wealth couldn't make him better. Or Warren Yates's mother. Same thing."

"Speaking of rich people, what are your plans for Andrea's

bachelorette party?"

"It's not a bachelorette party. We're flying to Maui for a girls' four-day spa weekend and her bachelorette dinner," she said, shaking her head in disbelief of what she was saying.

"See? Rich people," her father deadpanned.

"All the way to Maui? What was wrong with having it here in Oahu?" her mother asked.

"I don't know, Mama. I don't ask those things. Lani will pick me up in the morning so we can drive to the airport."

Her father looked up for the first time, his culinary trance broken. "You're flying private?"

"Mr. Yates, Warren's father, owns a twelve-seater." When she saw her parents' blank faces, she added, "A plane with twelve seats, I suppose."

"And you'll be okay? You haven't ridden a plane since—" Lolana swallowed her words. Father and daughter stared at her, waiting for her to continue. "The accident," Lolana said, her eyes downcast, her face full of regret.

"That was six years ago. I'll be okay."

Lolana reached out and gently tapped her daughter's cheek. "I know, kaikamahine. I know."

Her father finished dinner, pushed his plate aside, and leaned back in his chair. Mae knew what would come next. Slowly, he rested his hand on his stomach, sated after a delicious meal.

"Mama says you want to spend some time with your cousin and friends."

"Yes, I do." It was first a whisper, then she cleared her throat and repeated, "Yes, I do."

"What about school?"

Maele paused before offering an answer. "I'm done with my courses. I'd like to enroll in university next fall."

"University?" Her mother locked eyes with her father, who nodded slightly. A secret code.

"Yes. They will credit my two years and I will only have two years left."

What she didn't say was that she planned to make some money on her own. Maybe try touring the circuit, doing what she used to love—the thing that gave her life. It wasn't the time to say it out loud. She figured she'd spend weeks in Kauai building up her courage.

"And what is happening in Kauai?" her father asked. "Why spend your break there?"

"Koa is also home again. I miss him. It's been a few years, I thought I'd—"

"Are you going back into the water?" Her father leaned forward, staring at her, searching for the truth.

"I'd like to. When I'm ready."

"Okay," he said.

She could barely hear him. When had he gotten so docile? And when had her mother ever been this quiet? "Okay?" Who were these people and what had they done with her parents?

"Mae," he said. "You've been a good daughter. You want to take a break, go to school, and do something with your life. Why would I object?"

"I don't know what to say," Maele answered, overwhelmed and shocked at their submission. She was prepared to let this simmer for a few days. Now it wouldn't have to. "Thank you."

"I'll speak to your uncle Fudge about it; make arrangements. When?"

"Not sure, but maybe a week or so after the wedding. Definitely for Christmas."

"You're gonna miss Christmas, too?" Her father looked sadly at her mother, who nodded.

They were going to miss their only child. She rubbed the little blue diamond that hung around her neck for comfort. Maele was sad, too comfortable in her life, but she knew she had to push herself out of the nest.

"Well, maybe," she said, pausing to gauge her mother's reaction.

"Yes, maybe," Lolana said, turning to her husband. "Maybe we can celebrate it early, while we're still in Kauai."

"What? I'm supposed to pack all the gifts with us?" her father grumbled good-naturedly.

Lolana stood, walked over to Mae, and leaned down to enclose her arms around Mae's shoulders. "The world is yours for the taking. All you need to do is forget all your fears and go after it."

14

Kampai

They dug out the Porsche from the underground lot and tore over Coldwater Canyon to find a table at a little sushi place in the Valley called Katsu-ya. Adam took Warren to the one on Ventura in Studio City.

"This is the original." Adam pointed to the white neon sign that glowed in the soft night sky, still gleaming from the setting sun as he handed his keys to the valet in the bright blue shirt.

Adam and Warren walked into the restaurant to the shouted greetings of the chefs behind the bar and the three attractive ladies at the hostess station.

"Irasshaimase!" Their voices were loud and jarring, but it was the tradition of most sushi bars to welcome a guest this way and let them know the staff was ready to serve.

"Hey, guys." Adam raised a hand in greeting. "Danny, this is my brother, Warren." He turned his head toward Warren. "Danny's one of the best sushi chefs in Los Angeles which, I would argue, makes him one of the best sushi chefs in the world."

"It's nice to meet you, Danny." Warren nodded toward the chef and then arched an eyebrow at Adam. "In the whole world? That's a pretty big claim."

"Just wait."

Adam excused himself to use the restroom, where he took a bump of cocaine and then washed his hands. When he returned, a pretty young lady sat them at a table in the back of the room. It was a small space— sixteen tables plus twenty seats at the bar. Cozy, but it hummed with a warm buzz when it was full. The evening was filled with sounds of talking and laughter, with the intermittent "Irasshaimase!" thrown in. Adam saw Warren enjoying the ambiance, the food, and the company.

"Oh my gosh. What is this?" Warren asked as he took a bite of albacore tuna with crispy onions.

"Did you just say 'Oh my gosh'? Are we in first grade? What happened to my brother?"

"Sorry, it's something Andie says all the time and it's become a habit, I guess. So, do you come here a lot?"

"Yeah, once or twice a week. I love it here. I'll probably die of mercury poisoning from all this damn tuna I eat—sorry, darn tuna—but it's the best. Did you know that during World War II, the Japanese had submarines parked off the coast of California? So, not only were they able to strike our home state of Hawaii, but they were within striking distance of the entire west coast of the United States. This is so crazy. We're talking about this in a Japanese restaurant while eating sushi."

"In California."

"Ha, yes, in California. Dude, I'm so happy you're here. I'm so proud of you. Congratulations on getting married, Warren. Kampai!" Adam drank his saké. "You told me you were gonna get married. I remember the day well."

"You do? Because, as I recall, you were pretty out of it."

"You'd be surprised how well I function in any state of mind." He grinned. "So, anyway, the Japanese Empire told their entire submarine fleet to surrender, which meant Kamikaze. They sunk the entire fleet off the shoreline. The crews suffocated or starved, and the subs are now tombs at the bottom of the ocean. But here's the really messed up part— their giant-ass batteries leaked and have been steadily leaking mercury into the water for the past seventy-five years. More interestingly, this was told to me at the Post Ranch Inn by a man named Thomas, who happened to be John Steinbeck's son. Yeah, I was looking out at the water and this older man was standing there smoking a pipe and just started telling me about the mercury in the water and about sunken submarines. I mean, East of Eden. Come on."

"Don't forget Of Mice and Men or Grapes of Wrath." Warren interrupted his brother's monologue.

"Remember that Spielberg movie, The Empire of the Sun? Christian Bale was a kid in that movie and twenty years later he's the

Dark Knight." Adam was off on a tangent again, something Warren had gotten used to. "What a crazy career, when his character sees the flash of the A-bomb detonating in the distance. How eerie would that be?"

Adam had a few moods, most of them happy. But sometimes he had moods that got him talking for hours. Nobody could get a word in edgewise.

Adam wondered if his brother thought this dissonance was drug-fueled. He made a conscious effort to slow down. He knew his ability to dredge up random, unrelated thoughts made him a great writer, but Warren once told him that habit often made the conversation one-sided. He paused for a moment, consciously giving Warren time to say something.

"Speaking of movies, tell me about yours. What's happening? What's the latest?"

"I've wanted to tell you this news all day. Are you ready?"

"Yes, Adam, I'm ready. What's your news?" His brother took another sip of saké.

"Dude, everyone at Universal fell in love with my script and they bought it!" Adam was unable to control his excitement. He jumped up and waved both hands in the air before sitting back down. Warren leaned forward, his eyes as wide as the smile on his face. Adam felt love and admiration in that very moment. "The contract was signed last night, and I'm heading into script notes and, I guess, pre-production, in a few months. The film has a huge budget, in the hundred-million-dollar range. A well-known producer has signed on. They're projecting this could be the studio's next big franchise. It's beyond my wildest dreams. The deal is being announced this week, and my agents are telling me it's one of the richest contracts they've ever negotiated. What's more, I'm one of the youngest people to ever do it."

"So much for Father's plan B," Warren said, with a grin so wide it touched the corners of his eyes.

"Dad's relentless. Between Mom's suffocating love and his endless disappointment in my lack of interest in his business, I guarantee he'll say something to pull the rug out from underneath all this. But let's not go there. To Dad. Here's to Dad. Kampai!" Adam raised his glass.

"Kampai!" Warren raised his glass in return.

The brothers took their saké in hand. Before they drank though, Adam asked, "Do you know what it means, kampai? Kampai means 'empty glass' in Japanese, so every time someone shouts it, we will have to diligently drink what's left in our saké glasses."

The brothers downed their saké and then quietly poured more of the cold, cloudy rice wine from the frosted, tall pink bottle.

Adam watched Warren discreetly remove his cell phone from his pocket, read something off the screen, and smile. He then quickly typed something in reply. By the time Warren put his phone down, Adam was three pieces deep into the baked crab roll.

"I'm happy with the script. It's going to be a really good movie. It's about a dystopian world that's mostly underwater," Adam started up again.

"Oh ... So, you're remaking Water World?"

"No! It's totally different. The humans interact with sea life. Animals and man have learned to depend on one another, so the heroes can ride on dolphins and stand on sea turtles. Like, dude, the sharks are used for good! There's this cool scene where we see the hero and heroine way out at sea surrounded by nothing but water. They look triumphant, making their way across a desert of water. Think Lawrence of Arabia, but riding on a frickin' whale's back. And you see these sharks swimming closer and closer, as sharks do—"

Adam broke off as a memory popped into his head. "Do you remember that time at Waimea when I was chased back to shore by a bull shark?"

"Yes, of course, I do. I was there. One of the scariest days of my life. He was so aggressive. I thought he was going to attack you. I kept swimming behind him and hitting his tail."

"You were hitting its tail?" Adam asked.

"Yes. You don't remember that? I left my board floating out in the break and swam behind the shark as it trailed you, because if he took a bite, I was gonna be right there to poke his eye out, punch his nose, and pull you onto shore. All I could do was grab at his tail and try to steer it away from you."

"You were protecting me?" Adam asked, genuinely surprised. He tried to stop himself from feeling emotional about it, curtailed his smile, and shook his head at Warren. "I didn't know that."

"I will always look out for you, Adam."

Touched by those words, Adam took a deep breath, then a drink of his saké. He looked at Warren.

"I'm proud of you. It's enjoyable to watch all your hard work pay off."

As a boy growing up on Oahu, Adam had done one of two things almost daily. He would either surf, or make movies with his friends on a camera his parents had bought him. Most days, he did both. The movies started out as surf films. Young kids who were looking for the perfect wave, Endless Summer-type stuff. But as he got older, his stories grew in complexity. It was as if he was able to use his art to answer the real-life questions he was asking. By the time he was thirteen, he'd entered and won several film festivals. His IQ for filmmaking was off the charts, and his narrative voice was unique. Adam had been writing and directing films for almost fifteen years, at this point. Little films, but still. Films.

"I remember, after my mom's funeral," Warren began. "I didn't really know you yet, so you were already a young man of sixteen, and I just had all these not-so-great feelings toward you. I mean, you were the son that took my father away, right? So, I was prepared not to like you. But you filmed my mother's funeral and turned the footage into a short film about me and my dad. It was all love."

Adam remembered that it was his plan to go to the funeral and film this mysterious phantom brother, capture him on film and eat his soul. What he captured instead was the kindest, bravest, coolest person he'd ever met. He filmed Warren taking complete charge of his mother's burial, fighting back tears, being brave in a way Adam could never imagine being. He was a man in charge of his own destiny. At that time, Warren was twenty-four, but to Adam he seemed like a hero who could save the world.

Adam had cut footage from the funeral, along with clips he'd taken of his father on morning walks on the beach and during his meditations, capturing quiet moments that looked like regret and sorrow. This, along with old home movies he'd found of Warren's mother, Catherine, in a box labeled 'Lilly Cat,' which he'd always seen growing up and assumed it was a box of tapes with home videos starring a cat; until he learned of her nickname at the funeral.

Adam spent weeks editing the footage and weaved together a heartbreaking, twelve-minute film about grief, loss, and letting go. Neither man knew they were being filmed, but their narrative paths followed each other's, and their stories were interwoven, and the archival footage of Catherine made her come back to life for a moment and to show how she would have handled their broken hearts.

"That was your best work. It was personal and magical and when I watched it weeks after the burial, alone in my new apartment, with the sound of crashing waves below, I finally allowed myself to cry uncontrollably," Warren said.

Adam sat looking at his brother now. Warren was almost glowing with happiness and Adam remembered how that film dispelled his own myths about Warren once and for all.

"You allowed me to grieve my mother's death, and that film opened the door to forgiveness for the entire family. Art made understanding, Adam."

Art made understanding.

"Yes, it was genius. I'm happy for you," Warren said in the way of a toast. "Every ounce of your newfound success is well deserved. You earned it, Adam. You worked hard for this victory."

Adam teared up. Hard work was his best asset.

Warren shouted louder than the greatest sushi chef in L.A., his brother Adam, the three pretty hostesses, and all the other sushi chefs and guests put together.

"KAMPAI!"

Laughing, drinking, and eating the world's best sushi, Adam and Warren settled in for two weeks of pure pleasure and relaxation in Los Angeles before the big day.

Running Free

In December, harvesting season came to an end, which was good and bad for Maele. Good because she wouldn't have to feel guilty about leaving her parents for an extended stay in Kauai. Bad because, until then, life would continue at its frantic pace in the days leading up to her departure.

Maele took the morning shift at the coffee shop, but in the afternoons, she would return to the plantation and hold true to the promise she'd made to her parents. Ever the responsible one, she planned her daily activities, typed them all up on her phone, and checked them off when they were done. This was simply how Maele had been raised—believing her responsibilities as a daughter came first.

She tended to the animals while waiting for her friends to arrive. First up was her favorite horse, Romeo, who she longed to ride, but was afraid to because of her neck. She loved to ride as a young girl, but it became too expensive for her family to keep her in step with her peers, which is why she started surfing. If she couldn't ride a horse, she'd ride a wave. She led her horse, Romeo, down the alleyway and toward the vast expanse of land flanked by mountains and hills and sea and sky. In the clearing behind the barn, between the dense blades of grass and the red peppered coffee trees, Maele rubbed the back of her neck while Romeo galloped to his heart's content, slivers of slush, dirt, and clay flying into the air and settling in his mane and on his back, cramming themselves in the crevices of the hooves she'd just cleaned the day before. These were the moments that inspired her. The moments that brought her to life. They reminded her of all the times she was one with nature. Of all the times she was free.

"There you are." Maele's friend, Ola, waved as soon as she showed up by the coffee trees. "Where were you?"

Another friend, Makana, approached. "We texted you but no answer. You said you'd be here by one."

"I'm only ten minutes late."

"Yeah," Makana said, "but you're never late. And I can tell where you've been." He pointed at her face, smiling. "In the barn with the animals, you animal."

Maele swiped her hand across her forehead, surprised by the flecks of mud that cascaded down her face like snowflakes. She looked down and saw splatters on her jeans and on her top. The ends of her hair were soiled as well, the silt windblown and hardened like cement. She had looked worse. At least this time, the dirt on her face hadn't come from the pigpens. Besides, Makana and Ola were her friends from grade school. They'd grown up together—in the rain, the sun, the filth, and the dust. She had no shame around them.

"How can I help?" Maele asked.

That afternoon, tasks were divided between handpicking the cherries or running them through a pulper to extract the bean from the berry and prepare it for drying.

"You can help us fill the baskets so we can get done sooner," Makana replied.

Maele decided to stay with her friends, perched up on stools and shaking the coffee trees.

"What's up, chica?" Ola asked. "You've been so busy. We haven't seen you for a while."

"I've been working at the coffee shop in the morning and then helping my parents in the afternoon. Papa said this was the last week of harvest and I was needed more here."

"I'm kind of dreading the end of this," Makala said.

Maele didn't miss his downtrodden expression or the lines on his face that spoke of stress.

"There are no jobs out there during the holiday season," Ola piped in.

"Have you tried going to Kahala? I know of two restaurants that're hiring."

"He did," Ola answered. "They have already filled the open spots."

"Call me tomorrow night," Maele said, bending to pick up a few seeds that had fallen. "I'll ask Lani if they need someone to replace me while I'm gone."

"Gone?" Ola asked, stepping off the ladder and sitting on the ground. "Where are you going?"

"I'll be visiting Mama's family in Kauai."

"Why?" Ola persisted. "Is anyone sick?"

"No, I'm taking a break. Andie's wedding reception is there, and I'll just be staying behind for a month."

"Maele, you're so lucky to be invited to that wedding," Makana said. "All the beautiful, rich people."

"But they're just that. People. You talk about them like they are something special." If she had a dollar for every person who'd told her how lucky she was to know Andie, she'd at least have enough to buy the same shoes as Andie—the ones with the red soles.

"But beautiful and rich," he insisted. "What is the wedding going to be like, Mae? Did they pay for you to go?"

Maele was embarrassed to admit that the bride and groom were shouldering all expenses. The only things they weren't paying for were her shoes and the two dresses. Well, three, now that she'd insisted on paying for the bridesmaid dress eventually. Everything else—the trip, her, and her parents' accommodations—was at Andie's expense. She hesitated to answer, but staying silent would only make them more curious.

"I think they knew I couldn't afford to go. And as part of the wedding party, the bride is—"

"Maele," Ola interrupted, snapping her neck sideways to glare at Makana. "You don't have to explain it to us. She is your friend. Your parents run the plantation. The Floreses trust them. Your family has been living and working on this land as long as them, too. So, it's not like you're getting a free ride or nothing."

"It's just that I'm so uncomfortable, you know. Speaking about it."

"Don't be," Makana said. "You work hard, too. Do you know you're the only one in our generation who's going to college? You're also the only one in our group who doesn't sit around partying or getting drunk. While we're all doing that—"

"You're studying and working," Ola finished.

"The other boys in high school would always say, 'Don't bother going after Maele Moana. She's too good for us. She has big dreams,'" Makana said.

Maele hauled the wooden basket brimming with cherries from one tree to the other. Her friends followed along, more for the conversation. She noticed they were in no hurry to finish, while she had three more things to check off her list. "We all have dreams," she said, and exhaled loudly. Her forearms began to tremble. She was bone tired. Maele felt the exhaustion take over, pulling at her muscles and weakening her knees. She shot Makana a look of despair. He was like the brother she'd never had. He nodded, pushed the overflowing basket to the side, and brought over a new one.

"How about we fill one more basket and call it a day?" Maele smiled.

16

Always Worthy

Adam was asleep until exactly 9:17 a.m., only to be awakened by a gorgeous, wild-haired girl in a damp bathing suit jumping on his bed.

Rebecca Worthy was an actress and Adam's neighbor at the Chateau Marmont. She had a golden tan, was perfectly plump, and had a mane of shiny blonde hair which she usually wore side swept and wild. But this morning it was still wet from her swim. Her face was bright, fresh, and beautiful.

"Hey, sleepyhead. Look who I found in the lobby," she said, still bouncing.

"Ugh, what time is it?" Adam asked, afraid her knees would dig into his stomach at any moment.

"It's 9:17 in the morning, time to wake him up. 'Arise, ye sluggard! Waste not of life! There's time enough to sleep in the grave!'" Warren said.

Adam perked up at the sound of his brother's voice. This was something their father had sung to both brothers when they were growing up. Warren's rendition made Adam laugh.

"I'm awake, I am awake. And I see you two have met. Rebecca, Warren. Warren, Rebecca." He leaned up and planted a kiss on Rebecca's cheek, then wrapped his arms around her and pulled her onto the bed. She let out a laugh like a horse whinny.

Warren proceeded to tell Adam about his morning, which involved a walk up Laurel Canyon.

"I had breakfast at the Canyon County Store, and somebody

pointed out the house where Jim Morrison lived. Then I walked back here and met Miss Worthy in the lobby."

"The elevator actually. He was quiet and followed me down the hall to your door. I didn't know what to think," she said with a laugh.

"So, I had a vision last night. About today. I thought we'd have one of those days that just happens." Adam puffed out his chest in grand fashion. "An unplanned day. Maybe we can smoke a little weed, grab some food, and see what follows?"

"I have exactly nine days left of bachelorhood," Warren replied. "I am in your capable hands. We got our suits and a little gift for Andie, so I've ticked off all the items on my to-do list. As long as we don't wind up in a jail cell, I'm good to do whatever."

The trio had breakfast—Warren's second of the day—at the Beachwood Café.

"This place looks like what I always imagined L.A. would be like. The old-timey wallpaper, the blue and yellow triangle flag tile floor, and 1950s grandma-style décor. And this eggs Benny is awesome," Warren said as he devoured his food.

Adam chuckled at Warren.

"Is that Jeff Goldblum?" Warren tilted his head toward a booth near the back wall, visibly awestruck.

Goldblum spoke with his hands, in big fluid movements, like he was conducting an orchestra.

"It's The Fly in the flesh," Adam said. "Your first Hollywood celebrity sighting."

"Excuse me, Mr. Yates," Rebecca piped in.

Both brothers looked at her.

"He's already had his first run-in with a bona fide Hollywood celebrity—the star of one of the most streamed original shows on TV."

"Who's that?" Warren asked innocently.

Adam burst into laughter, a deep belly laugh.

"Me, Warren! I'm the star of a dang TV show! My goodness, what's a girl gotta do around here to get a little respect?" She let out her horse whinny laugh.

The brothers joined in and the three of them laughed without a care in the world, their happy noise catching Goldblum's attention. He turned around and smiled.

When the meal was over, the three of them walked outside and made their way to Adam's Porsche.

"I have an idea, a non-plan plan," Adam quipped. "Let's head up this crazy canyon and drive around Lake Hollywood. We'll drive right under the Hollywood sign, which—did you know this? The owner of the Los Angeles Times, Harry Chandler, built the sign as an advertisement for homebuyers back in 1923. He was also into real estate development. The original sign read 'Hollywoodland' and as time went by, the sign fell apart. Misfortunes abounded around the sign, and when the City of Los Angeles decided to rebuild it, they dropped the 'land.'"

"Yeah, a long time ago a failed actress killed herself by jumping off the letter H. That sign represents stardust and promise, but at the same time it reminds me of the struggle, heartbreak, and failure that so many people face out here. It's a contradiction," Rebecca said as they drove up the canyon.

In a lot of ways, Adam thought of himself as a contradiction. One side of him was so full of hope and promise, potential and goodness. But it was at odds with the side that was dark, destructive, dangerous, and a little in love with death. He yearned to kill that dark side; wished it would go away and leave him to the joy he once knew as a boy when he was innocent. He called it his better self. The Adam he knew he could be. If only he knew how to win that war.

Adam shrugged off the thought. "Nothing deep today. A No-Plan Day equals fun," he said with a forced chuckle. "Warren, where you at?"

"Sorry," Warren responded. "I was just thinking about Andie. I miss her." He grinned.

"Oh no," Rebecca interjected, mussing playfully with Warren's hair. "You've got mush for a brother, Adam."

"He misses his girl," Adam said. "Tell her. Text your soon-to-be wife."

Warren happily obliged.

The road up Beachwood Canyon was narrow, windy, and perilous. Every other moment, a native of the canyon came barreling down the road like they owned it. In a way, they did. But for Adam it was a game of chicken.

The Hollywood sign loomed like a roving, shifting target, growing larger as their car ascended. At each turn, Rebecca let out her crazy, equine laughter and flopped from one side of the car to the other. The little red Porsche was made for this kind of road.

They flew past the lake, which was in actuality a fenced-in reservoir. "Let's make our way to the ponies," Adam yelled.

The ponies in Griffith Park were a Los Angeles treasure, embedded in the park since 1948. Five dollars bought a child two rides around the track. It was a podunk attraction for generations of L.A. kids, like something out of a Roy Rogers film. Forgotten and irrelevant, but still operating seven days a week at the same prices they charged twenty years ago. Adam pulled into the parking lot.

"Would you guys care to smoke up a little bit and enjoy a slow train ride in the warm noon sun?" Adam offered his passengers a joint.

The look on Warren's face told Adam everything he needed to know.

"Or you don't have to smoke pot, Warren. Either way. But I'm gonna," Adam said, wearing a roguish grin.

Adam lit up a joint that looked like a miniature ice cream cone and offered it to Rebecca. She took a long, expert drag and held her breath for a count of twenty. Then she slowly let the smoke billow out of her mouth and nose with a gurgled laugh and half-shut eyes. She poured the smoke in Warren's direction, which he laughingly waved away. Rebecca was instantly high as Adam proved by making her laugh uncontrollably as he wiggled his fingers in front of her face.

Adam took a deep hit. "And I just became stoned very quickly," he uttered with a silly laugh.

"This is a sativa strain called Chibobo Blu. It hits the head just right. You sure you don't want a little?" He held the joint out to Warren again.

"No, I'm good."

Ten minutes later, the three were riding a miniature train around the mile-long track, past the ponies, through a grassy field, over a miniature bridge, through a little tunnel that looked like a set piece right out of an old Warner Bros. cartoon.

Warren looked to the right of the train, his knees almost to his chest because the metal seat was made for children. Adam and Rebecca shared the last row while Warren sat by himself in the seat in front of them.

"What makes you tick, Adam?" Warren muttered.

Adam considered the question. He had the uncanny ability to tell stories on film, genius level storytelling abilities, but he also felt too sensitive to live in the world without dulling his senses. Adam was often high or drunk—an addict with no shame—and he surrounded himself with people who were dependent on him to provide them drugs and a good time.

He'd put into place a royal court of enablers and codependents who bolstered his fraudulent empire. If their father had set up the Kingdom of Yates, and Warren was the heir apparent, then Adam was the prince who would never be king. In turn, he set up his own rogue dominion and his subjects were all drug addicts. Adam was the High King.

"Tick-tock," Adam mumbled.

Then Adam and Rebecca giggled and bobbed their heads to the rhythm of the train. The sun began to set, and the Los Angeles winter air grew chilly. The shadow of the Santa Monica Mountains crawled over the little train and its merry passengers, covering them in cool darkness.

The rest of the day was a wash.

17

Fools for Riches

Maele glanced at her watch repeatedly, trying not to stress about the time. She'd taken her lunch break early to make it to the bank before it closed for the day. Maybe she shouldn't have procrastinated so much, but working all hours at the farm and picking up extra overtime at the coffee shop was worth the delay. Now the bank was full. Corded ropes separated the customers in a line that snaked around the lobby. There must have been about twenty people waiting their turn.

Throughout the bus ride, she had been trying to decide how much to leave in the account after pulling out most of the cash for her stay in Kauai. The fact this trip would be indefinite—that it depended on this pie-in-the-sky plan to reclaim what she'd left behind—confounded her and made her uneasy. What would happen in an emergency? Or if her parents needed extra money to keep the business running? If she pulled everything out, where would they go? Every little bit helped.

Maele had never done anything this bold before.

She turned to wave the person behind her to move on up to the open teller. She didn't want anyone else handling her account but Neeta. Neeta, who had emigrated from India, was busy appeasing an older gentleman about fraudulent charges on his statement. Maele thought she looked especially beautiful that day—always perfectly matched in her sari and dupatta, dark hair and dark eyes peeking through the opening in the printed orange scarf. Her sons were grown and Harvard graduates—one a doctor and the other an engineer. Both lived in New York, away from their parents. It was Neeta who had befriended Maele when she'd taken her sons to the coffee shop before a day at the beach. Maele had been in

Oahu for only a year, newly recovered from her accident and walking with the aid of a cane. She hadn't been working, of course. But Lani had basically picked her up and dragged her there as a way of getting out of the house. Since that day, Maele trusted only Neeta with her deposits, traveling the twenty miles to Honolulu to see her. Sometimes, the deposits would be just coins or dollar bills–certainly nothing to travel twenty miles for. Neeta would never judge her.

Finally, the older gentleman shook Neeta's hand and moved to the side. Neeta smiled brightly while motioning for Maele to step forward.

"Hi there, young lady. When are you leaving for Kauai?"

"The wedding is in a few days, and the reception will follow after that."

Neeta turned her head from side to side, making sure no one was listening before leaning forward. "And you'll be staying for a while, right?"

"Right. So, I was thinking I'm going to leave three hundred dollars in the bank and take the rest."

"Okay. Please sign the withdrawal slip," Neeta instructed, while punching numbers on her keyboard.

Maele did what she was told.

"Are you excited?"

"A little. More scared, I think."

Maele was aware that the line of people behind her was moving in different directions. Not just in hers. She heard the shuffling of footsteps and the scanning machines going off around her. Neeta didn't seem to care about all that.

"Why?"

"For many reasons," Maele said.

"Like?" Neeta was unrelenting. "Don't worry about that line behind you. It's time the other tellers do their job, for once."

Slowly, Maele began to relax. She realized it might be the last time she'd see Neeta for a while, which saddened her. She wasn't going to rush through this. "First, this is all I was able to save for a whole year. I'm afraid I won't have enough money. Second, what exactly is it I'm chasing? How do I even know that whatever it is will be there for me?"

"You're chasing your dream. That's huge. And you won't take no for an answer. That thing, the whatever"—Neeta waved her hands; shiny golden rings reflecting the light and bracelets tinkling like wind chimes—"will be there because you will make it so."

"I've been preparing for a year, but now that I look back, I haven't saved enough," Maele said. "With all the house repairs we had to make, I thought about putting this off for another year. But there's a big competition in April I would love to try out for, and then I need to decide how I'm still going to pay for my school."

Neeta perked up, wagging her finger at Maele. "Do you know why I love this job? Because I love studying the human relationship with money. In this job, I see different types of people. People who are so attached to their money, it's like they visit it every single day. People who don't care about their money and spend it like drunken sailors. People who use their money to replace what they're missing. And there are people like you and me, who worry about it so much, it paralyzes us and gets in the way of living.

"Money has been separating us for so long. It's a sad fact of life, but it's also a motivator. If you work hard, you will have it. Even if you don't, you'll be doing something you love. That's probably more important. Don't let this separate you from success. I have so much faith in you. Enough faith that ..." Neeta lowered her voice and reached her hand out to Maele. "All you have to do is say the word. I can write you a check. Lend you some cash."

"No, no," Maele replied. "That's so kind of you, but my cousin Koa will be there, and I'll be staying at my auntie's house. I will be okay."

"I also know your parents are very proud of you."

"It's not like they have anyone to compare me to," Maele said. "Well, I suppose there's Koa and Maka and the other kids at the farm."

"That's our sin, as parents, to compare one child to another. My husband does that with the boys. One is kind and soft-hearted; the other is ambitious. At the end of the day, they choose their own paths and all we have to do is make sure they know how much they're loved. It's no different—it's a human thing. You used to compare yourself to others—to those rich kids who used to hang out at the beach years ago—remember how you told me?"

"Oh my, that was ages ago. But yes, I did."

"Well, don't let anything stand in the way," Neeta said. "You have worked so hard to get where you are today. Remember when I met you, you were just starting to walk again. Many people would have given up on themselves, but not you."

Maele paused for a second, pensive about what Neeta had just said.

"I remember. I was with a cane then. All I wanted to do was throw that thing away."

Neeta nodded before shuffling the one-hundred-dollar bills and laying them on the counter as she counted them. "And you did! Don't be afraid. You'll never know what's out there for you unless you search for it." When Maele nodded, she continued, "One thousand three hundred dollars in large bills. There you go. Let's put it in this envelope."

"Thank you," Maele said. As she opened her purse to stash her cash, she remembered something. "My tips," she said, sheepishly avoiding Neeta's eyes. "Can I please get bills for them, too?" Out came a plastic storage bag filled to the brim with coins.

Neeta laughed. "That's money too!"

With another $275.00 in cash, Maele was ready to go. Neeta asked her to wait and abandoned her post to bid her goodbye. "Text me once in a while to let me know how you're doing? And don't forget your friend Neeta when you're a world-famous surfer. I'll be here to deposit your first million-dollar check."

"Never. I'll never forget you," Maele whispered, holding her tight and wishing she had as much faith in herself as Neeta did.

18

Westward off Zuma

There was one week left until the wedding. Morning broke early in Room 64 at the Chateau Marmont. The brothers discussed their plans for the day over breakfast, agreeing the top item on the agenda was to spend the day at the beach and enjoy some California surf. Adam wanted to show Warren a sweet break off Westward Beach in the heart of Malibu. Rebecca got the memo and was at their door within the hour.

The three made their way through the lobby and out the private doors of the Chateau where Adam's car waited for them. Adam and Warren fastened three surfboards along its side. Rebecca got into the back seat and Warren sat shotgun. They drove along Sunset Boulevard, through Beverly Hills, over the 405, through Brentwood, and onto the PCH past impressive seaside mansions that housed the likes of Cher and Brad Pitt.

Adam yelled out above the roar of his motor and the rush of wind, "The Chumash lived in this stretch of coastline, then the Spanish, then a Frenchman owned it, and finally Mr. and Mrs. Frederick and Mae Rindge bought Malibu for ten dollars an acre and were the last private owners of these twenty-seven miles of scenic beauty."

"Why do you know so much about this place?" Warren asked.

"Because it's beautiful! Legend has it the only way into Malibu was to time the tides and ride in on horseback via the beaches. If the timing was off, riders would get stranded on the beach until the next low tide."

"Like we were yesterday." Rebecca laughed.

After engaging Warren and Rebecca in a one-sided conversation about the history of Malibu, Adam said with a bit of flourish, "Each one of those thirteen thousand residents wants to keep the land to themselves. They try to make the beaches private, and they want to keep the outsiders out, just like Mae Frederick did, Queen of the Bu!"

Warren and Rebecca clapped in response to his little presentation.

The trio saw signs for Zuma Beach but turned left off the PCH to the less crowded Westward Beach, parked on the roadside, and unpacked their boards.

"There is an incredible swell here. You're gonna love this ride, Warren."

"I can't wait to ride it. I've been hearing you talk about it for the past two years."

They grabbed their boards and headed into the cold, blue ocean where they played for the next few hours on a perfect, surging shoreline break.

Adam, Warren, and Rebecca sat on their boards, rising with the swell before it broke. It was peaceful and quiet out on the water. Moments like this were why Adam loved surfing. He was at one with the water, a part of its rhythm, belonging to the sea.

"It's transcendental," Adam whispered to himself. He floated alone.

"This is gorgeous!" Rebecca shouted, breaking the silence. "But why do I always have this feeling there's a shark below me?"

Adam laughed. "You know what I love about surfing?" He was just about to share that surfing made him believe in something greater than himself, made him feel plugged into the universe or whatever, but he didn't want to be laughed at. So, he went with, "The feeling of riding a wave you know you have no business on. At any moment, it can take you down and hold you at the bottom of the ocean until it takes your life away. That risk, that sanction from the ocean when it doesn't decide to take your life, that's what I love. The rush."

Warren and Rebecca nodded.

"I also love how hungry surfing makes me. Do you see that little house right there?" Adam pointed at a white building nestled on the south end of the beach.

"Behind the blue lifeguard stations?" Warren asked.

"Yeah, end of the beach," Adam said. "That's where we're gonna have lunch."

Warren caught the next wave and rode it all the way to dry sand. Rebecca followed on the wave after. Once she reached the shore, she ran up the beach and caught up to Warren. Adam watched all of this from the water and laughed. He looked behind him and saw the ocean stretch on forever, and scanned its untroubled horizon.

As if the sea was responding to his thoughts, a huge wave rolled into view, a swell that hid the horizon beyond. He faced the beach again, lay on his board, and paddled hard as the water pulled him toward the approaching wave. Before he knew it, he was standing on his board, surrounded by rushing water and foam and freedom and the feeling of flight. He broke to his right and there, in front of him in the green wall of water, rode a dolphin inside the wave. He laughed loudly and carved the face of the wave like a pro, like he belonged to the sea, and rode it all the way to the beach. He slowly walked to the white building called The Sunset Restaurant, in a state of bliss.

After lunch, the trio made their way back to the beach, where their boards and towels waited. Adam reached into his bag for a plastic baggie filled with an off-white powder, then pulled out a glass pipe and packed it with marijuana. Finally, Adam opened the plastic baggie.

"All right, Warren. I rarely insist that someone tries drugs with me, but I insist you try this. It's called DMT—or the god drug—so named because DMT is found in our bodies as well as in tons of plants. It's released in us during sleep and at the moment of our death. Shamans would drink this in a tea and have out-of-body experiences—it shows you the spirit world. I promise, this will take you to a place you've never been before. I think it's a necessary last stop before your nuptials."

"And if I say no?"

"Then the high lasts about fifteen minutes. Rebecca and I will transport ourselves to another dimension and report back to you."

Adam lit the pipe and offered it to Rebecca, who took a deep hit. Adam followed. He offered the pipe to Warren, who declined. Exactly one minute later, both Rebecca and Adam blacked out.

He found himself in the middle of brightly colored waves, translucent and sparkling, teeming with dolphins in and out of the water. He saw the color of yellow on a beach that was somehow familiar to him, as if a beach from his distant past had been rebuilt from different memories. Then he noticed a dancer on the water, walking on the surface of the waves. Before he could understand what was happening, he was the dolphin, then a bird looking down from great heights, suddenly he became all the things—transcendent. He heard the words ringing so clearly in his head, "It's time to put childish things away. When a boy, act like a boy, but now a man, act like a man." His body suddenly combusted, sparks of light blending in with the sky. The feeling of being set free. Totally free.

Just as quickly as he'd blacked out, Adam opened his eyes.

"Holy cow … You should see what I just saw … Everything's about to change."

19

Something Blue

The flight from Oahu to Kahului took all of forty minutes. Although she had never flown on a large airplane, the flight to Fiji she'd taken years ago had her subjected to so much security. This time, there was no check-in process. They drove a car right onto the tarmac and boarded the plane directly.

Maele purposely stayed back, observing the women who walked in front of her. She was keen on copying their movements, their reactions, their actions. Every single one of them—Andie, Api, Lani, and their mothers—all wore dresses and high heels. Only Lani didn't have the shoes with the red soles. Despite being in sneakers and jeans, Maele carefully followed the way they crisscrossed their legs, sort of like the way models did on the runway—shoulders back, flowing hair blowing freely in the wind.

Maele laughed to herself, was she supposed to be assigned a seat? Were seat belts still the same? The women around her seemed calm. The plane had twelve swiveling leather seats with solid oak armrests, tables, and a galley that was also a full-service bar. Plus a huge TV. The seats were so soft, she wished the flight was longer. By the time she'd begun to fall asleep, they were already landing.

After the plane touched down, a dignified-looking woman in a white pilot's uniform emerged from the cockpit and welcomed everyone to Maui. Andie addressed her as if she were part of the group. Maele surmised this was because the pilot worked for Warren. Andie never treated people as employees—she always treated them as friends.

The ensemble was stunning. Covered cabanas in white organza, tied to the side with a ribbon of lilies. Andie and the rest of the women dined on mahi, onaga, shisa, hamachi, and tuna. The rich, heady fragrance of plumeria in full bloom, alternating between the smell of citrus and the smell of the ocean, surrounded them. Api proposed a toast, to finding love when you least expect it. Mrs. Flores and Mrs. Matthews began to cry. Andie raised a glass in agreement. As they celebrated the glorious sunset, Maele thought otherwise.

I'd rather celebrate the sunrise. No sense in dwelling on the past. But, the future. Ah, that's where everything can change in the blink of an eye.

The next few days were much of the same. Resting, talking, drinking, laughing, gossip, and massages, more talking and drinking, and lots of sun. Not a bad life at all, one Maele didn't dare get used to. It felt too soon for Maele, but before she knew it, it was time to head back to Oahu. As the other women freshened up, Maele waited at the pool by the lobby. The water was warm, and the stars were just beginning to take their place in the sky. The flight back to Oahu was scheduled for eight that evening. They had over an hour to get back to the airport.

"Hey, there you are," Andie greeted, tapping Maele on the shoulder before sitting next to her.

Andie removed her shoes and lowered her feet into the water. Maele did too, bunching up her dress, careful not to get it wet.

"How are you? Did you have a good time?" Andie asked.

"The past few days have been amazing. The spa was great. The food … your friends. And, I think my cousin used to work at this resort."

"You looked pretty tense during your first massage," Andie said with a chuckle. "Your fists were clenched, and when the spa lady asked you to uncurl your toes …"

"It was my first massage ever! It tickled." Maele giggled. "I mean, I had physical therapy a few years back, but nothing like this."

Andie looked at Maele in wonder, squinting in anticipation, but Maele said nothing more.

They sat in comfortable silence for a while. The pool's tiny currents shimmered in the borrowed light, dazzling reflections from the moon and the stars. A mild breeze rustled the leaves of the palm trees and music from a nearby gathering drifted lightly across the air.

Andie seemed to relax, transfixed by the soft lapping of the water against the wall. "Look at the water. It's so blue," she said quietly. "This may sound silly, but I miss Warren. I used to drown in those eyes."

"And you don't anymore?"

"Oh." She laughed. "I don't drown anymore. I swim, fly, and live in them."

Maele thought that was the sweetest thing she'd ever heard. Love can do that to you, she supposed. She wasn't sure she'd ever felt that. When she was younger, there had been a boy, but that didn't really count as real love because they'd never said a word to one another. And while everyone else was busy focusing on their love lives, she'd learned that romantic love wasn't what she needed to survive. She didn't need boys. They were stupid and self-centered. And after her accident, she'd discovered love wasn't enough to protect her from the harsh realities of life. Friendships faded, loyalties changed. While everyone else had been experiencing young love, Maele had been trying to get over her paralysis, win over her body, so she could try to get her life back.

By the time Maele tuned back in, Andie was happily engrossed in her own thoughts. "So what do you think? Something old—my mom's wedding veil. Something new—Warren gave me a Love bracelet two weeks ago. Something borrowed is a beautiful hairpin owned by his mother."

Just as Maele was about to respond, Andie swung her feet out of the water and fell back on her elbows. "Oh, shoot," she groaned, reaching behind her to grab her purse. "Something blue! I forgot something blue!" She proceeded to type out a text. "I have to let my mom know."

"Wait," Maele said calmly, moving her hair to one side of her head and reaching behind her neck. "Will this work?" She used both hands to unclasp the long golden chain and handed it to Andie.

Andie cradled the cobalt blue stone in her hand, admiring the glinting stones surrounding it. "Is this a diamond?" she whispered before turning to Maele. "This is so valuable. I don't think I should be borrowing something so special."

"Isn't that the point? That you have something meaningful? Besides, I don't even know how much it's worth, like money-wise."

"You should have it appraised." Andie held the chain, carefully twisting so her hand was above the ground rather than the water.

"What does it matter? This is my most precious possession. It doesn't matter how much it's worth. My mom gave it to me after my—" Maele tread carefully. The last thing she wanted to do was scare Andie or, worse, incite pity. "Anyway, it's the color blue like a sapphire, which is a symbol of healing and strength. And you need something blue, so now I want you to use it for your wedding."

"I would be honored to wear it. Thank you, Maele." She smiled, then laughed a little. "It reminds me of Warren. He always talks about covering me in blue diamonds. It's perfect."

Maele smiled as she watched Andie securely clasp the chain around her neck with her dainty fingers, not realizing her hair was still pushed to the side until she caught Andie's gaze fixed on the raised scar that constantly changed color like a mood ring. She wondered what Andie saw, and wished the ugliness wasn't there as a constant reminder.

"What's this?" Andie asked, gently running her finger along the base of Maele's neck.

Her touch felt foreign, but welcome. "Long story, and we have a flight to catch. But it has something to do with the physical therapy I mentioned and, well, this necklace."

Andie placed her feet back in the water. "Well, that's one advantage of having a private plane. We can spare a few more minutes. Go on, tell me."

"Well, okay. Six years ago I had an accident and broke my neck."

"Maele! How did I not know this?"

"Hmmph." Maele exhaled loudly. "It's ancient history."

"For someone who's only been alive for twenty-two years?" Andie teased, nudging her elbow. "Tell me."

"I did love the water once. It gave me life, offered me purpose. I mean, it was my future."

"In what way?" Andie leaned closer.

From the corner of her eye, Maele saw Api and the two mothers emerge from their villas, engrossed in chatter, crossing the garden and making their way toward the lobby.

"I was going to be a professional surfer."

Andie blinked. "A what? As in the ones who ride waves?"

Maele nodded.

"You were sixteen?" Andie asked incredulously.

Maele nodded again. "Barely. And I could shred waves like a beast!"
Her laugh erupted from a place of ancient confidence. Maele used to
have a superpower—she could tear through waves better than anyone
else in the world.

"What? Wait a minute." Andie stared at Maele and reached out to
touch her hair. Gently, she smoothed it down, fingers between strands
of hair, as if detangling its ends. She smiled. "Yeah. I can see that. You
have the look of a champion. I guess I always saw it—natural. And
strong."

Without prompting each other, both women stood and reached for
the towels settled on one of the deck chairs. Slowly, they dried their feet
and slipped their shoes back on. Andie looped her arm around Maele's
and together they walked over to meet the others. She could tell Andie
had more to say—the stops and starts, her eyes wide, her mouth open,
the hesitation.

"But how can that be? I've never seen you near the water. I've often
wondered whether you were afraid of it. Like, last week, you seemed
terrified almost."

"I was terrified because of my accident. I've been afraid to go back
in the water. But I miss it, Andie, and I've decided to face my fears.
Partly—no, more than partly. In large part, because of you. You've
inspired me so much, taught me how to be strong. Ever since you came
into my life, I've been watching you. You're my hero. You represent so
much of what I want to be. Brave, resilient. Not daunted by failure,
heartbreak, or hardship."

Andie stopped and turned to her before taking Maele's face in her
hands. "Oh, Maele. Everyone experiences fear. Everyone is afraid.
Dealing with fear is much better than living with regret, though." Andie
clutched the little blue diamond that now hung on her neck. "I would be
honored to borrow this from you to wear on my wedding day. Thank
you."

20

Enough is Enough

Back in L.A., things had gone south ever since they had smoked the DMT. The trio made their way back to the Chateau and climbed into the elevator. Rebecca pushed the number three button for her and then the number six button for Adam and Warren.

"I'm sorry I asked you to kiss me," Rebecca said guiltily to Warren.

"Think nothing of it. You were high," Warren replied. They rode in silence the rest of the way up.

The elevator reached the third floor. Rebecca hugged them and stepped off. The doors slowly closed, and the brothers continued to ride in silence. They didn't talk as Adam opened his door.

As soon as the door was closed behind them Warren barked, "Enough is enough, Adam."

"Enough is enough of what?"

"Enough of your selfish, childish behavior. Can you go a day without getting high?"

"I could if I wanted to, but I don't want to. I'm self-medicating." He threw up his arms.

"Self-medicating for what? Depression from a perfect childhood? Chronic privilege syndrome? Fear of too much success? What on God's green earth do you need to be self-medicating for?"

"Mighty Warren! Man, you are so self-righteous. You've never gotten high in your life? You hypocrite. Says the guy who lived on Page Six for his antics just three years ago. Now you're too good for me?"

"Adam, if and when I did drugs, it was once in a blue moon and for recreational purposes—to be stupid and have fun. Honestly, in the past few years, the only drug I wore out was alcohol, and I've even outgrown that. But you, man … for the past six or seven years, I've seen you abuse every drug under the sun. You have so much promise, Adam. You have everything in the palm of your hand. From what I've seen since I've been here, the people you surround yourself with …"

"Rebecca? What's wrong with Rebecca?"

"Nothing. She's lovely. She would do anything you asked of her. Or like those people we hung out with in the lobby last week."

"Those people are my friends."

"Exactly, and a great deal of good they'll afford you! Carrying on about how stupid everybody is and how they should have booked so and so's part, all the while kissing your ass because, currently, you hold the keys to the kingdom. But what you didn't hear, because you were as high as a kite, was how everybody turned on you by the end of the night. How they all foresee your inevitable fall. One 'friend' of yours placed a bet that you'd be fired after the first rewrite is turned in. Another doubled down and said you'll be fired after the first script meeting, before you even have a chance to make changes. These people are not your friends. They're users! They use drugs and they use people. The only person there who cares about you, besides me, is Rebecca, who's incredibly insecure for no apparent reason. But I think she would hook up with a homeless person if it meant she would feel loved for a minute. Which tells me something about you—either you are taking advantage of her, or you are spiraling downward into your own black hole of insecurity."

"You are cruel, Warren, you know that? You take after Dad in that respect. You want to know why I self-medicate? Yes, I grew up super privileged. I wanted for absolutely nothing. I have a mother who loves me, a cool older brother, a great education—which I worked my ass off for—and don't forget all of Daddy's money. I also have a passion for making movies, and yes, I've been very lucky. I've had one really awesome break, which I'm scared shitless I'll somehow mess up. The thing that eats at me, every time I do anything, is that I hear Dad compare it to you and your accomplishments. You weren't there, Warren, when Dad would say, 'Well, Warren didn't do that in fourth grade.' Or, 'I don't know what's wrong with Adam—Warren was walking by now. Warren was talking by now.' Warren did this, Warren did that. You! You! You! I'm so sick of being compared to you, and it eats me up inside. I want it to end!"

"Hang on a second."

"No, you hang on. You are my Boogeyman, Warren. I went to your mother's funeral to bury you alongside her. Then, I found out you were everything Dad made you out to be. You were perfect and controlled and cool. Even Dad is afraid of you. When you say no, he respects you. When you wanted out, sure, he fought for you to stay in the business, but he was ready to back down. He never badgers you or bullies you. That's all I get. I never measure up! So yeah, if I want to escape the constant nagging in my head about how this script won't sell, or that script sucks, or how afraid I am that I'll have to crawl back to Dad and beg for a job if I don't make it, I get high. If that sums up my worth as a man, so be it. And, by the way, I'm freaking twenty-four years old, man. Where were you at twenty-four? What were you doing with your life? You didn't want to work for Dad, but look at you. His right-hand man. The 'yes' man. The good son."

The two brothers sat in silence with the hum of the city intruding from below. Adam carried deep wounds. He figured that Warren had no idea those wounds were caused by their father, who had weaponized Warren from day one, pitting brother against brother.

Warren's phone dinged, breaking the silence. He looked at the screen, smiled sadly, and mumbled into the speaker. "Give me a second. I'll text you back in a few minutes."

The brothers sat in their grief for another moment.

"Adam. I'm sorry. I didn't know. Why didn't you talk to me about this years ago?"

"Because I was living it. I was in the middle of it. I thought it was normal to feel like number two all the time. To feel terrified and afraid. Until recently. Those people who—and granted, you didn't see them in their best form—are very encouraging to me, and do believe in me. You watch, one day my little pack will run this town. And Rebecca loves me."

"Good. I hope you run this town one day, and I know she loves you, but you don't love her. When you love a woman, it makes you want to be the very best version of yourself. You would never dream of dragging the woman you love into your muck. You will want to rise to meet her. I know I did. I want that for you, but it's not here. Not right now."

"You want that for me ... You know something, ever since you met Andie, you've become so high and mighty and stupid in love, and I don't want what you have. I'm happy for you, I really am, but I don't want it. So, good luck with your wedding. Have fun and have a nice life, Warren."

"What's that supposed to mean?"

"I'm not gonna go to your wedding. I don't want to see Dad or have to bear witness to your holy matrimony, because I'll probably just bring it down anyway. Get high and say something stupid. Just be a disappointment. Right?"

Warren stood still in the middle of Adam's hotel room, visibly shocked. Those words hit him where it hurt, which was exactly what Adam wanted to accomplish. But when he saw his brother's face, something made him regret it. Adam watched Warren take a step back, shoulders stooped, lips pursed, his fingers pressed on his temple. He saw the pain he had inflicted. Visible, palpable pain.

The silence was deafening.

"If you ... are not at my wedding ... I will never forgive you, Adam. I don't care if you're so high you can't speak. You better be there."

Warren began to pack his things. "It's time for me to get back to Hawaii," he said quietly.

"But we have a few more days here in L.A.," Adam whimpered.

"Yeah, I think it's best if we cut it short. I have loved my time out here with you. I've enjoyed seeing your new home and meeting your new friends, but I'm disappointed. I love you. I love you no matter what, and you are my best man. But if you don't show up on the most important day of my life ... it'll break my heart." With that, Warren left.

Adam stood alone in his big empty apartment, Room 64 at the Chateau Marmont. Sirens blared from police cars as they raced up Sunset Boulevard. Night had fallen and loneliness crept around him like a demon. No one knew what an effort it was for him to project that self-confidence, that fake sense of achievement, when Adam knew deep down that everything he had was because he was a Yates. The drugs removed the agitation, made him think he was deserving of respect, made him feel worthy. Warren saw right through him, and yet, he couldn't stop. Babbling on and on, desperate to impress everyone. Why couldn't he stop? Exhausted and humiliated, Adam sank to the floor. Not knowing what else to do and fearing he had finally pushed his brother away for good, he buried his face in his hands.

And wept.

PART THREE:
Honeymoon Rising
Maele & Adam

21

Finding Him

The events from the wedding had Maele's mind reeling.

"Was it really him? The boy on the beach?" Maele muttered to herself as she dragged her feet on the sea wall along Poipu Bay. If she only had her childhood journal with her. She had intended to bring it but hastily changed her mind and hid it at the last minute.

She wasn't even running anymore. Her heels barely left the ground. What a way to start trying to get fit again. It used to be a breeze for her, taking on a six-mile run. Now, she could hardly do one mile. If there was one thing Maele had been blessed with, it was determination. She had a plan to be at six miles in two weeks. Needless to say, she hadn't had the time to begin training until the wedding was over. Training for what, though? She smiled when the thought crossed her mind. To get back into the water, of course.

She was deep in thought, trying to provoke memories of those times she'd surfed on the beach where the high schoolers hung out. The yellow sweatshirt. His face. She was kicking herself for not bringing her journal, and she even considered asking her mother to have it shipped to Kauai once they were home.

But then, if her mother had the chance, she would probably read it.

Maele didn't want to share anything on those pages with anyone. The joy, the elation, but most of all, the pain. Maele had learned firsthand that what you think of as a cosmic joke being played on you is really just a part of your path. There was a higher power that knew what was about to happen, plotting out every moment, every point on that curve.

Anyway, she was sure it was that boy. It looked like him. It felt like him. His eyes seemed a little different—more weathered, older, sadder. The eyes—the windows to one's soul, they called it. With time, they had turned ominous. More secretive. She made a note to really look in those eyes. She would know, once she did.

Maele stopped her watch at exactly one mile, slowing to a walk before sitting on the edge of the break wall, legs dangling close to the lapping waves. They were strong that day, forceful sprays blending with the beads of sweat on her skin. Everything around her, around the resort—from the tide pools that surrounded the cabins to the Nene birds that walked around the property—seemed different. The landscape was so perfect, she wondered whether it was manmade. Could nature be manufactured so you could experience only its beauty and not its wrath? That contrast, the conflict, was essential. Otherwise, there would be nothing to conquer. And how would destiny play a part? There'd be no place for miracles.

She was surprised that anyone would want to leave the resort.

Because she was in the bridal party, Maele had been in a suite with her parents, which her mom had embarrassingly told Andie was bigger than their entire house back on Oahu. Maele couldn't recall the last time she'd slept so soundly. The Egyptian cotton sheets and towels were so soft, she couldn't even begin to guess how much they cost. She laughed when she recalled her papa stripping off the sheets and tipping the mattress on its side to find out what brand it was.

"Wow," her mother had said, bouncing on it. "Look, Kaku, we need this. It doesn't squeak." Lolana had giggled like a young girl, giving Maele an unwanted visual.

"Here she is," said a voice which interrupted her reverie.

Maele shielded her eyes from the sun while looking up at Adam.

"How did I know I'd find you here?" he asked.

"I don't know," she answered with a touch of surprise. "How did you?"

"No clue," he said with a shrug, sweeping his fingers through his thick, wavy hair. "I'm Adam, by the way. Just in case you forgot."

"I didn't." For a brief second, she had a knot in the pit of her stomach. Had he been drunk last night? Had he forgotten their conversation? Had he forgotten about their dance? How he had held her, touched her, kept his face close to hers? Was she the only one who had been thinking about it all morning? "I'm Maele, just in case you forgot."

"I didn't." Adam took the liberty of sitting next to her. Same position, his shoes almost touching the water. "Okay, just wanted to make sure you weren't too wasted and forgot about me," he said, smiling.

This time, she didn't avoid looking at him. She saw him up close for the first time, and in the light of day. Andie was somewhat accurate. He was a mini-Warren in terms of height and build, but his hair was much darker, and his eyes were … well, strangely luminous. Deep green, like a forest of pines, illuminated by dancing flecks of gold like Christmas lights. If she looked closely enough, she saw the sunrise. He was the boy who had sat on the beach in a bright yellow sweatshirt. She'd seen those unforgettable eyes before. She remembered how she had been mustering up the courage to speak to him just before the accident.

Yes, it was undoubtedly him.

If she only had her journal. She could vaguely recall an entry she'd written that would solve this mystery instantly and put her mind at ease. Granted, it wasn't really a mystery, but six years was a long time to have not seen this stranger. So much had changed, and who was this guy, anyway?

"Huh. Dodgers," he said, pointing at her running cap.

Maele realized how she must have looked, with her hair pulled back and her forehead sticking out.

"Is that your favorite team?"

"Excuse me?" she said, still lost in the fog of her daydreams.

"I asked if they're your favorite team," he repeated. "I'm from L.A., you know."

"No, you're not. You live in Kailua. You travel to L.A. a lot."

He smiled again, his perfect white teeth flashing in the sun. "What don't you know?"

"Oh, no, it's just that Andie—"

"Relax, I was just kidding," he said, interrupting her. "I'm actually flattered Andie has mentioned me. I feel lucky to have her as my sister-in-law. Do you have any sisters?"

"No."

"Brothers?"

"No. Well, I have a cousin who has kind of been like a brother to me. Koa. I'm going to be seeing him the day after tomorrow."

"So you're an only child. Kind of like me for many years."

"I guess," she responded, peering around. "Is someone looking for me? Andie, maybe?" Surely, the only reason Adam Yates would be here was if someone had sent him.

"Nope."

"Oh …" She squinted in confusion. "Do you need anything from me?"

"Remember last night? Warren cut in while we were having fun on the dance floor, and I told you I'd find you."

"You did. Last night."

"I meant today, too."

When she remained still, eyes focused out on the horizon, Adam continued, "As I was asking—are you a Dodgers fan?"

"Actually, my dad just got this from someone who visited the plantation once. I've never been to a baseball game."

"Well, I'll tell you, you're not missing anything. Unless it's a Mets game."

"Mets?"

"The New York team. I am a die-hard fan. From my days of studying in New York."

Maele nodded, not really knowing what she could contribute to this conversation. She barely watched television, and hardly attended any concerts. "So, you're in L.A. a lot and you studied in New York."

"Yup. I'm a screenwriter."

Maele could have sworn he puffed up his chest when he said it.

"Like, what movie?" she asked, genuinely curious. She was certain she wouldn't know its title, but she planned to pretend she'd at least heard of it.

"Oh, well, I just closed a deal for my very first one."

"Ah."

"Yeah, I closed a pretty good deal," he said.

There was definitely some chest puffing going on.

"Is it much different? The West Coast versus the East?"

"Both are dog-eat-dog worlds, I think," he answered.

Maele wasn't listening. Just watching. She was captivated by who he was. What he represented. His lips weren't bad, either. No, really. What would a Yates want with her?

"But the pace of life in L.A. is definitely more like the islands. Slower. Not Island Time, but slower."

She nodded again, so stiffly her neck began to hurt. She

remembered what she had been doing thirty minutes ago. She had to go. She'd promised she'd call Koa, and now she wanted to tell him about Adam. How he seemed interested in knowing her. How weird it was because he was a Yates. Koa was an excellent judge of character. She swung her legs sideways, lifting them off the wall so she could stand. Adam seemed to expect her to do that—in one swift leap, he was on his feet. He held his hand out and pulled her up.

"Sorry, I have to go. I'm supposed to do another mile and then spend some time with my parents before they leave."

"Oh, I bet they're on the same flight as my friend, Shelley."

"Yes," she chuckled. "The ear licker."

"Let's go," he said, walking a few steps ahead as he laughed off her jab. "I'll run back with you."

She liked this boy.

Maele smiled as she looked at his shoes. He wore fancy leather sneakers with thick black laces and green and red stripes, and he wasn't wearing any socks. Maybe it wasn't the right time for her to ask, but he hadn't told her why he'd tried to find her that day.

"Hey, Daddy," she teased, recalling what Shelley had called him the previous night, before she dashed ahead and turned back to see his reaction.

Adam snapped his attention to her, wagging a finger at the same time.

"Try to keep up, okay?" Maele called.

It took a few seconds, but he laughed. "Game on."

22

Be Bold in Love

Adam got back to the resort when the sun was still low in the sky, sweaty from his run even if the day was not yet hot. A warm breeze, heated from the island, pushed past him toward the water. He felt a burning under his right big toe from a forming blister. He had to wear his designer sneakers that morning.

Adam shook his head and muttered, "If you can't wear designer sneakers to run in, goofball, why wear them at all?"

It was right then that he swore off designer sneakers, flip-flops, hats, and swimwear for the rest of his life. He would only buy practical goods that served a real purpose. His desire to flaunt his wealth, or his family's wealth, was suddenly distasteful.

I should sell my car. Nobody my age needs to be driving a car that's worth the price of a house. Speaking of houses, I should probably move out of the Chateau Marmont and buy a proper home. Put down roots. Adam laughed. This is so unlike you, man. You meet a girl, and now you want to upend everything! You simp!

He found a stone bench facing the water and undid the thick, black laces of his shoes. He slowly took off his right shoe. That was something else Adam was determined to change. If you're gonna wear tennis shoes, wear socks. You're not a cop on Miami Vice.

Miami Vice was a show he'd watched with his dad when they could find reruns late at night. One of the occasional shared moments when his dad had been human and accessible. Tennis was another activity they'd enjoyed together. Adam thought back to the time he'd played a match with his dad in full-on Miami Vice dress—Adam wore a pink jacket with the sleeves rolled up and a tank top underneath, pink

Converse shoes, no socks, and shades like Crockett's. The weather had been hotter than usual, meaning the court blacktop was scorching. Without socks on, his sweaty feet had slipped inside the shoes, so he'd played barefoot.

"You're gonna burn your feet, Adam. That's not a good idea."

"I won't, Dad. I play barefoot all the time. My feet are tough, you know, like a native Hawaiian. They never wore shoes two hundred years ago."

"Adam, I'm pretty sure they weren't making quick moves on a hot clay court two hundred years ago," his dad had said with a shrug. "But suit yourself."

Three sets later, Adam screamed at the top of his lungs. Not only had he gotten a blister, but the entire bottom layer of his foot had slid off—the skin from the base of his toes to his heel, gone. Adam had expected his dad to gloat, to say I told you so, but instead his father swept him into his arms as if he was eight years old again, and carried him off the court. He'd then removed a first aid kit from his tennis bag and gently washed the bottom of Adam's foot with hydrogen peroxide before blowing on it as the clear liquid turned into white foam. The sting had been painful, but his father's tenderness had soothed him. He'd felt completely loved as his dad had dressed his wound.

"Oh no, Adam, we gotta get this taken care of." His dad began to dress the wound. "Daddy's got you."

Daddy? Adam was fifteen years old. He had smoked cigarettes the entire spring semester of freshman year. He'd been a Puukumu Prep man, not a baby in need of a daddy.

Now Adam sat on a bench at the resort on Kauai, the sound of his big brother's laughter in the distance. Adam fingered the new blister under his toe and remembered how tender his dad could be and how much love his father had for him, especially when it really mattered most. Why, then, did he feel the constant desire to best his father, to conquer him and to prove he was a bigger man? What was this prison sentence and who had placed it on him? His father was complicated, but so was Adam.

Adam played with the skin that hung from his toe and tried to spit into the blister, thinking somehow that human spit would have the same effect on a wound as dog saliva, which is something he'd always believed as a kid. Get a cut, let your dog lick it. He laughed as he saw Warren and

Andie heading toward him.

"Hey, little brother," Andie called out.

"Hey, big sis," Adam replied. "That feels good to say. I've never had a sister."

She smiled. "Well, you got one now, like it or not."

They sat down on the bench, Warren on the right and Andie on the left, Warren's post-wedding gift on her wrist.

"Nice watch."

"I heard you helped pick it out. Thank you." She squeezed his shoulder and then placed her hand on Warren's back.

"What are you doing out here with your shoes off?" Warren asked.

"Well, I went running and got a blister."

"Ouch." Andie examined it as Adam spit on it again. "Eww, why are you spitting on your blister? Gross."

"I don't have any hydrogen peroxide to clean it with, so I'm cleaning it with my spit."

"I don't think that works, buddy," Warren chimed in. "I think it only works with dog spit."

Adam realized that the dog saliva theory had been passed from father to sons.

"Okay, who is Maele? How does she know you guys?" Adam asked.

"She's one of my best friends. She works at the coffee shop and her family works the plantation for the Flores family. She's amazing. I love her. In fact, she gave me this as my something borrowed, something blue."

Andie pinched the chain around her neck above the small blue diamond, holding it out to Adam.

"I danced with her last night."

They nodded in unison. "We saw," Warren answered.

"I used to watch her surf when I was in high school."

"What do you mean?" Andie asked, tilting her head toward him, intrigued.

"When I was here for high school ..."

"Adam went to a boarding school here on Kauai," Warren clarified.

"I used to walk to Secret Beach every morning before sunrise, and I'd watch a girl surf. She was amazing, she danced on the water. I went every morning until one day she just disappeared, like a ghost. I thought I'd made her up in my mind, until last night. It's her."

"She told me she was a surfer once, but she's terrified of the water now. I've never seen her go into it. Are you sure she's the same girl?"

"It's her. She's my mystery girl, manifested, and guess what?"

"What?" Warren asked.

"She remembered me. I used to have this crazy, bright yellow sweatshirt I'd wear on cold mornings, and she remembered. It's her."

"How crazy would it be if you found the love of your life at our wedding? Oh my gosh, it's so romantic," Andie said, clasping her hands in delight. "Like a story out of a fairy-tale book. Star-crossed lovers, who loved each other from afar, meet at a wedding years later, and live happily ever after. Oh, that's such a good omen for our wedding, Warren."

"You have no idea. I have the craziest story to tell you, do you remember the vision I had on the beach—" Adam was about to burst into the story when his brother cut him off.

"Omen or not, it was a good wedding," Warren interrupted. "But what are you gonna do about it, Adam?" Andie and Adam looked at Warren. "I'll tell you this right here, right now. Those things we talked about in L.A. Maele is not someone you toy with. She is one of the most dedicated and hardworking people we know. I've been trying to hire her for a year, but she's focused on graduating from college first. I keep telling her she doesn't need it, but she says, 'a commitment is a commitment.' She's big on commitments."

Andie and Warren looked at each other before breaking out in a laugh.

"A promise. Once I make it," Andie started.

"I don't break it," Warren finished.

They leaned in front of Adam to kiss. Adam had never noticed just how beautiful Andie was. Andie broke free and grabbed Adam's hand.

"She's also really virtuous, Adam. Like, she doesn't do any drugs and I've barely seen her drink. She's totally about her family and her work, but she's also fun and sweet. She's certainly not boring. She's just not, well, she's not like the women I've seen you with," she said, before letting go of his hand.

"That's okay," Adam said as he rubbed the stubble on his cheeks. "I think it's time I expand my horizons. As Warren so kindly told me, I tend to attract people who bring out my demons."

"So, I'll ask you again, what are you gonna do about it? Don't you need to get back to L.A. after Christmas?" Warren's concern was not lost on Adam.

"Yeah, I do, but I don't know what I'm gonna do. I feel like it's an adventure I want to take. Stay a while. Figure things out about myself, too. Didn't you once say to me, if you're gonna be bold in anything, be bold in love?"

"That sounds familiar, yes."

Adam smiled warmly at Andie, taking in her glow. He slowly turned to look at his brother. For the first time in his life, in complete contradiction to how he'd felt even a week ago, he realized he wanted what they had, and he wanted it sooner rather than later. He wanted to be in love and share the Hollywood ride he was about to go on from the ground up with someone he trusted. As quickly as possible.

Adam said, with a wide grin, "Well then, I'm gonna be bold in love!"

Trippingly Over

Maele spent the rest of the day with her parents, enjoying a little holiday celebration in their suite before they flew back to Oahu. Lolana insisted on a traditional Christmas dinner, which meant using the kitchenette beyond its design and capabilities. It was then that they exchanged presents, sitting cross-legged on the floor while nibbling on pork, chicken long rice, lomilomi salmon, and, of course, poi. Conscious about the cost of room service, her father had picked up some local delicacies at a gas station's general store a mile or so away. He'd also begrudgingly packed all their gifts in a suitcase and brought them to Kauai, since they weren't spending Christmas together.

"Mae, you shouldn't have. This looks expensive," Lola gushed when she unwrapped a brand-new juicer. It looked state of the art—very sleek and utterly white. A little bit of Andie had rubbed off on Maele, it seemed. Her father watched in earnest as her mother opened the box and pulled out gadget after gadget.

"You're always squeezing fruit for Papa. They say this one can even make vegetable juices."

"Anything your mom can make out of the vegetables in the garden, she does it." He winked and smiled.

Lolana playfully tapped her husband on the shoulder. "Saves money, doesn't it? Now, Mae, open yours."

Her parents watched her unwrap a black box, holding their collective breaths until Maele beamed with delight. "A sports watch!"

"Yes," her father said, his weathered finger poking at it. "Look at the numbers—they are big so you can see them in the water. The Apple thing was too pipi'i and the guy at the store said this was just as good. It's waterproof, too."

"Oh, wow," Maele said, lifting it up for them to admire. "And I like the strap. It's perfect."

"Not as expensive, either. Papa thought you could use it. It tells you where you are, and it can count your heartbeat or something."

That made Maele smile again. "Mama."

"We can't protect you forever, kaikamahine. Just promise us you will always take care of yourself. You have given us so much joy, you deserve to be free to choose your path in life. If going back to the ocean is what you want to do, we cannot stop you. But take it slow, okay?"

Lola's statement surprised Maele. "How did you know?"

"You put Koa and the North Shore together," her papa said with a snicker. "What else could you both be up to?"

Maele smiled at her papa and grabbed her mother's hand, and the two ladies danced a happy, swirling dance around the beautiful room while her father laughed his deep belly laugh. So much joy filled the room. The moment was perfect, and Maele couldn't have been happier.

The next day, her parents left for Oahu and she had the villa all to herself, if only for one more night before heading up to her auntie's house. This solitude left her with just one thought. Of the man who had danced with her, who had sought her a second and third time after that. What if she made herself forget he was a Yates? Or that he'd seen her before, when she'd been a different person? That girl was long gone, her confidence sucked away by an injury and the constant fear of failure.

She found herself wishing she looked like his actress-date. How beautiful she was, how perfect, how attractive. Maele stood in front of the mirror, pulling the hem of her shirt down, mimicking the low neckline that seemed to get Adam's attention. On the surfing circuit, she'd worn swimsuits all day, posed for pictures, and ran around with the boys in her group without a care. But this one was different. This man made her feel things she'd never felt before. When he'd touched her and pulled her close to dance, she'd felt an indescribable stirring in her body. Her skin burned and her stomach filled with butterflies. She wasn't that innocent. She'd been kissed during some truth or dare game they'd played when she was in high school, surrounded by surfer boys who treated her like one of them. Then another time, when a boy had confessed his love for her. She'd kissed him out of pity, really, because she'd felt no love for him in return.

But now she understood what love could be. That reaction. The one that made every part of her yearn to be touched. When she removed her shirt, her bra, then slowly peeled off her jeans, she felt the fabric rub against her bare legs. Her body trembled when she stepped out of her panties and stood in front of the mirror, staring at her reflection for a time. She wasn't a little girl anymore. With eyes closed, she placed her hand on her belly and imagined what it would feel like to be touched by Adam. She was a woman longing for the man she had just met. Maele laughed at herself before stepping into the large tub overlooking the bay. The warmth of the water against her skin felt good. To be stripped of everything was liberating. To shed the burden of fear, of shame, of remorse. To feel truly naked to the world and yet powerful. She resolved to carry this courage forward.

She thought of how they'd danced, how he'd held her, and how he'd looked at her. The more she remembered, the faster her heart paced. She wanted to be the girl she was in that moment for Adam.

Better yet, in that man's eyes, Maele wanted to be that woman.

There was a light rain the next morning and, as Maele woke up, the winter winds reminded her Christmas was in three days. The days leading up to and following the wedding all melded together in a fantastical blur. After a good night's sleep, just before sunrise, she walked to the beach, resolved to get in the water before she saw Koa. There was no way she was going to admit to him she hadn't sunk her feet in wet sand for six years.

Despite the overcast clouds, flashes of gold lit up the sky at sunrise. She made it to the beach early enough to avoid large crowds, early enough to do "the thing" without embarrassing herself. A small group of surfers congregated at a distance, far enough to give her the confidence of not being seen. After finding a spot on the sand and removing her cover-up, Maele set out for the shore. Hesitant but determined, she sluggishly placed one foot in front of the other, then paused when the water covered her ankles. She continued until the pull of the tide caused her to lose her balance, toppling her over so she fell on her knees.

"Are you okay?"

That voice, that man. Flustered by her thoughts of him the night before, she refused to face him.

"What are you doing out here?" she asked.

"I wanted to watch the sun rise this morning. It's something I never do, but I couldn't sleep so I thought, why not. Why do you ask? Am I not allowed out here?"

"Of course you are and to answer your question, I'm fine. I just tripped over a rock."

"Really? Because it looked more like you were getting into the water for the very first time. The way you were tiptoeing in."

She ignored him, even though she was tiptoeing in the water like a toddler. Her arms were stiffly lifted, like she was walking on a tightrope.

"Oh God," he said, walking up to her, his voice almost a whisper. "You *are* going in for the first time."

Her shame was back, so disconcerting to Maele that tears filled her eyes.

"No, don't," he said, reaching out. "Here, let's walk in together."

He took her hand and held it firmly until she was ready to keep walking. Maele could feel the strength of his grip, using his arm as an anchor to steady her against the rush of the waves. Soon enough, she was waist deep in the water. She wanted him to let her go so she could swim on her own.

Would he watch? Stay close, in case she lost her nerve?

She was about to say something when she heard someone call her name.

"Maele Moana?" A blonde girl on a surfboard drifted toward them. "Is that you?" The gusty, restless winds carried her voice across the horizon.

Maele didn't know what to do. She looked at Adam and tugged him in the opposite direction.

"Maele! It is you! Hey, guys," the surfer girl yelled at three people floating on their boards. "It's Maele Moana! Back from the dead!"

"Let's go," Maele said again, her voice shaking. "Please, let's go."

"Do you know those people? Are they your friends?"

"No. Let's go."

Adam remained motionless, confused, his head tilted, eyes fixed at their approaching company. She could tell he liked the attention, stepping aside and waving back so they could see her. "Why don't you stay and say hi to them?"

The group of surfers drifted closer, paddling furiously in the water. Maele panicked, and decided she'd need to get back to shore without Adam's help. With a quick snap of her arm, she broke free from Adam's grasp, took a deep breath, and forged her way against the tidal surges. Then, she gathered her things on the beach and disappeared through the dunes.

Free Ride

Adam found his way back to the hotel after Maele's hasty exit. He wondered what he had done, or if it had been the surfers. They knew her. Why didn't she want anything to do with them?

He knew the wedding party was staying in villas strewn throughout the hotel property. Adam quietly made his way from villa to villa, searching for Maele. He wanted to talk to her, see if what he was feeling was justified.

"If I'm going to be bold in love, after all," he said out loud, "then I better be sure I get to know who I'm being bold for."

He heard Maele's voice. She was talking on the phone through the speaker. The voice on the other end was deep and big and loud and very animated.

"Mae-Mae, my little sister-cuz! My Ohana. Hot damn, I missed you. I hate that you guys moved away, I don't get to see my little sister-cuz anymore. How was the wedding?"

"It was so beautiful, like a fairy tale."

"I bet you were the prettiest girl at the ball. Was the bride jealous? I bet she was jealous."

"Stop, Koa. No, the bride wasn't jealous. She's gorgeous and she's marrying a Yates."

"What's a Yates?"

"Not a what, a who. A very rich family on Oahu."

"They sound like a bunch of *haoles* to me, the kind who come over and buy up all the land and make these islands less and less like Hawaii and more and more like the places they come from. Are they New York jerks or some kaka like that?"

Maele laughed at her cousin's tirade. "I don't know, Koa, they are from here. They are local now, just like you and me. Like it or not."

Adam smiled at this last bit—she was defending his family to her family. That was a good sign. He didn't want to keep eavesdropping, so he made a lap around the lush area enclosing her villa. Each villa had its own veranda and back patio, surrounded by ulu or breadfruit and hala plants, which the Polynesians had brought to the islands and used to make sails for their canoes. He picked at a breadfruit and smelled it. This stuff can feed an entire country. It was funny how humans take a perfectly sustainable local plant that could feed everyone without irrigation and land management, only to replace it with something that wasn't native. Like coffee or pineapples.

"I guess pineapples and coffee are tastier than breadfruit."

He made his way to her window again and noticed Maele was off the phone. He gathered up the courage to knock on her windowpane. Without the aid of drugs, Adam found he wasn't always brave enough. Even to do simple daily tasks, like talk to people—especially people he really liked, and when he wanted them to like him in return. He paused for a moment, wondering for a split second whether he should run back to his room and maybe take half a pill. But Maele seemed to be in a hurry, shuffling back and forth and opening the dresser drawers. She might be gone by the time he returned.

He knocked gently and a startled Maele turned to the window.

"Hi, Adam."

"Hi, Maele. You're packing. Where are you going?"

"Oh, I have family on the island. My aunt and uncle, and I'm going to stay with them for Christmas."

"Oh, you're staying here for Christmas?" This was getting interesting.

"Yes. What are you doing for the holidays?"

Adam thought for a minute. He could go to Oahu and spend Christmas with his mom and dad. Warren and Andie would still be gone on their honeymoon. While family was nice, staying on Kauai and getting to know Maele would be nicer.

"I think I'm going to stay on the island and get some work done. I have a rewrite to do on the script I mentioned. I'll probably just stay here at the hotel," Adam blurted out rather impulsively.

"That's awesome! This place is beautiful. Am I crazy or does it have a special fragrance? I mean, it's like they spray perfume in the air."

"Yes, they do. They have a signature scent here, so when you smell it or something similar to it, you'll always remember your stay."

"It worked. I won't forget it," she gushed.

She stood in the light of her room, looking like a dream and holding a shirt she was about to put in her beat-up suitcase. Instead of zipping it up, she wrapped an orange bungee cord around it.

Adam's focus was on her long brown hair as it cascaded down her shoulders when she placed both hands on the suitcase. He had a habit of objectifying women, but the pleasure he derived from being close to this girl was somehow different. He saw her. Yes, she had beautiful legs—her arms were lean and strong—her collarbone was perfect, her face was gorgeous with high cheekbones, and her hair full and dark. And her coffee-colored eyes—warm and somehow so familiar to him. He felt inexplicably safe next to her. Simply put, he trusted her. Did he love her? Maybe. Whenever he saw her, he was overwhelmed with a feeling of wishing to grow old with her. As he was about to say something bold and lovely and foolish, he remembered he was a broken *haole* who had no business defiling this young woman.

"I ... I ..."

"What is it, Adam?" Maele looked up at him.

"I was hoping you and I could get to know each other better. Since I'll be here, and if you're gonna be here ..."

Maele's face grew two shades darker, and her pomegranate lips widened into a genuine smile. "I would like that very much. I'm about to check out and catch the bus. If I miss it, I'll have to wait two hours for the next one. Let me have your phone and I'll put in my number. You can call me after Christmas."

He handed her his phone, and she typed her name and number into his contact list.

"How far are you going?" he asked, saddened by the thought of not seeing her for a few days.

"I'm heading up north to the Hanalei, Kilauea area. That's where my family lives."

"Right, yeah, of course. Where I went to school." He nodded. "I have an idea. Would you let me give you a ride?"

Adam had a car on Oahu, but not on Kauai. That didn't faze him—

he could get one fast. He caught himself, wondering where this was coming from. He'd never tried so hard to impress a woman. "I mean, I don't have one here, but I'm sure I can get one. Are you in a hurry?"

"Not if I don't need to worry about catching that bus, but my cousin wants me to join them for lunch, so the sooner the better, I guess."

"Okay, hang tight. Let me see if I can find a car. I'll text you."

When Adam took his phone from Maele, his finger accidentally touched hers and a spark rushed up his arm and through his body. He ran to the front desk and found the lobby in full-on Christmas mode. He figured he could talk his way into borrowing one of their courtesy cars. He was right. The Yates name had worked once again. As soon as he was done with paperwork, he heard his brother's laughter and turned to see his worlds colliding.

Goodbye Christmas, Goodbye

The resort lobby was a madhouse. Suitcases and roller carts clogged the area by the indoor fountain while guests, cordoned off by rows of red ropes, zigzagged their way to the front desk. Maele was glad she didn't have much to take with her. Now all she had to do was wait in the long line to turn in her key. For a moment, she imagined herself in a slow-motion scene from a cheesy holiday flick. Santa and the North Pole in one corner, Christmas carolers in the other. Children danced to a pop rock version of "Silver Bells" under twinkling lights. Everything around her was glitter, gold, and ostentatious. She longed to get back to her comfort zone. Her family.

"Mae!" Andie waved her arms and zipped up the line, to the chagrin of the guests. Once there, she pulled Maele off to the side, appeasing everyone else. "You're checked out. You don't have to line up. I called and left you a message. Didn't know whether you booked a car to take you to the airport."

"Oh, oh. I'm sorry. Things were so busy, I forgot to tell you. I'm staying here for a few weeks to visit my mom's family."

"Really?" Andie smiled. "That's great."

Maele realized that Andie wasn't smiling at her, but at the man who had sidled up behind her.

"Hi, Warren."

"Hey." When Warren leaned down to give Maele a kiss on her cheek, she spied Adam in the distance behind Andie, signing papers at the counter.

"Baby," Warren said to Andie, "our ride will be here in ten." He turned back to Maele. "Can we take you somewhere?"

"She's staying on the island with her family," Andie said.

Adam stepped in, almost pushing his brother out of the way. "I'm giving her a ride."

Maele tried not to focus too much on him, but there they were again. The eyes that seemed to change color every time she looked into them. She kept her cool, addressing Warren. "He offered earlier." Maele couldn't pick up on the energy in the room. Adam wasn't acting the same as he had earlier. He seemed nervous and jittery again, like at the wedding.

"Don't you need to be on our flight home?" Warren asked his brother.

"Actually, I've decided to stay in Kauai for a few more days," Adam replied.

Warren and Andie stood silent, eyebrows raised, mouths agape, and flashing quick looks at each other.

"You checked this with Mom and Dad?" Warren asked. "You're supposed to be with them for Christmas."

"They'll understand. I'll work it out with them. I just want to spend some quiet time working on my screenplay. I'm gonna hang back a bit."

"Who with?" Warren furrowed his brow, squinting. He rolled his eyes in Andie's direction, ostensibly to get her attention, but she wouldn't bite. Maele thought it was Andie's way of staying out of the conversation, slowly putting one foot back and moving out of Warren's line of sight. Andie caught Maele's eye and gave her a slight nod. Now it was just Adam and Warren, face-to-face.

"Yeah, I want to catch some waves and get some alone time. And the rewrites. I mean, this place was my home for four years of my life. I get recharged here."

"And you're gonna miss the family for Christmas?" Warren asked.

"You guys will be on your honeymoon." Adam shrugged.

"Uh uh," Warren said. "That's not the point. When was this decided?"

"Um, just now. I just extended my stay here. I didn't check out."

Maele sensed a standoff between the brothers, the energy between them tense.

Haruto, the family chauffer, wearing a black suit and sporting a Don

Quixote mustache, came in. He reminded Maele of Mr. Flores, with his dark eyes and dark, slicked back hair. He made a coughing noise as he stood behind Warren, attempting to end the conversation.

Andie gently took hold of Warren's hand. "H's here, babe. Adam knows what he's doing."

Warren changed his attitude immediately, giving in to Andie. His face lost all tension as he bobbed his head.

It was now or never. Maele had to say something, assure the newly married couple she would take care of Adam. She owed them that. Why wouldn't she take him in, make sure he wasn't alone for the holidays? The Flores, the Yates, her family—their lives were all woven together in one way or the other. Adam was family. All she had to do was explain to her aunt that he was a Yates, part of the family who had employed her and given her a chance.

"He's welcome to join me and my family for our celebration. I won't be with my parents for Christmas either, but he's welcome to spend the holiday with me, at my auntie and uncle's."

Andie and Warren shot her a look, tilting their heads.

"What I mean is," she followed up, and paused, "if he doesn't want to be alone."

"Are you sure?" Adam asked, looking pleased. His smile was infectious.

Maele saw Warren's face soften and his shoulders relax.

"Yes, of course," she said. "That's the least I could do." Oops. That's not what she meant. Maele didn't want it to seem like a favor. She really didn't mind having Adam around. He was a stranger, but one she wanted to get to know badly. And sure, he was a bit arrogant and manic, but he was also kind. Maybe she needed the challenge. Maybe his confidence would rub off on her.

"Thank you, Maele," Warren said, before giving Adam a hug. "I'll have the company send you a car you can use while you're here."

"I'm good. I got one," Adam replied.

"All right, well, if you're good, you're good. Merry Christmas."

"Merry Christmas. Now … you two go and have an *amazing* honeymoon."

Andie and Maele smiled at each other. Adam held his arms open for Andie, who slipped into them and gave him a kiss on his cheek.

Maele was filled with an overwhelming sense of sadness. Who knew when she'd see Andie again? The newlyweds were off to start their life, make babies, and change the world.

As if Andie could read her mind, she pulled Maele aside and lovingly set her hands on Maele's shoulders. "So you, young lady, will take all that promise you have in you and do good in the world. The internship is open to you anytime. This year, next year. Whenever you're ready to start that chapter in your life. I know you have to finish this part, first. Face your fears, reclaim the bold awesomeness you had before your accident. And know I'm just a phone call away."

Maele couldn't help the tears. First a single drop and then an overflow that blurred her vision. She swiped her face with the back of her hand. "I'm going to miss you, Andie."

"I'm going to miss you, too. We'll see each other wherever life takes us. Promise me."

"I promise."

It wasn't the first time Maele had felt secure in Andie's arms, like the sister she never had. She cried because she feared it would be the last time she'd ever see her.

"Don't cry. I love you."

"I love you too, Andie, and I owe you for the dress, remember," Maele mumbled against Andie's silk blouse.

"Okay, I won't forget." Then Andie placed her mouth close to Maele's ear, stroking her hair at the same time and avoiding the gazes of both Yates brothers. "I love Adam. He's my brother now, but be careful. He breaks hearts."

Adam's Vision

While Andie and Maele were quietly talking, Adam pulled Warren aside.

"Hey, I just want you to know that I know what I'm doing."

"You always act like you know what you're doing—that's why the things you do are so infuriating. You are a drug addict, Adam, and until you're clean and sober, it isn't fair to rope Maele into your madness. She's an amazing young woman. I don't want to see you ruin her, or even show her a world she should never see. That would be the cruelest thing you could do." Warren held his brother's gaze. "You come from a place radically different from hers. Your money, your values ... I mean, she would never dream of missing Christmas with her family for a stranger. That says something about you, about your character, your loyalty. It just seems like another rash decision in a series of rash decisions in the reality TV show that's playing in your head, starring you."

Warren wasn't wrong. Despite the harshness of his words, Warren made a compelling argument. But Adam had seen something wonderful in Maele's eyes—a future with her that he wanted to claim.

"Do you remember when I said everything was about to change after my DMT trip on the beach?"

"Yes. I remember it well." Warren shook his head, his expression disappointed.

"Well, I never told you what I saw. I was sitting on a beach in Kauai, wearing a bright yellow sweatshirt I used to own. I felt peaceful, happy. I was watching something in the water. A wave. One that looked like a blue wall of glass. It was the bluest blue I'd ever seen, and on the wave was a surfer, a woman, who had dolphins riding on either side of her. Maybe she was riding a dolphin, like the character in my movie, but she was stunning, pure, and true. And as she rode the wave, I became the dolphins and, Warren, I can't explain it, but it was her." Adam motioned toward Maele and raised his eyebrows.

"Then I heard a voice say, 'It's time to put your childish things away.' And then, well, I know it sounds crazy." Adam pointed at Maele. "But I've never been more sober minded about anything in my life. Maybe all the chaos was meant to lead me to this moment, to right here and now. You have to trust me, you have to believe me, just this once. There is a bigger force at play, and I'm doing my part to fulfill the story. I feel it deep in my bones, Warren. I gotta be bold in love."

Haruto made his little coughing sound again. Like a horse trainer who clicks his tongue to get his horses to move.

"I gotta go," Warren said. "We have a plane to catch."

"It's private, the plane will wait."

"I know, but it's not good form to keep the pilot waiting. I gave her my word we'd be there at a certain time. I'll honor it."

"It's what I love about you, Warren." And Adam meant it. To take a stand, to be a man of your word. In that moment, Adam knew what all that meant, and he was seeing it through the eyes of his brother. "Have fun, see the world, send a postcard now and again. I love you," he called out as Warren began to walk away.

"I love you too, Adam." And, as if an afterthought hit him, Warren stopped and turned back to face his brother.

"Adam?"

"Yo."

"Happiness is all around you. It doesn't exist in temporary moments. You have to invest in finding it, be open to it, choose it. For all you know, it's staring you right in the face."

As if on cue, a band began to play, "Aloha Oe," the Hawaiian farewell song, as a bevy of zebra doves flew into the lobby from outside.

Adam watched as his brother walked away with his new bride and the family chauffeur. He felt a touch of sadness for the way of life that would no longer be. No more crashing on his brother's couch, no more Warren as his wingman. It was the start of a new era for Warren and Adam.

A brand-new chapter was about to begin.

Back on the Road to Kauai

I t was a beautiful day in Kauai. Early rains had cleared away the humidity and the citrusy aroma of plumerias filled the air. The winter sun was warm, not hot, and the sky was spotless. There was not a cloud in sight.

It wasn't a long drive from the South Shore to the North Shore. Adam told Maele he was going to travel his favorite route along Maluhia Road to get to the 50. A part of the road was known as the Tree Tunnel. Covered with a canopy of swamp mahogany, it stretched as far as the eye could see and made for a truly magical sight. Maele looked up at the trees as Adam drove.

"It's funny, I've always liked these trees. They're not native to these islands, but the islands are better for having them here," she said, turning to smile at Adam.

Adam smiled back.

"Do you know the story of how they were planted?" Maele asked.

"No, not really. All I know is they're some type of eucalyptus tree, and this road reminds me of an ancient kingdom or something. It's like a scene in a fantasy movie."

"Well," Maele began, "legend has it there was once a cattleman from Scotland who settled on Kauai about two hundred years ago. He came by boat, alone and with hardly a penny to his name. When he got here, he worked for other ranchers, but saw endless opportunity and soon became rich. According to the legend, he met and fell in love with a native girl from Poipu, but the times dictated he marry someone who was European. So, he married someone who would help his status rather than someone he really loved. The legend says this was the only road to Poipu. The native girl would walk this road on her journey home to the valley every day. The cattleman wanted to make it beautiful for the girl he loved, so she would feel special going to and from the town. He planted five hundred trees as an act of love."

Adam nodded, turning briefly to look at her.

"That's like my dad," he said. "Always telling me to marry someone who's equally yoked, whatever that means. A social arrangement versus true love. Shows you the kind of strength it takes to push against societal norms. I mean, the guy planted hundreds of trees for a girl he loved and turned an ordinary road into an enchanted canopy fit for royalty. I guarantee his wife didn't get a tree-lined road."

They turned onto the HI 50 while she touched the leather seat, thinking to herself. The seat was rock hard, and the red interior felt like plastic when she knew it wasn't. There was something to be said about the corduroy seats in her mom's white Impala. Those seats were so soft and comfortable, they could put an insomniac to sleep during long car rides. The humming of the motor and the clacking of the carburetor were also soothing.

Adam knew the way, driving north from Poipu as if he'd been there a thousand times. As they made their way onto Highway 56, he told her things she already knew. Like why Kauai was called the Garden Isle, and about the Royal Coconut Coast, which lined the east side of Kauai. Mount Wai'ale'ale, the wettest spot on Earth, was the shield volcano that formed Kauai, and is the source of the water collected high in the mountains. He asked her if she'd been to the waterfalls and whether she'd swam in the Wailua River. Of course she had, but she humored him, loved hearing his voice and enjoyed his rambling. She'd never seen anyone look so animated and happy.

It took thirty minutes for him to bring it up. She'd known he would, eventually. She was learning he wasn't the type to hold anything in and he had encyclopedic knowledge about a lot of topics. This boy could talk.

"So," he began, "do you want to talk about what happened at the beach yesterday?"

"Nope."

"Okay," he said, with a single shoulder shrug.

"I mean, not yet."

When he remained silent, she tried to deflect. "Just keep following

Highway 56 until it meets Kilauea. My aunt's house is right off that road."

"Okay."

They drove and talked about Christmas and family and film school and things that were light and breezy. The beauty of the island stretched into a green blur as they flew up the highway. This island was verdant. As they talked, she looked at Adam, took him in.

By then, she'd decided he had the perfect nose. And jaw. And chin. And face.

"Tell me more about film school," she urged. "What was college like? Were you in a fraternity?"

"No fraternities, but I had a group of friends who were like a fraternity," he said with a laugh. "I mean, we had so much fun. Too much fun. My dad wasn't too happy about my choice of career, so there were a lot of difficult times. He really made it clear to me how he felt about what I was doing."

"Are you doing what you love now?"

"Yeah. Even the rewrites," Adam said with a chuckle.

"Wow, is it difficult? To sell a movie?" She knew she was being relentless, but he intrigued her so much. He lived a life she was never going to know.

"Super difficult. There are so many of us pitching the same old stories."

"Ah, we're close," she said and Adam slowed the car. "You can turn into this driveway right up here on the left."

"Wow, you're practically on Secret Beach. My old school is just fifteen minutes down the road. Exactly how far are you from the beach?"

"It's almost a mile walk."

They pulled into the driveway of an old white bungalow with a white wooden porch and a dark shingled roof. A dilapidated VW bus sat on the grass with its doors hanging loosely and its wheels nowhere to be seen. Another ratty car nearby looked equally useless. Lots of old growth trees surrounded the property. Adam pulled the car to a stop.

"This is it. Kilauea road and the family estate." She stressed the last word. This was her family's home, and mansion or not, Yates money or no, it was theirs. Birthdays were spent here—holidays and barbecues, with so many memories. There was nothing to be ashamed of, and if it wasn't good enough for Adam, then he wasn't good enough for her. She looked at him. He didn't seem put off.

"Why don't you come inside and have lunch with us?" She wasn't normally this impulsive, but she wanted him to stay.

"Oh, thank you for inviting me, but I don't think I'm ready to meet everyone today."

She noticed how nervous he seemed, like he was back in the lobby. This man confused her—one minute he was calm and collected, in charge of the world, the next, he was manic and crazy. Then, a second later, he would be nervous like a small child, almost. What was his deal and what was he looking for? She contemplated him as he dug around in his pockets, searching for something without success.

"Okay," she said, disappointed. "Are you sure?"

"Maele, I don't know. I would hate for first impressions to be a surprise. What if your aunt didn't make enough food? I don't want to put her out. It wouldn't be right."

Maele answered by removing her seat belt and unlocking the door.

"Listen, can you wait here for a few minutes? I'll go see my aunt first and let her know I've brought a friend. She doesn't have a cell phone, and, yes, out of respect, I should ask her first, but I know she'll have enough food. Trust me."

"You think it'll be okay?"

"I'm sure it will be. Give me a minute, okay? I'll come and get you."

Suddenly, they both whipped their heads toward the front door when they heard a huge boom.

"*Mae-Mae!*" hollered a giant of a man, his arms outstretched in a warrior's greeting, hair like a lion bouncing in every direction. He ran toward them like a golden retriever, at least six and a half feet tall and all muscle. Tribal tattoos patterned up and down his arms and he had a beard that made him look like a pirate.

"*Koa!*" Maele met his energy pound for pound and jumped out of the car. Koa swept her up in his giant arms and twirled her around.

"My little sister-cuz! Holy kaka, look at you, you're a woman now. No more little girl for you, huh?" Koa stopped when he saw Adam, Maele still hanging from his arms. "Who's dis guy? Who you, bruddah?"

Adam smiled broadly. "Hey, man. My name is Adam."

"*Aloha*, Adam! Welcome to our house, bruddah. Any friend of Mae-Mae's is a friend of mine. He *is* your friend, right?" Still holding Maele, he pointed with her like an arrow toward Adam.

"Yes. Ugh, put me down, Koa. This is Adam Yates."

Instead of putting Maele down, Koa hoisted her up and over his shoulder like a sack of coffee. She quickly realized what Adam was smiling at. Her skirt had bunched up on Koa's shoulder and her bare legs were swinging in the air. Maele's attempt to reach behind her and yank her skirt down quickly failed when Koa started to spin her around.

"Agh, my little Mae-Mae is back. Come on, we're waiting to eat."

He took off with Maele over his shoulder toward the house. She looked up at Adam as he grew smaller and smaller, lifted both hands and shrugged, then waved for Adam to follow her in.

28

Giant Steps

A dam took a deep breath and decided if he was going to be bold in love, then major steps needed to be taken.

"Here we go," he muttered. Then he followed Koa and Maele into the little white house.

Adam wished he had his pills with him, or some weed to calm his nerves. He would love to go into that house, eat good food, and talk to Maele's family, but he was terrified. Getting over his social anxiety without using any drugs was one of those things he wished, deep down inside, he could change. He was going to sell his car, buy a home, no more designer tennis shoes, and no more needing drugs simply to talk to people.

Think happy thoughts. I did just see her underwear, after all.

He stood by the front door, observing the goings-on in the house. It was simple but clean—living room to the left, kitchen in front of him, and dining room to the right. He could instantly tell that the flamboyant house furnishings completely matched the colorful personalities who lived there. The yellow couch filled with printed daffodils and the green plastic chairs surrounding it were so seventies, but so spunky and spirited. Life. Full of life. This home had character, a history. If this was Maele's family's home, there was nothing he wanted to do more than to get to know it and her story.

Adam smiled with another thought. Koa was a presence in this house. Literally. His head almost scraped the ceiling, and for that matter, so did Adam's. Koa's body took up half the house.

"Koa, put her down," a voice boomed from the kitchen. Out

shuffled a middle-aged lady, plump and pretty, wearing an orange housedress. Adam thought she was a carbon copy of Maele's mother, whom he'd met at the wedding, though a little more tanned, and a little shorter.

"Ma, it's Mae-Mae."

"Koa, I said put her down. You are no longer children. You're making her flash her *palema'i*. Put her down, I say."

Maele ran into her aunt's arms, flushed and disheveled, her long braid unraveled at the ends. Adam remained by the door, his composure returning.

I got this.

"Auntie, this is my friend, Adam. He'll be here for a few days, so I thought I'd bring him up to meet you guys. Adam, this is my auntie, Nalani Leiva. She's Koa's mom."

Adam was shocked that something so big could have come out of something so small. He stepped forward and offered Nalani his hand.

She gave him a long hard look before narrowing her eyes and pursing her lips. She reluctantly held out her hand to him, curling the tips of her fingers so they barely touched his. "Whose son is this?"

"No one you know, Ma," Koa interjected. "Come on, guys, let's eat." He walked toward the kitchen table. "I texted Noe. He's on his way."

Nalani put a hand on her hip. "Does your friend eat poi?"

Mae grinned. "He's from here. He lives in Kailua on Oahu. Of course, he eats poi. You eat poi, right?"

Adam nodded his head.

Koa broke into a deep, hearty laugh, and Adam swore the house trembled.

"Oh, yeah, this is going to be fun!" Koa declared.

I'd hate to see this guy angry.

Koa added an extra place setting on the table for Adam. "Sit, bruddah."

His nerves were calming and the smell inside the house reminded him of a maid who used to cook for him when he was little. It smelled like things of the islands, raw, deep, rich—like soil. There was also the ever-present hint of oil cooking, things to be fried. He looked at Maele and she appeared relaxed, the most comfortable he'd seen her. She'd seemed uneasy at the hotel, like she felt out of place, constantly smoothing down her hair, her dress, and speaking in a measured tone. But here, she was confident and even feisty, dancing instead of walking from place to place. He suspected this was her true self and he dug it.

"Koa, your father will be home any minute. Make sure his plate is ready," Nalani said.

"Yes, Mama. Now tell me, sister-cuz, how is Oahu treating you?"

"It's really great. I'm taking classes at the community college—business classes. I work at this really great coffee shop, but it's also like a bookstore."

"Kinda like a bookstore, or is a bookstore?" Nalani interrupted. Adam could see where Koa came from—it was all making sense. This family was inquisitive. Asking questions without a care in the world and bursting with energy.

"It started out as a coffee shop. Well, not even a coffee shop, really just a place to sell some beans from the plantation ..."

"Yes, the plantation. The damned plantation that took my baby sister away. We had everything we needed here on this island. It still makes no sense to me. You can't divide family."

Adam couldn't hide his smile. This kind of passion was exactly what was missing from his family, the say-it-like-you-mean-it-and-then-move-on kind of passion. The Yates family was loaded with experts on passive aggression. Never really sure why the egg was there, but always feeling like you were stepping on shells.

"And that mother of yours," she said, looking directly at Adam, "she has always been trouble. Did Maele tell you she caused a scandal in my family? Engaged to a man, a family friend, and then going off and falling in love with Maele's father and eloping a few weeks before her wedding?"

"Auntie, you helped her elope."

"Yes, but your lolo doesn't know that," Nalani answered, putting a finger to her lips.

"Grandfather," Maele whispered to Adam, her lips barely moving.

"Ah."

"And it wasn't a scandal," Maele said, turning to Adam with a smile. "She's exaggerating." She addressed her aunt again. "Auntie, you love Papa."

"My sister always said, 'When you know, you know.'"

"When you know, you know," Adam repeated.

"Auntie, I know you hate the plantation, but that is the land Papa was born on, and he loves the work. You know he tried to make it here, but that plantation is his whole life. Mama loves the work too; it gives them purpose. They keep inviting you to come live there. There is so much to do, they could use the extra hands. You should see it now. The plantation and the coffee shop have changed so much. Him!" Maele pointed at Adam. "His brother just married the girl who changed our lives. Andie Mathews. Andie Yates, now."

"Andie Mathews Yates. I think she's now officially using her maiden name as her middle name," Adam said. He was in the flow.

"Nope. Not my wife," Koa declared. "I'm traditional. She's gonna take my last name—no middle maiden names, no hyphens. Old times."

Adam loved this guy. He cracked him up. Sure, he was still terrified of him, but the longer he sat there, the more he realized that Koa was a chief, or could have been if they still practiced tribal culture on the islands. He was sure of it. If the islands were still divided into tribes and clans, Koa would be the chief of Kauai. His voice would boom across the island. They would never need a messenger to deliver the proclamations.

"Anyway, I helped her with all of it. She left the coffee shop in my hands, and over the past two years it's become a popular destination for surfers, artists, writers, and musicians. It's a very cool place. You need to come visit us. You never visit, Auntie."

"You know I don't like the city. I don't even go to the South Shore on this island. Kapa'a is as far as I go. Too far, after that."

Just then, Adam met the patriarch of the house. It was abundantly clear where Koa had inherited his size. This man was huge. If Koa was a chief in the making, then here was the current chief. Tanned, tall, and full, but under a layer of fat was pure muscle. Barrel-chested, with huge arms and thighs like tree trunks. This guy could have played professional football.

"Daddy," Koa yelled and tossed his dad a can of beer. "Lunch is ready."

The Daddy came home for lunch?

Between the prickly mother, the larger-than-life cousin, and now the giant father, Adam had no room in his head to be nervous, anxious, or jonesing for his drugs. He was all in. Any counselor that advised you to remain in the moment would only need the Leivas to make that possible.

"Who dis?" Koa's father asked, and nodded in Adam's direction. "And who dis?" he said as he swept Maele out of her seat and held her against the ceiling. This was the second time today that Adam had seen Maele's underwear. He enjoyed the view until he felt Nalani's eyes on him, then politely averted his gaze toward the poi.

"Put me down," Maele squealed.

"Put her down, Fudge," Nalani barked.

"Ah. Look at sister-cuz, laying on the ceiling," Koa teased. "Why are you laying on the ceiling, Mae-Mae? Come down from there!"

Adam laughed out loud. If this was who he got to spend Christmas with, he couldn't be happier.

29

Like Old Times

"You're here!" Maele rushed into Noe's arms as he ran up the driveway. She noticed Adam watching, so she waved to him before walking with Noe back into the house.

"Look at you. You look different, hoaloha," Maele said.

"And you," Noe answered. "You look so grown-up. Even more beautiful."

The truth was, they had both changed. Separated for six years and altered by life's experiences.

"Noe, what the heck happened? Thought you were going to join us for dinner." Koa pounced on them, locking his arms around their shoulders and dragging them headfirst into the living room.

"Had to help my dad out." Noe made himself at home on the colorful couch. Maele followed suit and sat beside him. Koa approached with two Kona Pale Ales and a bottled water.

"Mae-Mae, you still don't drink beer?"

"Nope, but I drink wine now."

"Ooh," Koa and Noe mocked, pinkies up and fanning themselves at the same time.

"Stop."

"Who was that guy?" Noe asked. "The one who just drove away in the Land Rover?"

"Mae's boyfriend."

Maele swore she saw Noe's eyelids fly open before he looked down at his shoes. "Shush. He's not my boyfriend."

"You brought an Instagram influencer with you," Koa teased.

Noe remained quiet, still staring at his shoes. Maele remembered how long his eyelashes were. They were dark, like his wavy hair.

"What on earth are you talking about?" Maele asked.

"Did you see his clothes? I've seen those in magazines. You know, the fancy ones that only have pictures of models and clothing in them."

"You mean catalogs?" Maele corrected.

"He aha." Koa rolled his eyes.

"Don't *whatever* me. It's true. Apparently, you didn't hear a word I said when I called the other day. He's Andie's husband's brother. Kind of sweet, kind of lost, but self-confident, and I don't want him to be alone for Christmas. Which leads me to ask—"

"Any influencer boyfriend of yours is an influencer of ours, Mae-Mae."

Maele shook her head in exasperation. "So, you'll tell your parents he's spending Christmas and New Year's with us?"

"Hmmm. Christmas and New Year's might be stretching it." Koa leaned back on the couch with a smug look. "Okay, but only if you admit one thing." He clasped his chin and tapped it with his finger. "Noe, do you remember that boy on the beach? The dude who used to sit and watch us ride?"

Maele stayed silent, staring straight ahead without meeting Koa's eyes.

Noe snapped his fingers. "Oia ka! That's where I remember him from. The one never in a group of other malihinis on our beach."

"They're not strangers. They all live here on our islands," Maele muttered. "They were in boarding school."

"The filthy rich boarding school for problem kids." Koa pumped his fist in the air.

He shot Noe a look, and together they started elbowing poor Maele, who sat in between them ping-ponging from side to side. "Uy! It's the boy on the beach. The one you had a crush on. Uy!"

She tried not to smile. But, truth be told, she did want to gush—wanted to remember those happy times. When she'd had all the self-confidence in the world and the boy watching her had been enamored by her strength. Many times, while floating out on the water, she would watch him watch her, knowing their worlds would never collide. He would go home to his ritzy air-conditioned boarding school, and she would go home to feed the cows and the pigs.

"I did not have a crush on him."

"Maele, how long have we known you? Since you were born," Koa argued. A rustling sound from the next bedroom interrupted the ongoing torment. "Oh, shoot," Koa said, shaking the ground again as he jumped to his feet. "I'd better get your bedroom ready. Mama is going to be checking in a while."

When he left, Maele turned to Noe and took his hand. Her heart ached for him. She didn't realize how empty those six years had been until then.

"How's it been, Noe? I'm so happy you're here."

"Okay, I guess. My dad's still the same. He got sick right after you left and is just holding on. Mom still works with Nalani at the farm, and I help Koa in his new store a few days a week."

"Seems like nothing's changed. And everything."

"No, nothing changes around here. But tell me, Maele. What's been up with you all this time? Your family left pretty quickly after you—" Noe didn't have to continue. It was this unspoken thing, this life-changing event. But the ease and familiarity were why she was there now. She needed to get back that part of her life and the accident was, for all intents and purposes, a part of who she was.

"My parents wanted no part of anything that happened after the accident. They didn't think I'd ever recover, so they did what they thought was best. Touring the circuit was my life though. I went from that to not being able to move at all."

"How long did it take for you to get better?"

"Six months. For half a year, I could only wiggle my right hand and right leg. I never worked so hard in my life to move again. You know, being in the water came so naturally for me. I took that for granted. It took another six months to be able to walk with the aid of a cane. Almost two more years before I could run."

"Oh, Mae." Noe looked at her, his eyes pained.

In many ways, she felt responsible for causing time to stand still in Kilauea. They had been a good group, she and Noe and two other friends—sleeping in cars, meeting at dawn, and chasing the swells. When she'd left, everything stopped. That era, their generation—in keeping in touch with Koa, her friends seemed to be stuck in a time warp. Koa, fifteen years older than her, still lived at home after a crash and burn in Maui. Now that had been a family scandal. Noe and the rest still chased their dreams, never looking far enough into the future. In some ways, she was jealous. She wanted the same indifference, the contentment and simplicity of their joy. Maybe she could get it back while she was there. Maybe her thirst for achievement would be alleviated by the freedom she'd once had. Life didn't have to be more than what it had been before. She needed to reclaim that and see where she went from there.

Maele squeezed his hand and touched his cheek. "Don't feel sorry for me. I'm back, and I'm here to find the part of me that got lost for a while. Who best to help me get over the past than you guys?"

"You *maka'u*?"

"Yes. I'm afraid."

Nalani saved them from the silence that blanketed the room with Maele's admission of fear. She ambled in, wearing a bright pink nightgown overlaid with ribbons. Huge red rollers covered her head and a shower cap held everything together. Maele wondered why she needed them when Koa was proof there was no shortage of curly hair in the family.

"Koa!" Nalani yelled. "My sister already called to check on her daughter. Make sure your room is ready for Maele and that she has everything she needs."

"Everything is ready, Ma," Koa answered. "Mae-Mae, you take my room. You got clean sheets and I hung fresh towels on your bedrail. Next to your bed, I left you your favorite snack."

"Coconut chips?" Maele rubbed her hands together in glee.

"Yup, fresh from the grove."

Noe stood, running his hand through his hair. In the six years since she'd left, he had gotten bigger, more rugged looking. He was a man now. She could make out the bulk of his shoulders and arms through his shirt.

"It's late. You'd better get some rest, Maele."

"Yeah, it's been a long day. I am quite tired. Would you mind if I got ready for bed?"

"No, not at all. I'm going to get going," Noe said. "See you tomorrow?"

"At sunrise," Maele said, before planting a kiss on his cheek.

The Squall

Adam couldn't help but smile during the entire drive home. After having lunch with Maele's family, he had to excuse himself to allow them time to catch up.

The resort suite felt overwhelmingly empty. This wasn't usual, since he'd been there for the past week. He knew it was because Warren had left. Warren kept his goodness intact, it was his safe house. Every time he got a little too close to the edge, all Adam had to do was run home to his brother.

Literally. Home to the pool house. Where he would hide for days until he felt like going out into the world again.

As evening descended, Adam switched on the lights and moved from room to room, jittery from withdrawals and terrified of the next few hours of boredom. What should he do? He wanted to stay awake, rush back to see Maele at daybreak, spend the day with her. But no, he knew she needed time on her own. Besides, what did he have to show for himself? Nothing. Everything was a work in progress with him. For God's sake, he needed to see something through.

Anything.

A girl like Maele wouldn't want to be with someone like him. The opportunities were always stacked in his favor. His father had made sure of it. Even just through their limited interactions, something told him she wasn't interested in all the things he thought put him above the rest.

The villa was too quiet. He needed some noise. So, he walked over to the living room and turned on the TV.

He searched for something mindless, something just to drown out the voices in his head. He finally settled on a show that had characters in animal costumes singing in front of judges.

"That one's not so bad," he said as a frog with crazy eyes and a flamboyant hat sang its heart out.

Next, he fired up his laptop and found an outlet on the floor next to the couch. *Outlets in the floor, fancy. Need those in my future house.*

Wait, first things first. His heart was still palpitating. A cigarette. That should calm him. He smoked a special brand of cigarettes, from a light blue pack that claimed they were natural. Adam didn't consider himself a real smoker, but he always had a stale pack in his possession.

Disengaging the plug from the living room, he decided to walk out on the balcony and into the fresh air. His view was unrivaled. There it was, Poipu Bay—warm and placid, but also dark and chasmal. Its broad reach extended as far as his eyes could see—in the dark, it held on to its mysteries. During the day, it was as transparent as a sheet of glass. Adam sat on the teak-lined lounge chair, stretched out his legs, and crossed them at the ankles. He lit up a cigarette and took a deep, long drag. There. Better. Not as good or helpful as the other stuff, but it gave him something to do with his hands. He powered up his computer and began to think up a game plan.

First, he would make a few tweaks to his script in the morning before rushing off to see Maele. Then he would follow up and make sure his agent knew how excited he was about the opportunity. He stayed drunk after his brother left L.A. up through the wedding, so he hadn't talked to his team since the night he signed the contract. His agent, Chaz, had left close to twenty messages on his voicemail and twice as many texts.

Next, he would try to get into all the mindfulness mumbo jumbo everyone was swearing up and down about. He picked up the receiver to the phone that hung on the outside wall and pushed the button with the word Spa above it.

"Serenity Spa, may I help you?"

"Hi," he said. "Wow. I'm surprised you're still open. I was just going to leave a message."

"Well, sir, we are also a full-service gym, so we are open twenty-four hours."

"That's good to know," he said, smiling.

"How may I help you?"

"I'd like to enroll for your yoga classes. It says here ..." He reached with his other hand and leafed through the brochures inserted in the hotel book. "There's one at 6:00 a.m. every day. That one." He pointed to the spot on the page until he realized he was on the phone, and she couldn't see what he was pointing at. "Uh, Beginners."

"And this is Mr. Yates?"

"Yates, yes. Adam."

"Well, Mr. Yates, we have you down for tomorrow morning. Have a wonderful evening."

"Wait! Sorry, I have another question." He cleared his throat after catching himself yelling.

"Yes?"

"This will teach me balance, right? And peace? And calm? And also help me meditate?"

The lady on the other line couldn't help but chuckle. "Yes, sir."

"Sounds great. Really wonderful. In the meantime, you said you're open twenty-four hours?"

"That's correct, Mr. Yates."

"In that case, is there anyone available to give me a massage?"

"There is, actually. Ellen can set up in your room in fifteen minutes if that's acceptable."

"That sounds great. Thank you."

"How long would you like your treatment to last? Thirty minutes? Sixty? Ninety?"

Adam was itchy inside and lonely. He was craving transactional human contact, even if it was a simple massage. It would beat having to do battle with the voices in his head all night.

"Can she give me a three-hour massage? I know that's a lot, but she can use hot stones or a scrub. Whatever."

"Yes, Mr. Yates. She'll be to your room shortly. Or would you prefer to join us here in the spa where more treatments are available?"

"Yes, sure, I'll head your way. See you shortly. Thank you."

He heard the voice on the other end of the phone say, "Aloha." Then the line went dead.

Feeling good about his spa plans, he picked up his cell phone and video called his mom.

She picked up on the first ring. "Muffin, are you okay?"

Warmth radiated throughout Adam's chest, and the use of her

special nickname for him put a smile on his face. She looked pretty with her hair up in a messy bun, a pale, round face, and her skin so clear and young. She wore reading glasses, the blue frames accentuating her big brown eyes.

"What's wrong?"

"Hi, Mom. Nothing's wrong. I was checking in to see what you guys are doing for Christmas Eve." Adam leaned back in the chair and held the phone up to his face.

"It's so dark there. Where are you?"

"I'm on the balcony. Look." He turned the camera toward the sky. "There are no stars tonight, but the moon looks like it's floating in the water, doesn't it?"

"It looks so small to me through the phone, but yes, it kinda does look like it's floating."

"So? What are you guys doing? And what are you holding in your hand?"

"Oh, this?" Marta lowered the camera until it focused on the table. "It's a new paint-by-number set given to me by Auntie Elma. I'm waiting for your father to finish his laps in the pool so we can have dinner. And, for Christmas Eve? For the first time in a long time, we are going out on a date."

"Wow. Good for you guys. That'll be fun."

"Is everything okay? Where are you going to be?"

"Do you know the family of Maele Moana, Andie's bridesmaid? Her family is having me over for dinner. It'll be fun."

"Oh, great." His mom expertly tucked the pencil behind her ear to focus her attention fully on her son. Once in a while, her working-class habits would take over, like the pencil thing or darning Dad's socks, or rolling up her sleeves and caulking the bathroom floor. Adam always respected her for that. And his dad? Well, Adam would like to think his dad did, as well. "What else is up?"

"Nothing, really. I just wanted to call you, hear your voice. I just realize how much you took care of me growing up."

"Of course, you were my baby boy. You are the most important thing in the world to me. Do you remember what your dad used to sing to us?"

Adam laughed at the thought and sang, "Mommy and baby, stuck like glue. You think there's one, but really there's two!'"

"Are you okay?" Marta squinted at him, tilting her head, concerned.

"Yeah, yeah, of course. I just know I haven't made you very proud lately. But I will. I'm going to follow through on things. I'm going to make you so proud of me, Mom. I promise."

"Oh, Muffin. Are you kidding? You have always made me proud of you."

"Thanks. That means a lot. I'll let you get back to your coloring. I'll call you tomorrow."

"Okay. Please give my thanks to Maele's family."

Adam nodded. He blew his mom a kiss.

"Oh, and, Adam?" She brought the phone to her face. "You will find it. Your happiness. Sometimes, life needs to quiet down for you to see it. Just look closer, okay?" Her words hit him like a ton of bricks.

Adam had an epiphany and his entire world spun. He always used the excuse of not fitting in as a crutch to justify his vices, but that wasn't exactly true. He had a family that loved him very much. All the tension, the competition, the jealousy—it was all in his head. Why hadn't he seen this before? Perhaps he never looked close enough. He never put in the work or paid the price, he only succeeded at the things that came easy to him, and he never tried anything that made him afraid. Not anymore.

He hatched the biggest, most important plan he ever dared. It had nothing to do with being the best screenwriter in the world. Or making so much money he could afford the luxuries he was used to. The thought of constantly trying to please his father never even crossed his mind. His plan would be different this time. He would give up his heart. He was going to let himself fall truly and boldly in love with Maele Moana, and he was going to try his darndest to make her fall in love with him.

First Baby Wave

The sunrise was splendid on any day of the year. But Maele awoke with a blast of newness she could feel in her bones. It made her dizzy, just thinking about meeting her friends on Secret Beach. It was a brand-new day, a new beginning. She would be starting her journey.

The Leiva home was deceiving. An inconspicuous bungalow on a well-tended lot, it was humble but not impoverished, small but not cramped. Their family home for over forty years was unpretentious, yet well cared for. Its owner was constantly building something, fixing something, adding something. Evidence of unfinished projects lay scattered across the lawn. Despite its modest surroundings, the Leiva home sat on prime Kauai property. Nestled near Kilauea Falls and Kauapea Beach, it was a stone's throw away from the island's natural wonders. What Maele and Koa lacked in material things were more than made up for by the richness of their land. People paid to spend a fleeting moment in the midst of all that symmetry. Maele, Koa, and their friends lived in it every day. They never wanted for more.

One of Kauai's most impressive beaches was in the Leiva's backyard. Hidden and unobtrusive, Secret Beach was one that could only be reached by foot. Located off a nameless dirt road in Kilauea, the steep trail leading to the beach could be slippery when wet. But that world, miles from the busy highway and secluded by a wall of lava rock, gave the locals a place that hadn't yet been dominated by tourists. Dazzling views to the east included Mokuaeae Island and the Kilauea Lighthouse, which rested on top of a sea cliff. Rough surf and strong currents at times brought dangerous conditions. In the winter, especially, the often-treacherous water normally attracted only expert surfers.

Shortly before dawn, she rushed to their meeting place barefoot with one of Koa's old surfboards under her arm. She walked for thirty minutes down Kilauea to Kalihiwai, on to the first dirt road she reached on her right. Her heart stopped when she made it down the wet, muddy trail. In front of her, she saw her dream—the tidal pools and dribbling waterfalls of her childhood. All her memories of sunbathing, fishing, sandcastles, crabbing, and seashell hunting they had done when the swells were being obstinate, came flooding back. Not to mention the nudists who kept to themselves on the far east side of the beach. The ones her mother would nonchalantly engage in conversation. The waves on this beach were unpredictable—not as safe or as popular as Hanalei, ten miles out west on the same North Shore, off the world-famous Na Pali Coast.

But this was where Maele had learned to surf. As she took a deep breath and inhaled the smell of the sand and the sea—sweet yet pungent, stale, yet fresh—the sun in its copper glory broke out, fierce and radiant. That moment was one of contradictions. Maele was filled with fear, but also courage. The challenge wasn't just getting back into the ocean—it was going up against everything she'd lost and winning it back. She had been well on the way to becoming a professional surfer. The competition was steep among the locals and the not-so-locals, with the friendships she'd formed and sacrificed in the name of rivalry and the trust she'd held for a select few. Working at a coffee shop and living at home was the antithesis to this life.

Maele only had a few minutes to enjoy the quiet before groups of surfers began to line up on the shore.

She missed this. The low drone of chatter all around her. The swishing sound as the waves rolled in. Pretty soon, when the sun ascended high in the sky, their bodies would glisten with sweat and the salt from the ocean would get tangled in their hair.

"Girl, it's really you!" Soft, strong arms wrapped around her waist from behind. She'd know that voice anywhere—the thick Australian accent, the silky, husky purr. Maele spun around and hugged her back.

"Raelene." Yesterday rushed in like a tidal wave. Rae, with the killer blue eyes and unbound auburn hair. Rae, who had flown in on a circuit one day eight years ago and never left.

Beside them stood Noe. "Sorry we're late," he said. "Where's your wetsuit?"

"Oh, I'm not going in like that today. I just thought I'd paddle around."

If they were disappointed, they didn't show it. Raelene held a grin while Noe began to wax his board. When he was done, he gently chucked the bar over to Maele. "Here, do yours. Is that your old board?"

"No, I borrowed this from Koa."

"Sweet," Noe answered. "Hey, Rae, you coming out with us?"

"Of course, I am. The waves are relentless today. Let's stick close to the shore. We'll swim out and just hang in the water."

"Just like old times," Noe said.

"Yeah. Just like old times," Maele said, barely a whisper, her nerves getting the best of her.

The last time she'd done this, she'd had to be airlifted to Queens.

What are you so afraid of? You received clearance from your doctor. Your bones have fused. You are fine.

Something was missing. The confidence she'd felt over the past few days was gone.

"Where's Koa? I thought he was meeting us here." She felt her voice cracking. Panic began to set in. Her teacher, her protector, her brother-cuz. Maybe her nerves were getting the better of her because he wasn't there?

"Something came up with the kid who works for him, so he had to cover at the shop today."

That was new. Koa had grown up and become dependable. He'd set up his own surf store at the edge of Hanalei. There were no facilities at Secret Beach to set anything up. No bathrooms, no toilets, no showers. Hence, no businesses. All holding true to the spirit of secrecy.

Maele suspected Noe saw the worry in her eyes as he took her hand and slowly walked toward the water.

"No waves today. Let's just have fun and stay in the water. If we see a small beach break, you can decide."

"Waist deep only, I think," Maele said quietly.

"Waist deep."

Every surfer knew that riding the waves required balance. But the unpredictability of the energy that traveled under the water was the moving target they had to conquer. When Maele was young, Koa had used the following analogy to help her understand a wave's mechanics.

Waves weren't traveling water—they were the energy that moved through bodies of water. Professional surfers searched the world over for the perfect breaks, places where the sea floor rose dramatically, squeezing all that wave energy into the perfect swell. He'd always explained it like a game of Jenga, where the blocks get too tall and unstable to stand against gravity. Or like stepping on a tube of toothpaste. Waves were the same, and a good surfer knew where a wave would break and where to drop in. Waves that developed and broke slowly were best for beginners. Like a gentle spill, the wave would slowly roll in and touch the ground. Waves that began in deeper water could change abruptly when they hit shallow water. The steeper the slope of the sea floor, the bigger and more challenging the wave.

Noe stared out into the ocean for a few seconds, surveying the waves and determining where the breaks were occurring.

"You see there," he said, pointing to his left. "Looks like there are some good ones. Small ones."

The two women paddled out on their boards while Noe walked alongside them. He kept one hand on Maele's board while holding on to his, guiding his friends away from the lineup of surfers and in the direction he'd showed them from the beach.

"This is good, I think." Maele held on so tight, her fingernails dug into the board. The water was cold. Although her feet almost touched the ground, she noticed how much effort Noe was exerting to keep her steady against the strong current.

"Guys, over there. Who wants to try?"

Raelene was just as gentle with her as Noe. Maele felt safe now. They would watch over her.

"I will," Maele said, still afraid but determined to shake the jitters off. She figured she'd paddle around and take her time until the right wave came along.

Noe nodded with a smile. "Go. I'll be right here."

She left her two friends behind, paddling out to where she saw tiny crests of water oscillating at a distance. It wasn't a huge one. In fact, Noe later told her it was about four feet. She nixed her plan to warm up, decided it was then or never. Nevertheless, her heart pounded as she moved her arms and then her legs, kicking against the current with all her might. She spotted its peak and paddled to it, turning herself toward the shore as the mound grew beneath her, propelling her forward.

Just as Maele placed both hands on the side of her board, she froze. Nothing moved. Her legs felt like lead. She felt the energy rush beneath her and push her up and over.

"Now, now, now!" Noe screamed in the distance. "Get up, now!"

It was too late. Maele slung both arms over the side of her board as her body slammed against the wave. She summersaulted in the shallow water, her head barely touching the sandy bottom. Tossed around by the power of the current against her will, Maele knew her attempt was over.

In a few seconds, Raelene and Noe were at her side, pulling her up until she stood on her feet.

"No," she said, shaking her head, warning them not to offer her any comfort. She cowered with her head down, facing the water, and allowed herself to cry.

32

Romeo and Juliet

I
t was Christmas Eve, and Adam still hadn't been invited for dinner. Taking a chance she had no plans, he arrived at the Leivas at nine that morning. It seemed like the house had changed overnight. Garland made from pineapple leaves hung above the front door while tiny white lights twisted loosely around the porch rails. So understated, Adam thought. Yet, it made all the difference to him, and put him in the holiday spirit. Adam thought about his mom and the trucks that would pull in every November, filled with Christmas decorations to dress up their home. For many years, he'd never understood why all that production had to happen, only to be taken down immediately after the new year. But as time went on, he'd realized his mother had simply been trying to fit in with the rest of the neighbors. She hadn't come from money. She'd been born on the mainland and was his dad's office assistant. They'd always felt a little removed from society, which made Adam hurt for his mom. It was the life they had chosen, and it was a good one. Plus, it had given her the son she adored. She told him constantly that she'd do it all again.

His attention shifted to the pretty girl who answered the door. Maele wore shorts and a T-shirt, her long brown hair tied up in a ponytail. He was drawn to her face. Her velvety brown eyes were expressive and deep. But it was her dimples that got his attention, especially when she smiled. He realized he might have been staring a little intently when she self-consciously turned to look at the door.

"Hey," she said, smiling and stepping outside.

"Hey, Maele. I thought I'd come by to see what you're doing today."

"Nothing much," she said, a sly smile crossing her face. "Except I finally got in the water on a board yesterday." She dipped her chin down and fidgeted with her pockets.

"I know," Adam said. "I saw."

"You drove all the way to Kalihiwai? Why didn't you say hi?"

"You were with your friends, so I didn't want to bother you." Also, he could hardly move after the yoga class, but he wasn't about to admit it. "I saw you on the water, but ..."

She forced a laugh. "Yeah, I was crying. I was a mess."

"Right, yeah. It felt like you needed your space. Are you okay?"

She led him down the driveway. "Yes, I'm okay. I just have to keep trying."

"Well, I'm glad you got to spend time with your friends," he replied.

She had danced away from him, and he followed right behind.

She spun around to face him, her hair whipping in the wind. "Anyway, I'm glad you're here today."

She kept dancing away from him.

"You are?" He tried to keep up.

"Yeah," she said, doing the twirling thing again.

"I was going to see if you wanted to go hiking.

"But we have to be back for dinner."

He still wasn't sure whether he was included in that plan. Nevertheless, he was game either way. "Oh, for sure. I'll have you back then."

She came to a stop at the edge of the driveway and turned around to face him once again. "So? Where should we go?" Maele asked.

"On the way here, I saw a waterfall hidden past the bridge on Highway 56."

"Oh, Kilauea Falls? Yes, but boo! It's actually closed to the public. We can't get to it on foot. It's on private property now, owned by the founder of Facebook."

"I know." Adam smiled mischievously.

"Stop." Maele's eyes lit up, twinkling with matching mischief.

"Yup."

"Oh really, Mr. Yates. Let's go, then." She took his hand. "It's a mile down off Kolo Road. We can just walk from here."

Just off Kolo Road, security guards were planted at the entrance of the trail, standing by their ATVs and looking serious. They pointed to the DO NOT ENTER sign as Maele and Adam approached. Adam motioned for Maele to wait while he spoke to the guards in a hushed tone. He didn't want to look like a showoff, but he had called an old friend to request access to the trail.

"I'm Adam Yates. I believe the owner has allowed us to come in for a few hours."

The guards did their thing. Looking all serious as they spoke into their radios, the words from the other end were inaudible, scratchy, and unclear. "Copy that."

"Mr. Yates," the man in the gray uniform with a yellow beanie said. "Do you need us to escort you through?"

"I know the trail well," Maele interjected in an excitedly high pitch. "I mean," she said with her hands on her hips and then, clearing her throat, she added, "Before it became private land."

Adam tipped his head in her direction with a smile and the guards let them through.

"Way to stick it to the man, Maele," Adam said proudly.

"So, who did you call?" Maele asked as they began their trek down a rather wide path that ran alongside the Kilauea Stream.

"I just got lucky. I happen to know the guy who lives here."

"A little white privilege in action, maybe, Mr. Yates?" Maele said teasingly. "Or is there simply nothing you can't do?"

Adam stopped abruptly. So much so that Maele had to walk back toward him once she realized he was no longer next to her.

"What's wrong? Was it the white privilege joke? I'm sorry."

"Maele, there's a lot I can't do," he said, his tone darker. His stance went rigid as he looked directly at her. "As a matter of fact, you're going to find that I don't actually do much."

"I'm sorry, I—"

"No, it's no biggie. But you need to stop with the Yates thing. I'm just Adam. And if we keep getting hung up on my family, or my family name, I'll never be able to show you who I am."

Maele swiped her forehead with the palm of her hand. "Okay. Whoosh. I'm clearing my head. You're Adam No Name. 'A 'ohe inoa."

"Very good. Whatever that means, it's better."

Onward they went, talking incessantly about their daily lives. He learned about her family and their life on the plantation. He watched her move her hands, swing her head, and noticed how her eyes would light up when she spoke about her parents. And of Koa. Her life seemed so joyful. She was high on life. Tropical scenery and views of the river and the valley snuck themselves in between the banana plants, guava trees and skinny rails of bamboo. They walked in comfortable silence, their footsteps mostly silent, save for the crackle of a branch or the rustle of dry leaves here and there. The sound of tweeting birds grew louder. Lush green leaves and shrubs narrowed the path in certain areas, while stalks pulled down by the weight of their leaves formed arches that touched their heads. Adam was cognizant of the ground's gradual descent as they got closer to the waterfall.

"Can you hear that?" she asked, placing a finger on her lips. "We're getting closer."

He stayed silent, nodded, and kept walking.

"Wait. Look. Do you know what this is?" She bent to run her hands across a shrub filled with flowers.

She apparently liked testing him. "Of course. It's a naupaka flower, unique to Hawaii. My mom has them in the garden."

"I love the legend," she said. "Our very own Romeo and Juliet story. Do you know it?"

He didn't. "Of course, I don't." She stumped him. He liked that she could do that.

Maele plucked a bud and stood up. Half a flower with half its petals missing, white streaked with purple in the middle. "Well, one day a handsome fisherman named Kaui met a beautiful princess named Naupaka. They traveled far across the mountains and the forest in search of a high priest who could marry them. The high priest refused to marry them, asking them instead to pray to the gods for their permission. As the two lovers prayed, a heavy rain fell upon them, full of lightning and thunder. Princess Naupaka knew then their love was doomed. She tore the flower from her hair and ripped it in half. She presented the other half to Kaui and told him to return to his former life as a fisherman. Legend says the Naupaka flowers bloom in halves to mourn the tragic fate of the two lovers. They also look slightly different. The princess's flower is more fragrant, with a little bit of purple. Kaui's flower is white."

"I never learned that story."

"You can't know everything, Adam. What else would be there to learn and experience if you did?" Maele chided gently.

"I wonder if that's who they named the island after," he said.

She looked at him blankly, shrugged, and then smiled. Stumped. Now the game was all tied up. He returned the smile.

A few steps later, they reached the clearing. In front of them stood the Kilauea Falls—not too high, but wide. The thunderous roar of the water was muted by the exquisite poetry of its gentle cascade. Adam took Maele's hand and together they stood in awe and admiration. There was no one there. Just the two of them and the majesty of nature.

"Hi," he said, losing himself in her eyes as she looked up at him with a smile.

"Hi. Yes, hi. Always say hi."

"Are you thinking what I'm thinking?" Adam faced the dark, crisp pool, its tiny ripples fading as they moved away from the rushing torrent. Then he turned to her and allowed her big brown eyes to engulf him, ground him, and remind him that life could be beautiful when rooted, filled with peace and stability.

"Yes," Maele screeched as she let go of his hand, hopping on one foot and then the other, flinging her socks and shoes in the air. He followed suit. They were like children on a playground, running, laughing, and giggling, their shrill voices carried by the wind above the rush of the water.

Adam had never felt so free, so alive.

33

Silent Night

The two of them were on a mission, running back as fast as they could, arms flailing, ducking and maneuvering through the grass, the rocks, and the trees on the trail in the dark. Maele hopped on one foot while quickly slipping her shoes off. Adam grabbed a T-shirt from his car to replace the one he'd given her.

"Looks better on you than me," Adam teased, offering his arm for assistance.

"Shush," she said, playfully swatting his hand before barging through the front door.

"Sorry we're late!" Maele huffed, covering her mouth when she realized they had burst in on her auntie, Uncle Fudge, and Koa singing "Silent Night."

The bright colors in the home were muted with the glow of the warm yellow lamp light and colorful tree lights that wrapped around their tiny Christmas tree. The only thing missing was a fire in a fireplace, but since the home didn't have one, her auntie had lit candles and placed them strategically around the three front rooms. Christmas had come alive, and the singing was beautiful. Uncle Fudge sang bass, and Auntie Nalani sang with a rich tenor voice that glided in perfect harmony with her husband. Koa had a voice like an angel—a clean, clear alto sound rang out from his great wide chest. Maele regarded her family with pride. Not because this family could win a major talent show, but, rather, because of the heart with which they sang.

Maele was in an oversized borrowed T-shirt, no shoes, and damp shorts. Adam, looking like he'd just wrestled a bear, stood still and honored the moment with silence and calm.

Then, as if moved by an invisible spirit, Maele began singing harmony in the purest soprano voice. Adam drew his head back quickly and his eyes widened and grew misty as she sang. She looked at her family and their heartfelt expression of worship, eyes closed around every word about a miracle that happened two thousand years ago and taught the world how to love.

Their home was always full of song. It was like a rite of passage for Maele's family. To live, laugh, love, and learn through music. Every word had a meaning to life; every milestone, every moment, was marked by a song.

"Thank goodness you're finally here," Koa said when the song ended. "We needed more people to help sing harmony. Plus, these two are starting to drive me nuts."

"Just in time," Nalani exclaimed, her voice booming. "Dinner is warming up in the oven."

"Just in time? We started singing carols an hour ago. Late," Uncle Fudge chimed in, glaring directly at Adam. "Is dis the same boyprend? I told Lolana the other day dat her daughter has a boyprend. What's my name?"

"Uncle," Maele screeched.

"Uncle Fudge. I mean, Mr. Leiva," Adam answered.

"What is her name?" He pointed at his wife.

"Miss Nalani, Mrs. Leiva. She's your wife, sir," Adam said.

"And who dis?" He popped Koa on the top of his head.

"Well, that's Koa, of course. Maele's brother-cuz," Adam answered proudly.

"Bruddah-cuz, wha dat?"

"Excuse me?"

"I say, B-R-U-D-D-A-C-U-Z. What iz dat?"

"Oh, yes. What I mean is, he's a cousin that seems more like a brother."

"But Koa ain't her bruddah. Dat's weird you say dat. Unless you know something I don't."

He gave Adam a long, hard look. Maele pulled on her T-shirt. Andie had given back her diamond necklace the day after the wedding, and she nervously began to rub it. She couldn't tell if her uncle was joking or serious. She looked at her auntie with wide eyes, pleading for help by raising her eyebrows.

"Fudge, you let him alone. He is a guest in our house on Christmas Eve. This isn't how the Birthday Boy would act."

"I don't believe in Santa nor da Birt-day Boy! But I believe in showing up on time, not making a whole family wait while you drive da niece around in a fancy SUV. On Christmas time, too."

Koa caught Maele's eye just as he waved his hand under his chin. He winked to let her know his dear old dad, her sweet uncle Fudge, had been planning to scare the kaka out of Adam all night long, and to play along.

"You know dat. Hey, you. Oahu boy." Uncle Fudge was relentless. "Do you know what boyprend is in Hawaiian?"

Koa rolled his eyes.

Maele slid on the floor and sat next to him. "Help me, cuz."

"Not until you tell me where you've been," he whispered, wiggling his eyebrows. "You were gone for eight hours."

"Ugh. All of you?"

Koa's glare remained on Maele until she reneged.

"Geez, we went to Kilauea."

"The falls? That's on private land."

"I know," Maele answered, tilting her head toward Adam, who was conversing with her uncle. "He knows the guy who lives there."

"Dang. The Yates man. That's some sweet white privilege." Koa laughed.

"I made the same joke." She slapped his arm, laughing.

To get everyone's attention, Uncle Fudge said loudly, "It's ipo. Boyprend is ipo."

"Ipo," Adam repeated, looking directly at Maele with eyes as big as baseballs.

She felt the heat in her ears traveling to her face. "I'm going to get some dry clothes on."

Fudge leaned over to Adam as they watched Maele stand. "You know a lot about everything, don't you? What don't you know? You're like one of dees brightly burning Christmas candles, Oahu boy. Problem is, you take up all de oxygen in da room. You not leaving any for da rest of us."

Adam looked dumbstruck. He drew in a sharp breath before finding his seat at the far end of the couch.

Then Uncle Fudge broke out into a fit of laughter. "I'm just kidding you, A-Dam!" He grabbed Adam and pulled him into a bear hug. When he had him nice and close, he whispered, "Or am I?" Except it was more a stage whisper, since Maele heard every word.

Maele looked back before she exited the room and saw her uncle lifting Adam off the ground in a massive hug. Adam gulped loudly before laughing. She shook her head, knowing Uncle Fudge was all bark and no bite.

Alone in her bedroom, she combed through her hair and tied it up in a bun, then slipped on a fitted black sundress with matching straw sandals. Another one of her resale store finds, one that was a little loose in the waist, but hugged her elsewhere just right. Gently, she touched the little blue diamond on her neck again, this time thinking of Andie and everything that had happened in the past year. She was where she wanted to be—in the place she needed to reclaim her life—and unexpectedly, she had brought a friend along for the journey. She thought back to the events of the afternoon. What she remembered most was how carefree and confident he was, how bold and unencumbered. How he'd dived from the rocks into the water, and how he'd looked at her when nothing could be heard but the sound of crushing water and the rustle of the wind.

Exhausted after spending hours in the water, they lay under a tree and fell asleep. It had happened so naturally. The way he'd held her when they slept, her head on his shoulder. When she'd opened her eyes, she'd caught him sleeping peacefully, as if he hadn't a care in the world.

When Maele walked into the kitchen, she noticed Adam had managed to run back to his car to change. He wore khaki pants and a blue polo shirt, now—his hair had dried back into its natural curls. She still couldn't believe he was here.

"Wow," Adam muttered, low enough for only Maele to hear. Self-consciously, she turned to her aunt, who'd begun to set the table.

"Okay, I think we're ready," Nalani said, removing her apron and setting it on the counter. "Adam, you sit here, next to Maele. And don't mind her uncle. He is *lolo* these days, but only because Maele is like a daughter to him."

"Crazy," Maele translated for Adam.

"Oh." Adam subtly pulled Maele's chair out for her and took his place beside her. Same word, two meanings. Adam guessed it was a mix of two languages.

"We don't have traditional turkey and stuffing, here. This is our traditional meal. Hope you eat them." She pointed to each one. "Poke, sushi, kalua pig, and some pancit noodles." She turned to Maele, smiling. "And Maele's favorite, halo halo."

"Thank you," Adam said. "This looks so delicious."

"Well, feel at home and serve yourself. By the way, it's already eight o'clock and you still have an hour drive back to Poipu. Better if you spend the night and head out in the morning instead. There is an extra sleeping bag, and you can camp in the living room with Koa."

Maele saw Adam swallow loudly when they both saw the dreamy look and punch-drunk smile on Koa's face. He then winked at Maele and gave Adam a little wave with his hand; clearly, he was teasing them both.

Maele shook her head at him and smiled back. "Thank you, Auntie," she said. "But it's up to Adam if he wants to drive back tonight."

"I'm going to take you up on the offer, Mrs. Leiva," Adam answered. "Thank you for having me. Merry Christmas!"

With that, Nalani blessed the food and they all dug into the Christmas feast.

34

Who You Are

Adam breathed in the fresh, crisp air, filling his lungs to the brim and hoping it would cancel out the cigarette he'd just had. In the pitch-black night, he sat on the top step of the Leivas' porch, surrounded by peppered specks of Christmas lights that made up for the shortage of stars hidden by high clouds.

Everything was in its place—the wheel-less van and the verdant grass, the flower beds abundant with bloom. Despite the dimness, he saw everything in color. He thought about all that had happened that night. Not just about the hospitality Maele's family had afforded him, but of their genuine kindness. And the good joke her uncle had played on him. Of the closeness of Koa and Maele. Of the parents who enjoyed sitting with their children to tease and laugh and to play backgammon and checkers until the wee hours of the morning.

And geez, that girl could sing. Was there anything she couldn't do? Adam had been lost in her angelic voice. What he wouldn't give to hear her voice again.

For a while, he forgot about his addictions and his need to drown out the noises in his head. He was able to start building a new narrative that denoted peace and surrender. He knew it was his connection to Maele that soothed his spirit. But when all was dark and quiet, the bedlam in his head began to riot.

Hence, the cigarette.

Startled by a light tap on his shoulder, he turned to find Maele standing right behind him.

"Hey," she greeted, her voice gruff with sleep.

"Hey."

She wore yellow duck pajamas, but he thought she looked like an angel. Her hair swept to the side, her face clear and perfect.

"What are you doing out here? Are you okay?"

"Just needed a little air." Adam scooted to his right, giving her adequate space to fit beside him. She slid in, resting both arms on her thighs and clasping her hands together. They sat in silence for a good, long while. He wanted to kiss her right then and there, but his old confidence had betrayed him. He was paralyzed.

"You have a beautiful voice, by the way. Did you take any lessons?"

"Tsk," she said. "It's called karaoke. Many years of growing up with it."

Adam laughed, playfully tapping his thigh against hers. "Your uncle doesn't like me," he blurted out.

"He never likes any boy associated with me. He's a tough critic. Honest. But tough."

"You think I'm a know-it-all?" he asked, his tone hesitant.

"I think you think you know a lot about a lot. You are very confident. But I think it's attractive. You're the guy in the water that charges the wave. You're authentic."

There was that word, *authentic*. Adam thought Andie was authentic. He felt Warren was authentic. Maele, in her quiet strength and purity and commitment, was authentic. She was genuine, original, and true. Adam felt anything but authentic, but he loved that Maele saw him that way.

"Are you just not able to sleep? I mean, I guess I shouldn't even ask. Who could sleep with that freight train in there?" Maele said, referring to a snoring Koa.

They both laughed. "He's cool, actually," Adam said. "Did you know he's studying for the real estate exam?"

"Koa?"

"Yeah, he was telling me all about it. In a way, I think it's a really good time to do it. The housing boom here on the island makes it a viable career. He should take advantage, you know?"

"I guess. No wonder he hasn't had any time to spend with me. Selfishly, I thought he'd have time to help me get back to—" Maele paused. "Ah, never mind."

"No, tell me. To what?" Adam persisted.

"Well, I'd like to compete again. I thought he would help me train."

"Really? That's amazing. What happened exactly, Maele? Do you want to talk about it with me?" Adam asked.

"There isn't really anything to tell you," she said, her tone quiet. "Right before leaving for the U18 Junior Pros in Australia, I was at Tunnels. Nothing out of the ordinary. It was just a big set that day. I got pulled into an impact zone."

Maele turned to look at him, her face inches from his. She had the fullest natural lips.

She continued, "I fell off my board and hit my head on the sea floor. I blacked out for a few seconds and woke up when I heard my neck snap. I remember being under the water, thinking my head had been squished into my body." Tears filled her eyes.

Adam took her hand and held it tight. "Let's not go on, tell me another day."

"No, I want to tell you. I will tell you, I promise."

"When you're ready, I'm here."

"I'll tell you the ending first," she said, her eyes locking with his. "They flew me to Queen's, and I consider myself so lucky because the surgeons who looked after me were pioneering this new method that fuses the vertebrae with metal rods within the first twelve hours of accidents like this. They opened my spinal canal to relieve the pressure on the damaged cord, which stopped further risk of injury. Still, when I woke up, I had no feeling or movement in my right arm and both legs. It took three months before I could even start rehab. My mom and dad moved from Kauai and stayed with me on Oahu. We've been there ever since. They wanted me to have a fresh start, to take me away from anything that reminded me of my former life. It was the best they could think of to help me heal. I didn't want to look back, which I know wasn't fair to my friends and family here. They've been so welcoming to me, and forgiving too, but in the years that passed, I felt like a part of me had to die for me to survive the fact that I may never surf again. And here we are."

"Here," he said, offering her the sleeve of his shirt. She smiled and wiped her tears on it. "And what made you want to come back now?"

"The part of me that never died—it's who I am. I'm walking, dancing, and running again. There's a reason I was spared. I know it in my heart. And I want to feel alive again. The way I used to when it was just me and the water. I never really cared about competing. I did it because I thought I could help my mama and papa have a better life."

Adam was out of words. He wanted to hold her, tell her he'd be here as long as she wanted him to be. Yes, he was known to break promises, but this was the girl who made him want to keep every single promise he made from here on out.

Let me try.

"You were the bomb, six years ago. I know you'll pick it up again. I don't think it's an accident that we're back in each other's lives."

She didn't answer. He could tell she was deep in thought.

"Adam?"

"Uh-huh."

"Why were you in boarding school, then? Was it for sports or something? Or did your parents just like this particular school?"

"Not exactly. It was a school for broken kids," he said with a nervous chuckle.

"Oh," she said, staring out in front of her.

He could tell she didn't want to push further, but he was ready to share. Come to think of it, he'd never shared this with anyone before. All the girls he'd been with had never cared to know this part of him.

"I was expelled from my school in Oahu. I pummeled someone and sent him to the hospital."

"Why? Why would you do that?"

"This guy on the soccer team was ragging on my buddy one day. Teasing him about being Jewish, so I smashed him in the mouth. Took out two of his teeth. It's not cool to make fun of people, you know, and it just made me mad. The bully had been at it for a while—I'd just finally had enough."

"Wow, that's intense. And violent, Adam."

"Well, don't mess with my friends." He held up his fist like a boxer in mock protection. "But I haven't hit anybody since."

"And now you use those hands to write with."

"Yeah, from defender to entertainer. You know, the kid I was sticking up for wasn't even bothered by the bully. At least, that's what he told me. So, much ado about nothing, apparently."

"You got shipped away to boarding school and he wasn't even grateful? I bet he was. I bet when you stood up for him, it was one of the highlights of his life. When he sees your movie, he'll say to his own children, 'That guy once punched a kid's lights out for me. Just for me.'"

Adam liked how she saw the world.

"Would you like to read my script sometime?"

"Heck, yeah," she said, looking at him again and drying her face. Another flash of yearning to kiss her lit up the projector of his mind's eye. Kiss this girl, be bold, Adam!

"Like, tomorrow?"

"Like on Christmas Day? Will me reading your script be my gift to you, or yours to me?" She giggled.

"Ha-ha, okay, you're right, you're right. Not tomorrow, but soon. Whenever. I'd just like for you to read my script. I'd love to hear your thoughts."

They both sat quietly for a few seconds.

"Look at us, huh?" Maele said, squeezing his hand. "We make quite a pair. Two broken kids, but we have it pretty good."

"I know. We have it really good, actually."

Maele nodded as Adam gently took her hand in his.

"Does it feel weird, me being here?" Adam asked, genuinely curious and full of disbelief that he was actually sitting hand in hand with Maele Moana. He felt giddy inside, like he'd never kissed a girl before and didn't know what to do.

Maele looked at him and smiled. "No, it feels right. I'm glad you spent Christmas Eve with us."

"Your family is wonderful. Thanks, by the way, for the gift."

"It's nothing. I knew Auntie and Uncle Fudge would be opening presents, so I wanted to make sure you had something to open. It's from Koa's shop."

"Seriously, I love it." Adam fished a keychain out of his pocket and twirled it around his finger. It was in the shape of a surfboard. Blue and orange, like the sun and the sky. "I will think of you every time I use my keys."

Maele stood without letting go of his hand. He jumped to his feet, not wanting to lose her touch, but knowing the moment to kiss her had passed him by.

"It's three o'clock in the morning. Let's go in and try to get some sleep."

"Okay," he agreed, still gripping her hand.

With great care, she turned the doorknob and quietly pushed the front door open.

"It's technically Christmas Day. *Mele Kalikimaka*, Adam," she whispered.

"*Mele Kalikimaka*, Maele."

First Wave Redoux

I t was Christmas Day and Maele had never felt more inspired about being in the water. Though this was her first Christmas away from her parents, Adam made her feel like she was with family. It felt odd, the way she had just been so open with him about her past and her feelings. Not to mention how her heart felt like it was thumping out of her chest every time he was near her. A man had never felt this special to her, this close to her heart in such a short amount of time. It was frightening, at the same time—all these thoughts about never being good enough—but this was a new era in her life. She was facing her fears. She was doing the things that scared her, and today was no exception. She and Adam planned to spend the afternoon in the water.

"You know, I teach surfing for a living when I'm home. If I can teach little ones how to surf, you know I can get you back on your board."

So, there she was, her surfboard tucked under her arm and Adam waxing his in the midday sun. It was one of those beautiful Hawaiian days that stayed warm and sunny, save for the sprinkle of raindrops here and there. Rain falling from bright blue skies. An atmospheric contradiction found especially on these islands.

The waves were calm; there was no breeze. It was a good day to get out on the water and shake off the rust. They walked to a part of Secret Beach, near the nudists, where the break was small and gentle. Little white waves rolled in slowly, one after the other. It was a beginner surfer's paradise. Before her accident, Maele would have laughed at these waves, but today they terrified her. She hadn't ridden a wave since she'd broken her neck. What if it happened again? The other day was scary enough, and what if she wasn't lucky this time and ended up without the ability to use her arms or legs? Or, worse yet, what if she died? Was it worth it?

"All right," Adam said. "The best way to eat an elephant is one bite at a time. What do you say we get in the water?"

"I don't know. What if I don't need to surf anymore, you know? Like, what if I'm done, done?"

"Done, done? As opposed to just done?"

"Yeah." She forced a half-smile. Adam looked wild and free as he stood in just his black and white striped swim trunks. Something about him seemed solid, safe, and secure. Maele knew in that moment Adam would make a good father—patient, kind, and present. The kind of father who would teach his little ones to surf and seek out the wonder in the world around them. Her father was like that. Even when he was busy working the plantation, he would take time to show her how wonderfully made the world around her was.

She felt an explosion of love in her heart. In fact, she felt the warmth of love for Adam spread from her heart to the crown of her head and to the bottoms of her feet. It was a sweet, tender expansion that flowed throughout her entire body. She had never felt this for another human being in her life. She wanted to reach out and touch his lips with her fingertips and feel his hair. She wanted to taste his mouth and brush her face against his. She wanted to know what his stubble would feel like against her cheeks. She had thoughts about Adam that made her blush, but they didn't cause her shame. He gave her confidence and strength. She felt like a woman around him, not a little girl. Adam made her want things she'd never wanted before.

She wondered … was she falling in love with Adam Yates?

"I think we should get in the water while the kiddie waves are still going off." She laughed, picked up her board, and ran into the water.

They lay on top of their surfboards and paddled past the break and out to the lineup. There, they sat up, their arms akimbo and their feet dangling among the fish. Maele allowed the lapping sound of the waves to lull her senses. The water was relatively calm, an undulation that caused a subtle rise and fall of their bodies and boards, but nothing severe. There were a few other surfers in the lineup.

"How are you feeling?"

"I'm nervous. I feel like a newbie. I was in top form when I broke my neck. What if I do it again?"

"There's no saying that you won't, but by the sounds of it, you had a once in a lifetime wave and tumble combo. The chances of it happening again are like getting struck by lightning. While, yes, it could happen, it's really unlikely."

"The scariest part …" she said hesitantly. Then, as if a floodgate opened, she wanted to tell her story to Adam. "The scariest part after hearing the snap in my neck was being held under the water by the wave. I remember opening my eyes and seeing so much color. Then, nothing. It was like being in a washing machine filled with sand. Everything was brown and kicking up around me. I didn't know which way was up or down. Everything felt pressed in, compressed. I don't know how to say it, but I felt like I was being squeezed from the top of my head to the soles of my feet, like being squished together. I could feel it in my teeth. I couldn't move my arms. I couldn't stand, and my chest felt like it was going to explode. I needed to take a breath, but I couldn't get out of the water. I remember that panic so well. I heard once that drowning would be the most peaceful way to die, but the feeling I had in my lungs—the panic, the lack of control—was terrifying. I still wake up some nights and feel like I'm back in that moment, and it's awful. If it wasn't for Koa and Noe, I wouldn't be here. They were able to find me in the water just as I passed out, which in and of itself was a miracle, and lifted me out ever so gently, floating me to shore. They had someone rush out to bring them a towel, which they wrapped around my neck, like a makeshift brace, and Koa kept the waves from causing further damage because he stood with his back to the ocean, breaking the waves as he held my shoulders and head in his huge hands. He kept saying, 'You're gonna be fine, little sister. Don't you worry 'bout a thing.' He just said it over and over, and I believed him. Noe held my legs and they floated me to the shore and gently placed me on the beach. If they hadn't been so careful, the doctors said I would've been paralyzed, but it's because they stabilized my neck that I wasn't. The C4 and C3 were a micrometer from being broken in a way that would have caused permanent damage. That was the second miracle of the day. The paramedics showed up forty-five minutes later and the rest is history. God was with me on January thirteenth."

"Yeah, it sounds like something was with you. I've never put much stock in God, but you definitely had an angel, or something, watching over you."

They floated in silence for a moment.

"If you'd like to head back in, we can," Adam said.

"I think the only thing worse than having a reason to fear something is to let that fear run your life. Yes, I have a very good reason to fear the water, but I love it. I love surfing. It's a huge part of who I am, and I'm not gonna let my fear dictate what I do or what I don't do or who I am. I'm not going to let fear steal my joy anymore."

She lay back down on her board and paddled with all her might before rolling into a nice little wave. As the wave began to curl, she pushed herself off the board and sprang to her feet. It was like no time had passed at all. She felt free again, strong and sturdy. And away she went, once muscle memory took over, riding her first wave in over half a decade. She could hear Adam laughing at the top of his lungs and cheering her on. Maele responded with a laugh of her own, a signal to herself that she no longer held onto any anger or fear. There was a reason for her past pain. She needed it, like a metamorphosis. It had transformed her into a totally different person.

She felt the air as she pushed through it, the water churning white beneath her. She was surfing, flying and free for the first time since her accident. *Baby steps, little wins.* She had nineteen days to play with little waves and get her groove back.

On January thirteenth, she would head over to Tunnels, where the swells averaged seven feet. She would go back to where it had all gone wrong and close this chapter of her life once and for all.

36

Body Heat

A dam observed Maele from the water day after day, balancing on his board while she surfed back to the shore over and over. Just waiting out there to greet her every time she paddled back from the beach. He was her guard dog keeping watch for rogue waves and sharks. She took her time, but her confidence and skills grew. Adam knew the day was coming when she would ride every wave that came along, but today, the reef breaks were producing big enough waves to keep novice surfers away. Much more aggressive than her first day back on the water. Even though she was making incredible progress, today was different— today she wisely decided to head in early and read Adam's script while he stayed in the water and surfed.

Ke'e Beach was on the northernmost tip of the island, less than ten miles from Maele's home. At first, they'd had plans to hike up the Na Pali Coast, but as soon as they'd reached Hā'ena State Park, the ocean was calling their name. There weren't very many swimmers there, but since Ke'e Beach was the entrance to the Kalalau Trail, which ran along the coast, an abundance of hikers and beach bunnies was a common expectation.

It was two in the afternoon by the time Adam and Maele arrived. Adam wanted to catch the sunset. He thought sunsets were symbolic of his personality, the way the end of the day had more of an appeal to him, including the promise of a wild night. But Maele's love of the sunrise was slowly turning him around. Beginnings of a new day were starting to look hopeful and attractive.

Adam took his time floating on his board, not surfing now, just allowing the waves to push him where they wanted him to go, a true drifter. The beauty of Kauai converged around him. He knew it was called the Garden Isle, but his current view of the jagged mountains and the strange beauty of the greenery on the dramatic shoreline brought home its true meaning. There were mountains to the right and tide pools to the left. Before him, behind the stretch of sandy beach, was a tropical forest, covered with giant ironwood trees, their roots sticking out of the ground, their branches thick and grand. In a few steps, the clear blue sky and powdery white beach would end in a lush, green jungle made impenetrable by trees, rich, beautiful, and exotic. He began to paddle and made his way toward the girl of his dreams sitting on the beach when a wave swelled beneath him, and he stood to ride it. Just a moment ago he was a drifter, now he was a wave rider, how quickly he changed. Promise and hope were within his reach.

Adam got out of the water, tucked his board under his arm, and made his way across the beach toward her. She sat under a coconut tree, legs crossed, totally immersed in a pile of papers held together by three copper brads.

This beautiful woman is reading my script.

Maele was reading his words, his ideas, and his thoughts, and it rattled his nerves. None of his friends had ever taken the time to read anything he'd written. Maybe because he never cared to offer anybody a glimpse into that part of his world. The tableau made him want to kiss her so badly. At night, in his hotel room, he devised ways and means in his head to get her alone, to get her in the most romantic spot he knew. He wanted to get lost in her. He'd never been lost before. On the contrary, every woman he'd ever been with had failed to disengage him from his demons. With Maele, he forgot all about them; he actually believed he'd gotten rid of them completely. He regretted not kissing her on the porch on Christmas Eve. What he would give to relive that night again. Even with Koa's snoring and the deflated twin-sized mattress.

She looked up at him, smiling as he stood in front of her. "Hi."

"Hi." Grabbing a towel, he sat down and vigorously rubbed his hair. "I saw a school of tuna and some triggerfish."

"Awesome," she answered, her attention definitely not on him. Without another word, she swung her legs to the side and laid her head on his lap. He wanted to remember this moment forever. The weight of her head on his legs, the tan, smoothness of her skin, her big eyes, her hair wild like the coastline. Dark brown with streaks of gold, sun-kissed for sure. He studied her face, every line, every tiny pore. Scrap the scenery, the stunning views, the hypnotizing lull of the waves. He was mesmerized by her. There was so much beauty to behold, he didn't know what to do with it.

"What do you think?" Maybe if he rambled enough, he could release some pent-up energy.

"Shh. I'm on page seventy-five."

"Wow, you're a fast reader." He bravely brushed his finger on her forehead and pushed back a stray strand of hair.

"I looked. There are a hundred and fifteen pages. Quite short," she said.

"Do you know why? We try to condense an entire story into two hours, one minute a page, about one hundred and twenty pages."

"Hmm …" She sighed.

Not interested, he assumed. He just stared at her. She must've gotten the hint, mocking him by letting out a frustrated sigh and laying the script on her stomach. She looked up at him, her brown eyes searching his eyes. He wanted her to find his soul.

I am in love with you, he wanted to blurt out. There was so much truth and innocence in her eyes. The thing was, he felt like there wasn't very much of that in his.

"Okay, let's talk about it then," she said. "I have questions. First, I'm digging the world you've created. I've never seen anything quite like this. Floating cities striving for utopia."

"That's right. Thank you."

"So, these sea creatures that attack from the depths. They are symbolic, right? Do they represent our own hidden traumas?" she asked, her eyes gazing up at him.

"Traumas, demons. Call them what you will, they are monsters from the past, ancient sea creatures that try to stop the humans from, well, living in the moment, but also creating a new future for themselves. So, they need to find new tools to survive. A new way of thinking in order to live. That's how the animals get involved, because our heroes have evolved, and now they work together." Adam knelt on the sand next to her.

She nodded and stared up at the sky, lips unmoving and deep in thought.

Then, with all seriousness, hands clasped together on her stomach, she asked, "Will they cast Kevin Costner?" She let out a loud bellow, laughing so hard she lifted her head and sat up.

He was embarrassed, but he laughed along with her, throwing his towel on her lap.

"Come on! They are totally different movies!" he said as he started to stand up.

"Come back, come back," she said, taking his hand and pulling him down as he tried to stand. "I was just kidding."

He knew she was, so he sat again. Still clasping his hand, she leaned her head on his shoulder. "I could listen to you talk about your script all day. I love hearing you talk about it. You have such a passion for what you're doing. I think you're really good."

"You do?" he asked. "You said it was the first script you've ever read."

"Yeah, but your writing is sublime. You're a very good writer, Adam. I'm honored that you wanted me to read your script. Thank you for trusting me."

"Well, can I tell you what else I have a passion for?" he asked, his tone teasing as he gently brushed his hand against her cheek.

"Uh-uh," she whispered, allowing him to bring his face close to hers.

"You. Unexpectedly, you." He wanted to kiss her so badly, but it wasn't the right time.

There were other people on the beach, and he was afraid to embarrass her. If he was going to kiss this girl, it was going to be special and one they would never forget. A kiss to tell their grandkids about. He imagined what it would be like to kiss her. One kiss. Two kisses. The third one would last forever. Now that Adam thought about it, he had dreamed about kissing this girl ever since he was fifteen years old.

There they sat, facing each other. Engulfed in a warm breeze and flanked by people hustling, conversations, shrieks, Frisbees in the air, and sand being kicked around every which way. He brushed golden sand and tiny white shells off her thigh as an excuse to touch her, but when he felt her skin, his entire body surged with excitement. His heart pounded faster in his chest. A rushing noise filled his ears. He longed to kiss her so badly that it physically hurt. This girl had complete control over him. His hand began to shake which made him quickly remove it from her leg and adjust his body so he was sitting with his arms wrapped around his knees. He buried his feet into the sand. They sat quietly for a moment while Adam collected himself.

"Adam?"

"Hmm," he said, careful not to reveal how he truly felt about touching her.

"Why me? I clean pigpens and shake coffee trees for a living. On good days, I serve coffee to entitled tourists. I—"

He intended to act chagrined, but instead, she endeared herself more to him. The way she was so candid, so childlike with her curiosity. The hardship of her life had done nothing to taint her positive outlook on the world. He couldn't mask his awe for her.

She stared at him, waiting for him to answer. He swore he felt the heat emanating from her ears traveling to her face. She blushed.

"Shh," he whispered, placing his finger to her lips. Her perfect pomegranate lips. His body swelled at the contact of his skin on her mouth. He could feel her breath. "Why not you? What you do isn't who you are, believe me, I know. You have more integrity than anyone I've ever met. You're better. I honestly think if I had the guts to meet you when we were younger, I would have become a much better person."

"You're good now," she said, reaching out to touch his face.

The heat of her fingers seared his skin, driving all the madness away. He didn't have to think about anything else when she was near. He closed his eyes. His mind was calm.

"Well then, I have no more questions," she whispered.

He wanted to kiss her with every atom of his being, but not here. Not like this. He wanted to do it right. So, he rested his lips on her hair instead. A silly, rookie move. But any part of his body on her body was satisfaction enough.

"So, you really think I'm good at what I do?"

"I do. I really do," Maele said, leaning her head on his shoulder before turning her gaze back to the ocean. "Now, can I show you what I'm good at?"

Before he could warn her about the power of the waves, she picked up her surfboard and ran toward the water.

Starlight Before Sunrise

New Year's Eve made it the last sunrise of the year.

It was cold and dark in the early morning. The weather had turned, still warm in the height of the day but cooler before and after. She could see her breath, white like smoke, caused by the onshore breeze that brought cold air from the north. The radiant night sky lingered for a bit. In the quiet of the early morning, she was aware everything that had happened to her was God's plan for her life; the accident, the wedding, the cold front so she could pretend to be a fire-breathing dragon, standing in her aunt's yard waiting for Adam to pick her up and take her on an adventure. She felt loved beyond measure and carried a peace in her soul that she didn't try to understand. She was happy.

The moment was perfect.

Just then, Adam drove up and climbed out of his Rover. He carried a gray blanket and a throwaway drink carrier from the hotel coffee shop.

"It's colder than I thought it would be this morning." He held the blanket out to her.

She accepted and wrapped it around her shoulders.

"I also brought us coffee. I have packs of sugar and a cup of cream. How do you take yours?"

"Black is fine. Thank you."

He handed her a cup and she watched him as he walked back to the hood of his car and poured three packets of sugar and a healthy amount of cream into his coffee. She laughed a little. *He drinks his coffee like it's dessert.*

"Do you know what that constellation is?" she asked, pointing.

"You're always testing me, Maele. Are you aware of that?"

"Am I?"

"Yes, but I kinda like it. What constellation?"

"It's special because it's still dark and there is no moon in the sky. See the cloud-like mass?" She pointed to a giant swath of dim light streaked across the sky.

"The Milky Way." Adam gave her a high five.

"Good. Now, look a little to the east. See that bright yellowish star?"

"That one?" Adam said.

"Yes, that isn't a star—it's a planet. You can tell because it's not twinkling. Planets shine with a steady light because they're reflecting the sun. Stars twinkle because they're like our sun, made of gas, and so far away that their light is bent and bobbled as it moves through the universe. Did you know light from the stars is billions of years old? We could be seeing the light from a star that is dead and gone. And the air we breathe is the same air that has been on earth since day one? Think about that. You're breathing the same air that Jesus breathed."

"You mean I'm breathing the same O2 as Stanley Kubrick did?"

She had to laugh. Everything always related to movies. "Yes, JC and Kubrick. Same air. Now keep looking. Next to that planet, which is Jupiter by the way, which is a huge planet that has seventy-nine moons orbiting it. Think about that, Jupiter has seventy-nine moons."

Adam looked down at Maele and smiled the biggest smile she'd seen yet. He let out a laugh. "Tell me more."

"Okay, so next to Jupiter you're gonna see a faint little star. See it right there?"

She stretched her arm high into the dark morning sky. When Adam lowered his head, she felt his hair on her face and his breath on her shoulder. The smell of coffee on him was made sweet by sugar and cream. When she turned her head sideways, his lips lightly grazed her cheek.

"That one, do you see it?" she asked again. Adam nodded. "Well, draw an imaginary line to the next brightest star to its right and keep moving down, connecting the dots." She pointed to a series of stars, motioning with her finger so Adam could see how they formed a reindeer.

"This constellation is called Rangifer, or Tarandus in Latin. It is an extinct constellation. It's not in star charts anymore or in anybody's books, but every Christmas I like to come outside and try to find it. It was named by a French astronomer named Pierre Charles Le Monnier in the 1800s and somewhere along the way, people stopped caring about it."

They stood looking skyward in silence, then Maele went on. "Books or no books, little star nerds like me will never forget the great reindeer in the sky."

"You boggle my mind, Maele. You surprise me at every turn. Now, it's my turn to surprise you. You ready for it?"

She nodded in excitement, before rubbing her hands together in delight. "Ooh, yes."

"Sunrise at the lighthouse. I've packed us a picnic breakfast, too. The sun rises at 7:28 this morning, but I wanted to get here early and I'm glad I did, because you just gave me a very cool astronomy lesson."

They hopped in the Land Rover and headed up to the lighthouse. Visitors must park and hike a bit to see the restored landmark, which shined brilliant white in the dark and its red roof looked like a crown.

"Did you know Ben Stiller and his wife, Christine, donated a significant amount of money to see this lighthouse restored?" Maele asked.

Adam leaned toward her. "I did know that, actually."

She loved how he looked so intrigued, eyes just on her.

"And the restoration was completed in 2013. I remember reading about the donors and the senator who wanted to restore the lighthouse. It's too bad they couldn't get the light to work again, but it floats on a bed of mercury, so shy of replacing the original apparatus with modern technology, they just left it alone. They light it twice a year, though," he added.

"Yes, they do, and one of those nights is tonight," Maele said. After a moment she added, "A lot of people argue this is the first spot the sun hits on Kauai."

"So, we could be the first people to see it on Kauai," Adam said, nodding.

"Which would make us the *first* people to watch the *last* sunrise of the year in America. Think about it, this is the last spot of land the sun rises on in America. Did you know that?" she asked.

"I never thought about it," Adam said. "But it absolutely makes sense. And did you know that the first ray of sunshine rises on Cadillac Mountain off the coast of Maine?" She could tell he loved it when they were showing off what they knew. She loved it because they were learning from each other.

They parked and then walked along the paved road and stepped over the chain that kept the road closed off from vehicles. The ocean was loud, crashing two hundred feet beneath them on both sides of the narrowing point. The wind was calm that morning, and the glow of the arriving sun warmed up the sky. The lighthouse took on a ghostly shade of white against the silver light of dawn. They stopped walking when they reached the northernmost point on the island and settled on a spot where the sun would crest the horizon. Maele huddled close to Adam to feel the warmth of his body.

"I used to come out here as a kid to read or think, just to get away really," Adam began, while pulling Maele closer to him. "Boarding school was tough during my freshman year. I was terribly homesick. I'd call home every night from a pay phone on the wall outside the cafeteria. It was the only phone I never had to wait in a line to use. We weren't allowed to use our cell phones during the week, and they kept them locked up. But sometimes I would come out here and imagine the movies I wanted to make, or I'd write stories in my head. So much of *Oceana* was written right here, on this point, overlooking the Pacific."

They were truly in the middle of the ocean, so far away from the rest of the world. The sky was warming from purple to rose. Maele reveled in the sound of his voice, calm and deliberate, unlike most days when he was chasing his words.

"I used to feel so far away from everything standing here as a boy, but now, here with you, it feels like home."

Maele turned to face him.

"I've always loved the sunset," Adam said. "Yet, now, when I think of the sunrise, I see this giant wall of light coming for me—like a force field."

"I love the sunrise because it reminds me of rebirth and new beginnings."

Adam looked at her, prolonging eye contact.

"We can play, dance, sing, and fall in love. From sunrise to sunset. Life is short," Maele said with a quiver. She thought her voice sounded strange.

"I can hear you breathing," he said, shifting the topic.

Her breath had become shallow and rapid, like a little bird. She watched his eyes scan her body, wondering if he could see her heartbeat in the veins of her neck. She licked her lips and parted them.

The sky was red and silver, the air was electric, the birds sang in the glorious new day. Then, a warm golden light washed over the young lovers, the lighthouse shone with the glow of the rising sun as it broke over the horizon. Adam gently held Maele's face.

"It looks like the underside of an abalone shell. The sky is red!" Maele said with wonder.

"May I kiss you, Maele?" As he asked this, his face became illuminated by the gold and pink sunlight.

"Uh huh," Maele whispered, reaching up to touch his face.

Slowly, he leaned down and kissed her lips, tongue to tongue, breathing together tenderly and passionately. She inhaled deeply, making sure to take in every essence of his skin and body.

A new day was born, a new love was blooming, and a new year was about to begin.

New Year, New You

Adam awoke with a renewed sense of purpose. He didn't want the usual morning cocktail of uppers and weed. He didn't even want coffee, and it terrified him. He wondered what was going to happen when he finally crashed from this "Maele high." He feared *when* it was going to happen. He hoped in his heart of hearts it never would.

The young couple had agreed to meet at a trailhead called the Nounou East Trail, or as Maele called it, the Sleeping Giant Trail. Named so because if you are standing in the little seaside town of Wailua and look at the mountains to the west, it looks like a giant is sleeping on his back. For generations, families have climbed the giant's body to eat lunch on his chest. The brave ones even dared to climb all the way up to his face.

Maele told Adam to drive north on Highway 56 and to turn west once he found Haleilio Road.

"You'll know it when you see the traffic light."

"Why can't I just use my phone's navigation?"

"Because it's off the map. Everything on Kauai is off the map. Didn't you learn that while you were going to school here?"

He had the radio on when "Mississippi Moon" started playing. The song he and Maele danced to at the wedding reception. It was their song, and it sounded the way he felt, full of promise, hope, tenderness, yearning, and love. He lived in the song while it played and then saw a traffic light—the first one he'd seen yet—and made his left turn onto the road. He was told to keep an eye out for telephone pole number 38.

Where the heck is she taking me?

"Where the heck has she already taken me?" he muttered as he drove.

He saw an old car, the one that had been parked in front of her aunt's house, and leaning against it, looking like a movie star, was Maele Moana. His heart leaped.

I've never known a girl to make me nervous like this before.

Perhaps it was the fact he loved her from afar all those years ago, perhaps it was because she was formidable, not a woman you take lightly or for granted. What does that mean?

It means she's a "thou," she's not an "it."

The one and only thing he remembered from a philosophy class he took at NYU was a lesson about philosopher Martin Buber. Buber claimed that humans found meaningfulness in life through healthy relationships with the world around them and that every relationship existed between a person and an "it" or a "thou." An "it" was an object to be used, like a tool or food, but a "thou" was something special, cut from the same cloth, equal, and to be valued and seen as the same, another person. Adam recalled the joke he made about all the "its" he'd like to bang and it made him sick. Upon seeing Maele a few hundred yards away, he felt a lurch in his stomach.

The memory of Buber and the joke and a parade of memories that marched through his mind of all the girls he used like "its" made him hot with shame and regret. He quickly pulled the car over and threw up. There was no hiding it. Maele watched.

She ran toward his car and called out to him, "Adam, are you okay?"

"Ugh, I'm fine. Oh my gosh, I'm so embarrassed. I have no idea what just happened, but suddenly I had to pull over." He swished his mouth out with some bottled water. She handed him a piece of gum which he popped into his mouth.

"Do you feel sick? Do you still want to hike?"

Perhaps it was a case of withdrawals, he had experienced it before. That would be the easy excuse, but Adam felt it was something much deeper. Like something being forced out of his body, some nasty creature that had kept him in chains these past eight years which he just vomited onto the side of the road at the feet of a sleeping giant.

Epic changes were taking place in Adam's heart and mind and body.

Adam's legs were strong, but all the smoking made his lungs weak. Aside from that, Adam surely was undergoing the physical effects of withdrawal. He hadn't taken anything since before Christmas and he was dizzy and out of breath.

This girl is kicking my butt.

Maele walked a few feet in front of him, swaying her hips as she went. The short, gray shorts revealed strong, tanned legs. Her body was long, fit, and healthy, and the purple tank top she wore showed off her shoulders. Adam didn't mean to stare at her, but he couldn't help seeing how incredibly attractive she was.

They traversed up the switchbacks through the shade of the ironwood trees, guava trees, and the silk-oaks. The air was fragrant and thick with humidity.

"Have you made any New Year's resolutions?" Adam asked between breaths.

"Well, yes and no. Not the traditional ones. So, I told you what happened to my neck, but I never told you how it affected me after. You already know that until we went surfing after Christmas, I hadn't been on a wave. I'm so terrified of the water. On Oahu, I hadn't even stepped onto a beach until Andie showed up."

"That's crazy, considering you practically lived in the water."

"I know, and when Andie came, she said she felt all dried out and had to get wet immediately. Well, that's how I've been feeling for years, but I've been frozen by fear. So, my New Year's resolution, which I made a few months ago, is to go back to the place where I broke my neck, six years later, on January thirteenth. Back to the scene of the crime to surf it. To ride the wave that almost killed me. I think if I can go back and face my fear, then I can finally move on. Be like the heroes in your script and evolve to survive. Slay my monsters from the deep with the help of my new friend. I don't know."

"You were destined to ride waves and inspire people with your talent, Maele." Adam's tone was adamant. When Maele said nothing, he continued. "You were born to ride. I know what you're made of and that just doesn't go away. Sure, you've got to shake off the rust, but the wave rider is still in there. And your progress is incredible. It's been a little over a week, six hours a day, and you're already shredding like a pro again."

Adam saw her face turn a deeper shade. She smiled and looked away.

"What beach did it happen at?"

"Tunnels. I'm going back to Tunnels on January thirteenth."

"Dang. They have historic winter swells there. We better keep practicing."

She started hiking again and took his hand when they reached the top, revealing to Adam the most breathtaking view he'd seen in a long time. Far below was the small town of Wailua, the chocolate milk colored Wailua River flowing into the ocean and the homes in neat little rows. All those people down there, living their lives, going to work, eating and sleeping, rich with their own stories. Each story as important as his own.

Beyond the seaside town was the sea herself; mighty, raw, and indigo blue undulating under an azure sky, bright with reflected sunlight. Adam heard Maele laugh, and he knew he was in paradise.

"Maele."

She turned to face him. He gently placed his hands on her cheeks as he stepped closer. Usually, he towered over her, but she stood on higher ground this time, they were looking eye to eye.

"May I kiss you again?" Adam held her gaze. He knew how to do this, seduce women, and do it well, but those powers were malfunctioning.

Then she asked him, "Do you ask every girl if you can kiss them first? Is that like your signature move?"

"I learned from Warren to always ask permission from a lady first. It's the gentlemanly thing to do."

She did a little skip, yet passed on Adam's request with kindness, then beckoned him to follow.

"We still have to eat lunch on the giant's chest," she said, panting, looking at him with hungry eyes.

"Why don't we go back to my hotel room and eat there?" Adam was dizzy.

"No, why don't we finish what we started? It's good practice," she said, offering him more hope than a kiss would have.

"Yes, I like that. Let's eat lunch and ... do we dare climb to the giant's face?"

"I'm game if you are."

"Let's do it," he said. But what he wanted to say was, *I want this day to last forever. Let's hike up into the stars and become a constellation and hold each other for eternity, not caring whose books we are written in because we've*

completed each other's story. Maele, I will go where you go and live where you live.
I am yours ...

Instead, he just kicked at the dirt beneath his boots as Maele plodded gracefully up the mountain again. He took one last look at the little town of Wailua before willingly placing his fate in her hands.

39

Must be Love

She had been kissed by Adam Yates, and he'd asked to kiss her again. She hoped he wasn't too disappointed she'd turned him down, but she had her reasons.

No matter how much she intended to downplay their kiss by the lighthouse, the moment completely occupied her mind. Maele knew where the time spent in close proximity to him would lead. What she hadn't expected were the feelings that gripped her whenever she was close to him, whenever he touched her. Did she love him? Nah. How could that happen after only a few weeks?

Well, okay. Technically, they had many conversations with their eyes all those years ago. But was this really happening? He was into her, but she still wondered why. He could have anyone he wanted, be anywhere he wanted. Yet he was here, with her. Trekking through the rugged terrain on the Kalalau trail along the Na Pali Coast, its jagged mountains plummeting directly into the turbulent sea. Adam was walking in front this time, clad in camouflage shorts and a black T-shirt, with a sleek, black camera, tiny, compact, and light, slung across his shoulder.

He wanted to see another waterfall, so after an early morning session on the waves they headed into the mountains. Maele had asked Noe to help her get a hiking permit for the two extra miles past Hanakapiai Beach. The day before, they'd talked about New Year's resolutions. In the strangest way, she felt stronger, more confident about getting back in the water. Two things were filling her with electricity. Their kiss and surfing, and she was dying to do both again.

That kiss.

"Penny for your thoughts." Adam's voice broke through her train of thought.

"Just enjoying the view." She looked at Adam's body.

"The map says we should be approaching a stream soon, then we start climbing two miles up, seven hundred and sixty feet."

"Okay."

He reached back for her hand and held it tight. They found the stream and crossed it. Clear, ankle deep, narrow, and rapid. What they'd thought was one stream ended up crisscrossing through much of the trail up the valley. Apple trees and bamboo forests sprouted out around them, blocking out light as they moved farther inland.

They stopped here and there to take pictures, stealing little touches of shoulders, arms, and hair in between shots. His leg against hers, her face pressed against his, squeezed tightly together for the sake of a selfie.

The farther they went, the more labored his breathing seemed to get. Maele noticed him stifling a cough until he could no longer hold it in.

"Are you okay?" she asked.

"Yeah, I just got a little winded for a second."

"Well, let's slow down. We don't have to walk so fast. We have all day."

The climb was getting steeper and the air thinner.

He nodded and they walked on.

"Adam?"

"Yes, Maele?"

"You never told me what your New Year's resolution was."

"That's because I don't have one," he declared proudly, puffing his chest.

"Why not?"

He stooped down to take a picture of the bright pink flowers. "These are Philippine ground orchids. My mom loves these."

Maele decided not to push him. "Don't pull them, though. If you do, it will rain."

"Well then, I'm going to save that trick for later," he said with a laugh.

For a while, after his lungs calmed down again, the air was filled with the sound of chirping birds and crackling twigs. Maele was content with the silence. She breathed in the fresh atmosphere and focused on the feel of her hand in his. As they walked, she filled him in on her life before the accident. She told him about her friends, about Koa, Noe, and Raelene. How excited she was to see her pipe mentor, Dorian, whom she planned to visit soon. She had a tendency to grab the blue jewel around her neck as she spoke. Adam listened intently, nodding and turning to her every now and then to ask a question.

"You gotta go all the way," he told her. "Get back to competing. It's your life. It isn't really a choice."

Before Maele realized it, still caught up in conversation with Adam, the Hanakapiai Falls suddenly towered above them.

"That is insane," Adam shouted, taking his camera and shooting in succession. "Three hundred feet tall."

"If we continue on, there's another one that's five hundred feet tall." Maele said. She marveled at the majestic cliff face that glistened with green moss turned silvery in the sunlight. Thriving, lush, and green like his eyes.

"This is all I need," he said, smiling. "I'm so lucky I get to see this with you, Maele. These past several days, spending the holidays with you has been like a dream."

She said nothing. When he pulled her close, she folded herself in his arms.

"Although, there is one thing missing," he added.

"What's that?" she mumbled against his chest, the spray from the forceful cascade a relief from the heat.

He released her abruptly and ran toward a thicket of flowers. "Rain! I want to kiss you in the rain." He plucked up a bright, pink flower, and ran toward the pool at the bottom of the waterfall.

"No," Maele screeched, running after him.

The funny thing about Adam Yates was even nature was on his side. With a snap of his fingers and a pluck of a flower, the clouds opened and released a torrent of rain, so heavy and incessant they could hardly see. She ran to him and when she began to stumble through the current, her feet on slick rocks and rough silt, Adam swooped her up in his arms. Swallowed up by the storm, they held on to each other for dear life. Slowly, Adam tilted her chin up and aligned his lips with hers.

"Do it," she begged, certain she was going to drown if he didn't share his air with her. "Don't ask. Just do it."

When he cradled her face in his hands, touched her lips with his, crushed her body against his, and she felt his heart beating out of his chest, she knew. When Adam lifted her up and she wrapped her legs around him, and, when despite all that, she couldn't get enough, she was sure.

Maele Moana was in love with Adam Yates.

40

Grace finds Beauty

After their day in the mountains, Adam moved out of the resort on the South Shore and into a charming seaside hotel called the Hanalei Colony Resort. He made arrangements with management to stay until January fourteenth when Maele was supposed to fly back to Oahu. Adam decided he'd return to Los Angeles the same day. This was the place where Maele would reclaim her lost glory—the reason she was training up to ten hours every day. He was also a twelve-minute drive away from her aunt and uncle's place. Koa's store was smack dab in the middle, right off the 560.

"*Always something new with you, Adam Yates,*" Maele had said when he showed up that first day with a Jeep, explaining the Rover had been supplied by the old resort. "*So I rented this,*" he'd said with a shrug that made Maele laugh. They were as giddy as children, fazed by nothing and just happy to be together.

Every day, Adam and Maele went into the water, where he worked with her to make her dream a reality. She was an amazing athlete. Most days he'd meet her at Secret Beach, but as the winter settled in, the waves grew larger on the North Shore. Some days they would load their boards, head to the East Shore and surf a break near Anahola, or one near Wailua.

"Where are we surfing today?" Adam would ask.

"It's a surprise," Maele would respond. Every special place on Kauai was a well-guarded secret.

They went for a weekend trip to Kekaha and applied ahead for a pass to Barking Sands Beach, where there was a tasty little break deep off the west side. They laughed as they walked across the beach, their feet making barking sounds in the sand.

"I guess this is where they got the name from," Maele giggled.

On the West Shore, they ran down hundred-foot-high sand dunes, and off in the distance they could see Niihau, the private island.

"We should get on paddle boards and make our way over there."

"It's private. I bet they have sharks with lasers on their heads," Maele teased.

"Hey, are you making fun of my script?"

"No. First off, your sharks didn't wear lasers, that's a different movie. In yours, they just helped the humans fight sea monsters without lasers." She laughed.

Adam was in love.

He quit smoking. Without taking a single drug since the night of the wedding, he was clean and sober, and he loved it.

At night, he'd drop her off at her auntie's house where Koa or Fudge would be waiting outside for her. Then, he'd return to his room at the HCR to work on his script. Even when they went away for the weekend together on the West Shore, Maele insisted on two separate rooms and Adam respected that. Their friendship was becoming a relationship—an old-fashioned courtship Adam had only read about in books, or heard grandparents talk about. No, Maele didn't have a chaperone, but those passionately charged moments were kept chaste and pure.

One day, they hiked along the Na Pali Coast to an ancient surf spot that was so far off the map, it was even tough for locals to find. Most people got to it by boat, but Maele and Adam, boards under their arms, hiked the eleven miles in. They slept on the beach like nomads and surfed at sunrise amid a gentle swell that broke long and wide along the coastline.

And Kauai! He had lived here for four years, but he was like a little jailbird locked up on campus, minus his clandestine excursions to Secret Beach. He had never known the beauty, scope, and the rugged wilderness of this island until now. So much of Kauai was either off-limits or unapproachable unless by foot. The island, teeming with life, was a mysterious holdover from an ancient time.

Kauai was the only island in the Hawaiian chain with navigable rivers, so the young lovers took advantage of Maele's rest day by floating down the

Wailua River on a raft, holding hands and drifting slowly past the Opaekaa and Wailua Falls. They hiked up the river and blew up their rafts by mouth, so they were free to explore. Adam couldn't think of a better way to spend a day—floating on his back, hand in hand with the love of his life who, in two short days, would face her fear at Tunnels Beach. If she could do it, he could do it.

As they floated down the river, bodies warm and baking in the midday sun, birdsong filling the air, Adam wished he could slow down time. He loved feeling cut off from the rest of humanity. He knew he was in love with her—sold out and head over heels for Maele—and he wanted to do what he had to do for her. Drop any habit, right any wrong. He also knew he owed her the truth.

"Maele, there is something I need to tell you."

"What is it?" They floated in the sunshine, lazy and free.

"I have a ... well, I'm ..." He didn't know how to say it. "I have a substance abuse problem." There was a brief pause.

"Oh," she said, shielding her eyes from the sun as she looked straight at him. "Have you been taking anything in the past few weeks?"

"No, I haven't really had any since the night of the wedding. I haven't wanted any."

"Okay." This was followed by another longer pause in which Adam grew nervous and uncomfortable.

I shouldn't have told her. Not now. If not now, though, when? If she can face her fears and overcome at Tunnels, then I need to be able to burn this crazy empire I've built. Burn it to the ground. The truth is the only thing that can set me free!

"Thank you for telling me." When she spoke, there was no inflection in her tone. He had just shared his deepest, darkest secret with her, and she responded as if nothing he said troubled her.

They drifted down the Wailua, passing a boat filled with sightseers and then floated past a hollowed out volcanic grotto draped with ferns. "I'm going to be praying for you, because I want you to be the best version of yourself you can be. We live one life and it's short. Make the best of yours, Adam."

She squeezed his hand three times, and he held on to her for dear life in return, feeling grace wash over him and a sense of peace he couldn't understand.

For the first time in his life, he felt what it must feel like to be loved by God.

What's Found is Lost

When January thirteenth arrived, Maele had been kissing Adam Yates a lot. It didn't matter what they did or where they went—he would pull her close anywhere and kiss her. After a while, she found herself doing it, too. Like they both couldn't get enough of each other. Maybe he was making up for all the kissing he was used to doing, where she was making up for all the kissing she had never done.

And she wondered why on earth she'd taken so long to try it, but so happy she'd waited for Adam.

Maele greeted the day of the thirteenth with confidence and calm. Her friends came over early, and by sunrise, Koa, Noe, and Raelene were waiting to pile into Adam's car. Maele felt ready. The only time she hadn't gotten a little win had been her first attempt at Secret Beach, but even that scary moment had its lesson.

The clouds looked weighty, full, and thick with rain. As soon as they drove away, large droplets of water began to pelt the Jeep. Adam hit the brakes and pulled over.

"I should probably have checked the surf report for today," Adam muttered.

Koa answered from the back seat. "Kauai is this way. Always unpredictable. As long as there's no lightning, we'll be fine."

"We can head somewhere else, where the breaks are a bit more manageable," Raelene offered.

"Mae?" Noe asked. "What do you think?"

"No," Maele said, turning to address them all. She noticed how Koa took up half of the backseat. "I want to do this. It's today or never."

"Then let's go," Koa echoed. "It's today."

Adam drove in silence. Maele could see how focused he was on the road, windshield wipers working at full speed. They'd been talking about this for weeks now. Makua Beach was east of Hanalei Bay and adjacent to Ke'e Beach. It wasn't a swimming beach. Much of the shoreline was lined with rock, and only professional surfers could handle the ten-to-fifteen-foot waves that fired off during the winter months. Makua offered no amenities—no showers, no bathrooms, no service. Surfers and divers had nicknamed it Tunnels Beach, not just because of the myriad of lava tubes formed underwater, but because they were the source of Kauai's best reef breaks. Expert surfers from all over the world came to Tunnels to ride the "barrels"—perfectly formed waves that break into flawless tubes of crushing water.

When they arrived, there was a small cluster of three or four rain-soaked surfers lining up to drop in. Maele's group arrived, surfboards in arms, doubling the size of the crowd. There was also a group of onlookers, some with cameras, watching the brave and stupid souls who chose to surf that morning.

Noe warned the others. "Hey. You all know how contaminated the water gets after heavy rains. So, we're doing this 'ale'ale 'ino. But we get out of the water after Maele does her thing, okay? Everyone just gets one round and then we call it. And watch out for mano."

Everyone nodded, except Adam.

"He just said we're doing this storm surf and we need to be on the lookout for sharks," Maele shouted over thunderous, crashing waves.

"Oh," he shouted back.

They paddled out into the storm surge.

Maele had mixed feelings now, putting her friends at risk for this crazy dream. She watched as they began to paddle out, one behind the other. Noe and Raelene went first, then Maele followed. Adam and Koa closed out the rear.

They reached the lineup and watched in silence as huge walls of water crashed past them, the wave energy lifting the surfers ten-to-fifteen-feet high. Ahead of them was a lone surfer waiting to drop in, and when he paddled into the wave and broke to the left, he quickly disappeared.

"Where did he go?" Koa yelled over the thunder.

Everyone looked at each other. Raelene, Noe, and Koa were

excited; Maele was determined. Adam looked way out of his league. There's surfing and then there was big wave surfing. Tunnels was pushing into big wave territory that day.

The group wanted Maele to go first—she had the honors. She was about to lay on her board when Adam grabbed her arm, his face all seriousness. "Are you sure you want to do this?"

"I'm sure," Maele shouted, smiling and clutching her necklace at the same time.

"These waves are huge!"

"I've got this, Adam!" Maele squeezed the little blue jewel before tucking it into the neck of her wetsuit for safekeeping. She lay on her board, ready to paddle into the drop zone. The rain and the spray from the waves made it look and feel like they were all taking a shower.

Before she paddled into her future and closed the chapter on her past for good, Adam reached out and gently tucked a strand of hair behind her ear. "I want to tell you something," he began. "Do you know why I didn't have a New Year's resolution? Because I never saw anything beyond each day. But being with you, Maele, makes me want to create plans. So, this year, my resolution will be to watch you succeed, because you deserve to. And I'll be here, cheering you on."

"Thank you," she said. Maele reached up and caressed his face under the watchful eyes of Koa. "Now, can you please just snap your fingers and make the rain go away."

Adam snapped his fingers for her.

Off she went, paddling out toward her destiny. She felt strong, determined, calling up every single memory she had of the movements of the ocean. She allowed her instincts to guide her, closing her eyes and gauging the direction of the wind as the rain continued to pour. For a while, the water was an inky mass, sullen, stormy, and troubled. The tide began to pull, and she felt the equally rapid rise of her wave rolling in. The time had come. She started paddling with every ounce of courage she had.

The water felt heavy at first, but as she dropped in and veered left, her body adjusted to the movement and a song began playing in her head that told her to get up and dance. Gravity took over and she began to fly. She pushed against her board and stood up instantly, planting two feet and moving from side to side. Infused with the inner strength she had never lost, Maele rose to the occasion, lifting both arms in the air to welcome the spray of the ocean as the wave began to break. She rode down the face of the wave with force, speed, beauty, and grace. Her body felt weightless, like she was defying gravity and fighting G-forces all at once. It was an aquatic, electric rush. She was fully alive.

Out of nowhere, the sun joined her in her dance, her song amplified by the strong gusty wind and echoed by the mountains around her.

The song of her soul grew louder, a melody made just for her. A new anthem with new words. Something about love and how it makes you want to fly. A hymn about courage and second chances. She moved on the wave, graceful, wild, dynamic, and twisted. Maele danced like her life was just beginning. No pain, no loss, no past. A giant, tumbling, thousand-ton wall of rushing sea began to curl over her, closing in. White foam, like a hundred fire hoses, spraying out behind and beneath her. With her gaze bolted to the outside of the tunnel, her shoulders and hips centered, her right arm in front of her and the fingers on her left hand barely skimming the water, she tiptoed back and forth, careful to match the tune of the ocean. Too high and she risked falling off—too low and she risked hitting the lip of the curve right below the hollow.

It was the perfect barrel wave, a once in a lifetime, twenty-foot face, brought about by the wind and the rain—and she slayed it.

42

Foolish Idea

Adam watched Maele catch the biggest wave he'd ever seen up close. In that moment, she looked like both a princess and a warrior. He could feel the spray of the water, appearing almost black, as the break moved past.

All he could hear in his head was Noe saying, "Watch out for makos." But the feeling of being lifted twenty feet in the air when the swell moved beneath him, or the reduced visibility due to the rain and the spray, or the fact that, for the first time in his life, he was scared to be in the water, didn't interfere with how proud he was of Maele. She looked just like she did six years ago on a beach not far away. But instead of being a weirdo sitting on the sand in a bright yellow sweatshirt, he was out in the water with her. He was in her world now.

He lost sight of Maele behind the giant wall of water as the sun broke out from behind the clouds. Mist rose from the mountain sides. What had been black depth a moment ago was now a deep blue with green and turquoise mixed in, sunlight searing the horizon from every direction. He saw a flock of birds fly along the shoreline and if anyone ever asked him what he thought Heaven was like, Adam had an answer, now and for the rest of his life.

He was still terrified to ride his wave, but since Rae had gone, and Noe was dropping in, it was his turn next. He lay on his board and got himself in position. Looking over his left shoulder, he saw a beautiful swell rolling his way. With his forehead resting on the board, he began to paddle with all his might. Before he knew it, he was looking down the face of a wave that had to be at least fifteen feet tall. It felt like he was on ice when he stood, gravity taking hold of him and his board trembling under his weight. But he quickly gained control of his balance, his feet, his body, his board, and surfed. It was one hundred percent the biggest wave he'd ever been on, and he loved every minute of it.

"Chee-hoo!" Adam screamed at the top of his lungs.

As the wave formed a barrel and closed in on Adam, sunlight refracted through the perfect tube. He heard the roar of the wave and saw the sea in a blur underneath him, but he was in control, and he would ride this wave until it gave out. He bent low, placing one hand on his board as the tube got smaller until finally it spat him out with a spray of spume and foam. Adam lifted his hands high, and then dropped them to his sides, wrists loose and fingers relaxed. He'd done it. The wave was only about five or six feet now with water turning white and moving fast. Then, his ride was up.

When he got to the beach, his joy was quickly upended by the scene in front of him. Maele was down on her hands and knees patting her chest repeatedly and looking in the sand. Noe and Rae were mumbling and walking around in circles.

"What is it you guys? What happened?" Adam asked.

"I lost my necklace. I'm so stupid, I thought I had it tucked under my wetsuit, but I guess it got loose and fell off."

He noted an unmistakable quiver in her voice.

"When did you notice it was gone? Or when did you last have it?"

"I had it right before I dropped into the wave. I remember I had it before I dropped in. I tucked it into my wetsuit."

"Well, did you fall in the water or anything? Did you end up swimming after you rode the wave?"

"No, I rode almost all the way in."

Adam knew she didn't want her lost necklace to ruin her victorious moment, but he also knew how much sentimental value it had.

"It's lost in the water. I remember my hand catching on the chain— I thought it was my hair. I know exactly when it happened. After the tunnel, as the wave was dying, right there."

She pointed to a place between two distinguishable outcroppings of rocks. "I accidentally tore the necklace off my neck. Why did I surf with it, dang it?"

"It's gonna be okay, Mae," Noe said, trying to comfort her.

Koa swam up and joined them.

"That was awesome! That was the best surf I think I've ever seen. They were talking about a once in a hundred-year swell on the radio this morning. I believe it!" And then Koa looked around at each unhappy face. "What's wrong? What happened?"

"I lost my necklace."

"The one Lola gave you? Oh, ūhū."

"Yeah, ūhū is right." Maele whimpered.

Koa gently placed his huge arm over and around his cousin.

Adam didn't know how he would do it, or whether it was even possible, but he was determined to find her necklace, no matter the cost.

"I bet we can find it," he said.

The four of them looked at Adam. The old guard stood laughing at the new kid. Then, Adam was laughing, too. What a foolish idea.

Lost necklace aside, it had been a good day. Maele had rediscovered her superpower.

43

Peace and Wilderness

Later that evening, Maele and her friends celebrated her victory in Adam's suite back at the Hanalei Colony Resort. There was pizza, beer, and Maele's favorite haupia, which her aunt had made. Koa had brought it with him after he'd showered and changed. Maele watched as her friends celebrated the return of the girl they knew and loved. Maele Moana was back, and she'd ridden a twenty-foot wave like a pro.

"You know you're gonna have to try out for the circuit, right?" Rae asked.

Maele shook her head.

"Yeah, because you've got your flow back, Maele," Noe added. "Nothing's gonna stop you now."

Maele was still uncertain. "I don't know if I'll try out. There's the coffee shop and—"

Adam cut her off. "You should absolutely try out for the circuit. If you, for one second, think you have a shot at going pro again, then, Maele, you have to take it. You have to try."

Confused for a split second, she looked at him, her smile fading. "Yeah? You think so?"

"I do, I really do."

"Hell yeah, he does, Cuz. You were a little beast out there on the water today. I think that may be a record wave at the Tunnels. And did you see this? There was a photographer on the beach. Your photos are already online! Look at you, Mae-Mae. You're gorgeous." Koa picked her up over his shoulder like a sack of coffee again to parade her around the room.

Maele just laughed and swatted Koa on the back in protest, kicking her legs in the air. By the look on Adam's face, she knew they could all see her underwear, but she didn't care.

A few hours later, her friends were ready to go. "Do you want to ride with me, Mae-Mae?" Koa asked.

"I think I'll hang back with Adam for a while. He can give me a ride home later, or I can always walk." Maele looked at Adam, who nodded.

"No walking. I'll come get you, if you want. Noe, Rae, you guys want to come back to my house? My mom has made a ton of laulau and it's just gonna go to waste."

"Yeah, mate, I'm hungry again. I can eat," Rae joined in.

"Yum, sounds good to me. Hopefully, we'll see you later, Maele," Noe said.

"Then, this is it, eh? Will we see you before you leave tomorrow, girl?" Rae asked.

"My flight is at nine. I doubt it. Unless you wanna watch the sunrise with me, you know where I'll be."

Rae and Maele hugged and held on to each other while they rocked back and forth.

"Don't be a stranger, stranger," Noe said, breaking up the girls' silence. "It was good to see you these past few weeks, Mae-Mae." Noe looked at her long and hard.

"Noe, next time I see you, it's shaka 'till we die!" An old inside joke, which made Noe laugh. She wrapped her arms around his thick neck and squeezed him with all her might. "Take care of yourself and don't break any hearts." She glanced briefly at Rae and turned back to Noe. "Please tell your daddy I'm rooting for him. I'm glad I got the chance to visit with your family while I was here. And DM me, or whatever. I'm a short flight away."

"We gotta bounce, guys. It's time for my fourth meal. I'm frick'n starving. If I don't eat, I'll get angry. I love you, Mae-Mae. I'll see you soon. We got an early day tomorrow, so ... Adam, you touch her, and I rip your foot off and throw it into the water," Koa said with a maniacal grin, tongue out, eyebrows arched, and eyes squinted like a madman.

Rae and Noe followed, and the room went quiet. Maele was conscious of the silence—her anxiety soothed only by the popping of the fire from the fireplace and the roar of the crashing waves outside. It was their last day together, and she was exhausted.

As if able to read her mind, Adam walked over to the bed. He pulled off the silk comforter, laid it on the floor, and scattered throw pillows on top of it. Maele smiled when he sat facing the fire and reached for her hand. She took her place next to him, the two of them on a cloud surrounded by a rainbow of colors. Adam wrapped one arm around her and held up his phone.

"Look at these photos on social."

She looked like a model on a wall of glass—she hadn't recognized herself, at first. Maele crouched low, coming out of the tube like a beast. Her form was perfect.

"Look. There's my blue diamond necklace. You can see it in this picture."

In another photo, Maele's arms were held high as she looked skyward. The necklace was gone.

"Well, the necklace is in the water, one hundred percent. At least we know where it is." Adam scrolled up to the next one. "Would you look at that."

There, in the wave, a towering wall of glass illuminated by a burst of sunlight through gray skies, was a fifteen-foot shark. All that was visible was its dark silhouette.

"Maele Moana, you were surfing with sharks on a twenty-foot high, record-breaking wave. There's even a rainbow in the background! Look at this—the photo was posted three hours ago, and it already has 200,709 views. You're going viral!"

Adam tilted her head toward him and kissed her long and hard. Maele was overcome with a desire for Adam that she had never experienced before. She yearned to feel his hands on every part of her body—all of her. She wanted him fully and totally, her heart and soul one with his.

Minutes later, Adam and Maele were lying on the floor. Midnight was near, and the ocean was loud and raging as it pounded the shore. The wind had died down and all Maele saw was him.

They were lost in each other's eyes, finding ways to convey their love with their lips and hands.

"Stay, Maele. Stay until the end of the month with me. Don't go yet," Adam said between kisses, shirtless despite the fact that Maele was still fully clothed.

Adam slowly moved his hand from Maele's shoulder and across her breast. Her body rose in excitement. Soon, he found the skin of her stomach, which she tightened, drawn lean as she stretched out. Maele was on fire. Despite everything she believed in, she wanted Adam to be the one.

She was faced with a challenge she had never confronted before. Her carnal yearnings were rudely interrupted by thoughts of reason.

Maele was saving herself for marriage, which was all fine and well in theory, but while lying underneath the man she loved with her body screaming "Go for it," she desperately wanted to give in. Break that commitment and show him just how much he meant to her …

No, no, no. Stop thinking. For once, why can't you stop thinking?

Adam was lying on top of her, but Maele's mind had taken over. She was in full control. His hand was on her stomach and her skin rose under his touch.

"Your hands are so warm and soft, Adam," she whispered, taking his hands and bringing them to her lips. Adam paused to look directly at her. Those green eyes set ablaze by lust, love, and the glow of the fire. *Peace. He is my serenity.*

His hand drifted back down to her stomach again, this time trailing his fingers lower until they reached the elastic band of her red underwear. As he gently moved closer to the center of her body, Maele wrapped her legs around him and pulled him close, pinning his hand in place. She was conflicted. Adam's eyes were dark. She knew his desire had reached a peak.

"Maele, I want you. I want to make love to you."

She wanted him to, but long ago, Maele made a promise to God, and she'd given her word to Him. If she broke it—broke her word for this momentary pleasure, no matter how badly she wanted it—then her word would mean nothing.

Gently, she moved Adam off of her and sat up. "Not yet."

Adam was wide-eyed with confusion as he sat up too.

"But we can do other stuff." She flashed him a mischievous grin. "If you want?"

"I *definitely* want."

Maele giggled, pushing him back down to the floor and planted a kiss on his mouth.

Three Little Words

Maele stayed in Adam's arms through the night, and he reveled in her whispers and chaste caresses. They woke in the dark, knowing full well it was time for her to go. On the way to the airport, they drove to Hā'ena State Park to watch the sun glide its way across the heavens.

Wrapped in each other's arms, covered in blankets, and perched on the hood of his rented Jeep, they waited in silence. All around them, a misty fog blanketed the mountains, reducing them to dark lines carved into the giant shadows reflecting against the predawn sky. Adam could make out the ocean, its frosty tips shimmering against a canvas of indigo. No matter where in the world she went, the ocean would always be Maele's home.

But the sunrise? It would only have meaning because of Maele from now on. He'd been there to watch the sun rise with her and had given her the courage to embrace a new beginning.

If there was ever a time in his life where he harbored regret, it was that morning. As if she read his mind, she whispered to him.

"I want to stay."

But in that same breath, he knew. Those who stayed never got off the ground. Those who stayed never got a chance to live their dreams. You know those people, the ones who lived their lives regretting the moment they'd given up on their dreams? Those were the ones who stayed.

It was as if Adam read her mind. "We have to do this, right?" he asked, pulling her tighter against him while she sat between his legs, her back flush against his chest.

"Yes, we do."

Shrouded in silence, Adam had no words. The guy who had a theory about everything, who never ran out of things to say when they were together, whose brain barely kept up with his mouth—was dead silent.

"Are you okay?" she asked, concerned. "It's just not like you, you know. To be so quiet."

"Yeah," he answered, nuzzling her neck, inhaling every single inch of her, kissing her ear, her shoulder.

"What are you doing?" she asked, laughing as she caressed his hair.

"Savoring the moment," he answered.

"Why? I'm seeing you again, aren't I?" She looked at him, her face slack, her eyes clouded.

He knew what she was thinking. *Would he break her heart like Andie said he would?*

"Here it comes," Adam exclaimed, pointing to the horizon. They gasped at the sun's beauty. Rising from the water, a black spot at first, changing color right before their eyes. The sun rose quickly, and as it climbed, a surge of gold blasted across the horizon. Illuminating the mountains as its rays lit up the coast, the mountains were no longer black silhouettes but vivid, imposing, and grand. Small clouds swirled in greeting, and the colors of the world came back flooding to life. Like magic.

"Adam? What's the sunrise like in L.A.? Is it the same as it is on the islands?"

"I don't know, to be honest. I've never really paid attention."

"Will you remember this one?" she asked.

He knew full well they were going to be late for her flight. Lihue was thirty minutes away and her flight was in two hours. Yet, Adam couldn't move away from her. He wanted to cry, even though she'd given him no reason to be sad. "Always."

Sure enough, the traffic on Highway 56 was heavier than normal. On the drive to the airport, Maele called her aunt and uncle to thank them again and assured Koa she would call him in a few days to figure out her next steps.

Adam could tell she was in deep thought, but he didn't ask why. He admired her while she sat in the passenger seat, wondering how on earth the girl he'd first seen when he was barely a teenager—this beautiful, wounded girl—had come into his life.

By the time they got to the terminal, Maele had thirty minutes to board. Parking would have taken too much time, and with security being so tight, she thought it better for him to drop her off at the entrance.

"Well, I guess this is it," she announced once they were out of the car. Suitcase in hand, she planted a quick kiss on Adam's lips. "Let me know when you're back in L,A." Her voice cracked.

His heart was breaking, and he knew she was trying to show some strength. How could he have fallen in love so quickly?

Adam stepped forward and held her in his arms. Still saying nothing, he reached out to touch her face, brushing his thumb against her cheek. "Take care, Maele."

"You too, Adam," she answered, turning toward the crosswalk. In a few seconds it would separate them, and their time on Kauai, their time under the sun, would be over.

Maele crossed the street and walked toward the sliding doors to the terminal. As he watched her walk away, he heard cars rushing by, blinkers ticking, horns bleating, voices yelling. In that split second, when all the noise converged into one, and the sobbing in his chest found nowhere to go, he called out her name.

"Maele!" he shouted, chasing after her. Leaving his car double-parked and causing a ruckus of screeching brakes. She ran toward him, forgetting about her suitcase as it fell face down on the ground. Among the rushing crowd, the porters, and the silver luggage carts, bombarded by crying children in strollers and the irritated parents who hurried to tend to them, surrounded by humanity in all its untamed, hurried glory, Adam saw nothing but her. He felt nothing but her skin as he cradled her face in his hands, his lips brushing hers.

"I love you, Maele," he declared, breathless. "You're my sunrise, my hope for better things to come. I love you." The weight he'd carried in his heart was gone. He wanted to feel the burst of energy once again and so he repeated those words over and over – they set him free. "I love you. I love you."

"I love you too, Adam," she said, tears falling freely, her feet lifting off the ground. He said the words he never thought he'd say. He loved her. And she loved him in return.

"I'll be there soon, okay?" he said, lips against her cheek.

"Okay," she said, nodding.

"I'll finish up this thing in L.A. and I'll come find you."

"Okay," she said again. She looked lost for words, overwhelmed.

"I'm going to call you every day."

"Okay," she said.

He kissed her with all his might, laughing underneath, wishing her lips would burn an indelible mark on his. Adam's heart turned full and hopeful, right before a high-pitched whistle and a security guard pulled them back to reality.

"I have to go."

"Go," he said, smiling as he released her. First his arms, then his hands, until his fingers touched nothing but air.

"Wait for me, Maele. I love you."

PART FOUR
Heavy Waves
Maele

45

Rising Star

Maele's star was rising. Unequivocally.

In the first few weeks after returning to Oahu, she continued to work at the coffee shop part time, using her earnings to enter local surfing competitions. It didn't take long before she was recognized, not just by the locals but by foreign surfers who had seen pictures of her shredding the twenty-foot barrel off Kauai. That photo had made it on the cover of the largest surfing magazine in the world. She'd turned down the initial deals, wanting to prove herself first as a surfer. It was important she know that the barrel hadn't been a fluke. So, the plan was to accumulate enough points in three local World Surfing League competitions to progress to the World Qualifying Series. So far, so good.

Koa, Noe, and Raelene had moved to Oahu to be with her. They knew life would have to get back to normal eventually, but the excitement they shared as Maele ascended the ranks translated into full, all-out support. They traveled around the island in Duke's old Chevy, with Koa and the boards in the flatbed and the three of them scrunched up in front.

Still, she felt alone.

It was May, and she hadn't seen Adam in person since January fourteenth.

But they spoke almost every day, except for this week. She hadn't heard from Adam in five days, and she was worried sick. It had become a routine for her, looking forward to his calls. Saving his text messages to inspire her to keep going. Koa was on her case about it, but there was nothing anyone could do. Adam was in California, and she was here.

There was no sense crying about it.

That month, the summer swells in Oahu were just beginning. Maele and her friends, often presented with so many options, drove around and settled in different beaches each day. Located in front of a Canoe Club, Ricebowl was a spot where hollow waves were a gift from the shallow coral and the north winds. The water looked like it was almost solid and the breaks came fast, but the tubes were tight and near perfect. Ricebowl's waves weren't deadly, like the Pipe, simply because the deeper waters made for more gentle breaks. Even fearless groms and keikis could test their chops at the Bowl. And, for Maele's group, what started out as an easy ride gained momentum as the waves hit a series of hollow bowls for an intensely short set.

The daylight was winding down. The smell of sunblock and the line of surfers had dissipated. Some surfers gathered around with tents and sleeping bags. This was Maele's favorite part of the day. When she sat with her friends, she felt less alone.

"Mae-Mae, Auntie Lana's poke is the bomb," Koa said, swiping with his fingers to get the last of the food. "She asked us to stop by for dinner tomorrow."

Next to her were Rae and Noe, who were apparently a thing, these days. Rae had laid her head on Noe's lap and stretched out her legs on the powdery sand. There were a few other people in Maele's circle—her pipe mentor Dorian, his wife Alyssa, and three surfers from Australia. Soon, the glow of the fires scattered around the beach and the lull of conversation peppered the air. Maele's attempt to obscurely glance at her phone every few minutes didn't go unnoticed.

An acquaintance named Malik walked over to the group and crouched between her and her cousin.

"You shredded that hollow again today, Maele. Aiwaiwa! Everyone else wiped out on the break, but you didn't."

"Thank you," she answered. "Got lucky, I guess."

"The champion is being so humble," Raelene chimed in. Maele heard nothing except the incessant beeping of her phone.

"Sorry," she said, distracted. She shifted her eyes from side to side, trying to find a quiet spot. "I have to get this."

She found a row of wooden shacks, unlit, empty, and dark, a massive grove of trees behind them.

"Hey," she greeted, her heart skipping.

"Hey, babe."

"Where have you been? Are you okay?"

"I was out with the flu all week, I'm sorry, babe, I was too sick to call."

"Well, talk to me, how do you feel?"

"I can't. I'll call you tomorrow, I have to step into a meeting, I just wanted to let you know I'm okay and that I miss you."

"A meeting? This late, huh?" From where she stood, Maele saw that Koa was no longer sitting with everyone else.

"Yeah, you know, these people like to hold their meetings in restaurants or clubs. I'm just heading out in a bit," Adam answered.

"Okay. Good luck with it."

"I'll have more time to catch up tomorrow. I just wanted to hear your voice."

"Me too," she whispered. "I miss you, Adam."

"I love you, Maele. Just know that, okay?"

Maele heard voices in the background. He was around other people most of the time, but that was life in the big city, she surmised. A pit formed in her stomach.

When Adam hung up, Maele remained in place for a few seconds, deep in thought. Dropping her head with her eyes closed, she sagged to the ground, depleted.

"There you are," Koa said.

Maele looked up, careful not to show any of her disappointment.

"It's pretty dark and secluded here. Let's get back to the fire."

"Okay, in a bit."

"Malik annoys you, huh?" Koa said. "He's a really nice guy. His dad is the CEO of some drug company in Australia. And he's smitten with you. Maele this, Maele that. You're all he talks about."

"That's nice," she said. The wind lapped her hair around so much, she held it down with her hands. "I'm not interested."

"Was that Adam? What did he say?"

"Nothing much."

"You know how I feel about this whole thing. He promised he'd be back. It's been almost five months, Mae."

"He's stuck in L.A."

"Doing what?" Koa asked, staring straight at her, head cocked.

"His film. I already told you," she snapped.

Koa's tone changed. His delivery turned quiet and somber. "All I know is if I loved a woman as much as he says he loves you, I'd be here, with you. Watching you rise and succeed because you've blown up your universe, and the best gift he could give you is to be here with you so that people like Malik, over there, don't get a chance to steal you away."

"Wait a minute," Maele said, holding her hand up. "Are you telling me about Malik's dad because you think I'm with Adam for his name?" Her blood pressure began to rise and she felt her face flush. "*He aha ke 'ano?* What kind of crap is that?"

"He wowed you with his words, his status. His looks. And then what? Where is he?"

"Where is he?" Maele walked farther away from the group. Her footsteps felt like lead in the sand; she was physically exhausted from a long day in the water. "He's succeeding, doing really well. Do you know what the Chateau Marmont is? It's one of the best hotels in Los Angeles. That's where he stays. He's going to be a successful filmmaker. We agreed we would pursue our own dreams right now. I'm *okay* with that."

Koa stretched out his arms, inviting Maele to step in. She did. She loved him, trusted him, and knew that what he was saying was right. "All I mean is, he's this shiny, rich boy who has wrapped himself around your heart. You've always had a good head on your shoulders, Mae-Mae. Just see things as they are."

Maele nodded, her head buried under Koa's armpit. If the subject wasn't so serious, she'd be making a joke. But she loved Adam, and to her, love trumped every doubt, every pain, every uncertainty.

"As long as he loves me, I will go on."

Koa stayed quiet.

"Besides, you can't save me from everything, *kaikunane.*"

"I know, but I sure as heck am going to try." Koa took her hand and led her back to the crowd. "Be nice to that blond-haired puppy dog over there. He's a pretty good surfer, and he means well."

46

The Pain of Missing

Maele tried to convince herself that the third time might be the charm. The last thing she wanted was to keep calling, but she was so excited to tell Adam her news. When he didn't pick up the phone twice, she talked herself out of it. She slid off the bed and turned on the television, reminding herself that she had yet to check out of her hotel suite. It was strange to her, being in a place as luxurious as the one she was in, but at least she wasn't alone.

She padded out to the living room where Koa lay, spread out on the couch. He woke himself up with his own snore and opened one eye, following her every move. "What's up?"

"Nothing. I'm just so excited and I can't sleep. I know I should be jet lagged."

"Well, I'm jet lagged enough for you. It's 3:00 a.m. in Oahu, Mae."

"I know, but don't you want any breakfast?" She plopped onto the ottoman, facing him, running her hands along the suede material, then touching the Waterford glasses on the coffee table in front of her. "So fancy. We get to eat with all this fancy."

When Koa closed his eye, she knew he was down for the count. Next, she poured herself a cup of coffee and walked back into the bedroom. With the hotel's fine bone china in hand, Maele stood in the middle of the room and took in her surroundings.

A king bed with the softest chiffon comforter she'd ever touched. A giant curved TV. Blue and white antique jars complemented by modern bold prints of red and blue and orange on the wall. A bathroom as big as her home in Oahu. Drapes of satin and silk on every bay window. And a giant set of French doors that led to a wraparound balcony overlooking the ocean. Everything was bright, open, and breezy. Never in a million years did she think she'd be staying in a place like this. It was a dream, but she was wide awake. As she sank into the bed, she noticed the coup de gras—a domed skylight hovering above her—reminding her the world was getting smaller, and her reach was getting higher.

Then the sweetest sound she'd ever heard. Better than the sound of the crashing wave and more exciting than the droning of a barrel.

Her phone.

Quietly, she tiptoed to the open door and shut it. Her bedroom was far away from where Koa was, but she wanted to be sure.

"Hi," she greeted, jumping on the bed and crawling under the covers. Adam appeared on camera, and she smiled from ear to ear. He looked exhausted, hair standing on end, with dark circles under his eyes. Still, he was the most beautiful man she'd ever laid eyes on. He was also shirtless, and she acknowledged the heat running through her body.

"Mae? Is everything okay?" he asked, rubbing his eyes and laying his head back on his pillow.

"What time is it there?"

"Hmm," he said, bringing his phone closer to his face. "Oh, 7:00 a.m."

"Adam, I'm so excited," she said, half-squealing, half-shrieking. She leaned the phone against the pillow and began to clasp her hands together in delight. "I finally chose a sponsor!"

"Wow! I'm so proud of you. That's great, Maele. I know we've been talking about this for a while."

She wanted to get down to business. "I miss you." Those words had been like second nature to her for the past six months. She noticed two pillows side by side on his bed, but brushed it off, knowing it was normal to sleep that way sometimes. The sheets were in disarray, covered with his clothes strewn on top of the covers—a pair of jeans, his baseball cap, his wallet, and a leather jacket.

"I miss you, too," he replied. "Where are you?"

"Adam, did you just get home?"

"I mean, not right now, but we did have a late night. Where are you?" he asked again.

"In Rio, did you forget? I'm doing the Rio Pro. It's in Saquarema, about an hour away from here. But they housed us at the Copacabana in front of the beach. And guess what?"

He waited, smiling. She wondered what he was thinking. When he didn't say a word, she continued, "I'm in Brigitte something's suite, and it has a butler." She took the phone and pointed upward. "Look at the skylight."

That got his attention. He propped himself up on his elbows. "Wow, Brigitte Bardot. Wait, is that stained glass?"

"Yep, and look," she said, panning the camera around the room. "Everything is breakable around here. Only classy places don't care about the cost of breakable things."

Adam smirked. "So, which sponsor did you choose?"

"I chose Radcom. The surfboard company. They paid for all this, including Koa." She giggled.

"Oh, so Koa's there. That's good. How is he?"

"He's Koa." She snickered. "Oh, wait! I also forgot to tell you. They flew us first class. We had three courses, including an ice cream sundae bar, plus real silverware and place settings. You never told me how cool it was to fly that way."

He laughed, running his hands through his hair and lying back down on the pillow. "Did you do your time trials today?"

"Yes," she said, laying her head on her pillow, too, and facing sideways toward the camera. "I did so-so. The event will be in Itauna Beach. The water was really cold, but the waves were explosive." She smiled. "And I've never seen so many people in my life. The crowd is intense. I'm a little nervous about tomorrow. But today, Koa and I will just stay in and chill. Maybe take a tour to see Christ the Redeemer."

"Just be careful—I heard it's really dangerous down there."

"Always." She inhaled deeply and whispered, "I love you and I miss you. When will I see you, Adam?"

"Soon, baby. It will be over soon. We're just doing what we gotta do with the script and away we go. I won't have to be here while they're doing pre-production."

She drew a deep breath and pursed her lips. "I've gone so far without you. I wonder whether you miss me as much as I do you. Every time something good happens, I want to share it with you."

"I know, I know. Same with me, too," he replied, clearing his throat. "I'm sorry. It's taking longer than any of us ever expected. Please be a little more patient, Maele. I care about you. If you only knew how difficult it's been for me to stay away from you, but I'm doing this for us. I've been watching though, from afar, on social media, every post, every tag. It's like I'm there, kinda."

How could she explain to him that if he'd asked her to come to L.A. she would? Her chin began to tremble. She wanted to be strong, enjoy the success of her pursuit, but the pain of missing him overtook everything else. For a split second, she saw what Koa saw.

Maybe, just maybe, she was misconstruing his selfishness for intellect, his arrogance for culture.

But his eyes looked tired, his face was slack and expressionless. "Don't be sad. We'll be okay. We have to finish what we started, remember—we're chasing our dreams. Most of all, I love you."

"I love you too. And I'm so excited for you. Maele Moana, you're going places!"

"It'd just be better if you were with me. In person."

"I will be, I promise. Just a little longer, okay?"

"Okay. That'll make me happy." That seemed to be her favorite word these days. She knew exactly how to improve his mood, taking the phone in her hand and tilting it upward while she leaned forward. Maele was still bewitched by their intimacy. It was in those moments when she knew she still possessed him. The way he looked at her with glassy eyes and parted lips. The power she exerted over him was intoxicating.

Adam shot straight up, leaning against the headboard, shoulders back, eyes focused on the phone.

"You know what'll make me happy?" he asked, his tone low and husky.

"Uh-huh," she answered, unfastening one button.

"Then show me."

Kope Girl

Six months after that huge barrel at Tunnels, Maele Moana had become a household name. The first thing she did with her prize money was pay off her student loans and set aside another fund for her upcoming school year. She then gifted her parents with forty thousand dollars for some home repairs. She paid Andie back for the dress, even though it was like pulling teeth to get her to accept the money.

And, because he was strongly opposed to a handout, Koa agreed to make her a shareholder in a new business venture.

Together, they were going to package coffee and coconut chips. Forget real estate, for now.

Every single day she was followed around by reporters, photographers, and bloggers. The press capitalized on her story, dubbing her as the Kope (or coffee bean) Girl from the Plantation. They focused not just on the rags-to-riches angle, but more importantly, on her ability to rise and recover from her neck injury, like a phoenix rising from ashes. With endorsements and competition prize money, Maele had already made close to a million dollars.

Everyone knew that sponsorships and endorsements were few and far between. You had to have the whole package. You couldn't just be a good surfer. Sometimes, you could even be a mediocre surfer. But with good looks, a healthy lifestyle, and an interesting backstory, fame could catapult you into a different category. Maele had all this and more. When notoriety called on her, she had Koa as a crutch to steer her through the mad, invasive crowds and guide her away from the sea of people. He stood with her during interviews and coaxed her when she didn't have the words.

"Tell us how you stayed in the tube."

"How did you conquer your fear of the water after breaking your neck?"

"Do you have anyone special in your life right now? Are you dating?"

Koa would leave her to answer the first two. With all the innocence a bearded, robust, and powerfully built man could muster, he would jump in with a "No comment" to the third one.

"Why do you keep doing that?" she'd asked him, annoyed.

"Look around you at all those men salivating for a chance to get to know you. Keep the mystery alive. Adam's loss is everybody else's gain."

Was it his loss? Or her loss? She couldn't tell the difference anymore.

Currently, her crutch, Koa, was back in Kauai setting up their business plan, and there she was, all alone in Tahiti, in an overwater bungalow overflowing with contradictions. It was traditionally made with Polynesian bamboo and wood carvings, but equipped with all the modern amenities of the first world. Her favorite part was the glass-bottomed coffee table showcasing life beneath the incredibly tranquil lagoon. She welcomed this time alone, savored the stillness that had evaded her since she'd started this unpredictable journey. Tomorrow would be a different day.

The best part about these events was getting away from the crowd of surfers and spectators and into the water. She had altogether stopped watching the sunrise—that part of her life was hibernating. Rising at 5:30 a.m. to catch the low tide in Teahupoo, her adrenaline was on fire.

Teahupoo had the most dangerous and heavy waves in the world in terms of size, power, and speed, breaking over a sharp coral reef lying only twenty feet below the surface produced that energy, with a crush of water that could rip a wetsuit off a surfer.

Maele spent many hours with Dorian, going over the technical aspects of Teahupoo. She was well aware of the fast and hollow forty-five-foot drops and the dangers of wiping out on the coral reef. They drafted different scenarios regarding the potential conditions of the waves, the moves she would have to employ, and the bathymetry of the water's depth. This was the last competition she needed to complete in the circuit before qualifying for the big event—the Pipeline back in Oahu in the winter. Bottom line was, she needed to win at Teahupoo to place. Competitors were identified by the color of their Lycra. That day, she was in red. Red was all around me when we had our first kiss. It's perfect.

She paddled out to sea, fourth in the lineup and besieged by speedboats and jet skis. Her mind was empty. Maele glanced up to observe the spray of water lapping against volcanic rock and the thicket of trees in the jungle of Mentawai in the distance. Months ago, she had floated on the wings of love. Those wings were gone, and along with them, the inspiration that accompanied them. In their place was a different kind of resolve—strength from pain, from rejection, and confusion. How ironic that every awakening seemed to be stirred by pain, every win married to a loss, every gain coupled with something taken away.

Soon enough, it was her turn. As the unstable crest approached her, she took a deep breath and got ready to roll. Maele always garnered points for her maneuvers. Her goal was to position herself inside the wave as soon as it broke from the middle to the shoulder. The longer she stayed inside, the more successful she would be. She banked off the breaking wave and propelled herself in the air, riding the twenty-foot-thick lip before it turned into a hollow. It was tall, wide, and steep. One carve, two carves. She was riding the most dangerous wave in the world. All her movements were in sync as the thick gush of dense, green water began to spin and barrel around her, thinning out in seconds like a sheet of ice. The rolling vibration drowned out everything else. There were no boats, no motors, no people. Just silence. The onslaught of the rushing tide kept her focused, bent on throwing her over and then giving in to her resilience. Beauty and violence working in tandem with each other. Because Maele had been born with the waves, she respected them, allowing them to spin her around and whip her from side to side as they attempted to fling her off balance. Only so much of surfing was muscle and power—mostly it was heart, fearlessness, and mind over matter. Accident or no, Maele never skipped a beat on those qualities.

In the end, when the water crashed around her, she pumped her fist into the air. Not only had she survived—she'd crushed it in the heat with four other surfers. She had the best scores overall and made history and the news by catching the heaviest wave ever ridden by a woman.

She was picked up from the water by a guy on a jet ski and brought to shore. Back to the mayhem, back to the unrelenting stares and the fake adoration. She never understood why people killed themselves over that kind of attention. To her, it was superfluous—an accessory. A whim. She couldn't even work at the coffee shop without being sought out. The mayhem there was the mayhem everywhere.

And there they were. One, two, three, four microphones stuck in her face. Maele continued to move one tiny step at a time, weaving her way through the sweat-filled, heavy maze of people. The air was suffocating, nauseating. The smell of salt mixed with hot breaths and sticky, clammy skin.

"Congratulations! How are you feeling, Maele?"

"Great, thank you. I'm feeling great."

"Definitely a defining moment in your career. What's next?"

"I think I'll wait to see how my scores do against the competition, and then I'll know. Stay tuned."

"How did those waves feel to you?"

"Like riding on shaving cream filled with razor blades."

In a crowd full of people, while covered in sprays of beer, champagne, high fives, and embraces, Maele had never felt so alone.

Maele heard an unfamiliar voice before she felt a gentle grip on her elbow.

"Guys, guys, give her some room."

Her heart stopped when she turned toward the silhouette of a tall, lanky man. That hair, those shoulders, backlit—and she knew him in her bones. Her heart leaped for joy.

Adam ...

No, it wasn't him. This guy's hair was longer on the sides, his shoulders drooped, and his eyes weren't the color of spring. Maele felt faint, weakened by the realization of what she had just accomplished without anyone to share it with. Hadn't he resolved to watch her? He said, on the water, "My resolution will be to watch you succeed. Because you deserve to. And I'll be here. Right behind you."

Her feet began to sink into the sand. She allowed this Adam look-alike to take over, to lead her across the dunes and into a quieter area. People still followed, but the man carried her surfboard and lifted her onto a four-wheeler, and they left the crowd, their cameras blinking, cell phones in the air.

"I'd like to go home, please," she said, turning to this kind angel in disguise. He wasn't a total stranger. She had seen him around the circuit. A surfer, for sure, someone she'd seen with Dorian a few times.

"The resort, you mean."

"Yes."

"By the way, my name is Alex. Alex Brimley."

"Yes, We've met before, right?"

"Yeah, a few times."

"Thank you, Alex."

"We met in Fiji, or Bora Bora. Who can say, right?"

"I'm Maele."

"Oh, I know who you are. Everybody knows who Maele Moana is."

"I'm in that one there."

Carrying her surfboard, he walked with her down the wooden bridge to her bungalow. It was a far cry from the scene they'd just left. The place she was staying in was secluded and peaceful, and the surface of the lagoon was smooth and placid, like a painting. Alex leaned her surfboard against the railing. A thought occurred to her—one so true, it was devastating.

This man was here. Someone she didn't know. A witness to her success.

Where was Adam?

"Would you like me to stay?" he asked nervously, hands in pockets.

"No, thank you. Thank you so much for helping me get out of that—"

"Mess," he said, smiling. "It was a mess. No problem."

"I think I'm okay now. Thank you again for your kindness. I'm gonna rest." Maele slowly began to shut the door.

He leaned in. "Are you staying for a few more days?"

"No. I mean, yes, for a press conference tomorrow." The door was half shut; she couldn't wait for him to go.

He stuck his foot inside the door and looked at her for a beat too long.

"Maybe I'll see you then?"

"Maybe. Thank you again, Alex."

They just looked at each other while the air grew extremely tense.

He withdrew his foot and she closed and locked the door. Angry, sad, and terrified. Nothing had happened, but *what if it had?* It was so difficult, navigating the world as a woman alone. She took a deep breath and thanked God for keeping her safe today. In and out of the water.

She sank into the clean white couch, tainting it with sand and salt from the sea. Slowly, she picked up her phone and dialed a number. She saw the face of the big, burly man who'd been her brother, her strength, her friend. He was all smiles, his trademark gap teeth in full view.

"Mae-Mae, you freaking shredded it! You were amazing!"

His expression changed as he watched her face crumble and her shoulders begin to shake. She dropped her phone on the floor and masked herself with her hands. She knew he could no longer see her, but she was certain he could hear.

"Koa, why? Why did he stop loving me?"

"Mae-Mae. I'm sorry. I don't know."

"You don't understand. I almost–I wanted–"

You wanted what, Mae? Talk to me."

"Nothing. Nothing. I just want to come home, Koa. I can't do this anymore."

Run and Hide

Y ou can run, but you can't hide.

It was impossible to return to Oahu for the time being. So, Maele's parents packed their bags and met her in Kauai. Nalani was so thrilled her sister and her husband were going to be staying with her, she had unrealistic aspirations of fitting six adults into their two-bedroom home. Luckily, Maele's sponsor offered to house her and her three friends in a furnished bungalow right on the shores of Hanalei. It was a win-win for all, and Radcom's way of getting Maele to remain by the North Shore to participate in small events leading up to the championship.

"There she is, Sleeping Beauty," Noe greeted as soon as Maele shuffled out of her bedroom, still in the shorts and loose-fitting T-shirt she'd worn the day she'd gotten back from Tahiti two days earlier.

The sun was already high in the sky, the wretched, hot breeze wafting through the windows. She pulled up a barstool and sidled in next to her friends. Raelene and Noe were busy digging their chopsticks into a Chinese paper pail. Maele hadn't noticed the living space until now. Floor-to-ceiling windows looking out to the ocean, marble counters, and glass tabletops in every room. She missed her home on the plantation. Her curb-salvaged bookcase filled with memories of her childhood, her room, her ability to disappear for hours while ensconced in the security of her own dreams. This house felt too open, too obnoxious, with brightly colored abstract art screaming loudly against the obstinate white walls.

Koa gently placed a cup of coffee in front of her. "I don't think I've ever seen you wake up this late. Are you okay?"

"Yeah, just tired."

"We got you your chow fun noodles," Noe said, pushing a takeout box toward her.

"She's not supposed to eat that. She's in training," Raelene argued, pushing it away.

"No, I want it," Maele muttered, her voice still thick with sleep. "I'll eat it. I don't care." She tore the wrapper off a pair of wooden chopsticks and began to dig in. Her friends watched in complete silence, save for the sound of snapping wood, slurping, and the occasional swig of diet cola.

"Mae, are you okay?" Koa leaned forward, resting his elbows on the kitchen counter. "Wanna talk about it?"

"Nope," Maele answered. When she lifted her head up from her food, Noe and Raelene swiveled their stools toward her, their postures perked, giving Koa away.

"You told them," she said, more flustered than anything.

"Mae, you were in bad shape when you called me," Koa said. "I was so worried about you. I'm kind of inexperienced in things like that, so I asked for Raelene's opinion."

"We're your friends, Mae," Raelene said. "We were worried, too."

Rae glanced at Noe, who raised his hand in the air to stop her.

She paid him no heed. "Adam's called several times since you arrived. He's also worried about you."

Her heart skipped a beat. Maybe that was the point. Would it be possible to separate her head from her heart? "I'm sorry. I am just so embarrassed. I don't know how I got here. One moment I was fine, and the next thing I know, I'm looking for him everywhere I go. It's so stupid of me. I feel silly."

The four of them were startled by a loud bang outside the door, followed by a rustling sound and soft murmurs through the window. Maele turned to see three faces pressed against the glass right before she was besieged by blinding flashes of light.

"What the ..." Koa stomped toward the window. "Everybody get lost!" he bellowed, causing the delicate white jars on the glass coffee table to vibrate. "Move back! You can't trespass on our grounds." He pulled the shades down and locked the front door.

The entire house turned dark. What was the point of all those windows?

"They found you. The paparazzi."

"Photographers," Maele countered. "Paps are for celebs."

"Maele." Koa walked back toward the group, rolling his eyes as soon as she looked back at him. "What are you talking about? You are a celebrity, I mean, you just said paps are for celebs. Your sponsor is paying for this place. There are about thirty photographers and reporters outside of this house. The sooner you accept it, the easier it will be for you to evolve."

"This isn't going to work for me," Maele said. "Koa, can we work on getting back to Waialua? We can stay here for another week or so, fulfill my obligations, and spend a few more days here with my parents. Then, I'd like to go back to the plantation."

"They'll just follow you there."

"Not if we're smart about it," Maele said, smiling for the first time since she arrived. "We'll leave at night. We'll figure it out."

She knew she'd have to ask for favors, but that was a worry for another day. "I'm going back to bed. Thanks for lunch."

Koa turned to Noe who turned to Raelene. Maele just loved how obvious these three were.

"Mae, can we catch up for a second?" Raelene stood and took Maele's hand, leading her toward the bedroom. "Boys, go pae and I'll see you there in a bit."

"Dude," Noe said to Koa, "when she tells us to catch a wave …"

"Yeah, I know. It's code for *get lost.*"

Maele lay on her stomach, her head supported by a large green pillow, arms clasped underneath like a chain. Raelene sat next to her with her back against the woven rattan headboard. In the background, soft music played. On the TV, an old episode of *North Shore* was on, the volume off.

"Do you see that guy?" Raelene pointed to the actor on the screen. "Koa keeps saying he knows him, met him years ago when they filmed the show here, but I don't believe him."

"Don't believe him," Maele said. "He doesn't know Jason Mathews."

They laughed. Raelene slid down and laid her head next to Maele's.

"How are you and Noe doing?" Maele realized she hadn't even

checked on her friend.

Everything had just happened so quickly, and this erratic phase of her life left her clueless about what had been going on with everyone else.

"Great," Raelene answered. "He's so great."

"I kind of knew you'd end up together."

They both laughed.

"He's a good man. Taking care of his father and his family. You have a good guy there, Rae."

"You were his first love, Mae. I wouldn't even try to replace or compare to that."

"Oh, Rae, we were so young. Noe and I, we didn't even kiss, let alone know it was love. He was a kind and loyal friend to me. Maybe it was love for him. But my accident took away that chance for me to find out. What he has with you. That's love. You guys are figuring out your lives together."

Raelene nodded, but Maele could see she was distracted, by the way she stared at Maele's suitcase.

"So, what happened in Tahiti?"

"I had finished all three heats and scored well. I set a new world record for women, you know. No big deal." She laughed. "And it should have been this amazing, triumphant day, but when I got on shore, the crowd was so overwhelming, I couldn't breathe. This guy, his name is Alex, took me back to the resort. He looked just like Adam. Same hair, same build, and he wasn't creepy like most of the guys on tour. At first. He was someone who, in the middle of all the chaos, reminded me of a guy who was kind, and I felt so alone. I just lost any sense of safety or concern or reason." Maele switched positions, resting her head on her hand. "I don't know. I feel so *nalowale*. Lost at sea. Everywhere I turn, I feel rudderless. Where is this taking me?"

"It's taking you exactly where you wanted to go, even before you met Adam. You should be happy about that," Raelene said. "And you're sharing this incredible season of your life with me."

"Yeah, you, Koa, and Noe, a little bit, but not … It's like I'm living my childhood dream, but is it my dream anymore?"

The girls sat on the bed in silence for a moment.

"When I left Adam in January," Mae continued, "I thought we would see each other again soon after. It's been seven months, and he's not making any effort to be with me."

"Why can't it be the other way? Why can't you go see him?"

"What would that do?" Maele asked, desperate to assuage her pain.

"You can see for yourself what's going on with him. Hopefully, you'll just find him really busy working on the future he wants with you."

Maele shrugged. "I guess I never thought of it that way."

"Do you love him?"

"Of course, I do."

"Does he love you?"

"He says he does."

"Of course, he does. He followed you to Kauai, set aside his plans to spend an entire month to be there with you. When you guys separated in Kauai, you told me you were both off to pursue your dreams. Goals you'd already laid out long before you met. All he's doing is fulfilling his end of it like you're fulfilling yours, Mae. We've heard nothing that tells us otherwise."

"I guess," Maele agreed.

"Besides," Raelene said, puffing her cheeks and trying hard not to laugh. "Your cousin is the loudspeaker of the island." She chuckled. "The Megaphone. If he heard something that Adam was doing you wrong, we would've heard about it."

"Koa is not a fan of Adam. He tells me *all* the time."

Maele nudged her playfully before fully laying on her back and gazing up at the ceiling.

"The only guy Koa will ever like is the one who becomes your husband."

The girls nodded in agreement.

"What did Adam say when he called?" Maele asked.

"Well, he called Koa—said you hadn't been answering your phone so he wanted to make sure you arrived home okay."

Maele took a deep, satisfied breath. She laced her fingers behind her head and sank her body deeper into the cushion. Slowly, she began to relax. "I did just get offered a pretty cool job that would happen in L.A. I guess I should go see him."

"You should," Raelene agreed. "Support him as much as he supports you. Take it from me, my friend. Love always deserves a fighting chance."

49

Coming Alive

In mid-July, they pulled it off.

The trip back to Waialua in the middle of the night was uneventful. Maele had reached out to Dorian, who chartered a midnight sailboat from Hanalei to Honolulu. After a whirlwind of travels, she was finally home. Back in the room she'd missed so much, with its tiny twin bed with ruffled pink bed skirt and matching curtains. If you looked hard enough, underneath that plain white fitted sheet was a *Little Mermaid* bedsheet. She'd never removed it, just covered it when her friends were over.

Maele sat on the floor, sorting through the contents of her bookshelf. She wasn't sure why she felt the need to do it at that moment, but she did, so she kept removing items from the pile. Noddy hardbacks, Judy Blume paperbacks, her homemade Gymkhana ribbons (created every time she'd cleared a jump), high school photo albums, and amateur surfing medals. That bookshelf was like a capsule of her life, every row depicting a moment in time. Following those books and medals was a whole row of gifts given to her during her time at the hospital—devotional journals, prayer bracelets, and a stack of cards from her nurses and doctors. Finally, the picture of her life before that year. Business books, textbooks, and inspirational books were all neatly lined up on the bottom part of the shelf.

She heard a creaking sound, then spied her mother's nose sticking in through a tiny gap in the door.

"Maele? Can I come in?"

"Of course, Mama," she answered, watching the bed dip as her mother sat on the edge.

"Duke was able to find a way to keep everyone out of the farm. He closed the gate to the entrance and all of us are now coming in through the back."

Maele squinted in confusion.

Her mother continued. "He's stationed a few of the workers in shifts so tourists can still enter the visitor center, but no one can go past the building into our private farm."

"Well, I'll stop by later to thank him myself."

"Is it nice to be home?"

"Oh, gosh, yes. I don't ever want to leave again."

Lolana laughed. "I need to feed you more, put some weight back into that tiny body of yours. Which reminds me—where do you want to go today, aside from the resale store? Do you even want to go there?"

"Why not? Do you remember those outfits I got for Andie's wedding? They were so nice and cheap."

"But you can afford more now, *nani oha*."

Maele couldn't help but think about her younger days as one of the few girls on the plantation. They called her "beautiful daughter." She'd never felt that way about herself until she met Adam. Love makes you believe you can do anything.

"You never know what can happen, Mama." Maele snapped her fingers. "In the blink of an eye, it could all be lost. I would know. It happened six years ago."

"But you've taken it all back and more. I'm so proud of you." Her mother leaned forward with outstretched arms.

Maele scooted closer to grab her mother's hands. "Now tell me what's going on with you."

"I'd like to see Neeta at the bank to make sure my money is in placements. Neeta said I can earn more interest."

"Of course, we can do that."

Her mother nodded almost too quickly, a tell when she didn't fully understand.

"I'm asking about you. How are you? Papa and I never got to properly meet the Yates boy. Is he someone special to you?"

"His name is Adam."

"Adam," her mother echoed.

"Yes," Maele answered. Just hearing his name caused a thrill to run down her spine. "Aviator Nation just asked me for my schedule. I'm going to try to work in a trip to L.A. to see him, since they're based there."

"You're being sponsored by an airplane company? Will you get free flights?"

"No, Mama." Maele giggled. "Cool hats and clothes."

"Ah."

"Mama?" Maele stood and slowly lowered herself on the bed next to her mother. Thankfully, the bed stayed in place. Her mother took her hand while Maele leaned her head against her mother's chest. "I lost my necklace in the water."

"The one that your papa gave to me?" The pained look on her mother's face was like she just stepped on a tack.

"Yes, I'm so sorry, Mama"

"It's lost." Maele could tell the thought of it hurt her mother.

"It's an omen or something, like the ocean took it away from me when my courage came back. Like a ransom or an exchange. It feels like I had to trade my heart for this success. I thought getting back in the water would be the ultimate dream come true, but now I'm finding out that it isn't. There's more to life than being a champion surfer. Or being a champion anything."

"Have you ever thought," her mother said, nestling her daughter's cheek against her chest, "that maybe it's the opposite? Maybe that necklace gave you the hope and courage to get back into the ocean, and now you no longer need it. That diamond was a little token of our family's luck. The way your papa's father won it and then gave it to your lola like a prize. She passed it down to your papa who gave it to me. It's the only thing of material wealth we own, but I wanted you to wear it because it gave your nana strength and a sense of power which made her feel important. It gave me a sense of class and beauty which gave me strength to get through long, hard years, and I knew it would help you. And it did in its way. You no longer need it and this family no longer needs it. Plus, we don't put our trust in little blue diamonds, do we? We trust in something much bigger." She kissed Maele on the forehead.

Maele felt like she was seven years old and safe again.

"Look at you, Maele, everything is fine. Life is that way, my precious angel. It gives out and takes back in cycles."

Maele considered her mother's words. She had used the necklace as a reminder of her accident, as a crutch, or a brace, like wearing it helped hold her neck in place.

Maele lifted her head. "I'd love to think you're right."

"I am always right." Her mother smiled and waved her hand as if to clear the air. "Now, how serious is it with this boy?"

"I've never been in love or, at least, felt love like this. The kind that wants me to be better, do more, be more. The kind that makes me feel like I can do anything."

"You spent the night with him, Maele? You know, sometimes when a woman gives herself, the pain is deeper."

Maele was taken aback, blood rushing to her cheeks. Ashamed, for sure, but not shocked. She'd known word would get back to her mother. Aunt Nalani and her mother were two peas in a pod. They harbored no secrets from each other. Koa and Maele used to joke about their mothers huddling together to talk about the two of them, like the game of telephone.

"Nothing happened. I'm committed to waiting until marriage. The funny thing is, he said he was willing to wait with me. He's not like anyone else I've ever met. He's worldly, but so wise. He's not a Christian, but he is a better person than most people we go to church with, the way he loves. He's better than those who act all righteous but only when people are looking, you know how I mean? He's funny, kind, and so driven. He's lost, though. I see him sometimes—there's a sadness in him."

"You just said success isn't the end all of everything, and if he's a little lost, it is not your job to find him or fix him. Just like it isn't his job to fix you. You have to complement each other. He has to inspire you, and you have to inspire him. You know my story with your papa. Sometimes you must be brave and bold—move mountains to be with the one you love. That's how love is, daughter. That's how marriages last as long as they do. And that's also how marriages last as *short* as they do."

Maele nodded, absorbing every word.

"He took away my anger, Mama. He made me understand that life is a series of steps. We can't skip over anything to get there from here."

The bed shifted again. Her mother kissed the top of her head before getting up. "Oh. And let us meet this young man of yours. If you love him as much as you say you do, I am sure Papa and I will love him, too. We are a good judge of character. Take your time. I'll wait for you downstairs when you're ready to go."

Maele unlatched the windows, pushing out their panes as far as they could go. She gazed down at all the blossoming trees, their ripened blooms ready for harvest. The wind carried back the sounds of the barn. Loud horse, that Romeo. Always with something to say. She resumed her search for the diary she'd left behind. Looked under her desk, under the bed, and inside the closet, until a sudden inkling called her attention to the night table.

There it was, locked up by the little key she'd hidden in her left ballet slipper. With great care, she leafed through the pages, cautious about disturbing the letters and dried flowers she'd saved. And when she found the entry she'd been looking for, the one she'd remembered at the wedding reception, she sat on the floor and leaned against the wall to read it.

Closing her eyes, she imagined the first day she'd seen him. She dreamed about that time, how it'd been before the scars, pain, and sorrow. How fresh her perspective had been then, how the world had looked to her—simpler, clearer. She was there and he was there, and his presence had an impact on her life.

There it was in writing—she'd loved him then. She loved him now. He came alive again in those pages, and she took her time reading, remembering just how much she'd loved the boy on the beach, or the idea of him. Whatever love was for a teenager, she'd had that for him. Maele's heart leaped. She would take this journal to him—show him just how much time she had spent longing for him.

As she flipped to the last page, she saw it. A rough sketch of the necklace she had lost. Colored in yellow crayon and shaded in sapphire blue. It was gone from her life now, sitting at the bottom of the ocean, granting gifts to no one under the sea.

The memories were too much for her, being home and looking back at her life before and after her world had been turned upside down.

She realized just how much she had fought to get there, how far she'd come in the past eight months. And, all of a sudden, the magnitude of what she'd accomplished overwhelmed her, causing her chest to tighten. This was all so confusing.

How to be grateful for something she hadn't wanted after all?

And how to fight for someone she'd wanted all her life.

Flight for Love

"Miss Moana, would you like some orange juice or champagne before takeoff?"

The flight attendant in red, white, and blue held out a tray of glass flutes in her direction. Maele shook her head and proceeded to put on her headphones, checking the charge light below the tray table for power. Excitement filled her heart, causing it to flutter as she counted the hours until she would be in Adam's arms.

She reached for her purse and pulled out her laptop. She had downloaded Adam's original draft of *Oceana*. She planned to read it during the six-hour flight to L.A. To show Adam she'd read every word again, taken them to heart and understood his passion. Next to her laptop was her diary, its pages bookmarked, ready for him to see.

In the days leading up to her flight, Maele had been able to spend more time with her parents and friends on the farm. In the afternoons, she'd helped with the harvest, climbing the ladder, and shaking trees. Afterward, she'd cleaned the pens, fed the animals, and washed the windows. Despite being bone-tired, depleted after spending hours in the ocean, she kept on. These were pieces of herself she refused to let go.

The plane took off just after sunrise. Maele was transfixed by the ocean meeting the sky. Bands of pink and orange marked the horizon, as if framing it would guarantee the sun's luster. The clouds moved constantly, switching places in the sky until the sun was high enough to burn them out, leaving nothing but a canvas of blue.

"Adam, guess what? I've got an advertising deal with Aviator

Nation, based in Malibu. They're flying me to L.A. for a photoshoot. I'm coming!"

"Oh, babe, that is so great. I can't wait."

"It's been so long. I miss you so much. Adam? Are you there?"

"Oh yes, sorry. Do you know the exact date?"

"Sometime around August 5th. Then I can stay with you for a while."

"Like when, sometime? Can you let me know, in advance, the exact date and flight?"

"That was a weird reaction," Koa had said.

"Why? He's just super busy."

"You shouldn't have told him when. You should have shown up and surprised his ass."

"Koa!"

"What? That I said ass, or that you need to surprise him?"

It took Maele two and a half hours to read *Oceana* again. Hearing his voice, she discovered so much about Adam through his words. It wasn't just about searching for a place where mankind could flourish in peace—it was about surviving the struggle, the wars, and the strife humanity constantly battles to overcome to simply live. There was a surprise twist where the hero gives up his life for the good of the world. *What are you trying to say, Adam? What do we have to give up to stay together? Does fate take credit? Because I've lost six years of my life, and I'm just now trying to get it back.*

She made notes on the margins, determined to tell him she would go through any hardships with him. Whatever was hurting him or whatever battles he had to fight, she would be there. During her recovery at the hospital, through the excruciating pain of rehab and the setbacks from recovery, she'd had her parents and her friends, Koa, Noe, and Raelene. She'd had the people at the farm, the nurses at the hospital. Her parents often joked Maele had her own little community. They had helped her survive. She would be that for Adam. She could be his community.

An hour or so later, as the captain announced their descent into LAX, Maele whipped out her old diary and turned to the last empty page, a fitting ending to her story. She lifted the shutter and leaned into the window, wanting to capture the moment she'd been dreaming about for a while.

August 5th (22 years old)

The captain has just asked us to fasten our seat belts. Slowly, we are lowering ourselves from the sky. I no longer see clouds, and what lies below is covered in a heavy haze of smoke. Off in the distance, this raging billow of soot is carried over by the winds, caused by the blazing of wildfires burning the hills. Los Angeles burns in summer.

Grainy, gray, sooty, and dark. The ashes have reached the clouds.

For some time, there were mountains, but now that we've descended, all I see are highways, buildings, and houses. Every square inch of the roads is filled with cars. Sort of like the lineups we get on the water. Except no one is waiting. Everyone is moving.

Oh! I think I see the Hollywood sign.

As we glide across the air and the plane's nose begins to tip down, I think of living on a secluded island where I can stay in the water all day long with only you, Adam. There's no need for accolades or celebration.

You'll be crafting these epic stories of love, desire, and hope that come straight from your heart. And your words, your brokenhearted words, will help others heal, one day.

So, here I come, Los Angeles!

The City of Angels. Crushed by fame and inspired by success. For the past few months, you've been the home of the man I love.

I can see his face through the smog and the clouds and the damage.

I hear his voice despite the noises in my head (Koa's, mostly).

It's been a long journey, one rife with happiness and tears. And we all have a long way to go. While I must finish what I started with my commitments to my family, my island, and to myself, for the next few weeks, I will live in his world.

I am finally here. Where I belong.

With him.

In his world.

PART FIVE:
Riptide
Adam

51

1,621 Miles

Adam sat alone in his room, same old room number 64 at the Chateau Marmont, overlooking Sunset Boulevard.

Just three short days before, Maele's visit had started out so well. But now, she was gone.

Adam had picked Maele up at the LAX Terminal 5 baggage claim with eight-hundred dollars' worth of fragrant white flowers in his arms. He'd been taken aback by how tan she'd become. The photos of her online were one thing, but Maele in the flesh was quite a different story. Her hair was lighter, almost blonde, the streaks of brown and caramel slowly disappearing. Her skin was dark and toned, and her muscles formed on her shoulders and popped on her arms. She was strong and healthy, her body curated by the months in the sun and the sea. She carried herself differently too, magnified, and confident. Throw in the same authenticity and truth she'd always had, combined with a new self-confidence, plus a full wallet, and Maele Moana was a force to be reckoned with.

"Hi, Maele, welcome to L.A." He was awkward; she was reticent. Their comfort level with each other was not what it had been mere months ago. They both had changed.

They had a lot to catch up on.

Adam stood there as she threw her arms around him. He felt small. A knot formed in the pit of his belly, and that old familiar sense of dread washed over him. What had changed? Who was this girl?

"You look beautiful. Have you grown taller, Maele? Is that possible? Look at you. Wow. You look like a model."

"Well, I guess that's good, because that's what I'm in L.A. for. And to see you. I can't wait to see where you live. I've imagined what that famous hotel would be like and I wanna see your car. Can you take me to your office on the lot? I wanna see Universal Studios! I'm so excited to be here. I've missed you." She hugged him hard and held on to him as if she were saying goodbye.

There, he felt it—that old feeling to combat all the doubt and self-loathing, her ability to restore the best parts of him. Like sunlight for Superman.

"I have missed you more than you can imagine. I'll show you everything. Let's get your bags, and then—are you hungry?"

"Yes, I'm starving."

"Okay, we'll get you something to eat, and then I want to take you somewhere for the sunset. I think you'll love it."

"Where?"

"It's a surprise. Trust me." He hated himself for saying that. Wasn't that what she'd done all these months? Trust him?

He packed her suitcase into the back of his little red convertible, and they drove with the top down to a little Italian restaurant called Angelino's. There, Adam said, was the best penne con salsiccia she would ever taste. Right after dinner, Adam whisked Maele away to her surprise.

Nestled in the Hollywood Hills, under the Hollywood sign, was a stable built in the 1920s where folks like Charlie Chaplin used to come and ride. Beyond it, one could normally see Glendale, Burbank, and Pasadena, if it wasn't for the fires blackening the horizon with smoke. But today all they saw were the red rings of fire marching down the mountain sides. The entire city was laid out below, with a view that stretched from downtown to Long Beach to the Pacific Ocean. The smoke, like a thick, brown lens, allowed them to look directly at the giant blood red sun as it set behind the mountains into the sea.

Maele rode a horse named Otto. When they got to the top of the trail, she pointed out toward the water as the sun was beginning to dip low.

"If you swam 2,621 miles that way, we'd get to Kauai. I'll never forget our month on the island, Adam."

He smiled. That photo of Maele had become iconic. It had gone viral—over one hundred million people had viewed it. It had been printed in *Surfer Magazine* and a company had leased the rights from the photographer to print posters of it. Come the new school year, Maele Moana would be hanging on the walls of college dorms everywhere.

"Yeah, that wave changed my life. I rode it because of you."

"You were gonna ride that wave long before you met me."

"No, don't say that. Don't take that away from yourself. You trained me, Adam. You spent every day surfing with me, chasing down good swells on all parts of the island, and on my rest days you were willing to go wherever I wanted to go. You supported me. You believed in me so hard that you made me think there was no other reality than me riding a wave that day. And then ... God saw fit to send me a twenty-foot-high wave filled with a shark and framed by a rainbow. And He shined the sun on me and put a photographer on the beach who happened to take that photo. You know, small cosmic stuff." She laughed when she caught him staring at her. Adam was mesmerized by her presence, thinking of that day and how ridiculous and beautiful her life had been since then, like a wand was waved and, just like that, she was enchanted.

If Maele had been blessed that day, then Adam had been cursed. He'd flown back to L.A. on January fourteenth, and a week later his agent had called him.

"Adam, it's Z."

"Hey, Chaz. How are you man?"

"I'm good, I'm good. So, I don't know how to say this, but Universal is backing out of the deal. They are dropping the project."

All Adam could hear in that moment was his heart beating its way out of his chest and a loud ringing in his ears. His mouth went dry.

"What?"

"Yeah. They told me they started bumping on a few story-point issues and the property runs close to another idea they've already developed. Apparently, they're going to reboot an old IP from the 90s."

"Hold on. So, instead of moving ahead with a fresh concept, they're going to just rehash an old one? But are they using any of my ideas?"

"No, they don't need to. Plus, they still bought your script. They own it. It's theirs now. Which means the check they wrote you is good. That's the good news. It's just they want to pivot. The producer is going to call you this afternoon. I just wanted to break the news before you guys spoke. Listen, Adam, this is a high-class problem. They bought one script—the folks at Universal love you, they will buy something else down the road. I know you're disappointed but, buddy! Get cracking on a new script. We got movies to make."

"Well, so that's it? There's nothing we can do?"

"Adam, Universal owns it."

"Okay, but—" Adam was cut off mid-sentence by a third voice, his agent's assistant, Kimberly. He was in shock.

"Mr. Shaw, I'm sorry to interrupt. Steven is on the other line."

"Kimberly! What did I say about jumping on my calls? Sorry, Adam, I gotta take this. Call me after your chat with Frank."

With that, all of Adam's hopes and dreams were shattered.

Shoot Me

The photographer for the Aviator Nation shoot was a cool redhead named Elisabeth who really knew her stuff. She put Maele into more setups and sweats and swimsuits than anyone would have thought possible for a six-hour shoot. Adam was tired just from watching, but he knew a lot of money had been spent on this session. The crew, all thirty of them or so, did everything to cater to their talent. In addition to a table filled with food to snack on, Maele had her own trailer.

Besides, he had nothing to do, nowhere to be.

Adam hopped back and forth, determined to stay out of the way but not willing to miss a thing either. He'd watch a series of photos be taken, then wander over to the snack table and munch on M&M's or chips. The choices varied widely—from junk food to super healthy salads—nothing practical in between, like a turkey sandwich. *That would have been nice.* After grazing, he'd head back to the photoshoot and watch Maele crush it. One of the ad guys—Adam couldn't tell if he worked for the ad agency or for Aviator Nation—was obviously hitting on Maele. He kept telling her how she could become the next Gabby Reece, but for surfing. That her face and body were just so perfect.

Your face on the receiving end of my fist would look perfect, Mister Toothy Smile.

After he'd had enough of the smooth ad executive who was shamelessly hitting on Maele, he wandered back to her trailer and tried to work on a new script.

It had been a hundred and sixty-three days since he'd been fired. Well, since his project was shelved by the studio. And he'd had a new, awful idea for a script every single one of those days. Adam had a bad case of writer's block.

Maele entered the trailer to change into her thirty-third bikini. By bikini number twelve, she'd gotten used to Adam hanging around while she changed outfits.

"Oh. My. Gosh. How many bikinis are they going to make me model today? I'm so tired and hungry. Well, you know the drill. Look the other way, please." She peeled off her bikini bottoms.

"Do you want me to step outside? I can step outside."

"No, we have to change on the beach all the time, so I'm kinda used to it. Just don't stare at my butt, please." She wiggled her butt at Adam while laughing innocently.

This was the main reason Adam kept wandering to her trailer when he heard Elisabeth say, "Yes! I think we got the shot. A few more, then we'll move on to the next!"

That was his cue to head back to her trailer for a show that amounted to fireworks in his body. The comfort she felt to change with him in the room, and the fact he hadn't seen her in almost a year, let alone naked, was enough to render him stupid. It was also enough for Adam to count that day as one of the best days of his life.

It took all of his strength to simmer down his urges in the quiet moments when he stood alone in her trailer. Somehow, he mustered up his self-control, averted his eyes, got rid of his lusty thoughts, channeled all that energy and began to write a new screenplay. She was his muse, and it felt amazing to have her back.

The Party to End All Parties

The photoshoot ran long and, as expected, the ad agency wanted to take all the principal players from the shoot for drinks and dinner at the Soho House in Malibu.

Maele said she felt obligated, so Adam went along for the ride. The outdoor seating overlooked the water, and they witnessed their second sunset in as many days. As they both chomped on burgers, Maele made every attempt to show the smooth-talking ad executive that Adam was her man.

"So, Adam, what do you do?"

"He's a screenwriter," Maele said. "He has a huge movie being made with Universal called *Oceana*. They are spending over a hundred million dollars on it. It's quite a big deal."

Immediately the executive backed down, realizing who the apex predator at the table was. Adam was the alpha.

"Oh, wow. That's a really big deal. How old are you, if you don't mind me asking?"

"I'm twenty-four. I turn twenty-five next month. Why? How old are you?" He spoke with a tight smile.

Maele squeezed his hand, encouraging him to take the reins. She loved it when he was confident like that. For a while, he'd forgotten all his failures.

"Well, shoot, I'm forty-one-years old. Screenwriting. That takes some balls, man. Congrats on your success."

"Yeah, it's a big deal," Adam said, as if death itself was crawling inside of him. Hot sweat started to pour off his temples as he choked on the burning white-hot ash of his shame.

"You okay there, buddy?" the ad exec droned on. "You're so young, and you got a smoking hot girlfriend. I'm sorry, Maele, but you have such a bright future ahead of you. I don't mean to be crass …"

Adam tuned him out. How was he going to tell Maele the truth after all this time? Eight out of nine months of their entire relationship had been a lie—a massive omission of truth.

That was a deal breaker, and he was terrified.

Later that night, there was another afterparty. This time, an invitation from Elisabeth to a party in the Hollywood Hills. Adam thought it might be a good idea, since it was on their way to the Chateau, plus Maele was excited to go. When they arrived, the party was in full swing. Adam immediately saw a ton of people he knew—a lot of the same friends Warren had met. Then, as if the night couldn't get any worse, the absolute last person Adam wanted to see turned around to face him. Rebecca Worthy.

"Oh, Adam, my love, where have you been? I've missed you, you naughty boy. And who is this?"

"This is Maele Moana. I've told you about Maele."

"No, you haven't, but I'm intrigued. Hello, Maele, I'm Rebecca Worthy." Rebecca paused, waiting for some sort of recognition. When Maele had no clue who she was, she went on, "But you can call me Becca. I'm one of Adam's best friends out here in L.A. And his neighbor. I live at the Chateau Marmont, too. I used to date him, but that's neither here nor there. He's been a big, weepy baby all summer, so he's been a full-time job. Right, Adam?"

"Nice to meet you, Becca."

Adam saw Maele shrink for the first time since the airport. She loosened her grip on his hand and slightly turned away. Her eyes darted from Rebecca to him, and her shoulders drooped as she stepped back. He witnessed her misunderstanding of what she thought had been going on while he was away from her.

"What are you talking about, Rebecca? I've not been … whatever. Maele, do you want a drink or anything?" Adam asked, trying unsuccessfully to pry Maele away from Rebecca.

"Sure. Why don't you grab me a rum and Coke, please."

Adam looked at her, noticing a defiance in her tone, surprised by her order.

"What?" Maele stared at him. "I learned to like the taste of them on tour."

"And I'll have a vodka tonic, Adam," Rebecca said. "You know the kind of vodka I like. Thanks, hon."

Adam walked away, aware that Maele and Rebecca continued talking. While waiting for his order, he watched the two women. As Rebecca spoke, Maele continuously shook her head and shot looks at Adam. When they finally made eye contact, Adam saw Maele's eyes clouded with tears. There was a timestamp in those eyes when the present stood still and everything around him moved in slow motion. Rebecca had just told her the truth, but it wasn't her truth to deliver, and the timing was all wrong.

As Adam approached with a drink in his hand, Maele turned away and began a slow walk toward the restroom.

The truth was coming out, so Adam did what Adam knew to do.

He walked back to the bar and ordered three shots of Jack Daniels and hit them back, one after the next. He bummed a smoke from the guy next to him and took a huge drag. He'd stayed faithful to Maele. Since leaving her side in Kauai, he hadn't slept with anyone. He was doing fewer and fewer drugs at first, but the news had hit him hard, and the struggle was overwhelming. There were weeks when he would take pills and float away on a cloud of indifference, one week in May, he drank until he blacked out every night. It was Rebecca who had tended to him. She would stay in his room, nursing him back to health. Then, three weeks later, he'd gone on a coke bender. Rebecca had been there to catch him when he came down. Her TV show had gone on hiatus in April, so the timing couldn't have been more perfect. It was scheduled to resume in September, so this entire episode of the Adam drama timed out quite nicely for Rebecca.

The only problem was that while Adam had kept the news about his script a secret from Maele, he'd also kept Maele a secret from Rebecca. Somewhere in his warped mind, he'd thought that was the best plan. Now he realized if Rebecca had at least known Maele existed, had he said, "I'm in love with a girl named Maele," it would have given all involved a wash of dignity. Honoring his relationship with Maele and upholding his friendship with Rebecca at the same time would have afforded both women the respect they deserved.

But I kept it hidden, he thought right before he took a fourth shot. Tonight was going to be a rough one, so Adam buckled in.

54

Before the Sunrise

Adam didn't remember arriving back at the Chateau nor did he know where Maele was. Room 64, where hours ago there had been laughter and life, now there was silence. All that was left of Maele was a handwritten note.

Dear Adam,

This is a really difficult letter for me to write. I can't find the words, other than to say I am sorry. I'm sorry you didn't think you could trust me with the truth about your screenplay. I'm sorry you continue to battle with your addictions. I'm sorry if I led you on in Kauai, made you think I would be fine with your excessive drinking. I've never seen you like that before. It really scared me. You getting high and blacking out at the party was awful. I didn't know what to do. I felt so helpless. As much as I love you—and I do love you, Adam—I can't wrestle with your demons.

I've never been in a photoshoot or invited to a Hollywood party before, which made your behavior doubly hurtful. Not only did you embarrass yourself with the things you said to everyone, but you ruined a first for me.

I'm sorry you're hurting. I'm sorry your script didn't get made into a movie. I'm sorry you can't control your desire for drugs and alcohol. But what hurts me the most is my love wasn't enough for you. I was here for you. All you had to do was tell me.

Fear can be debilitating. Of all people, I can identify with that. When doctors told me I would never walk again, it took me a long time to get up on my own and prove them wrong. I was terrified of the water, but with your help, I relinquished that fear. Told it where to go.

I'm so sad that I couldn't do that for you.

I don't want to preach, but you need Jesus in your life. That's the only advice I know to give you. I know it's hokey and provincial, and I'm sure your professors at NYU would ridicule me for dragging God into our conversation. But the only one who can heal you from the pain, my love, is Christ. That's who got me walking again. That's who gave me the wave that changed my life. That's who gives me life.

The only way forward for us is if you realize how much you can give to this world by choosing to live. That masking your pain or your struggles with drugs and alcohol will only serve to end *your life. And because I am terribly frightened at that thought, I must do what I can to protect myself, I suffered with you these past eight months and I didn't even know why I felt so brokenhearted. That's not fair. I don't care if you sell a script. All I care about is you. I want to be here for you, but you have to do your part. When you do, I'll be here waiting.*

You know I'm good for it. Once I make a promise, I don't break it.

I'm sorry to leave you so early and unexpectedly, but you're so good with words that if I stayed, you could have talked me into marrying you in a rush wedding in Vegas.

You have my heart, my prayers, and all my love. I believe in you.

MM

Adam looked at his watch. It was almost four in the afternoon. His head felt like it had an ax wound in it and his mouth tasted like an ashtray. He needed to hear what happened. Maybe it would finally allow him to own his actions.

Moments later, he was knocking on Rebecca's door. She opened it, looking like someone out of a Ralph Lauren ad.

"Hiya, doll. How's my baby doing today?" She reached out and patted Adam on the face.

"What happened last night?"

"Um, you don't want to know."

"Yes, I do."

"Well, okay, if you're sure you want to know … I filmed it," she said, handing him her phone.

Adam pushed PLAY. What followed was a six-minute video of

Adam standing on an enormous white stone jar, holding court at last night's party. He was repeating a lot of what Warren said to him almost a year ago about the nature of his friends, but a lot worse. He was speaking about himself as the king of a broken-down kingdom and that all the people gathered below him were his bad and unfaithful subjects. Sycophants and users. From high on his perch, Adam looked at every guest and flipped them off as he "knighted" them with the words "You're an 'it, you're an 'it', you're an 'it.'"

The worst part was when Adam repeated what Warren had said about Rebecca. That she'd go to bed with a homeless person, if it meant she could feel any kind of love for a brief second. When Adam got to that part of the video, he looked up at Rebecca, who was just holding the phone as she held his gaze. He couldn't read her. His eyes darted back to her phone and, by the end of the video, the camera slowly panned around from face to face, finally landing on Maele who just watched Adam and cried.

Maele was the one who'd walked up to Adam at which point he announced she was the only "thou" in the room. She held his hand as he stepped down off the planter, but he still fell when he landed. Maele was the one who helped him stand, brushed him off, and then slowly walked him toward the exit.

It was rock bottom.

The video stopped and he handed the phone back to Rebecca.

"You're an asshole, Adam. A selfish, entitled little punk. I actually liked you. And I'm not insecure—I'm the star of the second most-streamed show on TV, and they pushed season three back four months so I can film a movie with Austin Butler. I'm sorry you see me as such a pathetic bimbo, but I was your only real friend, bucko, and now you got none."

She quietly shut the door in his face. Adam stood in the hallway of the Chateau Marmont as a housekeeper vacuumed the hallway.

It was time he made some changes.

It took another week for Adam to gather up the courage to face the music with Rebecca. He stood guard by the elevator in the hotel lobby, waiting for her to show up. He'd tried calling her, left notes under her door. He simply couldn't close this chapter of his life without explaining himself. He assumed she was at some shoot, since he'd been trying to contact her since Sunday. It was Wednesday, late afternoon, and even the doorman had no idea where Rebecca was or when she'd be returning.

He was about to give up and head back up to his apartment when he heard that familiar laugh. It was no longer a whinny, but more a cackle—higher pitched, but her head still turned upward and her spine still flexed forward as she reacted to whatever the doorman had to say. God, he loved that sound. It was familiar and warm and embodied everything else in his life he had taken for granted.

"Go away, Adam, I don't have any." Rebecca shimmied past him and pressed the button on the elevator. "I'm not your supplier. Go find your other friends."

"I'm not here for that," Adam said, his voice low, solemn. "And besides, I don't have other friends, remember?"

When he followed her into the tiny elevator, Rebecca rolled her eyes. He stood next to her, shoulder to shoulder, riding in awkward silence except for the dinging of the bell on every floor.

Rebecca stepped off first, and he kept right behind her. After taking a few steps forward, she turned to him. "Wow, this is the longest time you've ever gone without saying a word. What? No smart quips from you? No words of wisdom, stories, fables? Myths?"

"No," he said, head hung low. A random thought crossed his mind about the conversations that must have taken place in this same hallway for so many years. The scandals, the affairs, all absorbed by the yellowed concrete walls and the dark red Moroccan printed carpet.

"Then what, Adam. What do you need from me?"

"Listen, Rebecca, I wanted to apologize. For everything. For using you when you were my only real friend, for not telling you about Maele, for not telling Maele about you. For lying to you all these years. When Maele left me after that party, I—" He cleared his throat and prodded himself to continue. These words were as difficult for him to say as they were for him to accept. "I realized that I need help. The one person in my life who was going to make me a better man is gone, and the only other person who can help me get the help I need, won't talk to me. I'm sorry."

"You hurt me," Rebecca said, her voice shaking with emotion. "After all we've been to each other. You insulted me in front of your friends, you looked down on me."

"I know," Adam responded. "I am very sorry. You are the only one who stayed with me, through everything. Through my success, which turned out to be a failure, through the crash and the burn. I was a jerk. I'm truly sorry."

"Okay."

"Okay? As in you forgive me?"

"Adam, I don't have any friends, either. I'm stuck with you. You're all I got."

"Thank you."

"So, what are you going to do now?" Rebecca reached inside her purse to pull her keys out. Adam welcomed the sound of clanking metal. It echoed across the halls and broke the silence in that long, hollow space.

"Start over. Find a way back to her."

"Good plan," Rebecca said, smiling. She turned her back to Adam and slipped the key into the door.

"Here, this is for you," Adam said. "It's a gift. Maybe it will help you remember me when you're even more famous than you are now." He handed her a green, leather, script binder that had been tucked inside his jacket.

"What is it?"

"I wrote you a script. I wrote it last year, before my life imploded, and made some recent changes to it just for you." They held each other's gaze for a moment. A truce was made.

"Oh!" Rebecca grabbed the binder and began to leaf through its pages. "What is it about?"

"Maybe it's about a famous actress who falls in love with a homeless guy."

"Sweet," she said, shaking the binder in front of him with glee. "That's *so* my role. You turd. Like a twisted version of *Notting Hill*?"

"Sure. But this is way better."

"You think I can play it even better than Julia Roberts?"

"I know you can," Adam said, smiling. He reached out to touch her hand, the one that held on tightly to the binder with her nails digging into the leather. "But all jokes aside, it's a love story and it's the best thing I've ever written. It is truly the best and only gift I can give to you that is worthy of you, Miss Worthy. It's all I have."

Adam was sad, he knew they would go their separate ways and that this chapter of his life was officially over. Rebecca felt it too because she hugged him long and hard.

"Take care, Rebecca. And thank you for helping me during the most difficult weeks… no, years of my life. I'm sorry I didn't open up to you the way a friend should. You were a good friend to me."

Rebecca leaned over and planted a kiss on his cheek. "Goodbye, Adam. I sure did love you a lot. Now, get out of here, go on. And take care of yourself."

Jerome and Esther

I t's easy to buy a $250,000 car if you have the money, but much harder to sell it.

Adam had spent the last three weeks cleaning up his mess, getting rid of the things that gave him a false sense of security and made him think he was somebody he wasn't. He had given the Chateau his notice and asked if they could keep a few boxes in storage in the hopes he would one day return to the city he loved. It was an act of faith, in himself mostly, leaving five small boxes behind. With his accommodations easily taken care of, two large suitcases packed and ready to go, a one-way plane ticket purchased, and a destination, all he had left to do was sell his car. That was the last thing tying him to L.A.

He finally stumbled across a gentleman named Jakob who worked at a place called Bonhams, a privately owned international auction house based out of London. Jakob was sending someone over to appraise the car and put it up for auction. There was a Supercars on Sunset auction being held in November, and he was certain Adam's car would "fetch a fine price." Adam was going to miss driving the streets of L.A. in his Porsche and the attention he thought the car earned him. He used to love that attention. Now, he just felt sorry for those who used their material wealth to measure their self-worth. It meant they hadn't found real love. He had. And he didn't need to look anywhere else. He wanted to be where that love was.

Along with selling his car, he was getting rid of all his designer shoes and clothes. They were ridiculous and where he was going, he wouldn't want them. He kept one pair of sunglasses because they were practical and looked good on him.

He was driving to a homeless shelter off the 405 called Hope of the Valley. The shelter was about to get the mother of all drop-offs. He'd taken Sunset all the way to the 405 and was about to exit onto Victory Boulevard when his phone rang.

"Hey, Z."

"Adam, player, what's this I hear from my assistant that you're leaving town?"

"Yeah, I'm taking some time off," Adam said, turning down the volume of the call.

"I don't understand. You leave now and it looks like retreat. You stay, we sell your next script. That's how this business works. It's optics and momentum, and momentum is based on optics. You understand this. Once you hop off the treadmill, you're done."

"What do you mean, I'm done?"

"I mean, how the eff am I gonna sell the next big thing in Hollywood if you aren't in effing Hollywood?"

"Dude, lower your voice."

"You want me to lower my voice?" Chaz screamed. "Do you know how many people would kill to be in your shoes? Where could you possibly be going that's better than here?"

Adam took a deep breath and began to practice what he'd learned from Maele. A louder voice doesn't mean a better message.

"Dude, Chaz, Z. I just realized something … I don't like you. I pretend to, but I don't like your fancy agency or your lies. I don't like the way I constantly feel compared to your other clients. You make it seem like I work for you. It's supposed to be a team, where we work together toward a common goal, right? Now, I'm not sure how, but you got that all twisted up along the way, and you're always trying to make me feel like I'm lucky to be repped by you. Thing is, I know men who make more money than you will ever see in your lifetime, who have more power than you'll ever know, and they treat people so much better than you do. Kimberly, for example. I know she has to listen to all your calls, so … hi, Kimberly, I'll miss you. Now, Kimberly is a great assistant to you. She puts up with so much and she's smart and kind, and she will make a fantastic agent one day."

Kimberly, who was on the line listening per the requirement of her job, chimed in, "Thank you, Adam."

"You're welcome. You will be one of the great agents out there, if that's what you want. Heck, I'd be your client. But you, Chaz, you're not one of the great ones. You're a troglodyte. You're a bully. And you're fired. Bro."

Adam had cleared another obstacle from his path. He had faith that if he had a story to tell on film, the universe would let him tell it, not Chaz.

It felt invigorating, this thing called honesty.

Adam pulled into the parking lot and was met by a tall, thin black man who wore a bright blue shirt with yellow embroidery that read *Hope of the Valley*.

"Hello. Are you the one that made the drop-off appointment?"

Adam was still all adrenaline and nerves from his phone call. "Yes, hi, my name is Adam Yates and I'm here with some goodies."

"Wonderful. My name is Jerome, and I'm in charge. Thank you for thinking of us. And, may I say, that is a beautiful car."

"This? Yeah, it's a classic. Spartan luxury, and she purrs when she moves."

"I've always wanted a Porsche, but that's not in my cards, I guess. The good Lord had other plans for me."

"Well, I think what you're doing here is awesome. If this was the plan, it's a good one."

"You know, this is only half of it. We have a women's and children's shelter out in Pacoima. We've housed nearly fifty families who were homeless."

"That's incredible. How much does something like that cost to run, and this place? You feed and clothe people?"

"Don't forget the showers. Making this place a rest stop for these people is our mission—rest, food, shade, showers, companionship, and safety from the streets. All they have to do is commit to staying the night with us. We sing worship songs and whatnot at a church nearby, but in exchange they get three meals, a bed, new clothes if they need them, and a shower if they want it."

"Sounds like a win-win for them. Sounds like you offer a lot of hope."

"That's it. That's the name of the game."

"And how much does it cost to run this place?"

"Close to a million dollars a year. We survive off donations."

"Do you make that every year?"

"By the grace of God, we do. Miracle after miracle. I've seen so many miracles, I've come to count on them." Jerome laughed with an ease that made Adam happy, and he joined in with laughter of his own.

"Well, I guess I should unload these bags. Now, I don't know if homeless folks care about this kind of stuff, but all these things are designer."

"Oh, they're just like you and me, they care. They'll love whatever you have to give."

Adam and Jerome made their way across the parking lot to a little shed that acted as a clothing store—people could come in and get what they needed for free. Adam saw at least twenty people sitting outside under the trees, next to a church building now used as a rec hall to feed the homeless. He felt grateful for his lot in life. He'd done nothing for it, had just been born into the right family. Luck.

The two men started unpacking tens of thousands of dollars' worth of goods from the black plastic bags Adam had placed them in.

"Wow, Adam, you weren't kidding. These clothes are beautiful, and most of them don't even look worn. You sure you want to give these away?" Jerome held up the fancy tennis shoes that had given him blisters that morning on Kauai. The morning he'd sat next to Maele and dangled his feet over the water and known he'd found his mystery girl and the love of his life.

He missed her so badly, it hurt deeply. He could no longer breathe easily those days, even when his lungs had cleared of the cigarettes. Something was always sitting on his chest. It felt like she had died, and he wanted to bring her to life again. The items in the bags didn't mean anything now. Which was exactly what he wanted to convey to Jerome. Sure, the monetary value would help as a donation, if you thought of it from a cash perspective. But, to Adam, he was giving away his past. Unfortunately, material things signified most of it, but what he was letting go of was the core of all his misgivings.

"Yes, especially those."

Jerome shot him a look, eyebrows crossed like he just wasn't getting it. "Are you okay, Adam? Did you want to talk?"

"You see, Jerome, these things weren't really mine. Most of them were from my parents. I need to start from the very beginning. I need to start with nothing. I think my life will have more meaning that way, if you know what I mean."

Jerome nodded pensively, still trying to figure Adam out. "I'd like you to meet my wife. We run this place together. Esther! Hey, Esther?"

A beautiful woman dressed in bright colors—orange, pink, and blue—came out from the office.

"Hello," she greeted Adam.

"Hi, Esther, I'm Adam. Jerome was telling me how much you both do for the homeless folks in our city, and I'm humbled by it."

"It's God, Adam, not us. We wouldn't have the strength for it, otherwise—too many problems, too many complaints, too many bureaucrats, never enough money. But it's amazing. God provides, and somehow it always works out. So, we just keep being obedient and saying yes." As she spoke, she removed a small leaf stuck in her husband's hair.

"I see how you can stay encouraged, Jerome. That's an awesome story." The three stood there for a moment as Adam wrung his hands. "Well, I've got a meeting a bit later, so, I'm gonna head back, but it was such a pleasure meeting you both. Bye, now."

"Bye, Adam." Esther gave him an unexpected hug, which he needed badly. He missed his mother.

"I enjoyed your company," Jerome said, putting a hand on Adam's shoulder as they walked toward Adam's car. "Thank you so much. You have blessed so many people today. Sometimes—we can call them residents or guests—they get job interviews. Your clothes will give them pride and dignity. Thank you."

"No, it's really my pleasure, and I've got to be honest, it feels good to give." Adam stood quietly for a moment, staring off, then asked, "Have you ever known God to change His plans?"

"What do you mean?"

"Like you said, He has a plan for you. Have you ever known Him to change His mind abruptly and write a new plan?"

"I suppose. I've seen men come in here with only the clothes on their back, but one lucky break, and they were productive members of society again. And I've also seen it work the other way far too often. People who have jobs and families, but live month to month. Then, one bad turn and, boom, they're homeless. Poverty is a nasty cycle that's hard to break. But, to answer your question, yes. Yes, I believe God can change His plans at will."

"Well, I agree with you. See, God just changed his plan about you ever owning a Porsche. He just dealt you some new cards, Jerome."

Jerome stared blankly at Adam with his mouth hung open.

Adam went on to say, "I want you to have my car."

"What?"

"Yeah, you heard right. I'm giving you my car."

"No, Adam, that's insane. You can't give me your car."

"I can and I will. It's all paid off. That's the good news. So, it's yours free and clear." He went around to the passenger side and reached into the glove compartment and pulled out the title and a business card. "The second bit of good news is I have the title on me, as I was about to sell this car, anyway. I mean, put it up for auction. Which is what this is for." Adam handed Jerome the title to the car and the business card. "This business card belongs to a guy named Jakob. He works for that company there, and when you are ready to sell this puppy, he'll fetch you a fine price. I paid $250,000 for it. I'd say it's worth a bit more, now."

"Esther! *Esther!*"

That was the second time Adam heard someone scream today, but this was for the right reason. Esther came running out.

"What is it? What's wrong?"

"Not wrong. Right. It's so right. This young man is donating his car to us."

"What? Well, that's sweet, Adam. That's a very old-looking Porsche. It must be worth six or seven thousand dollars, Jerome," Esther said with glee.

"No, my love, no." He leaned over and whispered into her ear. She quickly looked at Adam. Her face froze and her dark eyes filled with tears.

"Praise Jesus. Oh, my goodness, thank you, Lord!" Her response made Adam cry with laughter.

"So, drive it until November, if you want—that's when the auction is. Or, call him today and he'll come pick it up. Or keep it. It's yours, Jerome. It's yours."

Adam called an Uber, swung by the Chateau for his luggage, and took one last look at his Los Angeles home.

"Goodbye, L.A."

He wondered if he'd ever come back for those five boxes.

56

Treasure Hunt

As soon as Adam's plane landed, he called a taxi to take him to his new home—a five hundred dollar a month back house rental located ten minutes away from a beach. He planned to spend as many days as it took to accomplish his mission. It was two-fold. The first part of his mission was to dry out once and for all and get his life together. The second part of his mission, and how he was going to accomplish the first, was to find Maele's necklace.

It was nearly impossible. He knew roughly where the chain had broken off her neck, based on the photos, and he had the two rock outcroppings to use as markers. The questions would be, how deep was the area? How big were the waves? What did it look like at high tide versus low tide? Were there any riptides, and was it home to many sharks?

Questions he'd soon know the answers to.

His plan was simple. Adam was going to buy scuba gear and he was going to go to Tunnels Beach every single day. He would be true to the commitment he'd made. For once in his life, he would honor a promise, even if it only had been made in his heart. He would swim every day, be out in the sun, in the water, fighting the elements come rain or shine. He would find her little blue diamond necklace or die trying.

"Why? Why is this so important, Adam?" his mother asked on their last phone call. "Your father and I are sick with worry. Your father is furious about the fact that you gave your car away, and I'm wondering why you fired Chaz. He seemed like such a great agent, and that agency was powerful. You are acting irrationally. We are worried for you. And now this insane treasure hunt. It makes no sense to us."

His mother had wept when she learned her baby was a drug addict, and he was ashamed of who he had become.

"Mom, everything in my life has come too easy to me. Dad paved the way with money, and you with your love. Even my script, which now nobody wants, and the agent and all the fuss out in Hollywood. It all happened so easily. I am incomplete, for some reason, and I feel lost. I'm constantly competing with Warren and Dad, and nothing I do is good enough for me.

"I feel trapped, lost, and angry. I'm sorry I'm scaring you, but this, this totally insane plan of mine is the only way I know how to heal myself. I have money from the script sale, which I'm gonna make last as long as I can. I have a strict budget. And I made a promise, standing on the beach in the rain with the girl I love, that I would find her necklace. That's what I'm going to do.

"It's going to take discipline, effort, and hard work. I will either succeed or I will fail. If I fail, then the die is cast. That's my answer. If I find it, then I know I can be the man you think I am, the man Maele sees, and Warren believes I am, the man Dad always hoped I'd be. The man I want to be. But that's gonna take work, and as weird as it sounds, this is that work. I called to let you know where I am, so you wouldn't worry. I'm close. I'm on Kauai, but I need to do this. I'm asking for your blessing because I need it."

"Adam?" His father's voice jumped onto the line.

"Hi, Dad," Adam said, surprised.

"I overheard you and your mother's conversation, and you have our blessing. Find it, if you can. Be careful. We love you."

And with that, Adam began his treasure hunt.

57

September

Adam landed in Kauai on September fourth and took five days to settle into his rental and buy food—mostly cans of tuna fish, crackers, cereal, milk, and a tub of red licorice for his inevitable sweet tooth—and his scuba gear. He also spent time making a list of the drugs he liked to take and why he took them. He catalogued their effects on his body and mind, the pleasure levels each registered at, and then rated how much he liked each one. He wanted to record this information as an act of understanding himself not just so he could quit for a while, but also understand the levels of his addiction and break them for good. This was a mental and emotional act, like ripping a tree out of the ground that had gained a deep-rooted foothold. In place of these old footholds, he would symbolically plant new trees, ones that gave life instead of death.

He turned twenty-five on September ninth and began his hunt. The beginning of a new year was symbolic to him; his new life on this island, filled with brand-new goals. His parents called to wish him a happy birthday, and Warren and Andie did, too. Maele texted him a sweet message. She was doing so well, winning competition after competition. Adam continued to watch her progress every night on social media and the web. Although he was literally fulfilling his New Year's resolution to watch her succeed, staying away from her just wasn't the way he'd expected to do it. But he did say, *"My resolution will be to watch you succeed. And I'll be here, cheering you on."* So technically he was exactly where he'd resolved to be.

He watched her get more confident in interviews and with the press. She was officially the real deal—a professional surfer, and quite the popular one at that. The photos she'd taken that day in LA for Aviator Nation exploded on the internet. She was a star, and she inspired Adam to dig deeper than he ever had before in his life.

He started every day by watching the sun rise from the beach, drinking coffee and eating almond croissants, that he got from a nearby bakery. His first few days in the water were strictly exploratory. The first order of business was to figure out how deep the area was he'd be searching. The answer was between thirty to forty feet deep. The range was about the length of two football fields and the width of three. It was a massive area, but also not the entire ocean floor or even the entire length of the beach. It helped him keep a good perspective on the task at hand. Large, but not insurmountable. There was normal underwater tidal activity. It wasn't a channel, there were no constant riptides or pulls out to sea to worry about—just a nice, flat area with plenty of rocks and huge outcroppings of coral and ancient lava flow. Being a point, the area was a convergence of two separate wave systems, but Adam couldn't feel that when he was underwater. The only issue was the coral—there was lots of coral. A million little places for a thin gold chain to get hung up on or fall into. Which forced him to buy a piece of equipment he hadn't planned on buying.

It hurt him to invest in an underwater metal detector. There were so many types, he knew he needed one that had a long battery life, GPS for tracking and mapping, and sensitive omnidirectional antennas. And that meant shelling out $3,500 for the one he wanted. That amount put a huge dent in his monthly budget, five months' worth of rent, in fact. His lifestyle over the summer had evaporated a significant chunk of the money he earned from his script, and what was left had to last at least a year and a half, if not longer. He couldn't ask his parents for any more money. He wouldn't.

He was investing in this knowing this would be the only way to save his life. Or what was left of it.

Each oxygen tank held about an hour's worth of air. At first, Adam had four tanks he placed into rotation, using one until it was empty, then heading to the beach to replace it, but that ended early on when he surfaced to find that somebody had stolen his three reserve tanks. More money gone. He called it quits that day and headed over to a shop where he bought six steel tanks, lengthening his day to almost seven hours, but again at a great expense. He also bought a flotation contraption, some cord, and an anchor which he used to devise a makeshift floating buoy of reserve tanks. He also kept his lunch and drinking water in a nasty old bag to camouflage it from thieves, from that day forward. Adam would take about a forty-minute break for lunch, and then work until he no longer had enough light to continue. He was diligent and meticulous, using his underwater metal detector to sweep the bottom of the ocean floor. He also carried his long paintbrush to comb through the sand, or in case he needed to brush off the coral. His eyes were his only other tools.

The end of the day was the worst. His body was tired and waterlogged, but once back on dry land, he would still have to drag six empty tanks up the beach, get them refilled with oxygen, make dinner, and finally go to sleep. He knew Maele's friends were on the island, because he was scuba diving one day when they'd come to Tunnels to surf. He'd hidden under the water from them, not wanting anyone to know he was on the island. Not wanting anyone to tell Maele he was there instead of with her, but there because of her. He didn't want to hurt her any more than he already had.

October & November

By the end of the second month, Adam began to feel at home under the water. There were rocks and outcroppings of coral he recognized. He had his very own buddy in the form of a red octopus, or *he'e*, as it was known in Hawaii. Every morning on his way to his search zone, surrounded by the blue world of the sea, Adam would see the same octopus playing, changing color and shape. He did see the hole where the octopus lived, one morning, but the octopus remained evasive, as if playing a game of hide-and-seek with Adam. There was also a shark that liked to call Tunnels home—a reef shark, about five feet long. Once or twice a month, she'd make a pass through the area.

Adam had become accustomed to the rhythm of this underwater neighborhood. He knew the *he'e* and the reef shark, he saw so many fish, and he noticed where different schools gathered, perhaps based on the food that grew on the coral. It was a wondrous sight, spectacular and overwhelming for snorkelers who visited the island, even more so for Adam who began to learn the secret rhythm of that underwater world. By late October, Adam had become a regular. Day in and day out, he learned the slopes of the seafloor where ledges were versus cave formations in the rocks. He knew it better than the L.A. streets he'd loved so much. The waves broke over him soundlessly all day long, and that, in and of itself, was special. The ever-shifting, liquid mosaic muted the noise in his head, made him feel calm and collected as it rolled on above him.

When he wanted a rest from searching, or to simply be overwhelmed by splendor, Adam would look up and watch the waves move over him in shades of green, blue, and white in the dancing sunlight. They didn't bother him at all down there, nor did the surfers who often passed overhead.

Day after day, his world was filled with colors—teal, aqua, azure, indigo, cobalt, sky, beryl, cerulean, navy, ultramarine, turquoise, and even emerald in the right light. Adam experienced every shade of blue while he was thirty feet below the surface of the Pacific Ocean. Some days, the temperature was colder than others, and some days he'd be lucky enough to bask in a column of warm water. On odd days, there would be the occasional riptides that moved him quickly from one spot to the other. He recognized the pull as it was happening, which signaled the need to swim parallel to the shoreline.

He covered new ground and thought about Maele every day. Adam treated his body roughly, to train and discipline it. He was staying clean. Some days were harder than others. Physical withdrawals were replaced by mental ones. The occasional desire to lose himself in something was always present. But the water, the pressure, and the creatures he was surrounded by, calmed him in a way he had never been calmed before. The sea was changing him on a molecular level. The saltwater dried Adam out and healed him at the same time. This world, where he floated among sea turtles and swam with sharks, was his healing place. He was being made new.

December

When December came and winter moved in over Kauai, the water was noticeably colder and the waves choppier. Adam had run into Koa's mom a few weeks back, and he worried Maele would know he was on the island. She'd left him four months ago. When she made that choice, it gave him the freedom to do whatever he needed to do, but the mission was not easy. In fact, it was nearly impossible. *But there's still hope. Her necklace is down here somewhere.*

I will find it.

Adam had searched for nearly ninety days. He had been faithful to his task, fervent in his mission, but it hadn't paid off. He began to dream about being pulled out by a riptide to the deepest, darkest parts of the sea, which scared him immensely. Death didn't frighten him, but the thought of never seeing Maele again did. That thought spurred him to bravery. He fought through his phobia of plunging past the shallows, because there, on the ancient lava that acted as a footstool for the island of Kauai, on this ledge of coral and rock, he felt safe. One year ago to the day, Warren had come to L.A. to visit Adam. In two weeks' time, a year ago, he'd met the girl who changed his life, twice.

Adam swam to the surface of the water to change his oxygen tank out with a fresh one, and what he saw took his breath away.

The clouds were huge and gray—a storm looked like it was rolling in. Huge waves rolled past him, the water surface was jittery, and down the coast, the waves made a vast spray of white mist along the jagged shoreline. Thunder rumbled through the mountains. Adam feared they would tumble into the water. The sky turned a dark hue of brown.

Just as Adam was going to pack in his gear for the day, the sun broke through the clouds in bright golden rays. Adam remembered what his mother used to say when she saw sun rays, "It looks like God's hands poking through the clouds."

Adam saw it as a sign.

Adam broke his silence and prayed for the first time in his life as golden pillars of light streaked across a sepia sky.

"God, if you're up there, please help me. I need to find Maele's necklace. and I know you know where it is. I mean ... you're God." He paused for a moment. "I kinda need a miracle. No, I really need a miracle ... Um, Amen."

Adam clung to his little makeshift buoy of oxygen tanks as the endless sea rolled on and he became a part of the wonder surrounding him. It was his last hour of the day. The light was growing dim, and the sea was getting worse. Adam made his decision to pause his search for the winter and pick back up in the spring. He would go home for Christmas, at least. He couldn't justify a second Christmas away from his mom and dad. Plus, Warren and Andie would be home and said they had some exciting news to share. He thought it was probably a baby, but he didn't know for sure. Maybe a job in another city. They had been in Chicago all year.

Adam dove to the bottom of the ocean for his last search of the year. He weightlessly sank thirty feet until he was floating above the bottom of the sea. He could feel the pressure in his ears. It was getting dark down there. Adam pushed off and headed to the edge of the reef. About ten feet in front of him was the sheer blackness of fathomless depths. Inky black water. He felt the strong tidal pull of a riptide and his pulse raced. He kicked against the drag of the current, gliding over the coral, toward the edge of the island as he was pulled out to sea.

A small vibration in his hand startled him.

What was that? He had used the underwater metal detector for nearly ninety days, but it had never gone off. Until now.

He saved his strength by activating the buoyancy control device and sank to the bottom of the ocean. Adam wedged himself against the sea floor and crawled his way to where the detector had buzzed, but felt nothing. He waved the wand in broad, circular motions. Nothing. What was that? Where exactly had it happened? He searched frantically for another vibration.

And then there it was. Buzz.

It happened again, reminding Adam of a game his father used to play when he was young.

"*Warmer, Adam, you're getting warmer. Ah, colder, colder, warmer, warmer, hotter, hotter! Adam, you're getting scalding hot!*" And then Adam would find whatever his dad had hidden.

A little buzz, and another, then he would be pulled away by the motion of the ocean and he'd have to kick and drag himself back to find another little buzz, but he couldn't keep himself in one place and his tank was running out of air.

He finally grabbed onto a rock and fought his way to a stable place between an outcropping of coral and a rock formation. He waved the wand, again a bit higher, then angled it to fit in a divot in the rock. He turned himself around to face the coral and waved his metal detector again.

Buzz.

Adam let out laughter in the form of a huge burst of bubbles. *It's probably an old fishing hook.* He pulled his paintbrush from its little side pouch and began to search the coral for a gold chain or a blue diamond when he saw it. Gently wrapped around a piece of coral and made to look alive by the movement of the water, was Maele's necklace. Hanging like a precious, ripe grape from the underside of a coral branch was the little blue diamond, still attached to the chain by way of the clasp. A warm feeling washed over Adam and filled every part of his being with light.

He had done it. He made a promise and fulfilled it.

Adam had found Maele's little blue diamond necklace.

PART SIX

Undulation

Maele and Adam

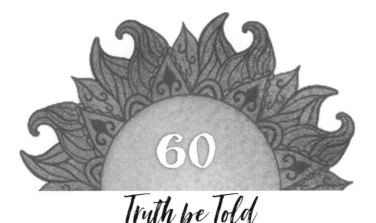

60

Truth be Told

Maele sat quietly in her dressing room, waiting for the interview to start. Everyone looked so professional; she was glad she'd taken her mother's advice and splurged on a dress for this occasion. Truth be told, Maele was beginning to get comfortable in her own skin. She knew what she was there to do, and she knew how to do it.

This interview wasn't one of those held in a tent or a shack right after a surfing competition with the suffocating smell of grease and sunblock permeating the air. It wasn't a reporter in a baseball cap or board shorts spewing out words only surfers understood, like *break, shore, swell, tube, curl, reef, heat.*

This one was in a studio with a live audience and a famous talk show host. Maele had a publicist, now, another part of the public life she wasn't keen on, but needed. Her name was Holly and, in a way, Maele had gained a friend. No one had ever expected her career to branch out as it had. She'd become a role model, received letters from young girls who wanted to be like her someday. Girls who, like her, couldn't afford surf classes or ballet lessons or gymkhanas. She'd become the spokesperson for non-profit organizations that championed underprivileged girls, providing them with opportunities where they could excel both in and out of school. She'd also made the rounds of the Pediatric Orthopedic Center at Queens Hospital.

No questions were off limits except for one. Holly knew what it was, and so far, she'd done her job and kept those questions at bay.

"You must understand. You are a young, bright, beautiful woman. Everyone will want to know that part of your life."

"That part of my life isn't for them," she would answer.

"Okay, they're ready for you." Holly rushed in and went straight for her hair, tucking in a loose strand that had fallen to the side.

Sometimes, little gestures like that would make her remember. She shook her head. *Not now.*

"I still think this dress is too short," Maele sighed, finding another excuse to voice her nervousness.

"It's perfect," Holly said. "Green is your color. Shows your nice, long legs. And I'm glad you wore those heels. You look stunning."

Maele looked down at her feet. The shoes had red soles.

"Thank you," Maele answered as Holly guided her down the hall. When they reached the interview area, she was shown to a sofa and asked to sit on a marked X underneath bright lights. In a few minutes, she sat face-to-face with Jenny James, mesmerized by the bluest eyes she had ever seen. The host of TV's top nationally syndicated daytime show waited for the team to count them down and they were off to the races.

"Maele Moana, you are even more beautiful in person. Welcome, and thank you for taking the time out of your busy schedule to stop by the studio."

"Thank you for having me."

"So, two days before the Pipe Masters. Is everything set?"

"Well, Jenny, as you know, surf conditions are being monitored as we speak. So far, so good. I think it's happening."

"Just for the audience's knowledge ..." Jenny turned to face the camera. "Nature is as unpredictable as can be when it comes to the swells and waves on the island. There's a window of time for the competition, but it can change depending on conditions. This year, it was set for December sixteenth to the twentieth." She swiveled her chair toward Maele. "So, Maele ... wait a minute—am I pronouncing it correctly?"

"Yes, it's Mae-leh."

Jenny nodded. "You have a very interesting story. At sixteen, you were well on the way to achieving success in the amateur world of surfing. Then your life changed dramatically. Was it six years ago?"

"Yes. Well, it's been seven years, now. I was a high school sophomore at the time. I caught a shallow break, got dragged on the ocean floor, and broke my neck."

"Ooh," Jenny said, cringing. "But look at you now. How long did it take you to recover? Did you ever think you'd be here today, doing what you love?"

"It's funny. It took six months for me to feel anything on my left side. But once that feeling came back, the doctors performed a miracle, and the rest was up to me. If I worked hard enough, I would make it. No one in my family made me believe otherwise. I'm still one of the lucky ones, but I'm not going to say it wasn't one of the darkest, loneliest times of my life. My parents moved the family from Kauai to Oahu so I could have a chance at life without the ocean." Maele realized what she'd said and laughed. "I mean, farther away from the ocean, at a coffee plantation … still surrounded by the ocean. I live on an island."

"Amazing. That is an amazing story, Maele. You are a true picture of courage. Now, tell us why you're here today."

She'd noticed celebrities used that word often. *Ah-maz-ing.*

"I'm soliciting donations on behalf of Queens Hospital, from my island, and their pediatric orthopedic department. There are many young people who are not as fortunate as I am. Some of them are debilitated for life, and we need to keep doing research so we can find innovative ways to give them hope for some normalcy, however that's defined. You know, my surgeon, Dr. Davis—if he hadn't tried the new technique to ease the swelling of my spinal cord just hours after my accident, I wouldn't have been able to heal like I did."

Jenny listened intently, legs crossed, hands on her knees, leaning forward. Maele was slowly growing more comfortable. *This isn't so bad.* She glanced at Holly, who was watching intently.

Throughout the entire interview, Jenny hadn't looked down at her cue card. Until then.

"So, Maele, I want our viewers to get to know you," she started, bringing the card closer to her nose. "It looks like you were here in Oahu exactly one year ago, celebrating a wedding."

"Yes, my friend Andie got married and I was in the wedding party."

"The socialite Andrea Yates, correct?"

"Yes, correct." As soon as she heard that name, Maele knew. She knew this was going to take a turn for the worse. All of a sudden, she was that girl in the coffee shop. The one who had no business being friends with Andie Yates.

"So, friend and boss."

"I'd like to think just friend, now," Maele answered, smiling tightly. If this was Jenny's toughest question, she could handle it. She leaned back and stretched her legs out. "I'd love to talk a little bit more about the orthopedics wing at Queens. They have a fantastic team of doctors who—"

Jenny continued to peep at the evil card. "Take a look at the screen behind you, ladies and gentlemen."

To her horror, a picture of herself and Adam flashed on the screen, life-sized and in living color. The image was an innocent one, from the days of falling in love. Strolling along the seawall, hands hardly touching, Adam in sunglasses and designer sneakers, laughing. "This was taken after the wedding reception in Kauai. And this one ..." Another picture of her, wrapped in Adam's arms at the airport. If she closed her eyes, she could still feel his lips on her neck, smell the scent of his skin. "I think this has been the best kept secret in Oahu, Maele. From Hawaii to Los Angeles. You're dating young billionaire, Adam Yates."

"No, no," she stammered. "That was—"

"Will we see him at your event, Maele? We tried to reach him, but it seems he's left Los Angeles."

"No, no, I'm. We—" There they were. All one hundred days of her suffering out in the open. She felt trapped. All the inconsistencies of her thoughts regarding the time she had spent with Adam, how it had happened, why it had happened, and how she'd let herself fall so deep she couldn't seem to rise above it. No matter how many people you have around you— your friends, your family—misery is a solitary process. She still thought about him. Some days it was bearable, a nice memory here and there, a tame yearning to hear his voice, see his face. Other days, the lump in her chest would persist, sucking the life out of her and knocking her down.

"Wow, you are every woman's envy, at the moment. A world champion surfer, a survivor, and, what inquiring minds want to know— you're dating the son of the richest man in Hawaii. And so hot, too. Was it a tough adjustment? Working on a plantation and now—"

"N-no. That's not—"

"That's enough!" Holly snapped, storming onto the set with the click-clacking of her stilettos and pulling Maele out of her chair. "This interview is done."

"Mae-Mae, it's me. Koa. Can I come in?" he whispered through the door.

Maele nodded, forgetting he couldn't see her. After a few seconds, he entered anyway and shut the door behind him.

"Holly called me. I came right away."

Maele said nothing as he looked around the room, his gaze shifting from the wads of Kleenex on the dressing table to the ones on the floor. She saw him take in the mess of dresses on the couch, on the floor, and shoes kicked around on the carpet.

"Are these all yours?"

"No. They brought them in this morning and had me try on a few in case I liked one more than the one I brought."

He took a seat next to her on the black leather couch, offering her his hand. "I would have come sooner, but I had to iron this suit. Didn't want to embarrass you."

Maele smiled weakly.

"Oh, Mae-Mae."

"I thought, how bad could it be?" Maele said, sobbing and struggling to pronounce her words. "I'm here to promote the hospital. Even if she's known to be controversial, what could she ask me that would be so bad?"

"That was Holly's job. She should have made sure nothing like that would happen."

"I don't think she knew. It just came out of left field. And it was live!" She sobbed louder, hiccupping between shallow breaths. "Oh, Koa, the worst thing about it is, I miss him so much."

"Here," he said, reaching for the box of tissue. He pulled out the last one and blotted her eyes with it. "Remember, we've talked about it. You can still walk away right now. Leave all this behind. You said you wanted to go back to business school. You can afford it, now. I bet that, with your brain, you can get into Yale or Harvard. Didn't Andie go to Wharton?"

"Warren did. Andie went to Brown."

"Whatever, same thing."

"Everywhere I turn, I see him. I don't know why he didn't try to explain himself," she said, calming a bit. Her eyes were still so clouded with tears, she could hardly see. Maybe this was the cleansing she needed. Until she'd seen those pictures splattered on a screen, she had tucked away her pain, masking it in the guise of success.

"What was there to explain?" Koa asked. "That woman told you everything. I respect him more for not denying it."

"I would have loved him with or without that movie."

"I know. But I suspect Adam has been wrestling with his demons all his life."

Maele nodded. No argument there. "He didn't love me enough. I have to accept that."

"Oh, Mae. Channel that pain. Channel your love for him into your energy, your resolve into what you need to do tomorrow. Win for your love for him. No love is ever wasted. It goes back into the universe and comes back in different forms. It never really goes away."

"When did you get so philosophical?" Maele forced a laugh, sniffing as she swiped the tears off her face.

"When my baby cousin fell in love, I guess."

"College," she said, standing and moving around the room. She gathered her things and then gestured for Koa to turn around as she removed her robe and pulled her jeans back on. She hung the dress she'd worn and zipped it up in a black leather wardrobe. Koa followed suit and led her to the door. "Sounds really good right now."

61

Ruin

Adam could spot Koa from a mile away as he stood at the entrance of The Island Coffee Company. He saw the commotion outside. Throngs of reporters camped out in vans and trucks, and some were on motorcycles. A *Do Not Trespass* sign in large red letters blocked any entrance past the chain-link fence. Adam didn't know who to call. His only hope was to try to get Koa's attention as he checked in with the plantation workers who formed a human gate across the perimeter. He supposed they were there to protect Maele's privacy. They all stood together, turning those away who tried to push their way inside the plantation.

Love and loyalty were so prevalent in this place, and Adam longed to be a part of it.

"Excuse me," he said, squeezing himself between people and camera equipment to get to the front of the line. He raised his arms and waved frantically. Koa turned to him and glared, then slowly walked closer and closer, eyes narrowed, as if he'd seen a ghost.

"Adam?"

"Koa!"

"What are you doing here?" Koa asked, barreling through the mass of reporters and clearing the way for them to cross the barrier.

"I need to see Maele. Is she here?"

"No way."

"No way she's not here, or no way I can see her?"

Clouds of dust rose from the asphalt as trucks began to trail in and out of the driveway.

"Why are you here?" Koa's stare was like a drill to Adam's eyeballs. He didn't even blink.

"I just arrived this morning. I know she's here."

Koa tilted his head and pursed his lips, confused.

"The Coconut Express—it's a small island, word travels fast," Adam said.

"Great," Koa said, slapping his thigh and walking away. "She's not here. Go home."

"Koa," Adam pleaded. "I saw the interview."

"So did the whole world. It doesn't matter."

"But it does," Adam cried out, the roar of the harvesting machines competing for attention. Tiny white blossoms drifted through the air as the photographers snapped pictures of the cascading flowers. It was harvest season, and the plantation had come to life. "I saw her reaction. There is hope for us. It broke my heart to see her that way, but I'm here now."

"Really? You made no effort to see her for the past three months. You been creeping around Kauai like a stalker. Why you wanna see her now?"

"Can we go somewhere quieter?" Adam asked, turning his head from side to side.

"Fine. Come with me." Koa marched over to the tourist center with Adam right behind him. He pushed open the heavy door to reveal a modernized coffee shop complete with souvenirs and travel books. Adam saw his sister-in-law in every single corner. Her trademark books and coffee—a concept that gave the business a new life. He missed Andie and his brother.

"Sit." Koa pointed to a wooden bench right next to the romance books. "Why now, Adam? She needs time to heal. Your being here isn't going to help, especially right before she goes for her qualifiers tomorrow."

"Everything she found out when she saw me in L.A. was true. I was a fake. I didn't even know who I was anymore. So, I had to take the time to fix myself. I had to get better. Maele ..." He paused to catch his breath. "She was the only good thing in my life, and I lost her because I was too proud to admit I had fallen. Not anymore. I'm not too proud to admit I'm still trying to find my place. That I'm in love with someone who is better than me. But, because of that, she makes me better."

"In love, everything's the same. The way she was with you. You made her better, too."

Adam nodded, wondering when Koa had become so thoughtful. "How is she? How is Maele?"

"Well, since she came back from L.A., she's been training. I'm amazed at how that woman sets her mind to something and does it. She still cries. But when she does, we're there for her."

Adam saw an older gentleman scurry in hurriedly, eyes wide to see Koa with someone else. He glowered at Adam and pointed a finger at him. "You look familiar," he said.

"Duke, it's Adam."

Duke turned away from Adam and addressed Koa as if no one else was in the room. *He had every right to do that*, Adam thought. It made him feel small, and he deserved nothing less.

"The truck is ready. I know you wanted to go pick up—" He looked at Adam. "You know."

"Yeah, I gotta go," Koa said. Adam followed him out. Koa turned and held up both hands. "I told you she wasn't here. She's out with Noe and Raelene. Don't see her today. It isn't the right time."

"I have something to give her."

"I can give it to her for you." Koa held out his big hand for whatever Adam may have for his cousin.

"No, I need to be the one to..."

"Where's your car?"

"About half a mile down, before the barricade."

"I'll drop you off. Hop in."

Adam and Koa rode in silence, slowly making their way through the mob. When they arrived at his car, Adam nodded his thanks and jumped out. Koa leaned out the window as soon as Adam approached his side.

"Adam," he said, his loud booming voice carrying with the wind, "she believes in the sunrise again! Don't ruin it."

62

Full Circle

Maele had come full circle. She was sad for the love she had won and lost, joyful that she'd had it at all, and grateful Adam had given her the courage she needed to face that wave almost a year ago and anchored her in the storm that had been her life these past eleven months. She had loved the idea of him from afar, all those years ago. She had loved him these past several months—perhaps this short period of time was their fate. Not every love story had a happy ending, and maybe young love wasn't meant to survive. It was there to open your heart and make you experience it once, so you'd remember it all your life. That one special time when you lived in such pure joy that nothing, not even the darkness, could pull you out of that light.

She was heading into a massive competition. Any day, the perfect swell would roll in and she would be called to the water to do the thing she was born to do.

"I'm ready to go, Duke. Where's Koa?"

"He'll be right back to fetch you. Now, you go bring us home a victory, eh, little sister?"

"I will. I promise."

"The one thing I know about you, Maele, is once you make a promise, you don't break it."

That was absolutely true. What if she had broken her promise to wait for Adam and then pulled the same disappearing act he'd pulled on her? She imagined how much worse she'd feel right now, but because she'd kept her word, deep inside, she was satisfied. She had a little victory over Adam and his bad behavior. Mostly, she felt badly for him.

Just as the sun began to fatten on the horizon and deepen into a golden color, Koa tore over the ridge along the dirt road. Dust kicked up behind him into plumes that stretched skyward.

"Hey, hey, Mae-Mae," he called. "Here we go. I'm so excited, I can't contain myself. My cousin is about to claim the crown as the best female surfer in the world and nothing is going to stop her. Nothing!"

Maele smiled weakly. She still saw Adam's face in her dreams.

"Let's get you to the water's edge. It's time. Tomorrow morning is the big day, according to all the reports." The reports were predicting a world-class swell, offering conditions that dreams were made of. The entire island was buzzing with energy.

"Why are you yelling, Koa?"

"If you're not careful, I'm gonna pick you up and carry you into this truck."

By now, he had the truck parked. The suicide doors were wide open, and he was tossing her gear into the bed. He took more care with her surfboards, but he was excited. Hasty.

Maele's parents stepped out of the front door, arms around each other, beaming with pride. Maele ran to them and squeezed herself in between her parents like she always had when she was younger.

"Calm down, Koa, you're gonna stress me out. I want to make sure I've got everything I need. Mom, Dad, you guys gonna meet us there tomorrow? You sure you don't want to stay on the shore with me tonight?"

"No, you go with Koa and your friends. We'll be there at sunrise with warm bread and coffee to fill your stomach." Her mother released her and led her husband back into the house.

When her parents left, she stood alone, looking over the fields of coffee, the sun low in the sky, but still high enough for her to shield her eyes. Koa and his truck, with her surfboards jutting out the back, dust still hanging in the air, cut a beautiful silhouette in the golden light. The animals in the barn were making noise as if to send her off. A year ago today, she had left this place to go to a wedding and her life had changed, even if she hadn't. She'd been nervous about the dress she was going to wear. She'd felt good that she'd paid back Andie long ago and even better that she'd been able to add the gift of a mountain of merchandise from her sponsor. Acts of generosity were fun. She loved overwhelming the people in her life with kindness, material and otherwise.

She breathed in the air, the smell of water from the irrigation system on the soil, the coffee plants, the hay from the barn, the humidity in her hair. All the elements of her life—where she came from and the heritage of her ancestors—were present. Little white flowers were floating with the breeze, adding a magic charm to the moment. She remembered Adam saying they call this the "Magic Hour" in the movie making business. The hour of the day when the sun was golden and soft.

She took this moment in and prepared for the next chapter of her life. It was going to be big, loud, and fast. She was ready to go it alone and with no regrets. Maele Moana was about to be the champion of the world.

Maele got into Koa's truck. They headed into the sun as it set, past the main plantation house with its blue roof. Past the barricade and the line of photographers who hoped to catch a glimpse of the rising star. A photo of Maele Moana in her natural habitat could sell for fifteen thousand to *Stab Magazine.*

In the last twenty-four hours, Maele had been linked not only to Adam Yates, but to a movie star who had a penchant for dating younger models. That last PR stunt had Holly's fingerprints all over it, as the movie star was also Holly's client. Maele was in the white-hot center of the public's attention, like it or not, and she had no other choice but to ride the wave.

Worth Waiting For

Adam got into his car after Koa dropped him off and began to head back toward Honolulu. He thought about what he'd wanted to say to Maele if he had been given the chance. He wanted to tell her he was sober. That he hadn't had any alcohol in over five months. His system had been cleaned out, and he hadn't taken a drug or even smoked a cigarette since the party in L.A. He hated the idea of telling her. *Showing her*, spending day after day with her, sober, month after month, sober, year after year, showing her he had turned over a new leaf—that was what he wanted to do. He wanted to stand in front of her and wrap her necklace—the necklace he'd scoured the ocean floor for and found against all odds—around her neck, kiss her, and walk into their future with her. He didn't want to explain a thing.

As Adam drove, he thought about his life, his future. What next? What was he doing with his life? Where was he going? *Where was he going?*

Adam suddenly slammed on the brakes and made a U-turn. He floored the pedal and raced back toward the plantation. The sun was low and shone straight through the windshield. He couldn't see well, making it a dangerous drive. The road was a two-lane highway and as he came around the bend, a pineapple truck driver blew his horn—they barely escaped a head-on collision.

Adam pulled up to the plantation and saw the photographers waiting for Maele. That's when he spotted it—Koa's truck. Koa was driving, Maele in the passenger seat with dust kicking up behind them. They made a right turn onto the highway, heading north. Adam gunned it. He sped up and tried to pass Koa, but another truck was coming, so he swerved back into his lane. Koa was looking at him in the rearview mirror, shaking his giant lion head. He observed them talking before Maele turned around to look in his direction. Could she see him?

He tried to pass them again—this time he made sure it was on a long straight section of the highway. He sped up, but as he did, so did Koa. Koa wasn't going to let him pass. At one point, Adam pulled up next to the truck and rolled his window down, hoping to get their attention when Koa turned to Adam, smiled, and then flipped him the bird. Followed by the hang loose hand sign.

"That son of a ... Okay, Koa, you want to play it that way?" Adam let his car drop back. The road curved, but Adam knew there was a long straight stretch of hill in his favor coming around the bend, and if he timed it just right, he could blow past Koa and his big, stupid truck.

It was on.

They climbed the hill for a while, and Adam settled into place. He kept his distance, watching the truck disappear around the last bend before the straightaway. Then he floored it—sixty miles an hour, seventy miles an hour. He hit eighty as he came around the corner at the top of the hill and saw Koa's truck below. There was a cement truck climbing midway on the opposite road, but Adam felt it wouldn't be an issue. Adam tucked and rolled like a speed skier down the hillside, reaching ninety miles an hour.

His brother's words echoed in his head. "If you're going to be bold in anything, be bold in love." Adam was sweating. Adam wasn't sure if this was bold or stupid. Adam was right, the cement truck slowly drove by as Adam zoomed past, and then he made his move. He gently drifted into the left lane and prepared to pass them. He surprised Koa, who tried to speed up, but there was no way his old pickup could out power Adam's car. Adam sailed past Koa and Maele, and not a moment too soon, as another pineapple truck was headed straight for him. He swerved and pulled in front of Koa and then gently applied the brakes—seventy, sixty, fifty, then forty miles an hour. Koa tried to pass Adam, but Adam kept him hemmed in, swerving to ensure the pickup truck stayed behind him as he slowed even more. Thirty, twenty, ten miles an hour, full stop.

Maele got out of the truck. So did Koa, all three hundred pounds of him, and he charged toward Adam.

"I told you to stay away, bro!"

"Koa! No!" Maele shouted.

"I'm gonna kill you!"

"I'm prepared to die for you, Maele!" Adam shouted at the top of his lungs.

That stopped Koa cold in his tracks. It stopped Maele, too. Adam was the only one still running. He stopped when he got to Maele and grabbed her shoulders. He looked at her and a thousand words flooded his mind but got jammed in his mouth. He just looked at her.

Adam saw his reflection in the truck's window. His eyes were white and bright, his skin tanned and made perfect from endless days in the ocean. His hair was long, and he had grown a beard. On the outside, his body was in perfect shape and on the inside his soul was at peace. A different Adam stood before Maele, and he hoped she saw the changes in him. Even Koa was not as confident as he had been a moment ago.

"Bro, that was crazy." Koa said with awe in his voice.

"Yes, Koa, yes, it was. But sometimes love calls for crazy." Adam gently rested his hands on her shoulders. He wanted to drop to one knee and ask her to marry him. He wanted to declare his love. He wanted to tell her everything, but instead he said the words that were bursting out of his heart.

"I needed help. I've gotten help and will continue to receive it. I'm so sorry I hurt you. I never meant to, but I was embarrassed and didn't want to drag you down with me. When I want to remember life's goodness, its promise—all I have to do is think of you. I've been watching you every step of the way, rooting you on, and I'm so proud of you, Maele." Adam dug his fist into his pants pocket and held the necklace tightly in his hand. He had searched the ocean for this treasure, risked his life to bring it back to her. He wanted to tell her how it all happened, how he was given the miracle he asked for.

Maele gently touched his face, her eyes filling with tears. "Come with me."

Those words.

They were all he needed to hear. They changed everything for him. Gave him the strength to do what he needed to do next. He needed her strength. Before he committed to finding her necklace, he had never followed through on anything in his life. She had worn this necklace for six years like a talisman, grieved its loss on the same day she won over the wave. He needed to offer it back to her, give her back her treasure.

"I found it," he said. "I found it for you."

He stepped back from her and pulled his hand out of his pocket, still holding her necklace tightly in his fist. He held his clenched hand out to her and slowly rotated it so his fingers faced upward. Adam opened his hand to show her what he had searched for and found. The stone glistened in the setting sun's light and the gold shone pure and untarnished.

Maele stared at the little blue diamond nestled on the gold chain curled in Adam's big hand. She gasped as tears filled her eyes. She looked at Adam.

"How?"

He wanted to tell her everything, but the words stuck in his throat. Maele's reaction surprised him. Her shoulders began to shake, and a wail escaped from her lips, the sadness seeping from her crumpled face. With a heaving sob, she placed her hands on top of his, both of them holding on to the blue necklace. Then she looked directly at him, with a smile that immediately erased all their sorrow.

"Please. I didn't mean to make you cry. I don't want to make you cry anymore."

"No, no, I'm crying because our love is bittersweet, isn't it? Look at how blue it is, blue like the ocean. Blue like the sky." She looked at him for what felt like eternity. Koa seemed to disappear as did the rest of the world around Adam. In that warm sunlight, inches away from the love of his life, he met heaven.

Then Maele said, "You can't come with me quite yet. I see that now. You have some work to do, don't you? And I need to keep going, don't I?" Tears still flowed down her face. "This diamond was given to the women in my family for two generations by the men in their life. From my lolo to my lola, and then it was passed down to Papa who gave it to Mama. If I'm to have this in the traditional way, then I suppose a man needs to give it to me. Finders keepers, Adam." She laughed and it made Adam cry. "My mama gave it to me because she said it would give me strength to heal, and I am healed. But you have already given me back the part of me that I lost in the ocean all those years ago. You gave me back my courage, and now you've found my heart. And because of you, I don't need this anymore." She wrapped her fingers around his hand, both palms pressed against the golden chain. "I want you to keep it. Wear it close to your heart and let it remind you of mine, Adam, until another day. It's something worth waiting for. You are someone worth waiting for."

"Can I tell you how I found it?" In that moment Adam was inspired with an idea and he knew exactly what he had to do. "Nope, you know what? Better yet, I'll *show* you." He said, with a smile that matched hers. Purpose, direction, permission, and most of all love. She offered those and so much more to him.

Adam slipped his hand back into his pocket.

She no longer needed her necklace to win—she was winning.

He was the one who needed something to hold on to, something he would return to her at the end of their journeys. Something she cherished that he could hold in his hand. Something worth waiting for.

"I would go anywhere with you, Maele, but, yes, you have to keep going. Take as long as you need. Win. I will wait for you," he finally had the courage to say.

Silently, he released his grip on the necklace, feeling its weight as it settled back into his pocket. He would keep the little blue diamond safe and close to his heart until the right time. It would have a new meaning then, and everything would be different.

"I'll be out there in the world rooting you on, Adam. I'll always love you. I've committed myself to what we have already, and you know what they say about me?"

"You and a promise. Once you make it, you don't break it," Adam said as they both laughed a bit sadly. "As the sun rises, it shines with the promise of a new day and the adventures that wait to fill it. I'll make it worth the wait, that's my promise to you, Maele. And I won't make you wait too long. The adventures we are about to have together are going to be—"

And, with that, Maele Moana stopped his words with a kiss. She kissed Adam Yates deeply one last time as the sun began to set in a magical explosion of color. It was a kiss so tender and yet filled with so much passion that it sealed Adam's fate to hers forever.

The kiss was a testament to their unfinished story.

A promise that there would be another day.

And, because of this, it was enough.

For now.

Acknowledgements

Anna Gomez

My heartfelt thanks to the usual suspects – **Vesuvian Media Group** and **Rosewind Romance** for taking a chance on us. My manager, **Italia Gandolfo** for your tireless belief in my words. **Liana Gardner** for your support, **Holly Atkinson**, for such never ending patience and **Hang Le** for another stunning cover. Thanks to my publicist, **Meryl Moss**, for always coming up with the most fun events and to **Leslie Sloane** and the **Vision PR team** for your partnership.

Thank you to my **#BraesButterflies** for holding my hand throughout this journey. And to our new friends from the **Polaha Fan Club** and the **Polaha Chautaqua** group who have welcomed us into your family. Special thanks to **Rachel Schneider, Gayle Meyer, Kiki Chatfield** and team for your help and support. I couldn't do this without you guys. To all the bloggers who have taken the time to read and review our first book, _Moments Like This_ – and for those who are sticking around for this next one – we are so humbled by your love.

Thank you, **Jhoanna Belfer** from BelCanto Books, for making me feel included. And for bringing **Bren Bataclan** into my life.

Thank you, **Bill, Tim, Gigi, Marco and Izzy** for the blessings you bring to me every single day.

And to **Kristoffer Polaha** my partner and my dear friend. Somehow, we pulled it off again. A second book, a second journey. This time, life was a little more demanding, a little less patient. But the world we've created, its characters and our stories – is still a product of the most joyful collaboration I have ever had. Thank you, Kris. No matter what the future brings, you have given me the experience of a lifetime.

This book is dedicated to my father, **Gary Torres**, who passed away during the final edits of this book. I pay tribute to all he was in my life— my friend, my father, my avid supporter. He had no expectations from me even if I had so much from him. I miss you so much, Papa, but I am comforted by the fact that you are now at peace.

Choose love always. And don't ever regret following your heart.

xo

Kristoffer Polaha

First and foremost, my thanks goes to **Anna Gomez** without whose trust, enthusiasm, organization, passion for story telling, and encouragement I would have never even dared to venture into the realm of writing a book, let alone two, in the first place. Anna, you have taken me on an unbelievable journey and I have loved every second of it. From the bottom of my heart, thank you. I'd also like to thank **Nina**, whom I have the pleasure of calling my friend.

I could never write another acknowledgment without shinning a light on the members of the **Polaha Chautauqua** community. Truth is, there are simply too many of you to name here and I certainly don't want to leave anybody out, but you know who you are and you have been fervent supporters of the first book in this series and of me and my career! You stop at nothing to show your support and I have been overwhelmed by your electric word of mouth campaigns and social media blitzes. And, of course, a warm thank to **Brae's Butterflies** for your invaluable support! Thank you, thank you, thank you!

To everyone at the **Vesuvian Media Group** and **Rosewind Romance**, especially **Italia Gandolfo, Liana Gardner**, and our editor **Holly Atkinson**. Thank you all for making this book and the From Kona With Love series a passion project. The reader can feel how much care and attention goes into these books with every turn of the page.

And thank you, **Hang Le** for another perfect cover. We actually want people to judge these books by their covers!

Thank you to **Leslie Sloane** and to her entire **Vision PR** team, especially **Jami Kandel**. Leslie, you have been a valuable member of my team for almost 20 years! That's no small thing and your support and dedication to my career has been remarkable, not to mention our friendship, which Julianne and I cherish. Thank you.

To my family; my **mom and dad**, **Esther** and **Jerry Polaha,** and to my brothers **Erik, Jon**, and **Mike**, to **Elaina** and **Kristen**, and in loving memory of my little Nana, **Mae Smalley** who loved these books and had to hear how this one ended before she departed. And to the entire **Ulleseit** and **Gates families**. All of you have endlessly supported any and every artistic journey I've ever ventured into. Thank you for making art feel like the noble and important effort is it. I've never once been made to feel ridiculous for dreaming big dreams. Thank you.

And to my three boys; **Caleb**, **Micah**, and **Jude**, whose late-night desires for stories from their daddy has forged me into the story teller I am today. You boys gave me exacting practice which helped me discover the joy of telling a story that will keep the attention of three young, wild, and brilliant boys. Thank you.

And to my wife, **Julianne**; you are wisdom, patience, grace, service, and love personified. It was your daddy that tightly tied our knot with his "it versus thou" wedding speech and it has clearly stuck with me ever since that wonderful day. You are the best thing about me. I love you. Thank you for giving me the time to write this book.

And lastly, to you **gentle reader**. Thank you for spending your hard-earned money and invaluable time with Anna and I throughout the pages of this book. I'd simply like to acknowledge how much I appreciate you. And since you made it to the last line of the acknowledgments page you win the added bonus of an extra thank you, so … Gracias, Merci, Danke, Tak, Spasibo, Xie Xie, and Mahalo!

About the Authors

Award-winning author **Anna Gomez** was born in the city of Makati, Philippines and educated abroad before moving to Chicago. She is Global Chief Financial Officer for Mischief at No Fixed Address, a consolidated group of advertising agencies. Gomez was recently selected for the 2020 HERoes Women Role Model Executives list, which celebrates 100 women who are leading by example and driving change to increase gender diversity in the workplace. Gomez has championed various ERGs for Black and API colleagues as well as resources essential to address challenges of ageism. She has sat on several boards and served as treasurer for Breathe for Justice and The Jensen Project, both focused on socio-economic issues, particularly violence against women and human trafficking. She was a keynote speaker in the 2020 Illinois CPA Society Young Professionals Leadership Conference, as well as the Northwest Indiana Influential Women's Association's Breaking the Glass Ceiling Event in August 2021.

Gomez, also writing under the pen name of Christine Brae, has published seven novels which have received various literary awards.

She lives in Indiana with her husband Bill and their Sheepadoodle, Izzy.

www.AnnaGomezBooks.com

Kristoffer Polaha is best-known for his long starring role in the critically acclaimed series *Life Unexpected* (The CW). Other TV series credits include *Get Shorty* with Ray Romano and Chris O'Dowd, the limited series *Condor* opposite William Hurt and Max Irons, The CW's *Ringer* (Sarah Michelle Gellar) and *Valentine*, as well as *North Shore* (FOX).

In addition to co-starring with Rainn Wilson in *Backstrom* (FOX), he had a multi-season role on the acclaimed series *Mad Men* (AMC) and *Castle* (ABC). Polaha is also well-known for starring in Hallmark Channel movies such as *Dater's Handbook* with Meghan Markle, and the *Mystery 101* franchise on Hallmark Movies & Mysteries.

Polaha first received attention for his portrayal of John F. Kennedy, Jr. in the TV movie, *America's Prince: The John F. Kennedy Jr. Story*, opposite Portia de Rossi. He has appeared in numerous independent features, including *Where Hope Grows*, *Devil's Knot* (Colin Firth, Reese Witherspoon), and the Tim Tebow film, *Run the Race*.

Polaha has a featured role opposite Gal Gadot in *Wonder Woman 1984* and is in *Jurassic World: Dominion*.

Polaha was born in Reno, Nevada, and he is married to actress Julianne Morris. They have three sons.

www.KrisPolaha.com

Made in the USA
Middletown, DE
15 November 2022

14952738R00191